S

'Ha,' Perak Shah comme g at the women, and then suddenly stroking h beard. Teng Lee uttered a mental oath. What he had most feared had happened. 'By Allah,' Perak Shah said, 'a goddess!' He walked through the English people, who shrank away from him, to stand before Elizabeth Blaine, who was as usual by herself, separate from the other women. 'By Allah,' he said again, and stretched out his hand to take her hair between his fingers.

Elizabeth, keeping still with an effort, stared at him, eyes wide, breathing a little laboured, pink spots in her cheeks, but maintaining a high level of courage.

'By Allah,' Perak Shah said a third time. 'You may have the others, Teng Lee. But this one I will keep for myself.'

SINGAPURA

Christopher Nicole

**THE SHERIDAN
BOOK COMPANY**

This edition published in 1994 by
The Sheridan Book Company

First published in Great Britain by Century 1988
Random House, 20 Vauxhall Bridge Road, London SW1V 2SA
Arrow edition 1990

Printed and bound in Great Britain by
Cox & Wyman Ltd, Reading, Berkshire

ISBN 1–85501–661–3

CONTENTS

Prologue

The Malay ran up the beaten-earth roadway, panting, perspiring; it was not quite noon, and the equatorial sun penetrated the thick-clustering trees to beat full upon his head. The heat caused his sarong, his only garment, to cling to his yellow-brown flesh like a second skin, and his thick black hair gleamed with sweat. He reached the first of the wooden houses, little more than huts perched on four-foot-high stilts to keep out the flood waters from the turgid river which flowed only a few yards away on the other side of the path, and slowed. Here the trees were less dense, and naked children stared at him from dark doorways; their veiled mothers peered from behind them, wearing only sarongs, for all the care with which they concealed their faces. Dogs barked, and men gathered to shout questions. But he had no replies for them.

Still panting, he reached the dock, where the prahus of the Singapura fleet lay alongside the worm-eaten wooden piles. Facing the dock, on the far side of a tree-shrouded open space which in a more civilised clime might have been called a square, was an altogether different building to those of the village itself. This was large, if also made of wood, and low and sprawling; it was fronted by a wide verandah, which in turn gave way to steps leading down to the earthen forecourt — there was no gate, and the forecourt was part of the street.

The man ran to the steps and there dropped to his

1

knees, looking up at the figure which had risen from a stool and now stood at the top of the wide staircase. 'The Chinese comes, Perak Shah,' he gasped. 'The Chinese comes!'

Perak Shah stroked his straggling beard. A beard was a necessary part of being a Muslim, and of being a leader of his people, but, as a Malay, he did not find it easy to maintain. He was tall, for a Malay, and had powerful shoulders and legs. His black hair was smoothed back from his forehead, half concealed by the bandanna he had tied around it to keep it from his neck. His face was suggestive of great strength of will, even when disguised behind the beard and equally thin moustache; the chin jutted, the mouth was flat and hard, the forehead low and thoughtful. His black eyes could be dull, and angry; at this moment they sparkled with pleasure.

He wore a white tunic over his red sarong, and sandals on his feet. His only decoration was the gold earrings which glinted in the sun, and his only weapon an ornate kris, the fearsome double-edged knife of his people, which was thrust through the red sash holding his tunic close to his stomach. 'Then prepare to welcome him,' he commanded. 'He will have much to say to us.'

The man nodded, and having partly regained his breath, ran across the square to the ornate mosque, which was very nearly as large as the chieftain's house. He seized the wooden club which hung on the door and struck it against the large brass gong. The noise reverberated across the village and into the trees, and people hurried from their houses to play their part in welcoming the new arrivals. Perak Shah watched them with a satisfied smile, and turned to the young man who had just emerged from the interior of the house. 'Teng Lee will have news from Siam,' he said.

'News which will please you, Father,' the young man said.

'News which will please us both, Bodaw Shan,' the

2

chieftain said. 'And our people. News which will please all of Singapura.' His smile widened. At best it was a tight-lipped smile, a mere elongation of the already wide mouth, and conveyed little humour, but, again, a good deal of satisfaction. 'And which will strike fear into the heart of the Sultan of Johore,' he said confidently.

The booming of the gong reverberated down the river, seeming to bounce from the trees, heard long before the houses came in sight. Teng Lee walked to the forward rail of the high poop of the junk, the *Dragon's Wake*, gazing at the dark water in front of him, snapping his fingers impatiently. Entering the Singapura River always quickened his heartbeat, and he had done so on so many occasions now that he no longer feared the sandbanks and snags which lurked beneath the brown water. But there was more to his excitement than just the pleasure of seeing his old friend.

He had first come to the island nineteen years before, when he had been a lad of hardly twenty. That was in the year 53 of the Ch'ien Lung Reign of the Emperor Kao Tsung, or the year 145 of the Ch'ing Dynasty, or the year 1167 A.H. to the Muslim Malays, or AD 1789 to the Christian Europeans – Teng Lee dealt with and understood all the peoples who scrambled for wealth and power in South-East Asia.

Teng was only second mate then, but because his father owned the junk he had stood beside Perak Shah as the junk had been conned through the rocks and the shallows, and into the magnificent natural harbour that lay beyond. It had still been blowing very hard, if perhaps not up to the storm-force strength of the previous week, when the Chinese had gone to the assistance of the sinking prahu. 'We should let them drown,' old Su had growled. 'They are pirates.'

'We do not know that, Captain Su,' Teng had argued.

'All Malays are pirates,' Su had declared, but he had

3

made the rescue, because the owner's son wished him to do so. It had been no easy task, for the junk was difficult to manoeuvre into a strong wind, while the prahu was clearly sinking. But with four men hanging on to the helm, and the sails lowered by several boards, Su had managed to bring her about and gradually steer her to a position just upwind of the stricken vessel. Then lines were thrown, and eagerly taken in by the Malays. That Su had been correct in his judgement was by now evident, both from the swivel guns mounted on the smaller craft, and by the personal weapons carried by all her crew.

'If they come aboard with those, they will take our ship,' Su complained.

Teng had solved the problem by disarming each Malay as he gained the junk, and throwing the swords and pistols into the sea. The rescued men were too grateful to object.

The rescue had been an inspired act, quite apart from its charity. Because if Perak Shah, then a youth hardly older than Teng himself, most certainly was a pirate, he was also capable of showing gratitude, and as he had grown in stature and power amongst his people, that gratitude had become important. From that day to this, not a single ship belonging to Teng Wong's vast fleet of trading junks had been attacked in Malayan waters; no investment could ever have been more amply repaid. But for Tengee it had meant even more than that: the friendship of a strange, often cruel and treacherous but always attractive man – and an acquaintance with Singapura.

The island was not one ever visited by the average trader. Situated just off the southern tip of the long, south-stretching peninsula of Malaya, and itself surrounded by small islands and shoals and rocks, known evocatively as the Dragon's Teeth, it was best avoided on purely navigational grounds, quite apart from the reputed character of its inhabitants. These included huge

4

tigers, even larger snakes and enormous crocodiles. But it was the men who were most dangerous.

Once, in the early days of history, Singapura had been a prosperous and independent nation, a halcyon period which Perak Shah was fond of recalling nostalgically. But the island was only twenty-three miles long by perhaps half that wide, and thus the limited population it had been able to sustain had acted against either expansion or even self-preservation. The men from Malacca had conquered it, as they had once conquered all of south Malaya, and when their power had dwindled, Singapura had become part of the Sultanate of Johore, which dominated the mainland across the narrow strait that made Singapura an island.

But the sultans had thought little of their southernmost province. They had neglected it, preferring not even to acknowledge its existence. Thus the jungle had swept across the ruins of what had once been fine buildings, and the creeks and harbours had become refuges for men who would earn no honest living, and for whom the bustling trade of the Java and South China seas had provided a continual, tempting harvest. Perak Shah was only the latest and most successful of these.

In the strongest possible physical contrast to Perak Shah, the Chinese Teng Lee was no more than medium height and nowadays slightly running to stomach, with smooth hands more used to holding a pen than either pulling on a rope or firing a pistol. But if his figure no less than his clothes, from the richly embroidered green silk jacket with its matching loose trousers to the splendid kid of his brown boots and the jewelled green cap he wore on his head, indicated a man over-fond of the very best life had to offer, he was still Teng Lee. He was one of the six sons of Teng Wong of Canton. There was no greater trading concern in the world, whatever the airs given itself by the 'John' Company, the British merchant consortium which sought a monopoly of the Far Eastern carrying business. Even if the sons of Teng Wong campaigned with their brains and their wealth rather than with swords, the friendship of so well known a house had worked out to Perak Shah's advantage as well, and not only in Teng Lee's regular visits to the island, bringing the best of the outside world for the delectation of the pirates.

It was perhaps a good thing, Teng thought, that his friend had never taken the trouble to consider that trading empires, like any other, need to be preserved, and even, from time to time, defended.

Perak Shah was on the dock to watch the junk bring up, a simple matter of dropping the huge, wood-ribbed sheets of canvas — there were no yards on which the sailors might perch precariously to furl the sails. Then the anchor plunged into the still waters of the harbour, and the varnished hull came to rest. Perhaps to the eyes of the Malay the Chinese ship looked incongruously top-heavy, with her high stern and bow, and impossibly decorated, with lanterns and streams of coloured ribbon — he was aware that the stern cabin where Teng Lee lived was far superior in its luxury to anything he possessed — but he also knew, from experience, that the junk was a surprisingly good sea boat. It was a well-manned one, too: already one of her boats was being lowered to convey the captain ashore.

For the occasion, Perak Shah had hastily donned his gold necklace, from which there hung a gold replica of a lion's head. This was Perak Shah's emblem, as indeed Singapura meant Lion City. The name had been bestowed by the legendary Prince Nila Utama, son of a Malay king and a mermaid. The Prince had been washed ashore following the wreck of the ship on the island then known as Temasek, or Sea Town. Even then it had been a haunt of pirates, but the first creature Prince Nila Utama had encountered was a fearsome beast, which the Prince

6

had later been told was a lion. Hence the name he had given the land he had first brought to greatness, and if no one in South-East Asia had ever actually seen a real lion, the story was nevertheless a satisfactory basis for a national mythology; Perak Shah was not going to let it die.

With the chieftain were several of *his* captains, and several of his sons as well, amongst them the eldest, Bodaw Shan. Another friend, Teng thought as he stepped ashore. At Perak Shah's request, Teng had once taken Bodaw Shan, then a boy of fourteen, to Canton, to show him something of the world which lay beyond the horizon of any Malay. Bodaw Shan had been awestruck at the wealth and power to which he was introduced; Teng liked to feel that the tour had perhaps made him more civilized than the father he would undoubtedly succeed.

'Teng Lee,' Perak Shah said, and clasped Teng's hands. 'It is good to see you.' He looked at the sky, where heavy dark clouds were gathering. 'I had not expected you for another month, the weather has been so unsettled.'

He spoke Malay, a language which Teng understood perfectly, as he had also made it his business to understand and speak Thai, and Flemish and English, all the tongues which were used in the countries with which he traded. It was Teng Wong's way, and the source of his enormous wealth, to have his sons command his trading junks; if they cheated him, then in the long run they cheated themselves. And of them all, Teng Lee, only the third eldest, was the most successful.

'It is good for me to see you too, Lord of the Five Villages,' he now replied in the same language. 'We have outrun the weather to get here.'

Perak Shah grinned. It was a title he had chosen for himself, denoting his overlordship of the five villages which had grown up around the river and the harbour. If ambitious, he was also cautious, and for all his acknowledged leadership of the pirate fleet when it put to sea, he would not yet call himself Sultan of Singapura. That step had first to be prepared carefully, with Teng Lee's help. 'What news from Bangkok?' he asked anxiously, as they walked together back to the palace, as he would have his bungalow known; the other men followed at a respectful distance.

'Little, I am sorry to say,' Teng reported. 'Rama was away, campaigning against the Vietnamese. I spoke with his son, Prince Nobhalai. His father is interested in expanding Siam to the south, certainly, and contemplates an invasion of Malaya, but Prince Nobhalai asks what a mere pirate can offer him to make him wish an alliance with a country so small and remote as Singapura.'

Perak Shah was beginning to frown, but Teng did not look disturbed, even if the men behind them were clearly alarmed — there was no one else in the world who would dare so to address the Lord of the Five Villages.

'So I told him of your greatness, Perak Shah,' he said. 'Of your dream of restoring the independence of Singapura, in alliance with the great power of Siam. I told him how an invasion by you of Johore, just as the Thai armies were marching on Kedah from the north, would distract the sultans from helping one another and make his victory certain. I told him that all you require of the alliance would be the assistance of the Siamese fleet.'

Perak Shah climbed the steps to his verandah and sat on his stool; another was hastily produced for Teng — the other men remained standing. From inside the house the veiled women of the chieftain's harem peered through bead curtains at the richly dressed visitor. They all knew Teng Lee, knew that his presence meant fine things for them. 'By Allah,' Perak Shah said. 'Did he believe these things?'

'Are they not true, Perak Shah?' Teng asked, innocently. 'The Prince undertook to report my words faithfully to his father, with whom I am to have an audience on my homeward journey.'

8

'And I am, as always, lost in gratitude for your work,' Perak Shah said. 'To achieve the independence of Singapura, to free ourselves of Johore, to be a sultan . . . are these things idle dreams, my friend?'

'They are legitimate ambitions, Perak Shah,' Teng told him. 'And confirm the greatness of your spirit, that you will seek the aid even of those whose beliefs are alien to you, against people of your own race and religion, purely for the greater glory and prosperity of your country.'

Teng, of course, was a Buddhist himself, as were the Thais, and Perak Shah was well aware that he risked the condemnation of the mufti for seeking infidel aid against his fellow Muslims of Johore. But if he considered that he had been either warned or reproached, he gave no sign.

They ate many of the delicacies of which the Malays were proud. The meal was known as a *nasi padang*, which indicated that the several dishes, as many as fifteen, would be served with rice and spiced with curries. It commenced with satay – marinated pieces of chicken delicately speared on thin wooden skewers and roasted in ground peanut sauce; this was followed by *nasi goreng*, the traditional fried rice of the Malays, containing small slices of chicken and lamb; then there was *pepesan* – pieces of fish coated in coconut cream and broiled in banana leaves; and *rendang* – boiled hunk of meat smothered in coconut and spices – this last was a very special dish in honour of the visitor, for Perak Shah's herd of cattle was small and intended for milk rather than meat. With all of these dishes there was a huge bowl of sambal, the hot curry mixture which was essential to the preservation of food in this steaming climate, and with the meat was served a dish of *gado-gado*, delicately steamed vegetables which, like the satay, were dressed in ground peanut sauce. To wash it down there was coconut milk.

Although the food was exquisitely tasty; it was not a

meal that appealed to Teng Lee to any great extent. He found the curries too hot to enjoy, and the food itself was cold and clammy. This was because the Malay women, who had also the responsibility for tending the rice paddies and the flock of sheep and the chicken run, not to mention their children, did all their cooking first thing in the morning; the food was eaten cold as required during the rest of the day. Nor did he appreciate the Malayan habit of eating with the fingers. It was a delicate operation, the rolling of the rice into little balls before it was dipped in the sambal, the vigorous licking of the fingers after each mouthful – but he would have preferred to use the foodsticks he kept in his sash.

He found it equally distasteful to eat in public, sitting on the verandah. It seemed almost the entire village had squatted in the palace forecourt to watch the great men. Presumably there was little enough to entertain the people of Singapura, and the arrival of the trading junk was an important event, but he could not help but wonder how often those people ate on this scale. In any event, in Canton he preferred to eat in private, with only Wu Chang at his side. But then, no doubt he was more happily married than most.

'You are a good friend, Teng Lee,' Perak Shah remarked. 'The best of friends. And yet . . . I would ask you a question.'

Teng Lee bowed his head.

'You have now acted as a go-between for myself and King Rama for a year,' Perak Shah said. 'This must have been at a great expense in time and trouble to yourself, and yet, you have never asked for any reward for your services. I find this disturbing. I would not have you act out of friendship alone. That would put me too deeply in your debt.'

'I understand, Perak Shah,' Teng agreed. 'And I shall ask for my reward, when it is time.'

'I would have you ask now.'

10

'It is simply this: when you have achieved your ambition and made Singapura an independent country, and a great one . . . I would ask your permission to settle here and build warehouses, and carry on my business. From this very spot.'

Perak Shah was amazed. 'You wish to leave China?' He had never been to China, but he had heard about it from his son. There could be no place on earth to compare with China.

'That is my intention,' Teng said carefully. 'In the course of time.'

'But why? Your father. . . ?'

'Will not approve,' Teng agreed. 'But fathers do not live forever. Then, perhaps, my brothers also will not approve. But perhaps I think more deeply than they. You know, because I have told you, that ten years ago the Emperor Kao Tsung died?'

Perak Shah nodded.

'As was prophesied at the time,' Teng went on, 'that was an evil day. Kao Tsung was the greatest of the Ch'ing, and greatness permits justice. If the gods seem to have decided that it must be the fate of China ever to lie beneath foreign domination, his rule was the most just, the most correct, of all foreign emperors. Since his death, there have been hard times. China has fallen into revolution and chaos. There are old men with long memories who speak of what their fathers told them of the last days of the Ming, when a man could not walk abroad without guards to save him from being beaten and robbed.'

'In Canton?'

'Not as yet. But it will happen there soon enough. And then, the Manchu are not as we. They treat the men of Han* as inferiors. This was not apparent in the early years of their rule, because of the justice of Kao Tsung

* The Chinese

11

and his father, and because the Eight Banners were confined in the north. Now they roam the country, exacting taxes, and we are forced to bow before them. This seems not to matter to my father and my brothers; the Manchu at least do not interfere with our trade – they only seek to tax us afterwards. But to me, such demeaning servitude is abhorrent.'

Perak Shah looked even more surprised; he had not thought to hear this normally mild-mannered and quiet-spoken Chinese so vehement.

'Besides,' Teng added less forcefully, 'can there be a better place to trade from than Singapura? This island is the very centre of the world, for those who would deal with other countries, as it has perhaps the finest harbour in the world, too.'

Perak Shah smiled. What his friend had to say pleased him. In pursuance of his ambitions for himself and his country, he had studied the vital forces which made other countries strong. Trade was one of those forces, and the Malays knew nothing of trade. To have a man like Teng Lee operating out of Singapura would be a great asset. 'Then you shall be welcome,' he promised. 'We shall celebrate the independence of my people together.'

Teng spent several days on every visit to Singapura, as he did in every port at which he called. He moved through life in an orderly, but inquisitive fashion. He liked to watch other people at work and at play, sometimes even at war, as long as the war did not affect him or his profit. Thus he enjoyed waking in the morning to the call of the muezzin to prayer, just as in Batavia or Penang he enjoyed listening to the pealing of the church bells, and always wondered at the impiety of the Europeans in worshipping only once a week.

But in Singapura he had more than a passing interest. This was to be his home. Thus the almost human call of the mynah birds, the rustle of the lizards, the wild orchids

12

which bloomed in such abundance, all held a special significance for him. Yet he could not help but wonder what impact his coming would have. These people were desperately poor, desperately primitive. They lived at subsistence level by Chinese standards, their existence garnered from and limited by the sea and their pitiful flocks and tiny rice paddies – whatever profit they made from their piracy went either to Perak Shah or the mosque. Even their Mohammedanism was a survival from the past, in many ways tinged with the paganism to which it could so easily revert, the subtle eroticism of the Hinduism it had replaced. He did not think that Perak Shah, with his grandiose schemes, was truly aware of these things. But Bodaw Shan was, and in him there was hope for the future. Nor were Perak Shah's dreams unattainable. If Rama I, who had himself within recent memory usurped the throne of Siam, did indeed invade north Malaya, then all things were possible. Certainly Teng intended to do what he could to make them happen.

He knew that his wife Wu Chang and the boy Teng Chiang would be happy here. He could hardly wait to show Wu the island, the strange combination of primitive people and even more primitive jungle, with the exquisite, if warm climate, balmy sea breezes, blue skies . . . even in the monsoon season, Singapura was blessed. And it *was* the monsoon season; his ship had come to shelter just in time. For a week the rain poured down and the wind howled, bringing down trees, even overturning some of the Malay huts, while great waves pounded the beaches and the river mouth, and the beaten-earth pathways which were optimistically known as streets themselves turned into rivers of mud.

This was another reason for delaying his departure; the junk, securely riding to four anchors and surrounded by land, was in no danger, and Teng could spend his days walking by the river beneath his umbrella, and selecting in his mind where his warehouses would be sited, and

13

where he would build his house and where his personal dock would be placed . . . and a great many other things besides. He intended to bring civilization to this place. But it would be civilization of his own choosing, and based on the writings of Confucius and the thousands of years of Chinese culture which had produced them, not that imposed by the barbarian Manchus, who galloped to war behind their Eight Banners and thought only of conquest.

He might even civilize the people, he thought, watching the men running from the trees, splashing through the puddles. Like the messenger of the first day, they were panting and excited, and they had not come down the path from the river mouth, but through the jungle itself, from the west coast beaches. Now they pointed behind them as they knelt before Perak Shah. 'A big ship, O Perak Shah,' the first man shouted.

'She has lost her masts,' said the second.

'Drifting,' said the third. 'Badly damaged by the wind.'

'And close to the land,' said the first, continuing the theme.

Perak Shah stroked his beard. 'European?'

'Undoubtedly, Perak Shah.'

European ships invariably carried everything a man about to fight a war might need, so much so that they were as a rule too strong to be attacked. But, drifting and dismasted. . . .

Teng hurried into the forecourt. 'Allow me to offer my advice, Perak Shah,' he said.

'I will have her,' Perak Shah declared. 'It will be a great victory.'

'It would be unwise,' Teng argued. 'These Europeans are powerful people.'

'Powerful?' Perak Shah asked. 'Where is their power?'

'I have seen their ships, and their soldiers. And their guns.'

'So have I seen their guns,' Perak Shah pointed out.

14

'When that Dutch ship sank off our shores three years ago. They are great things. But they are too few to fight against us.'

'They are not few, Perak Shah,' Teng insisted. 'They may seem few to you, but they are many, very many.' He pointed to the west. 'They are only far away.'

'Well, then, that is too few, here in Singapura,' Perak Shah pointed out. 'This ship is crippled. We shall have her.'

'No doubt,' Teng agreed. 'But what if the Europeans seek to avenge her, and send a fleet, each ship more powerful than any you have ever seen? They would destroy you, Perak Shah. Destroy Singapura. Destroy all of your ambitions.' And mine, he thought, although he did not say so.

Perak Shah considered for a moment, then grinned. 'You are not a soldier, Teng Lee. You do not understand the true source of power. I do not think these Europeans are as powerful as you pretend. I will have this ship, come what may.'

Teng hesitated. 'Then allow me to accompany you, Perak Shah,' he said. He might at least be able to save a few lives, he thought.

PART ONE
The Orient

CHAPTER ONE

The Pirate

'Ladies,' said Mr Small. 'The wind is dropping. The seas are going down. We shall commence our repairs immediately, and hope to be underway very shortly. The captain send his compliments, and says to tell you that cook is now relighting the galley fires, so there should be a hot breakfast for you all very shortly.'

'But the land?' asked Major Phillips. Although an army officer, he considered himself an experienced sea-traveller, and had been one of the few passengers to venture on deck during the storm. 'We are too close to land.'

'Well, the Strait of Malacca is narrow, to be sure, sir,' the mate agreed. 'Should we approach the land too closely for safety, we shall simply anchor until our jury rig is complete. There is no longer any danger.'

He closed the cabin door and there was a great stirring. Four months at sea, even in the relative comfort of a big East Indiaman, made for intimacy of a physical kind. Three days in a typhoon had added an entirely different sort of intimacy to the forty passengers. Those who had been most aggressive and bombastic in fine weather had been found to be afraid of the howling wind and the roaring seas; Mr Anstruther, stout and florid, fond of standing on the quarterdeck and holding forth to a large audience on any and every subject that came into his head – he had set himself up as a universal expert – had fallen to his knees, his wig slipping from his bald head, and

19

prayed when the first of the masts went overboard. Those who had been most timid had proved to possess quiet courage, or at least resignation. The children had been terrified, but this was understandable. The storm had broken – sadly, when they were almost within sight of their destination, the tiny British colony of Penang off the west coast of Malaya, and swept them past their goal into the strait which separates Malaya from Sumatra. But, at least, by that time they had all found their sea-legs, and the distressing stench of vomit, which had long afflicted them when crossing the Bay of Biscay so very long ago, was absent. But fear has a smell of its own and is difficult to shake off.

Now the male passengers buttoned their waistcoats and replaced their jackets, discarded in the heat of the storm; in the cabin, with all its ports tightly battened, it had been like the antechamber of hell, as Clive Hammond had put it. Women straightened stockings and gowns, and flushingly mumbled apologies if the arms in which they had been nestling during the tumult were now found not to have been those of their husbands.

Elizabeth Blaine stirred and sat up; Mr Hammond's arms fell away. If she gave him an apologetic glance and a smile, she was unable to muster a blush. Too much had happened, after too long, these last four days.

Elizabeth Blaine's husband was not on board; he had gone to Penang as ADC to the Governor two years previously, only a month after their marriage, and had not felt it suitable to take his bride to so insalubrious a climate. He remained, therefore, a man she hardly knew save as a distant and to her mind elderly friend of her family who had approached her father after a decent period of mourning for his first wife, and had been happily accepted as suitor for Harry Townsend's only daughter. Edward Blaine was an army officer with considerable prospects; apart from a private income, he was a staff rather than a line officer, and therefore did

20

not have to risk life and limb charging about a battlefield.

That he was thirty-eight years old and his bride only twenty-two had seemed about the right ratio, in the England of George III. Certainly Elizabeth had not fought the decision; she had been too well brought up for that. Instead she had determined to make the best of her marriage, and might even have succeeded but for that unfortunate separation. Two years is a long time in the life of a young and beautiful woman and Elizabeth Blaine, with her long, pale golden hair, her wide-set blue eyes, her straight nose, perhaps a trifle long, and matching chin, her surprisingly wide mouth and her slender body, was certainly beautiful. But, worse, the two years had had to be spent in the home of her husband's parents, as she was now a member of that family. The result had been not the slightest chance of even a flirtation to pass the tedious hours.

Thus when Major and Mrs Phillips, old friends of the Blaines, had come to call and announced they were also on their way to Penang, where the major would command the garrison, and furthermore had hinted they would chaperon her, she had not thought twice about accepting. There had been no time to inform her husband and obtain his permission, for she was going to arrive as quickly as any letter could. She had no doubt he would understand that she had been almost driven mad by her continual confinement.

She had boarded the *Henry Oliver* in that admirable frame of mind, and had then found herself surrounded by ship's officers, all magnificent in their uniforms if not terribly handsome, and the passengers included several young men, all aware that there were four long months ahead, a good portion of which would be spent beneath a tropical moon.

'Well, Mrs Blaine,' Mr Hammond said, 'shall we go

21

on deck and get some fresh air, and perhaps see if we can discover what cook is preparing? I have to confess that I am very hungry.'

'Why, so am I, Mr Hammond,' she agreed, and gave him her arm, avoiding looking at Mrs Phillips. Undoubtedly there were problems ahead. Harriet Phillips, although a good-natured woman and indeed a broad-minded one, was also practical. She had interfered with none of the invitations Elizabeth had received to look at the stars or to learn how to take sights with a sextant, which required a good deal of shoulder to shoulder manoeuvring, until the captain had announced that by his reckoning they were within a week of Penang, and indeed the next day they had sighted the Nicobar Islands, and soon after that the mountains of Sumatra. Then the good lady had felt obliged to point out to her charge that she would very shortly be back in the arms of her husband, about to undertake a life of domesticity, and that it was time to start thinking about her wifely duties, rather than which companion she would choose to walk with on the quarterdeck after supper each evening.

Remarkably, that warning had acted as a catalyst in Elizabeth's mind. She had certainly not come on board the *Henry Oliver* with any idea of adultery. If she knew she did not love her husband, she was still determined to be a good and faithful wife, however much she might enjoy being admired by other men. And anyway, adultery was not a practical proposition on board a crowded ship, where passengers of both sexes shared a single cabin with only curtains over their bunks for privacy. Besides, at the beginning of the voyage she had taken little notice of Mr Hammond. She knew who he was, of course; he had quite a reputation as a novelist, even if he had published only one book. But that book, *The Cardinal*, had made him a notorious figure, for while purporting to be a fictional life of Cardinal Mazarin and telling of his amour

22

with Anne of Austria – the mother of Louis XIV and regent of France during the King's infancy – it had quickly been recognized as a most scurrilous satire on the Prince of Wales, his entourage and lady friends. Rumour had it that the author had hastily been found a position as an apprentice clerk to a factor in Penang, just about as far away from England as one could get without actually being despatched to Botany Bay as a convict, to save him from imprisonment for sedition.

Elizabeth had never read *The Cardinal* but she had gathered from one of the passengers who had that the book was not only defamatory and libellous, but in places, obscene. This discovery, which she had made during the voyage down the West Coast of Africa, had aroused her interest in the author. In addition she had realized that Mr Hammond was an attractive man, tall enough to tower above herself, and she was tall for a woman, gauntly handsome, with long thin features and straight black hair above a high white forehead and startlingly luminous dark eyes. He was in his late twenties, entirely the best age for a man to be in Elizabeth's opinion. Closer inspection had revealed flaws, of course. His slender build and pale complexion, while suggesting a possibility of poor health which aroused the motherly instincts in most of the other female passengers, indicated to her someone who had spent too much time indoors with a pen rather than on horseback with a whip, and he had been seasick during their first week out of Bristol.

But during the following weeks and months she had found his allure growing. When the weather warmed up and he had removed his jacket and rolled back his sleeves, she discovered him to be far stronger and more athletic than she had supposed possible: he alone of the passengers had responded to the officers' challenge and proved his courage and ability by climbing the main-mast to the crow's nest. Unfortunately for her interest in him, even if

23

he wrote obscene books, he was also most certainly a gentleman, and unlike most of the other men never attempted to flirt with her. But his conversation was witty and well-informed, and if he had every reason to consider himself hard done by since what had been a promising career was now ruined, he seemed to take it very well and be prepared, like her, to make the best of his situation. They had spent more and more time in one another's company during the crossing of the Bay of Bengal, after venturing ashore together when the ship stopped in Bombay, mutually fascinated by their first glimpse of India and the Orient.

She had come upon this strange world unprepared, and her senses were assailed and titillated by the sights and smells with which she was surrounded. Beggars in rags lying by the roadside, handsome women in diaphanous saris, fiercely moustachioed men whose eyes seemed to burn her flesh, the minarets, domes and exquisite decorative work, were as stimulating as the stench of cow dung or rotting animal flesh was revolting. Elizabeth knew she had led a sheltered life. Visits to London had been rare excitements, and her marriage to a man so much older than herself a total disappointment. Yet she also knew that beneath the manners, carriage and dress sense which had been hammered into her from childhood there was a creature longing to break free and experience life in the raw. It was not an ambition she ever expected to realize, but in Bombay she could sniff at it.

Clive Hammond had been the perfect companion on such an occasion. Indeed, as she got to know him better she found him a most exciting man, with his fascinating tales of London society, for his fame as an author had gained him an entree into some of the great houses, and his immense knowledge, obtained from reading rather than experience to be sure, but none the less valid for that.

When he confessed that he had been falling in love with

24

her from a distance, ever since the voyage began, she had not known what to do, except that she had wanted to do *something* and Edward had seemed further away than ever. She wasn't sure who had actually instigated that first kiss, but Mr Hammond had not only kissed delightfully, he had also been prepared to carry things a stage further, and even to find solutions to all the problems that lay in the way. When they had looked into each other's eyes, and she had remarked that according to the captain in only forty-eight hours they would be in Penang and her last freedom would be ended, he had said, 'It is a terrible thing to give up one's freedom, without ever having used it.' He had a peculiarly roguish smile. 'Or abused it.'

His flippancy did not disguise the desire in his voice. Elizabeth had not lowered her gaze, even as she understood that he was inviting her to commit adultery, and that he had perhaps been planning this from the very beginning of the voyage, luring her with his studied aloofness. Adultery! It was hardly a word she dared to think, and had never uttered aloud in her life. But she had come to realise one thing during the voyage: that she did not love her husband. It might be possible to do so when they were again living together, but it had not been achieved in their one month of married life. And if it were not possible in the future, then her whole life was cast away, with nothing to remember save perhaps the voyage and this man. Adultery would be a sin, but to die without ever having lived was surely not what God intended.

So she had said, 'It is sometimes very difficult to abuse one's freedom.'

'If you were to find it too hot to sleep tonight,' he had suggested, 'and came on deck for some air, we might be able to resolve the dilemma.'

She had had no idea how he meant to go about it, nor did she feel she had as yet committed herself, but she was certainly not going to refuse at this stage. And in fact that night had been unusually hot and still, the *Henry Oliver* had done no more than drift, yards banging, the peaks of Sumatra still visible astern, the mountains of the Malayan Peninsula not yet visible ahead. Trembling with fear and excitement she had crept from the cabin in her nightdress at one in the morning, when everyone else was snoring, except for Mr Hammond, who was already on deck.

He had found that the cover on the ship's gig, which was stowed on chocks just aft of the mainmast and thus in considerable shade from the moon and in a part of the ship seldom used for routine duties, could be rolled back a couple of feet, sufficient for two people to insert themselves, and once replaced, providing they did not make any noise, they were totally concealed from the view of anyone else on board. He had even had the foresight to lay a couple of blankets in the bottom of the boat to soften the boards.

It had been difficult not to make a noise, because Mr Hammond had lifted her up to the boat by sliding his hands up her legs, beneath her nightdress, until they lodged beneath her buttocks. She had never been held like that in her life before, and gasped with a mixture of consternation and pleasure. Then of course a ship's boat is not usually intended to be used as a bed. There were some two and a half feet between the thwarts and the spread blankets, but she still had to insert her body beneath the thwarts, banging her head as she did so and aware that her nightdress was now riding up to her waist; although it was dark, she was even more aware that Mr Hammond, clambering in beside her, was wearing only a nightshirt.

Once inserted, she understood there could be no changing her mind; with Mr Hammond beside her, movement was very restricted, except against him. She had also been very aware of the wooden ridges pressing into her back. But these were rapidly forgotten as Mr Hammond's hands started to slide over her body.

Edward had never stroked her at all; a perfunctory clutch at her breasts, a crisply slapped indication that she was required to spread her legs, a grasp on the inside of each thigh to arrange her to his satisfaction, and a fiercely thrust entry which had hurt her as much at the end of their month together as on their wedding night – that had been the sum of his lovemaking, or her experience. Mr Hammond's hands were at once a torment and a delight. They slid up her legs, carrying her nightdress ever higher. They moved over her buttocks and to her horror went between. But it was a delighted horror, and she understood that because of the darkness he was using his hands as a blind man might have done, to know her. How she wanted to be known by Mr Hammond.

Even so when his hands had come round in front and sifted through her pubic hair she had stiffened, and felt she should reject him. She had made herself relax. His fingers had parted her legs and then the lips of her vulva, so gently, to move between. Elizabeth had never known such a sensation, she seemed to be reaching towards some goal of explosive passion, reaching . . . when he had taken one of his hands away she had again wanted to protest.

However, his intention had only been to take one of her hands and place it on his penis. Another first experience. She could not imagine herself touching Edward there, or his reaction if she did. But what a glorious, glossy sensation, especially as it hardened beneath her fingers.

All this while he was kissing her mouth, playing little games with her tongue. Then his hands came up to her body to stroke her nipples, and she had nearly screamed with ecstasy. His entry was perfection, because she was so ready. When he thrust he seemed to touch the entry of her womb. And when she felt the huge damp warmth flooding her, she thought, oh no, why so soon.

There had followed another delight, as, again totally

27

unlike Edward, he had not immediately commenced climbing out of the boat, but had stayed to play with her again, and have her play with him until he was ready again.

'Oh, Mr Hammond,' she whispered. 'I love you.'

'Elizabeth,' he replied, 'you are the most wonderful woman in the world.'

Her natural cautious commonsense kept telling her that to love a man solely for his prowess as a lover was a recipe for disaster. But then she could answer that she loved Mr Hammond for a great deal more than that. They liked the same things, laughed at the same jokes, held the same opinions on so many subjects. Those were all parts of the recipe for friendship; the sexual compatibility turned friendship into love. She wanted nothing more.

But she was married to another man! A horrible fact which did not need to be faced for another twenty-four hours. She felt no guilt, only resignation that such was her fate, total happiness that she had known one night of ecstasy. No matter what happened, she would love Mr Hammond forever. And if she did that, then surely all things were possible.

The very next morning the captain announced they were going to experience a storm and would not, after all, make Penang the following day. The passengers had been intensely disappointed, for by now they could see Malaya even if they were not yet able to make out any of the offshore islands. To Elizabeth it seemed as if God had bestowed a blessing upon her criminal act, and was permitting her one final unforgettable hour with Mr Hammond. But by nightfall it was pouring with rain, and by dawn the wind was howling and the sails had to be shortened. There had followed seventy-two hours of frightful buffeting by the sea, which she had not enjoyed at all. There again Mr Hammond had come up trumps; he had not appeared to be frightened, telling her that

28

from what he had read, well-found ships could survive even a typhoon. She had been obsessed with propriety, inspired by a guilty fear that the other ladies might suspect her secret, as the passengers were confined to the cabin all day, for when the ship had broached, losing a mast in the process, she had collapsed in terror in his arms, and stayed there as the other two masts had also gone by the board. That had not seemed so very improper, as every woman was in the arms of some man or other, expecting momentary death. Perhaps Mrs Phillips had not even noticed.

But now the storm was over. Elizabeth was very conscious of this as she emerged on deck, inhaling the still fresh breeze with pleasure after the stuffy confines of the overcrowded cabin. There were still whitecaps and the seas remained big enough, some fifteen feet from trough to crest. But the terrifying black clouds had gone, taking with them the searing flashes of lightning, which had struck the surface of the sea like giant whip cracks, and the tumultuous crashes of thunder that had followed immediately, and now the sun was giving a glow of wild beauty to the scene. Of course the ship itself was a mess, with cordage and torn sails and broken wood all over the place, but like any vessel on a long and arduous voyage she carried additional spars, and already men were hard at work bending these onto the stumps of the masts, while others cleared up the chaos on deck. Most important, everyone seemed perfectly cheerful, whilst during the height of the storm Captain Manners had been chewing his lip anxiously. Neither captain nor crew now doubted that they would be able to re-rig the ship sufficiently to get her underway again and after all make Penang with only a slight delay and even with most of her cargo intact.

'How long will it take us to get there, Mr Hammond?' Elizabeth asked.

'With a jury rig, three, maybe four days.'

'Four days.' She had been looking down into the water; now she turned.

But Mr Hammond was looking at the gig, which remained on its chocks but had been smashed by the falling mainmast and resembled a collection of driftwood.

'I doubt there'll be an opportunity, anyway,' he said. 'Elizabeth . . . will I be able to see you in Penang?'

Now she did flush. 'Will you want to?'

'Want to? My God . . . I love you.'

'Can you, Mr Hammond? Can you?'

'I have loved you for four months, from the moment I first set eyes on you. I have told you that.'

'And I believe you,' she said. 'Oh, my Lord.'

'And you?'

'I?' she asked. But she could very easily love this man, she knew. And she certainly did not love Edward Blaine, nor ever could, she now felt. 'I am sure we could arrange a meeting from time to time. Do you know Penang?'

He shook his head. 'I have no idea what to expect.'

'Neither have I,' she confessed, 'but there must be a way.'

'To meet from time to time? Surely, if we approached Blaine and told him of our love . . . he might agree to a divorce.'

'Never,' she said. 'He would kill you.'

'I can look after myself.'

'He would,' she insisted. 'He'd call you out. Can you shoot a pistol?'

'I never have before.'

'He's a marksman, and an expert fencer. He's a soldier. He'd kill you, Clive. And what he'd do to me . . .'

She was really alarmed. Clive Hammond patted her hand. 'Then we will have to meet clandestinely, as you suggest. But I could not live without seeing you again.'

She gazed into his eyes. Words might come easily to a writer, she knew. And yet she could not doubt his sincerity. Besides, having betrayed her marriage to him, she had to trust him. 'You will see me again,' she promised. 'I swear it.'

They continued to gaze into each other's eyes, so wrapped up in themselves they were unaware that there was a sudden tension and commotion on deck. Now Mr Small touched Clive's arm, 'Mr Hammond, I say, Mr Hammond, would you mind taking Mrs Blaine below?'

Clive frowned at him, 'We've only just come on deck.'

'Quite. But I'm afraid there's going to be some trouble.'

'The storm isn't coming back?' Elizabeth gasped.

'No. Something rather more serious than the storm.' He was looking past them and they followed the direction of his gaze. The land, which appeared to be an island, although there was mainland immediately to the north of it, separated by a narrow strait, was really quite close. Low-lying except for some hills a few miles inland, it was green and forbidding, looking darker than it actually was because the still rising sun was shining from behind it. It also looked devoid of any kind of life, but now they could just make out, leaving the heavy backdrop of the trees, several small sailing vessels, single-masted and rigged fore-and-aft, seeming to leap over the waves as they sailed closehauled into the breeze. 'Those are Malay pirates.'

'Pirates?' Clive snatched the mate's telescope and levelled it. Each of the prahus was certainly crowded with men and he was sure he could make out the glint of weapons in the sun.

'Pirates?' Elizabeth whispered, grasping his arm.

'But surely they would never attack a ship of this size,' Clive protested. 'Why, your guns could blow them out of the water.'

'Indeed they shall, if we can bring them to bear. Just as if we possessed our masts we could outsail those cockle-shells without difficulty. Oh, we shall fight them off, do not be concerned about that, but in our crippled

31

condition it is possible that one or two of the rascals may get on board. I therefore must ask you to take Mrs Blaine below. The cabin door will have to be battened until we have dispersed those people.'

Elizabeth gazed at Clive, her eyes wide. He gave her a reassuring smile, and escorted her back to the companion hatch. 'I'm sure Mr Small is right and it will take only a little while to disperse those fellows.' She observed that there was a slight tremor in his voice.

Teng Lee, standing aft beside Perak Shah as the lead prahu surged over the still boisterous waves, was aware of a tingling of the blood. He did not approve of piracy, or indeed of violence in any form, but the prospect of seeing a battle could not help but stimulate him; he had been in one or two battles against pirates himself in his youth, but never had he sailed *with* them. At the same time, he was more than ever concerned that Perak Shah might be creating a situation he would bitterly regret. Whatever the Malay's contempt for Great Britain – a country of which he knew nothing – he had never laid eyes, to Teng's knowledge, on a British man-of-war. Teng was well aware that a single British line-of-battle ship, such as he had seen lying off Calcutta some three years previously, could destroy the whole of Perak Shah's fleet, his villages, and even probably his island. And the British, from what he had seen of them, did not easily forgive an injury.

The ship was undoubtedly British. He had had some hopes that, this far south of the nearest English colony, she might be Dutch, caught out on her way to Malacca or Batavia. But quite apart from her lines, her captain had defiantly nailed a Union Jack to the stump of her mizen mast. She was not a warship, but as an East Indiaman she had been designed to withstand pirates, and there were at least a dozen guns in her broadside. As Perak Shah could see. Just as he could see that she was an unmanoeuvrable hulk. 'Steer for the bow and the stern,' he commanded. 'Do not let them bring their guns to bear.'

The orders were shouted to the other prahus, and signalled to those more distant. There were now a dozen of the small vessels at sea, word having been sent to the neighbouring villages that there was an exceptionally fine prize to be had if they acted promptly. As each prahu carried fifty fighting men, there was a formidable force closing on the Britisher, whose crew, Teng knew, would be exhausted and dispirited after at least three days of fighting the elements.

But she intended also to fight the pirates, if she could. As the prahus steered to get in front of or behind her, she opened fire, and soon plumes of water were leaping out of the sea, but none came near to the pirate ships. 'By Allah,' Perak Shah remarked, 'but the sound of guns stirs the blood, does it not, Bodaw Shan?'

He was clearly in his element. He had discarded his tunic and his gold necklace, added a brace of pistols to his sash, and was also carrying an ornately carved musket.

'Yes, Father, it stirs the blood,' the young man agreed, clinging to the rail as the little ship bucked and danced across the waves. Teng wondered what the boy really thought of the prospect of killing, or being killed – he looked serious enough, but quite unafraid.

Again the Indiaman fired – without success – and now the pirate fleet had reached their appointed positions, six in front of the drifting hulk and six astern. Perak Shah led the stern squadron. '*Now!*' he bellowed, firing his ancient musket into the air. The steering oars were brought across, the sheets let go to increase speed as they turned to run before the wind, and the prahus rushed down on the exposed stern of the merchantman. Teng Lee gazed at the men lining the taffrail, who were also armed with muskets, and at the puffs of smoke rising above them – and realized that those people were actually firing at him. Not that any of their bullets even came close to hitting the

33

dancing prahus. He was more interested in the faces to be seen at the stern windows below the poop, staring anxiously through the glass. The ship would be carrying passengers, of course; he had not thought of that. More than ever, if he dreaded what he was about to see happen, he was glad he was here.

With a thud and a crackling of splintered wood, the lead prahu struck the stern of the Indiaman; the jolt was so severe Teng was all but thrown from his feet. Instantly grapples were hurled to shatter the glass of the cabin windows and send the watchers there reeling back with shouts of alarm. Others were lodged on the taffrail itself, and before the English sailors could begin to free them and throw them back, Perak Shah was leading his men up, now joined by the crews of the other boats which came surging alongside; those at the bows were also boarding at this moment.

The English captain faced aft to defend his poop against what he considered the greater threat, while one of his men discharged a swivel-gun loaded with small-shot at the pirates. But that checked them for only a second, and Perak Shah was unhurt. Now he gave a roar and ran at the captain. Rapier was pitted against cutlass, but the lighter weapon was quickly swept aside and the captain fell to the deck with his head half severed from his body.

Teng Lee clung to the rail of the now abandoned prahu bobbing at the end of the grappling ropes and thudding into the big ship again and again, as well as rubbing strakes with the other boats at either side of her. He watched the swirling kris, listened to the exploding pistols and muskets, saw the smoke rising into the air and heard the shouts and curses from the deck — and the even louder shrieks of fear from the women and children in the cabin, where a good number of the pirates had entered through the shattered windows. It was time to interfere if he was going to accomplish anything.

Carefully he made his way forward, grasping the trailing ropes, and swung himself up; he might look soft but his muscles were as hard as any other man's, and he possessed the additional blessing of supreme self-confidence. His feet caught the strake beneath the stern windows, and gingerly he crawled through, coming to rest on the cushions of the nearest bunk. He stared at the scene in front of him. The male passengers had given a good account of themselves against the initial assault, for one of the Malays lay on the deck, clearly dead, and several more had been wounded by the discharge of pistols, the smoke from which still filled the large room. Three of the white men had also been wounded, but none seriously, and they had retreated against the far bulkhead. They had clearly been preparing to defend themselves to the death when they were assailed from behind by more pirates coming down the companion ladder and breaking through the cabin door. Now they looked left and right, panting with fear, while their women and children huddled behind them; several of the ladies appeared to have fainted and were being supported by others.

The Malays had paused for breath, but their eyes were fixed on the women, and particularly one striking young female with long yellow hair. She would have been worth looking at even had she been a brunette, but the hair was unlike anything Teng had seen before – and yellow was the most important of Chinese colours, the imperial shade, forbidden to anyone not of the Ch'ing house.

Equally attractive, to his eyes, was the young woman's look of defiance rather than fear. But the Malays too had obviously never seen yellow hair before. Teng realized he had to hurry, and decided to ignore the blood into which he had to step to reach the deck. There he picked up a pistol lying on the cabin sole, which he had observed was unfired, pointed it at the ceiling and pulled the trigger.

The noise was deafening, and the Malays turned in

alarm. 'These people are Perak Shah's prisoners,' Teng Lee announced.

The pirates glared at the diminutive figure in the green silk, but they all knew who Teng Lee was, and that he was a friend of their commander. Teng stepped past them to face the passengers. 'Throw down your weapons,' he said in English. 'Otherwise you will be killed.'

They were regarding him with equal consternation, confounded even more by his almost perfect command of their language. Then one of them, wearing the red jacket of an officer in the army, demanded, 'You are the captain of these murdering scoundrels?'

'Alas, no,' Teng said. 'I am a passenger, you might say. But I believe I can save your lives, if you cooperate with me.'

The man hesitated, then looked at his companions.

'It is our only chance,' he said, and threw his sword to the deck. The others followed his example, and the pirates gave a whoop of triumph.

Teng checked their forward movement with outstretched arms. 'They have surrendered,' he said. 'They are not to be harmed. Fetch me Perak Shah.'

The Malays looked at each other. The idea that anyone should peremptorily send for their captain was clearly preposterous. But the dilemma was solved by the appearance of Perak Shah himself, stamping down the companion ladder. His kris dripped blood, and blood had splashed all over his arms and chest; Teng realized why he had discarded his white tunic. He presented a fearsome sight, and the Europeans insensibly drew closer together; the men, who were binding the wounds of their fellows, stopped to reach for their discarded weapons.

'By Allah,' Perak Shah said. 'They put up little resistance.' From on deck there came a wailing cry and a splash, followed by several more. 'But these . . .' He stood in the centre of the cabin, hands on hips. 'We shall have sport with these.'

36

The passengers did not understand him, of course, but they could understand the tone of his voice. The men looked at Teng, the women shuddered in anticipation of imminent murder. The blonde girl tossed her head, but as she was now at the back of the throng Perak Shah did not notice her.

'These people are our prisoners, Perak Shah,' Teng said.

'Prisoners? They are Europeans. Christian infidels. They are mad dogs who make free with our seas and invade our very lands. I know of these Europeans, Teng Lee. They should be exterminated. I will not permit a single Christian infidel to live that my sword can reach. This I have sworn.'

'And I have promised them their lives if they surrender,' Teng said. 'As they have done.'

Perak Shah glared at him. '*You?*'

'I,' Teng said. 'I did it to save you from disaster, Perak Shah. I would also recommend most strongly that you spare the lives of all the crew who did not perish in the initial assault.'

'Bah,' Perak Shah said. 'We have already killed them all.'

'Then I pray you do not live to rue this day,' Teng said. 'But let me most urgently entreat you not to compound your crime. These people will not trouble you. I will take them with me when I leave Singapura.'

'You seek to command me?' Perak Shah shouted, still clearly excited by the battle and his easy victory.

'I seek to advise my friend,' Teng Lee said severely. 'Should a friend decline my advice, then I can no longer regard him as my friend. Neither can I again break bread with him, nor negotiate on his behalf.'

Perak Shah gazed at him in frustrated bewilderment.

'Teng Lee is right, Father,' Bodaw Shan said, coming into the cabin. 'We have killed enough.' He too was

37

splashed with blood. 'These people's lives are not worth the friendship of Teng Lee.'

'Bah,' Perak Shah said, and turned back to the ladder. 'You try my patience, Teng Lee. But you are my friend. And once you saved my life. I give you the lives of these miserable creatures in return. Take them away. My men have work to do.'

'I find it difficult to express our thanks sir,' said Major Phillips. He stood in the stern of the prahu with the rest of the male captives capable of remaining on their feet. Amongst them was Clive Hammond. Hammond had, in fact, much to the major's surprise, given a good account of himself in the skirmish with the pirates, even though it had been apparent he knew nothing of weapons.

'I am only sorry that so many men were killed before my intervention,' Teng said, thinking of the blood-stained shambles that had been the deck of the ship. The English sailors had fought bravely, but, exhausted by their earlier battle against the storm, they had been overwhelmed at once by the numbers thrown against them and by the ferocity of the assault. So they had been slaughtered to a man, pitilessly hunted down when they had sought refuge below, their still breathing bodies tossed over the side to summon the sharks.

Fortunately, the passengers had been made to climb down to the waiting prahus through the broken stern windows, and had not seen the horror above them. They had of course been aware of the sharks and the floating bodies, and had shrieked with fear, but in the main they were more concerned with their own immediate fate.

'You say you are not the master of these men,' Mr Anstruther said to Teng. 'And yet they obey you.'

Teng smiled. 'I am a humble trading captain, sir. But I happened once to have done Perak Shah, their leader, a service.'

38

'And what is to happen to us now?' Major Phillips inquired.

'Why, one of the ports at which I shall be calling on this voyage is Penang. That is a British colony. I will take you there, if you wish.'

'Penang?' the major cried. 'Why, sir, that was our original destination. We shall be even more grateful were you to deliver us there.'

Teng bowed his head. 'It will be my responsibility.'

'Penang,' the major said loudly, addressing the women, who with the children and the wounded were huddled in the bottom of the prahu – much as they had been in the cabin of the ship, Teng thought, as if they had congealed together – staring anxiously at the half-naked Malay seamen who surrounded them. Only the yellow-haired girl remained apart, watching the approaching land, her magnificent tresses flowing in the wind. But every few minutes she turned, holding her hair from her eyes, to look aft. At the youngest of the adult male passengers, Teng surmised. He had observed how the young man had been most solicitous about helping her down to the prahu and given her hand a reassuring squeeze once she was safely on board. The young man now addressed him. 'May I ask how you come to speak English so well?'

'I trade with Penang,' Teng said simply. 'Is the young lady your wife?'

There was a dash of colour in Clive's cheeks. 'No,' he said. 'No. We are friends.'

The prahu had surged back to the Dragon's Teeth and was now shortening sail to enter the harbour. Behind it came the others, laden with swords and muskets, pistols and ammunition, powder and food, clothes and ropes; the Indiaman had been anchored, and was now riding to the wind, to remain there until the prahus had been unloaded and were able to return again. Perak Shah would like to get one or two of those cannons ashore,

39

Teng had no doubt. But he did not think he was going to be able to do it.

The English people gazed at the river and the mangrove swamps which fringed its mouth, then at the huge trees, the houses beyond and the mosque. Some of their fear had begun to abate, and now the children were complaining about how hungry and thirsty they were, but even these complaints became muted as they took in the strange savagery of the scene. The half-clad, brown-skinned men and women, the naked children, the beaten-earth tracks, the refuse heap, the heat and the insects which swarmed everywhere were beyond anything they had ever suspected to exist.

'By God,' Major Phillips remarked. 'A pirate community.'

'A community which lives by what it can garner from the sea,' Teng said carefully. 'Now you must go ashore.'

The prahu had handed its sails and glided up to the wooden dock, alongside a ladder. The ladies and children had to be assisted up. Now their apprehensions were back, and they panted and clutched their skirts, sweating at once with the fierce heat and from their exertions, staring around themselves in continuing anxiety, and being stared at in turn by the Malay women and children who gathered around them.

'That is my ship,' Teng said, pointing at the big junk, which was not very much smaller than the Indiaman. 'You will be transferred as soon as I have summoned my boats.' He wanted them away from the Malays as rapidly as possible, and clucked his tongue as he realized he was not going to accomplish that in time; Perak Shah had also returned with the first boats.

'Prisoners,' the chieftain said disparagingly. 'Infidels. It goes against my ancestors to release them.' He had clearly been brooding on the matter.

'Nevertheless, you have granted these people to me,' Teng reminded him.

'I wish to look on them,' Perak Shah declared, and stalked to where the Europeans were gathered, while Teng hastily signalled the junk to put down its boats. 'Are their women totally shameless?'

Teng hurried behind him. 'It is not the custom for women to cover their faces in Europe, any more than in China.'

'This is true, Father,' Bodaw Shan said, having joined them.

'Ha,' Perak Shah commented, gazing at the women, and then suddenly stroking his beard. Teng Lee uttered a mental oath. What he had most feared had happened. 'By Allah,' Perak Shah said, 'a goddess!' He walked through the English people, who shrank away from him, to stand before Elizabeth Blaine, who was as usual by herself, separate from the other women. 'By Allah,' he said again, and stretched out his hand to take her hair between his fingers.

Elizabeth, keeping still with an effort, stared at him, eyes wide, breathing a little laboured, pink spots in her cheeks, but maintaining a high level of courage.

'By Allah,' Perak Shah said a third time. 'You may have the others, Teng Lee. But this one I will keep for myself.'

CHAPTER TWO

The Merchant

Elizabeth Blaine caught her breath. She spoke no more Malay than did any other of the passengers from the *Henry Oliver*, but she knew when she had been admired, and she could recognize the possessiveness in Perak Shah's voice.

Teng also drew a long breath. 'I must advise against it, Perak Shah.'

'One woman?'

'Yet does she belong to another. And the British hold their women as objects of great value.'

'Bah. They will have to do without this one. By Allah . . .' He was still holding Elizabeth's hair, and now used it to draw her closer, her mouth twisting with pain, while he stroked the flesh of her arm; yet she still did not cry out. 'She is as if made of silk,' Perak Shah said admiringly.

'Take your hands off that woman, sir,' Clive shouted, stepping forward and being followed by several of the other Englishmen, led by Major Phillips. But instantly they were surrounded by the Malays.

'Is this man her husband?' Perak Shah inquired, releasing Elizabeth and allowing his hand to fall to the haft of his bloodstained kris.

'No, her husband was not on board,' Teng said.

Perak Shah snapped his fingers to summon two of his men. 'Take this girl to my harem. By Allah,' he said, 'what a prize. Truly this has been my lucky day.'

'Your unlucky day, Perak Shah,' Teng said. 'If you take this girl, you will suffer great misfortune. I prophesy it.'

'I am sure Teng Lee is right, Father,' Bodaw Shan said. 'Have you not women enough? Malay women. What do you want with an infidel?'

'I am surrounded by advisers,' Perak Shah sneered. 'I do not need advice.' But he was looking at Teng, not his son, and Teng realized that he must make up his mind very quickly. Perak Shah was still riding a high of excitement and blood lust, and now sexual lust as well, and so were his men, with the exception of Bodaw Shan. Teng doubted that threats of ending their friendship would really work again, at this moment. And besides, he did not wish to end their friendship. He wished Perak Shah to prosper, so that he could come here to live, away from the heel of the Manchus stamping on his neck. All he really feared, as a result of today's crime, was a British punitive expedition to destroy Singapura and end that ambition. Even if he had not been able to save the ship or the crew, he had yet felt sure that if he could take the passengers to Penang he could avert the worst. He was still sure of that. Was one girl, however beautiful, worth risking all of that? It was not even as if her life was at stake, although she might equate honour with life. But that was a European concept.

'If the woman so pleases you, Perak Shah,' he said.

Perak Shah smiled. 'Had you blood in your veins instead of Chinese dollars, Teng Lee, you would be disputing which of us should have her. Take her inside,' he commanded. 'Tell my women to prepare her for my bed.'

The two men who had come forward at his earlier summons immediately grasped Elizabeth's arms. Now at last she gave an exclamation of alarm, and turned toward her compatriots. 'Help me,' she gasped. 'Clive! Help me.'

Clive pushed the restraining Malays to left and right as he attempted to dash forward, but Teng caught his arm.

43

He turned, and aimed a blow at the Chinese man. Teng avoided it without difficulty, placed his right leg behind the young man's while still holding his arm and exerted pressure; Clive fell heavily to the ground with a grunt of pain.

'By Allah, but that was well done,' Perak Shah remarked. 'Truly, you are a man of many talents, Teng Lee. Let us strike off this fellow's head. He will cause nothing but trouble.'

Teng shook his head. 'I will not have him killed. Have him bound and placed on board my ship.' He turned to Major Phillips. 'Now sir, please embark all your people in these boats and take them to my junk as quickly as possible. Or I may no longer be able to protect you.'

'Help me,' Elizabeth screamed, as she was half carried across the square to the palace steps, helpless against her captors, who had been joined by two more men to suppress her wriggling efforts to escape them; she was also now surrounded by an excited group of Malay women and children. 'Help me,' she shrieked.

The Englishmen shifted their feet and gazed at the drawn kris of the Malays surrounding them. They knew they would be committing suicide if they followed their instincts to go to the girl's aid.

'Can you really mean to abandon that young lady to a fate worse than death?' Mrs Phillips demanded.

Teng Lee bowed. 'There *is* no fate worse than death, good lady. And death is a fate which will overtake you all' — he pointed — 'including those children, if you tarry here a moment longer.'

Harriet Phillips looked at her husband, who returned her gaze, flushing as he did so. 'I'm afraid there is nothing we can do,' he muttered.

'We can die like men,' Clive shouted, attempting to get up as his arms were bound behind him, and then trying to stop himself as he was pushed towards the steps leading down to the waiting boats.

Clive Hammond watched Teng Lee come through the gangway on to the junk and give a series of sharp orders. Instantly the Chinese sailors sprang to work, hurrying to and fro; the sails were hoisted to the mastheads, their clews secured with sheets to pins set in the gunwales, and the anchor was brought in; the three storm anchors had already been weighed and stowed.

They were about to sail away and leave Elizabeth. For the tenth time he strained against his bonds, unavailingly, save to cut his wrists on the rope. He had been placed on deck against the gunwale, and had been left there, even by his fellow passengers, as if they feared contamination from his greater danger. No one had even offered a word of condolence. Now they had gathered further aft, gazing at the shore, unwilling even to look at each other, much less speak. None of them had covered himself with glory this day.

As if he cared what *they* felt. His own misery was all consuming. Had the Chinese not bound his ankles as well as his wrists he would have run to the side and thrown himself over. Better to drown than to live without her, knowing what she would be suffering in the arms of that thug. Besides, would she not also seek to end her own life the very minute she could?

He panted with frustrated anger because he was in love. It had happened with such overwhelming power he could still hardly believe it. Not the love; that had grown over four months. But the realization of it, the understanding that a girl as beautiful as Elizabeth Blaine would actually yield herself to him . . .

He had never loved before. If he had had a juvenile adoration for his governess, and then for a friend of his older sister's, that period of his life between the ages of eighteen and twenty-six, when he should have been sampling the delights of womanhood and falling in and out of love like a jack-in-the-box, had been entirely without romance. The reason was money, or rather, lack of it. His father, although descended from a long line of on-the-whole respectable and even, occasionally, wealthy country squires, had inherited a bankrupt estate, thanks to the weakness of his own father for cards and women. With great diligence John Hammond had set about restoring the inheritance which would eventually fall to his eldest son, but he had found it difficult with England's prosperity restricted by the war against France, and prices rocketing in every direction. Thus Clive had not been able to attend university. Instead, he had been confined to a bucolic Surrey existence, his principal occupation, when not helping his father about the farm, being playing cricket with the village lads and reading.

The perusal of every book in his father's library had inspired Clive to write. He had done so as a hobby, to relieve his boredom, never intending that his manuscript should see the light of day. He had been ashamed when his father had shown it to a visiting friend, a London bookseller, and utterly amazed when Mr Squires offered to publish it. But that was as nothing compared with the consternation aroused in the entire family, himself included, when it had been an instant success. For a glorious few months he had been the literary lion of London, invited to all the best homes, hovering on the edge of society, until the axe had fallen. Rumours had circulated of the official disapproval of Carlton House, and of the anger of the Prince, who had readily identified himself with the portrait of the Cardinal. After such august condemnation, invitations had disappeared overnight, and another friend of John Hammond, who was connected with the Prince's circle, had suggested that it would be best for Clive to see something of the world for some years and as rapidly as possible: there was more than one itinerant scribbler languishing in prison for having published a scandalous libel on Prinny. Useless to protest that the satire had been unintentional, even had that been true. With the King's health in such a precarious state there seemed little doubt that the Prince of Wales would soon have to be named Regent, if he did not succeed to the throne; certainly he was not one to have as an enemy.

Fleeing England would probably have become a necessity even if the Prince of Wales had never heard of the book. Being lionized by society had involved spending a great deal of money on clothes, an equipage, a valet, on cards and on presents – money Clive did not possess. The royalties which had accumulated from sales of *The Cardinal*, while sufficient to keep him in modest comfort in Surrey for some years, had hardly lasted a month in London society. Thus Clive had gone into debt, and his creditors pressed even harder when they discovered that he was *persona non grata* with the aristocracy. He had fled, before being gaoled on two counts.

As a penniless fugitive, Clive had been forced to take what he could. Another friend of his father's had a cousin, a Mr Gresholm, who was a factor in a place called Penang, one of the East India Company's stations beyond even India, and virtually at the end of the earth, who, he was certain, would welcome an assistant. For a twenty-seven-year-old man about town who had tasted the heights to become an apprentice merchant, a humble clerk, in the most remote part of the globe had been only one degree better than accepting Newgate . . . but that had been before he saw Elizabeth.

For if Clive had never been in love, that was not to say he had never *loved*. Adultery was the rage amongst the great ladies of London, although a game played to strict rules, naturally. There could be no dallying before marriage, or after marriage, until one had given one's husband a son and heir. Then the barriers went down. And this seemed to be accepted by the husbands, as long as it was done discreetly; after all, they benefited from it by the use of other men's wives. Clive, brought up in the highly moral atmosphere of his father's house, had been shocked – there is all the difference in the world between imagining great ladies falling into bed at the crook of a finger and discovering that they actually do so – then alarmed, and finally delighted. In a short space of time he had come to regard every woman as attainable provided she had reached the necessary marital status; that many of them had no desire for pregnancy, and were just as entertained by hands slipped beneath the skirt while drinking afternoon tea had been more exciting than offputting – it had taught him the use of his hands without which no man can aspire to be a lover.

Elizabeth Blaine had certainly been married. That she had not yet produced a son and heir was accounted for by her early and long separation from her husband. But that very separation suggested that she might be willing. Clive had therefore approached her as a hunter might stalk his quarry, content to take his time, plan his campaign, let her flirt and then become bored with all the other men on the ship while he gradually insinuated himself into her favour. It was a strategy which might have snared the Duchess of Devonshire herself.

But he had fallen in love while carrying it out! That might have been amusing had it not been so tragic. He had, he supposed, loved her before she had allowed herself to be seduced; he had spent the months watching her, listening to her, inhaling her, and dreaming about her. That night in the lifeboat had been an unforgettable experience, with a girl so fresh, so nearly virginal, and yet so relaxed about the whole thing, so eager to receive, and to share. He had known then that he had sought such a girl all his life, and that having found her he would never love again, as long as he lived. Her marriage had not seemed an insurmountable obstacle. But now he had lost her to a heathen pirate.

Teng Lee, having given his orders to his mate and seen

the junk begin to slip down the river to the sea, now went up to the other survivors and gave them a reassuring bow. 'I know you are weary,' he said, 'and no doubt hungry and thirsty as well. Will you come below and allow my people to care for you?' He tousled the hair of one of the little boys, who was obviously half delighted and half terrified.

The English exchanged glances, and then allowed themselves to be escorted into the after cabin. No one appeared to spare a thought for him, Clive thought bitterly; they felt he had endangered all their lives, as well as shown up their own spinelessness, by his futile attempt to rescue Elizabeth. And no doubt that attempt had also confirmed the suspicions shared by some of the most discerning women, that Mr Hammond and Mrs Blaine had been conducting more than merely a ship-board flirtation. But after a few minutes Teng returned on deck, accompanied by one of the servants he had mentioned. The man carried a tray, on which there was a bowl with rice in it, another with stewed meat, and best of all, a glass of coconut milk. This he held to Clive's lips, and despite his resentment at his treatment, Clive drank deeply; he was very thirsty.

'I am sorry I had to knock you down,' Teng said. 'But had I not done so, you would surely have been cut to pieces.'

Clive did not reply.

'My name is Teng Lee,' Teng said. 'What is yours?'

'Clive Hammond,' Clive said, without thinking.

One of the Chinese sailors had brought his captain a chair, on which Teng now seated himself. To Clive's consternation, the servant, kneeling beside him, produced a pair of ivory sticks, each just under a foot long and scarcely a quarter of an inch wide, squared but gently tapered and decorated with what he took to be Chinese scroll; with these the man expertly rolled some rice into a ball, then picked it up between the two sticks, almost as if

49

these were elongations of his fingers, dipped it into the stew, and held it against Clive's mouth. Again Clive would have refused, but he was too hungry, and the food was delicious.

'I should like to release you, Mr Hammond,' Teng said. 'Providing you will promise me that you will not throw yourself over the side.'

'Would it matter?' Clive asked, swallowing and immediately being fed again.

'Are you so in love with the young lady?'

Clive turned his head in surprise.

Teng smiled. 'Are you supposing that because I am of a different race I do not understand about love? I am perhaps more fortunate than you, in that I have a wife to love. You do not?' It was only half a question.

'No,' Clive said.

'Thus you have the misfortune to love the wife of another. Where is her husband?'

'In Penang.'

'Where the major says you were bound. Then, would you not have been about to lose her to the arms of another, in any event?'

Clive frowned at him; that had not seemed important, before.

'Or is it the concept that she should now be loved by a man of different colour, different culture, different religion, and therefore different sexual habits to yourself that angers you?'

'My God,' Clive said. 'If you only knew . . .'

'But I do know, Mr Hammond. Far more than yourself. And I can assure you that the sexual act is not so very different, no matter by whom it is practised.'

'Easy for you to say,' Clive remarked. 'Has your wife ever been raped?'

'No, I am happy to say. But then, neither has yours.'

'It amuses you to play with words.'

'Words are but the expression of thoughts, of ideas,'

50

Teng told him. 'They have no value in themselves. You are grieved at having lost your lady love. You suppose she may be gone forever. But is not forever a very carelessly used word? Certainly a very negative one.'

Clive had been staring at the Dragon's Teeth drifting by as the junk reached the open sea, while he swallowed the last of the stew. Now he turned his head sharply.

'We have a philosophy in China, which is called yin-yang,' Teng said. 'It represents the entire universe, and men's fates within it, as being of a whole, rounded and equal. The concept is itself represented by a globe with equal parts of black and white. Black is evil and . . .' he smiled, 'is regarded as female. White is masculine and good. The important thing, however, is that the two halves fit perfectly. So it is with life, we believe. A man is composed of both good and evil in equal parts. It is not easy to decide in every case which half will eventually triumph. Similarly with the events of a man's life. It is supposed that where a man suffers great misfortune, he will, in the course of time, achieve an equal measure of great good fortune. Or vice versa, of course. But it is better to suffer the ill fortune first.'

The meal was finished, and Clive felt considerably better; the servant had removed the tray, and now returned with another, on which were two steaming cups of green tea. One of these he served to his master, the other he held to Clive's lips.

'Explain to me the good fortune achieved by the sailors who were murdered by your friends,' Clive challenged, interested despite himself. 'Or by Mrs Blaine to make up for her being abducted and raped.'

'A true believer in yin-yang might say that they must have had great fortune at some previous time in their lives,' Teng said. 'However, I agree that is unlikely where so many people are involved.'

'Which ruins your theory,' Clive pointed out, unable, despite his misery, to resist an argument. 'And there is no

51

good fortune which could possibly compensate Mrs Blaine for her fate.'

'In which case, we must take refuge in another Chinese philosophy,' Teng said urbanely, 'which indeed should always be taken in conjunction with the belief in yin-yang. That is the principle of wu-wei.'

Clive waited. He understood that this strange man was trying to help him recover his spirits.

'It is difficult to translate wu-wei into English,' Teng said. 'The most literal translation would be "inaction". And basically, the principle of wu-wei is that more things are achieved in this life by inaction than by action. Thus, when a strong man armed with a sword bullies a weak man who is unarmed, it is better for the weak man to accept the blows and the harsh words with bowed head, than attempt to defend himself and perhaps be killed.'

Clive nodded. 'We have a similar tenet in Christianity. It is called turning the other cheek. I am afraid in that regard I am not a very good Christian, at least where the lives and honour of those I love are concerned. Nor would you be in similar circumstances.'

'No doubt,' Teng agreed. 'However, the point I would make is that I, and a good many people, consider that "inaction" is a mis-translation of the true meaning of wu-wei. We would prefer to translate it as "patience".'

Clive's frown had returned.

'Thus we would say that the true meaning of wu-wei is that more things are achieved in this life by patiently waiting for the right moment to occur than by hasty action. Thus the weak man who is bullied by the man with the sword should indeed bow his head and accept the blows and insults that are offered him – until the man with the sword lies down to sleep. Then the weak man should take the sword and chop off his head. That is a primitive example, of course, but I am sure you understand me.'

52

Clive gazed at him. 'I had thought that the pirate captain was your friend.'

'He is, and an important one. I will attempt in every way I can to prevent you from chopping off his head.' Teng smiled, because the idea of this inexperienced young man ever challenging Perak Shah was absurd, at least, without help. 'However, that does not mean that, if I were you, I should despair of ever regaining the young lady. Providing I were patient enough, and were prepared to leave the matter in the hands of those who would be my friends. And providing' – he returned Clive's stare – 'that I was sure I wished to repossess her, when it became possible.' He snapped his fingers. 'We have talked long enough. Release this man,' he commanded his servant in Chinese, and then reverted to English. 'I am sure you feel like a rest and a change of clothing, Mr Hammond. We will talk further tomorrow.'

For all his determination to regard Teng Lee as an enemy who had carelessly insisted on abandoning Elizabeth to an unthinkable fate, Clive soon realized that the Chinese was one of the most remarkable men he had ever met. As he got to know him better he discovered Teng to be urbane, learned, a philosopher, and yet a man who could use his hands to defend himself, and, Clive did not doubt, use a sword with equal ability; he was, on top of all that, an experienced and expert seaman and navigator.

He was also a witty and fascinating conversationalist. If his philosophy had been irresistible, at least as a source of argument, Clive found himself captivated the following day as Teng talked. He seemed to have visited almost every seaport in the East Indies, and stopped at several places which contained no port at all. He could speak with equal ease of Burma and Siam, of British India and Dutch Java, of the Philippines, where the Spanish held sway, and Macao, an island off the Chinese coast where there was a Portuguese trading station. And, of course, of the immensity that was China itself, for on his father's business he had travelled up the great canals to the Manchu capital city of Peking, and from there had even visited the Great Wall, only a hundred miles north of the Forbidden City.

He was clearly a very wealthy man; his silk clothes, the silver plates and cutlery on which his food was served, the quality of the food itself, amply proved that; but he was saved from complacency by his own nature, which was apparently one of compassionate curiosity about all living creatures, and especially those he regarded as less fortunate than himself. Thus he would spare the time to pat the English children on the head; talk with their mothers, pouring reassuring words into their still terrified ears, and produce silk robes for them to try on in place of the badly soiled and torn garments which they had worn since leaving the ship; and discuss serious matters with the men, whom he also invited to adopt Chinese clothing for the duration of the voyage.

'I think he really is quite a trustworthy fellow,' Mr Anstruther ventured that afternoon. 'Although I cannot help but feel that he will expect some reward for his services.'

'If he does not mean us some mischief,' Major Phillips growled. 'I should like to know why we are still sailing south. I had supposed he was standing well out from the reefs before turning back up into the strait, but I will swear we are now in the Java Sea. Mr Hammond,' he suggested, 'why don't you ask your friend what that land is over there?' It was generally accepted amongst the passengers that Teng Lee was more Clive's friend than theirs; he had spent far more time during the day in the company of the young writer than with anyone else.

Clive looked at the islands which had appeared on the starboard bow, and asked Teng Lee about them.

'Those are the Lingga Islands,' Teng replied. 'If you look beyond them, you will just make out the mountains

54

of Sumatra. Tomorrow we will sight the island of Bangka, and pass between it and Biliton. Then the day after that we will come to Batavia in Java.'

'Batavia?' Clive inquired.

'Batavia?' Major Phillips shouted, having come close enough to overhear the conversation. 'You are taking us to Batavia? You told us you would take us to Penang.'

Teng Lee bowed. 'I am taking you to Penang, Major. After I have called at Batavia. I have business there.'

'But you don't understand, Mr Teng,' Mr Anstruther protested. 'Batavia belongs to the Dutch. And Great Britain is at war with Holland. They will place us in prison.'

The women began to talk excitedly, voicing their concern.

Teng waited for them to calm down. 'I doubt they will do that, please,' he said. 'You will remain on board my ship, at least until we have ascertained that the Dutch mean you no harm. But I'm afraid I must call at Batavia before going north.' He smiled. 'I am carrying goods for the people there. If I do not deliver them I shall have lost a profit.'

On the morning after passing between the islands, they were now steering south-west, and could see mountains on both the port and starboard bows with a narrow strait between. But right in the middle of the strait, rising like a finger toward the sky, there was another, very small island, above which there were wisps of smoke.

'That is called Krakatau and is the greatest volcano in the world,' Teng said, and offered Clive the use of his telescope.

'Is that so?' Clive asked, thinking of what he had read of Vesuvius or Etna, as he studied the distant peak.

'Perhaps not the highest,' Teng conceded. 'But the most powerful. There are more than one hundred volcanoes in Java alone, and many of them are active, but none can compare with Krakatau.'

'When did it last erupt?'

'Many years ago. More than a hundred, in fact. But men still speak of it as told them by their fathers.' Now he pointed to the other land. 'To the north is Sumatra.'

'Still Sumatra?' Clive inquired. 'We sighted it before the storm. That was more than a week ago and a long way to the north.'

'It is a very large island,' Teng agreed. 'To the south is Java. It is also very big, but not so large as Sumatra. And there is Batavia.'

Clive swung the glass. The junk was approaching a rather low, flat coastline – although there were mountains behind it in the distance – which could just be discerned as a very shallow bay. There he could see ships at anchor, and in the very centre of the bay, a walled town consisting of a very European collection of buildings; indeed, he immediately thought of pictures he had seen of Dutch seacoast towns. The houses were clearly made of wood, with steeply sloping roofs to throw off the rain, and like the Malay huts in Singapura they were raised on stilts to keep out flood water, although these were much more solid affairs. There was, needless to say, a church, its steeple towering above the rooftops, as well as a town hall, in the tower of which was set a large clock, while as part of the enclosing wall he could make out a solid, square-built fort. Outside the wall there were several warehouses, and the wall itself was pierced in several places by what he made out to be canals.

'It is the Dutch way,' Teng explained. 'Wherever they go, they build canals for drainage. They have told me that in Holland this is very necessary or the whole land would flood.'

'That is so,' Clive agreed. 'The Dutch are a very industrious people.'

'Industrious,' Teng observed. 'But also destructive. There was a fine town here once, built by the Javanese themselves. The Dutch destroyed it, to create their own.'

'You sound disapproving of them,' Clive ventured.

'It is easy to disapprove of conquerors. Even would-be conquerors.'

'Yet you trade with them.'

'Only a foolish man permits his personal feelings to interfere with his business ventures or his opportunity for profit,' Teng pointed out.

The junk was anchored off the town and Teng went ashore, leaving a very apprehensive group of passengers behind him.

'By God,' the major growled. 'If he sells us short . . .'

'Why should he do so, Major?' Clive asked.

'You are a very trusting young man,' Mr Anstruther admonished.

In a few hours Teng was back, with several big, blond Dutch officials and factors, who saluted the major and then the ladies. 'Captain van Essenling, at your service,' said their leader, who wore uniform and had a sword at his side, and who spoke very passable English. 'Mijnheer Lee has informed us of your sad misfortune. That scoundrel Perak Shah is indeed a menace.'

'You know of him?' the major demanded.

'Indeed, sir. He has occasionally led his pirates in raids as far south as this, and he has taken many ships in the Straits of Malacca and the South China Sea.'

'Then why do you not smoke him out?' Clive asked. 'You should know, sir' – he glanced at Teng, who as ever stood impassively by, his hands buried in the sleeves of his green silk jacket – 'that the pirate is currently holding an English lady and subjecting her to the most unspeakable insults.'

Captain van Essenling sighed. 'Believe me, sir, I can appreciate your feelings. But it is not possible for us to take any action against the pirates of Singapura. We have a perpetual war of our own here in Java with the native princes, and lack the resources to bring it to a successful

conclusion. I could not spare a man for such an undertaking, especially as I know it would not benefit the
young lady; Perak Shah would certainly cut her throat if
he felt himself endangered. But now let me speak of
happier matters. Mr Teng informs me that he proposes to
convey you to Penang. This is perfectly acceptable to me.
But while he transacts his business here, which will take
several days, may I invite you to come ashore as you wish
and exercise yourselves? I am sure you will find much to
interest you.'

'You mean we will not be considered as enemy aliens?'
Mr Anstruther blurted, earning himself dirty looks from
the rest of the English.

'Why, sir, you are travelling under the aegis of the
Chinese flag,' the captain said, nodding to the red dragon
on the white background which hung at the junk's stern.
'Besides, Great Britain is at war with the Emperor
Napoleon and his satellites, of which, alas, Holland at
present happens to be one. But we in Java look forward to
the day we can regain our freedom. Perhaps even with
English assistance.'

'My God, sir,' the major cried. 'Let me shake your
hand. No damned Jacobins here, eh?'

Van Essenling smiled. 'Oh, there are a few, Major, a
few. Now, will you not avail yourselves of our
hospitality?'

'I'm afraid we have only rags to wear,' Mrs Phillips
said. 'Or else these heathen robes. The pirates took
everything else.'

'I am sure our good ladies will be able to assist you,'
van Essenling reassured her.

Suddenly everyone was very jolly and good-humoured,
anxious to get ashore, the women smiling, the children
chattering in shrill voices, the men squaring their
shoulders and endeavouring to appear less beaten by
their circumstances.

Teng drew Clive aside. 'There is someone I would have

you meet,' he said, and led Clive to the hatchway leading to the main hold, into which several of the Dutch factors had disappeared, accompanied by various of the Chinese crew. One of these factors was now re-emerging, a big man, like Captain van Essenling, but dark-haired and considerably older; Clive estimated him as perhaps fifty. His face was red and his arms sunburned – he wore no coat over his white shirt – but he looked fit and strong. 'Pieter Pieterszoon Hoorn,' Teng said. 'This is the young man of whom I told you. Mijnheer Clive Hammond.'

The Hollander peered at Clive, then extended his hand. 'Welcome to Batavia, Mr Hammond,' he said in very good English. 'Yes, Teng has told me of your misfortune. I am very sorry to hear it. You will come ashore and dine with me.'

The invitation was couched more as a command, from a man who was not used to being denied. Clive looked at Teng in surprise, and Teng gave a brief nod. 'I shall accompany you, Mr Hammond,' he said.

'Pieter Hoorn is a true success story,' Teng explained, as they were rowed ashore some time after the rest of the British party had departed. Clive was dressed in Chinese tunic and breeches, somewhat short in arm and leg, as even the loose Chinese garments were not designed for anyone quite so tall. 'He came out here as a young man, probably younger than yourself, apprenticed to a factor, just as you are, oh nearly thirty years ago. And by hard work and absolute honesty he has made himself into the most wealthy man in Batavia. So now he buys silks and spices, such as ginseng, which he cannot obtain here in Java, from me, and pays me in hides and sugar and even in fine silver. There are some mines quite close to the town.'

Clive could not decide whether or not he was being shown a path to follow. But any scepticism he might have felt about Teng's estimate of Hoorn's wealth disappeared when they gained the shore and were met by an equipage driven by a Negro coachman in livery, and thus conveyed through the narrow, cobbled streets of the little town and over bridges crossing the canals, to a remarkably large house, set almost in the centre of all the others. Here there was a walled garden filled with tropical flowers and stone statuary, and also tended by Negroes, whom Clive now realized must be slaves. He had never seen a slave before, nor, since Great Britain had abolished the slave trade two years before he left England, had he ever expected to see one in his life; certainly he had no idea they were used in the East Indies. It was not a subject he had ever considered very deeply, save to be happy that he had never been exposed to such a fate, and now he took it as evidence of Hoorn's wealth that he should possess such creatures. That wealth was even more readily displayed within the house, where the polished wooden floors, in places covered by magnificent Persian carpets, the whispering drapes, in a similarly rich material – obviously supplied by Teng – the paintings and the exquisite Leyden and Delft chinaware, were all superior to anything he had ever seen except in the great houses of the English aristocracy.

Waiting to greet them, apart from their host, was a pretty, buxom lady, and with her, three girls who were clearly her daughters, whose ages, Clive estimated, ranged from twelve to sixteen. All were as pretty as their mother once must have been, dark-haired but blue-eyed, making extremely attractive pictures in their pleated gowns, broad sashes and white stockings.

'Now,' Pieter Hoorn said, when they were sitting down to drink arrack, the sweet, strong, sugar-based alcohol produced in Java. 'Tell us the news from Europe.'

Clive had to consider. It was now late November, and the *Henry Oliver* had left England in July. But there was no telling how long before that the Dutch in Java had received their last news. 'Well, sir,' he said, 'were you

60

aware that following the Battle of Friedland, in June of last year, which was a resounding victory for Bonaparte over the Russians, the Frenchman met with the Emperor Alexander I at Tilsit to draw up a peace treaty?'

'Yes, indeed,' Hoorn said. 'It is the outcome of that treaty that concerns me. Did it not virtually divide the world, save for America, between France and Russia?'

'Why, I suppose it did,' Clive agreed.

'Giving Russia a free hand in the East,' Hoorn went on. 'Now, Mr Hammond, what has been the British reaction to that?'

'Well,' Clive said. 'I am not sure there has been a great reaction. I do know that late last year Bonaparte invaded Spain and Portugal, with a huge army, which was not at all to the liking of the Spaniards, by all accounts. He said it was to protect them from British incursions, but I think most people accept that he is merely rounding off his domination over western Europe.'

'And what is Great Britain doing about it?' Hoorn insisted. 'I will tell you, sir, that the death of Mr Pitt two years ago, and the succession, virtually to the primacy, of that libertine Charles Fox –'

'Ah, but Mr Fox is also dead now,' Clive interjected. 'The Duke of Portland is prime minister.'

'I have never heard of him.'

'Well, neither have many other people,' Clive conceded.

'But will he make peace with Bonaparte?' the Dutchman persisted.

'Never,' Clive declared. 'I can assure you, sir, that there is no risk of that. We shall oppose him to the last drop of blood in our veins. And we shall defeat him, too.'

'Well said,' Hoorn shouted. 'Well said.' He refilled Clive's glass.

'What I would like to hear is your experience at the hands of the pirates, Mr Hammond,' Mevrouw Hoorn said. 'If you can bear to speak of it.'

Her English was not as good as her husband's, and Clive gathered that the girls did not speak the language at all, because as he related that more recent story of the storm and the pirate attack, either Hoorn or Teng himself translated.

He told them what had happened exactly as he recalled it, very conscious that Teng was there to monitor his words, and thus not forgetting to praise his Chinese friend, for so he now certainly regarded him.

Teng deprecated the end of the tale. 'I feel that I failed,' he said, 'in that many good men were murdered. And Mrs Blaine taken prisoner.'

'But that is terrible,' Mevrouw Hoorn agreed. 'Oh, these pirates . . . this place . . .' She gazed at her husband under arched eyebrows.

'My wife would like to sell up and return to Holland,' Hoorn explained. 'Of course, that is impossible while Bonaparte treats our country as a province of France. Besides, sell up? Who would buy at this time, my dear?' He patted her on the knee. 'Tomorrow I will take you to see one of my plantations, Mr Hammond. If you would care to come.'

Clive was delighted at the prospect; he wanted to occupy every minute of his time. And somewhat to his relief, Teng did not this time accompany them; if Hoorn was his principal Batavian customer, he had business to conduct with several other factors and planters. So Hoorn and Clive drove out in a shaded trap, the factor himself taking the reins, although they were accompanied by four other white men, on horseback and very well armed.

'Not that I would have you think there is a great deal of danger here by the coast,' Hoorn explained. 'But our soldiers are trying to push back the frontier of the colony, and meeting with resistance from the native princes in the interior; and occasionally parties of marauders do come down here, seeking whatever they can find. They are usually dispersed by a few well-aimed shots.'

It seemed to Clive an appalling way to live. 'Would it not be more sensible to leave them alone?' he asked. 'Surely you have all you need here.' For the plain across which they were travelling clearly stretched a considerable distance, mile after mile of rice fields, broken up with copses, flowing streams and occasional villages – many with ruined mosques and temples to suggest a once prosperous past – with the blue mountain peaks forming a perpetual backdrop. 'And to what use could you put the mountain terrain, anyway?'

'We will not consider Java truly a Dutch colony until the entire country flies our flag, Mr Hammond,' Hoorn said quietly. 'But lacking real support from Europe while Bonaparte dissipates our strength in his dreams of conquest, it is a long, tedious and costly business. There.'

They were entering a sugar estate, which Clive gathered was only one of several large plantations owned by Hoorn. Now he looked at acre after acre of waving ten-foot-high cane-stalks, divided up into fields, each field separated from its neighbour by an irrigation ditch which was bordered by a high dam, along which they made their way, towards the boiling house, or factory, which lay directly in front of them, a low, roofed accumulation of vats and rollers, out of the midst of which there rose a tall chimney, like a finger pointing at the sky. Here again there were armed guards, and these also carried whips, for in addition to looking out for marauders, they were supervising the work being done by large gangs of Javanese labourers, who were weeding the fields, or repairing the roadways, or clearing the irrigation canals. They seemed to work well enough, although every so often there was a crack of a whip and a stifled shout of pain.

'And have these people accepted Dutch rule?' Clive

63

asked, feeling distinctly upset by this blatant overlordship.

Hoorn snorted. 'They never accept anything worthwhile. They are part of the corvée.'

Clive frowned. 'You mean you employ forced labour?'

'We have no choice. It is our policy, you see, to interfere with as little of the native ways as possible, but of course we have to impose taxes, and we must have labour for our plantations. But these people have no money, and no concept of money — paying them a wage would be a waste of time. So while we leave those Javanese princes who have sworn allegiance in control of their lands and people, subject of course to our ultimate jurisdiction, we demand of them taxes, paid in kind, and the labour of their subjects.'

Clive had read *The Wealth of Nations*, Adam Smith's monumental work on economics, and as usual could not resist an argument. 'There is a body of opinion that holds a much better return is obtained by free men working the soil than by slaves.'

Hoorn grinned. 'Your Mr Smith. Oh, indeed. But I am afraid he never visited the tropics, and that makes his argument invalid. These people simply would not work unless forced to it. Nor would the blacks, for that matter. As I have said, they do not understand the use of money, they require very little on which to live, and they are all thieving rascals at heart. Besides, these Javanese are not slaves, you know. When they have completed their required labour they return to their own homes, and it is the decision of their prince which of them are sent to us. And then, while they are working for us, they have had the opportunity to observe, and perhaps imbibe, some of the principles and achievements of our civilization, and even more important, some of the beliefs and practices of our church.'

'You mean they are heathen?'

'The next best thing; they are Muslims.'

'Ah,' Clive said. He had also read of the immense achievements of the Arabs in Spain and North Africa, their architecture and their medicine, their mathematics and their piety. But he decided not to risk antagonizing this man who rather surprisingly seemed to wish to be friends, and instead of arguing further Clive allowed himself to be suitably impressed as he was shown over the factory, where the stalks were crushed to yield both sugar and molasses, and the various houses where the products were stored and tested for quality. He was given some more arrack.

It was a thoroughly enjoyable, if exhausting day, which ended with another delightful meal at the Hoorns' house. To his surprise he was invited to return again the following day for another tour and, indeed, for each of the next four days he was shown some part of the Hoorn estates, for the factor did not only deal in sugar, but had substantial acres under rice and some under corn as well, while he also cattle-ranched on a large scale.

Clive was fascinated, especially by the many varieties of fruit, such as mangoes and bananas, which he had never tasted before. But he was even more interested when Hoorn took him into the foothills of the mountains, twenty-five miles inland from Batavia, where the peaks seemed to rear some ten thousand feet above their heads. Here there were immense forests of teak, which Hoorn called the hardest wood in the world, as well as formidable groves of enormous bamboos.

They saw wild pig and ox, and several fearsome-looking crocodiles basking on the river banks, while snakes abounded and had to be watched because, as Hoorn told him, some had bites which could be fatal to a man within a few seconds. On the other hand there were also innumerable varieties of brightly coloured butter-flies. The contrast between the beautiful and the deadly seemed to epitomize the island.

Java was, as Teng had suggested, a large island

covering an area very nearly the size of England, although longer and thinner. Hoorn confirmed that there were active volcanoes in the east, which was where the Javanese who had refused to accept Dutch rule preserved their independence. Everywhere there was evidence of the long pre-Dutch history of the place in some quite spectacular ruined Hindu temples, while traces of a Buddhist past were also to be found, contrasting strongly with the more recent Muslim mosques and the comparatively new Christian churches, although the Dutch had apparently had a foothold on the island for some hundred years.

Hoorn also took him hunting, for rhinoceros, he claimed, a rare variety with but a single horn, but they never saw one, although they did bring down a tiger. For Clive it was an unforgettable occasion. The white men sat on a raised platform on the edge of a thick wood where tigers were known to be living, and their servants rode round to the far side and raised a tremendous noise, beating drums and blowing trumpets. For a while nothing happened, then Clive became aware of stealthy movement, and above all, eyes gleaming through the undergrowth. At last, loping directly towards them, he saw a magnificent beast, which could not have been less than seven feet long.

'Your shot, Mr Hammond,' Hoorn said.

Clive hesitated, then raised his rifled musket and fired. The beast did not check, and one of the gun bearers pressed another weapon into his hand. This bullet struck home, and the tiger reared back, giving a tremendous scream of outraged agony.

'Another,' Hoorn shouted.

A third musket had been given him, but Clive knew he was not going to use it; he could not bring himself to destroy so much splendour. 'I have had my turn,' he said.

'Bah,' Hoorn shouted, seething with excitement. His own gun exploded as the beast turned to escape, and his second shot had the tiger on the ground, writhing in its death agonies. 'A noble fellow,' Hoorn shouted.

'Yes,' Clive agreed. 'Far more noble than either of us.'

Hoorn glanced at him, then grinned. 'Why, you are quite right. But he will still make a splendid trophy.'

And always there were the meals at the house in Batavia, served by silent Negresses in long white gowns and with white turbans on their heads, at which Mevrouw Hoorn and her three daughters were most attentive. Clive was quite overwhelmed by such hospitality; he gathered that his fellow passengers were also being well looked after, but none had been entertained on quite such a lavish scale, if only because there was no one else in Batavia with the wealth of Pieter Hoorn.

He enjoyed it all as best he could, but after nearly a week he could not help but broach the matter to Teng, although, as Teng seemed such a good friend of the Dutchman's, he did so under the guise of a question as to the Chinese attitude to slavery, during an after-dinner smoke on the poop deck of the junk. They were listening to the excited conversation from beneath them, amongst those of the passengers who had returned on board from their day's excursion, as usual loudly discussing the things they had seen.

'Slavery is a fact of life,' Teng pointed out. 'The Dutch believe it is their God-given right to rule over those they choose to regard as the inferior races. We in China have the same problem with the Manchus.'

'And the English?' Clive asked.

Teng smiled. 'Oh, the English are the worst of all. As a people, not as individuals. But tell me, do you like Mijnheer Hoorn?'

'Oh, very much,' Clive said, grateful for the cue.

'As he likes you.'

'Yes. I was going to ask you why.'

Teng smiled. 'You mean you cannot understand why someone should like you?'

Clive flushed. 'I mean, there is no reason for *him* to, certainly. He has only just met me, he can surely see that I am both destitute and young enough to be his son, and yet he treats me as an old friend.'

'Well,' Teng said, 'he knows a great deal about you.'

Clive looked at him.

'Oh, indeed,' Teng said, without embarrassment. 'I told him what you had told me.'

'May I ask why?'

'I thought it would interest him in you. As it has done. Like me, he regards you as hard done-by. And yet you are a man of courage and intelligence. Neither is rare individually, but they are not often found together. When one does find them, then one has a man worth knowing, or perhaps, employing.'

Clive gazed at him.

'So,' Teng went on, 'perhaps we both feel you might be better employed here than in Penang. I should add,' he continued, 'that no man does anything in this world without an ulterior motive, and it is because I have known Pieter Hoorn for years, and understand his problems, that I recommended you to him. You may recall that on your first day in Batavia, Captain van Essenling told you that there are only a few Jacobins amongst the Dutch in Java. This is certainly true. But in expressing the hope that perhaps Holland may one day be freed from the grip of the tyrant Bonaparte with English help, he was presenting a rather personal view. Most of the Dutch in the East Indies regard the English as far more dangerous to their trading prospects than, say, Perak Shah and his pirates. You must remember that the Dutch have been in these waters for more than three generations. They came here expecting to have to fight those they quaintly call the "natives", and knowing that they would have to fight the Portuguese, who at that time had a monopoly of European business here in the Spice Islands. These things they did, successfully, and estab-

68

lished themselves. But barely had they done so when the English appeared. The Dutch of course, regarded them as interlopers and trespassers. Mijnheer Hoorn is an exception to this point of view, but then, you see, he was not born here, as are so many of the Dutch residents today, but came here fresh from Europe as a young man. He thus shares the captain's opinion, and this is why he finds it difficult to locate trustworthy aides from his compatriots. Or even trustworthy friends.'

'I am beginning to understand,' Clive said. 'Teng, you are an intriguer.'

Teng bowed his head. 'In China, to be so called is by way of being a compliment. You should also consider that Mijnheer Hoorn, while lacking a son, is the father of three handsome daughters, one at least of whom is of marriageable age and the heiress to a great fortune.'

Clive got up and went to the rail to stare at the lights of the town. Then he turned. 'You must think me a very shallow fellow.'

'I think you are a man who has suffered and must now seek to redress his fortunes.'

'And you think I will do that by forgetting Elizabeth and foresaking my nationality?'

'It is the course I would recommend. Given all the circumstances. I certainly do not believe you can do yourself anything but harm by continuing to think about that unfortunate young lady.'

'I am afraid that is not the English way of doing things.'

Teng sighed. 'So you will continue with us to Penang? I can only hope, my dear young friend, that you find its people as pleasant as you hope. And as eager to help you. But I shall be surprised if that were so.'

CHAPTER THREE

The Dreamer

The voyage from Batavia to Penang took just over a week, and was a sombre experience for the English passengers. Teng was his usual kind and considerate self, and the food and comfort on board the big junk remained of the highest quality, but it was necessary again to pass the reef-shrouded island of Singapura, with all the memories that aroused, and in addition, as they proceeded up the Strait of Malacca they were assailed by another gale of wind. Perhaps this was not as severe as the one which had dismasted the *Henry Oliver*, or perhaps the junk was more expertly handled, something which none of the English was prepared to admit, but they came through this second ordeal unscathed. Yet the howling wind and brilliant lightning, the huge seas and growling thunder, once more evoked sensations of fear and horror. Clive was more perturbed than any of the other English passengers by the voyage north. Whatever their memories, they were at last moving towards their destination; and whatever their misfortunes, none of them had been bereaved. For him it was different. The Hoorns had seemed genuinely sorry to see him leave. Pieter Hoorn had invited him to return whenever he wished, and the eldest daughter, Amalia, having apparently been rehearsing, had burst out in English, 'I like you very much, Mijnheer Hammond,' blushing pink amid screams of laughter from her sisters.

Thus he was keenly aware that he was leaving what

appeared to be a definite haven for an unknown prospect, all on the chance of being able to find the help necessary to rescue Elizabeth. He did not doubt he would do so. Edward Blaine himself was in Penang and surely a husband would not just abandon a wife in such horrifying circumstances. Of course, finding help in Penang would mean concealing his own feelings, not only now but perhaps for a considerable time in the future, but as Teng had said, forever can be a very negative word, and he was prepared to practice wu-wei as best he could, once Elizabeth was out of the clutches of Perak Shah.

Yet he could not prevent his blood from surging with anger and outrage as he gazed at Singapura again and tried to stop himself imagining what might be happening behind that curtain of thickly matted green.

Penang Island was situated only a few miles off the coast of the Sultanate of Kedah, the northernmost of the Malayan states, whose northern border was contiguous with the military empire of Siam. The narrow strait which separated the island from the mainland was blocked at its southern end by shoals, and so it was necessary for the junk to sail right round the island before approaching the port of Georgetown, which was situated on the sheltered, eastern side, facing Malaya itself. This gave the passengers an opportunity to inspect their future home, and they were all disturbed to find it exceedingly small, although there was also some British territory on the mainland, named Province Wellesley after the Governor-General, elder brother of Sir Arthur, during whose tenure of office it had been created.

The island itself was attractively forested, and rose to a considerable range of hills in the centre, behind which Georgetown lay only three miles from Province Wellesley. Clive had read his history, and recalled that the East India Company, in the person of Captain Francis Light, had established the colony as recently as 1786, only twenty odd years previously, having noted its strategic position at the very top of the Strait of Malacca: it could be used to observe and perhaps deter any Dutch eruption from their Javanese strongholds. The actual seizure of the land had been legalized in 1791, when the Sultan of Kedah had agreed to a treaty ceding the island, for which he had no use, and in 1800 the mainland province had been added, again entirely as a defensive bastion, for the place remained very definitely a frontier. Indeed, the town compared inadequately with Batavia, for if there were one or two fairly substantial houses, there was no such indication of prosperous industry as had been immediately apparent in Java, although of course the alluvial-plain on which Georgetown was built was only a fraction of the size of that available on the southern island.

The arrival of Teng Lee's junk, the *Dragon's Wake*, caused only mild interest at first; he was a well-known and regular visitor to the community, and at this stage it was merely supposed that the East Indiaman was overdue because of the bad weather. But when the passengers went ashore there was instant pandemonium. The church bell was rung, the garrison stood to arms, and people gathered on the dockside to stare at the decrepit band of survivors and listen to their shocking tale, themselves watched by a crowd of curious Malays. And however recovered the passengers of the *Henry Oliver* were after their warm welcome in Batavia and Teng's unfailing hospitality, they were yet willing to pour out the story of their misfortunes with the utmost pathos.

The bulk of the talking was as usual done by Major Phillips, and listened to with horror by the English residents. One of these was a striking-looking young man, no more than medium height, and extremely thin, as if not altogether in the best of health, a suggestion increased by the pink patches which glowed in his sallow cheeks; but he had a face of tremendous intensity, with a

72

thrusting jaw and burning eyes, which in turn suggested that part of his ill health, if indeed he were unwell, could be the result of some inner fire which was threatening to consume him.

This man waited until Phillips had to pause for breath, and then said. 'You'd best come with me and report this to the Governor.'

'This is Mr Raffles, the Governor's secretary,' Teng explained.

'And of course you are right, Mr Raffles,' Phillips agreed. 'I shall attend his excellency right away, if he will pardon my undress.' For although he had donned his sadly tarnished red jacket to come ashore and his white breeches, the latter were now a dirty grey and torn in several places.

'I am sure his excellency will not be concerned with your dress at a moment like this,' Raffles said. 'I'd like you to come as well, Teng.'

'Of course. I also think Mr Hammond should accompany us,' Teng said.

'What has Mr Hammond to contribute?' demanded Mr Anstruther, clearly annoyed at having been left out.

'I think his opinion may be of value,' Teng said quietly.

Raffles had been observing the slight difference of opinion with interest, Clive noticed. Now he intervened. 'I am sure you will be a great help, Mr. . . ?'

'Anstruther is the name,' Anstruther said, having regained all his pre-storm belligerency now he was again safely on British soil.

'Mr Anstruther . . . in helping the ladies, and these fine fellows' — he patted one of the staring boys on the shoulder — 'to get acclimatized. Our people will be happy to make you all as comfortable as they can. Martin.' He turned to a man standing beside him. 'Would you be so kind as to take charge here while I take these gentlemen to see the Governor?'

73

'Of course,' Martin agreed, raising his beaver to the ladies.

'We have lost everything,' Harriet Phillips told him. 'Everything.'

'Then it will be our charge to see that as much as possible is replaced,' Raffles assured her. 'Now, if you will excuse us, Mr Martin here will be in charge of showing you to your quarters and seeing to your necessities. But I am sure you will agree that his excellency must be informed without delay so that we may decide upon our best course of action.'

Obviously he was a difficult man to argue with and the rest of the passengers allowed themselves to be escorted away by Mr Martin, with promises of warm baths and cups of tea and clean clothing and everything that might be considered dear to the heart of a memsahib, as well as, clearly, endless sympathy. Raffles himself escorted Teng and Major Phillips and Clive up the slight hill to the imposing residence where the Union Jack fluttered from a flagpole erected between two cannons, before which red-jacketed soldiers presented arms. The major returned their salute, although he had lost his bicorne with the *Henry Oliver*. Clive had remained wearing the Chinese dress Teng had given him, finding it vastly more comfortable than any clothes he had ever possessed, however ill the fit, which earned him many curious glances as they climbed the slope.

On the verandah of Government House, a tall, spare, somewhat severe-looking man with a bald head, wearing a blue undress uniform, was waiting to greet them. Clive knew instinctively who he must be and his heart thudded down to his boots. 'Ah, Raffles,' this individual said. 'What on earth was all that commotion?'

'A most serious matter, Major,' Raffles said. 'Major Blaine, I'd have you meet Major Phillips, our new garrison commander.'

The two men shook hands.

74

'Teng Lee you know, of course,' Raffles went on. 'And this is Mr Hammond.'

Blaine allowed Teng a brief nod, and merely glanced at Clive. 'And the serious matter?' the ADC asked.

'Must be placed before HE at once,' Raffles said.

Blaine considered for a moment, then allowed them inside. Sarong-clad Malayan houseboys bowed as they passed by, and they were shown into a large, high-ceilinged office, where fans circulated above their heads, worked by other Malay boys in the corridor outside. The Lieutenant-Governor of Penang Colony, Sir Charles Wilmot, was waiting to receive them. He was short and stout, red-faced and white-haired, and looked very hot and bothered, if somewhat more pleasant than his ADC.

'Major Phillips.' He shook hands, ignoring Teng and Clive. 'I understood you were arriving on the *Henry Oliver*. Have you news of her? And what was that tumult down by the shore. And,' he was now frowning, 'whatever has happened to your dress, man? You are positively incorrect.'

Phillips stood to attention, very red in the face. 'The answer to all your questions, your excellency, can be given in one sentence. The *Henry Oliver* is lost, sir, taken by Malayan pirates.'

There was a moment's silence. Then the Governor asked, 'Taken by pirates? An East Indiaman. That is not possible. It has never happened before.'

'We were dismasted during a gale,' Phillips said miserably, 'and were drifting when attacked. Our guns could not be brought to bear. But that is not the worst of it.' He stared at Blaine, unable to make himself continue.

'You mean there were casualties?' the Governor asked inanely.

'A great many. The crew was massacred. But . . .' He visibly came to a decision to get it over with. 'The pirates also took one of the passengers prisoner. Mrs Blaine.'

There was another brief silence, then Blaine said,

75

frowning, 'My wife? She was on board the *Henry Oliver*?'

'Yes, she was,' Phillips said. 'I suppose she could not let you know of her intention in time. I believe she had been trying to secure a passage for some time before our departure.'

'And you say she has been . . .' Blaine's jaw dropped as if the import of what he had been told had only just sunk in.

Phillips looked at Teng in the hope of some support.

'It is a very sad business,' Teng said. 'Is it permitted to sit down?'

'Good heavens, yes,' the Governor said. 'Unforgiveable of me. Mr Teng, is it?' He looked at Blaine, who had already sat down, or rather collapsed on to a chair. 'Raffles,' he told his secretary, 'you'd better organize a glass of brandy. But this is terrible news. Terrible. Mrs Blaine . . . good heavens.'

'She is still alive, sir,' Clive said eagerly.

'My wife?' Blaine shouted.

'She was taken by the pirates,' Phillips said again, giving Clive an angry look.

'Oh, my God!' the Governor commented. 'You mean she was taken *alive*?'

'My wife?' Blaine asked again.

'There was nothing we could do,' Phillips explained, more miserably than ever. 'The Malays were in overwhelming force. They murdered the entire crew. They would have murdered us as well, had Mr Teng not intervened.'

'I happened to be there,' Teng said. 'And I had some influence with the Malayan chieftain. He owed me a favour.'

'And we are eternally grateful to you,' the Governor said. 'Who else was kept by these people?'

'Only Mrs Blaine,' Teng said.

'But why. . . ?' the Governor swallowed, and looked

up in relief as a servant hurried in with a glass of brandy for the ADC.

'My wife,' Blaine muttered, staring into the sparkling liquid. 'My Elizabeth, taken by those heathen dogs, to be raped . . .'

'Here, I say, we don't *know* that's what they intended,' the Governor protested, reverting to inanity.

'Whatever they have done to her,' Clive said. 'She is alive. She can be rescued.'

Their heads turned.

'You cannot just abandon her,' Clive shouted.

'You impudent young puppy,' Phillips snapped. 'Oh, he was all for dying like a hero. I had the women and children to think of.'

'Oh, quite,' the Governor said.

'My wife,' Blaine muttered. He had now finished the brandy, although he continued to stare into the glass. But he had made no attempt to support the idea of rescue, and Clive was beginning to wonder if even his grief was as heartfelt as he was trying to establish.

'You *cannot* abandon her,' he said again.

'Who *is* this fellow?' the Governor asked, gazing at Clive's Chinese clothes.

'His name is Clive Hammond, and he is to be clerk with a Mr Gresholm . . . that's right, isn't it, Hammond?' the major snapped.

'Why, yes, but.'

'I believe he has found it necessary to leave England for his health,' the major added, meaningfully.

'Does that matter?' Clive shouted. 'We are talking about Eliz – about Mrs Blaine, an Englishwoman held prisoner by the Malays. She *must* be rescued.'

Blaine raised his head. 'She is *my* wife,' he said, as if resenting anyone else being concerned about her.

'Your excellency,' Clive begged.

The Governor looked at Phillips. 'Where did you say this happened?'

77

'The bottom end of the Malacca Strait,' Phillips said. 'They took us to an island, called. . . ?' He looked at Teng.

'Singapura,' Teng said.

'Never heard of it.' The Governor turned to Raffles, who had remained a silent spectator of the scene. 'You know all about Malaya, Raffles. Ever heard of Singapura?'

'Yes, your excellency. It belongs to the Sultanate of Johore and is well known as a haunt of pirates.'

'Hm. I suppose we could make some representation to the Sultan of Johore. Has he accepted our credentials?'

'No, sir,' Raffles said.

'The scoundrel. Then I don't suppose we'll obtain much help there. Would it be practical to launch an expedition against this island?'

'I think we will have to ask Mr Teng that,' Raffles suggested. 'As he has actually been there.'

Clive turned to Teng, anxiously.

But Teng's face was as impassive as ever as he said, 'I do not think it would be practical for you to attack Singapura.'

'But — ' Clive protested.

'It would require a great fleet,' Teng went on. 'Several ships of the line. Do you have any ships of the line, your excellency?'

'Why, no,' the Governor said. 'At the moment I do not have a single one. I am expecting a frigate any day now. I suppose one or two more could be procured from Calcutta . . .'

'Then it would be a matter of navigating the reefs,' Teng said. 'The danger to ships and men would be considerable. Then, a large force of soldiers would be necessary to land and take possession of the Five Villages, and hold them while the operation was carried out.'

'You rascal,' Clive muttered.

'My God,' the Governor remarked. 'It does sound a formidable business.'

'Nor would any of that rescue Mrs Blaine,' Teng finished. 'The moment a single warship appeared off the island and was revealed to have an aggressive intention, Perak Shah would undoubtedly have her throat cut.'

The Englishmen stared at each other, except for Clive, who stared at Teng in angry consternation.

'So nothing would be served by such an expedition, save grievous loss of life,' Teng pointed out. 'Mrs Blaine would certainly not be recovered.'

'Oh quite,' the Governor said. 'I do take your meaning, Mr Teng. And I imagine you know more about the situation than any of us. Blaine . . . Edward, my dear fellow. . . .'

'However,' Teng went on. 'That is not to say Mrs Blaine *cannot* be regained.'

Their heads turned.

'Providing this is what you wish,' Teng said.

'My dear fellow,' Wilmot said, 'if you know of any way . . .'

'I have an idea that I may be able to persuade Perak Shah to relinquish the lady,' Teng said, 'when I return there in a month's time.'

'Good heavens! If that could be done . . .'

'She will, however, have spent that month, and some weeks besides, in Perak Shah's harem,' Teng said very carefully.

'Well, really, I don't think we ought to go into that,' the Governor protested.

'I must be sure it is the will of everyone present that I attempt this task,' Teng insisted. He was looking at Edward Blaine.

The ADC realized that, and squared his shoulders. 'Do you suppose I care what has happened to my wife, sir, so long as she is returned to me, safe and sound?' he snapped.

79

Teng bowed his head. 'I expected nothing less from an English gentleman. Then, sirs, if it is your wish, I shall attempt to negotiate the release of the young lady and return her here.'

'My dear Mr Teng,' Wilmot said. 'If it is a question of ransom . . .'

Teng shook his head. 'I do not think a ransom will be involved, your excellency. I would just ask you to be patient.'

'Well, should you succeed, we should be forever in your debt. As we are already in your debt for bringing us the rest of the passengers from the *Henry Oliver*. If you could indicate in some way how we can possibly repay you. . . ?'

Teng gave another little bow. 'That I am allowed to trade with your colony is reward enough, your excellency. I will ask for nothing more.'

It seemed an eternity before they finally escaped the office. 'I thought you were my friend,' Clive said bitterly.

'I am,' Teng said. 'Or I hope I am.'

'But you will let . . .' He hesitated, because Blaine had accompanied them, with Phillips, 'that poor lady linger in such vile captivity for another month?'

'I find Hammond's concern for your wife's fate positively offensive,' Major Phillips remarked in a loud aside.

'A month in captivity is better than an eternity in a grave, Clive,' Teng said. 'Believe me.'

'I think,' Raffles interjected, as he could see Clive was about to lose his temper, 'that I had better see about getting you some proper clothes to wear, and informing Gresholm that you are here. I take it he is expecting you?'

'No,' Clive said, unhappily.

'Oh?'

'Well . . .' He glanced at the major. 'I had to leave England in rather a hurry and was carrying letters of

80

introduction with me. But I'm afraid the pirates must have destroyed them.'

'Hm,' Raffles commented. 'You really are in a bad way, Mr Hammond. I think I had better take you along to Gresholm myself. You'll excuse us, Teng.'

'I must return to my ship.' Teng bowed to them all. 'Gentlemen.'

'But you'll dine with us before you leave,' Raffles said. 'Flora would not like to miss you.'

Teng bowed again. 'It will be my great pleasure.'

Blaine and Phillips watched him go. 'You do not mean you entertain a Chinese in your home, Raffles?' Phillips demanded.

'Teng is a very good friend,' Raffles said. 'Now come along, Mr Hammond, let us see what we can do about you.'

'Insolent puppy,' Phillips growled, before they were out of earshot. Whether he was referring to Teng, Raffles or himself, Clive had no idea.

Mr Gresholm, the factor, turned out to be short, thin and aggressive. His red hair was speckled with grey, and his beard was almost entirely white. He seemed to bristle whenever he spoke, as if daring anyone to argue with him, for all his lack of inches. 'Davenport?' he barked. 'Davenport? I knew a John Davenport. At school with the fellow.'

'The very man, sir,' Clive said, with great relief.

'Sent you to me? What confounded effrontery. Why?'

'I wished to leave England, sir, and find myself a place in the colonies.'

'You'll understand that Mr Hammond is one of the survivors from the *Henry Oliver*,' Raffles put in. 'He has had a very difficult time.'

'Am I running a charitable institution?' Gresholm demanded. 'How do I know he isn't some scoundrel, eh?'

'You don't, sir,' Clive said, beginning to lose his temper.

Both men looked at him in surprise. Then Gresholm said, 'I suppose I could do with some help. Better than thieving Malays. You'll use the attic, boy. And I'll pay you what I can spare, when I can spare it. Understood?'

Clive looked at Raffles, who shrugged. 'I would say you have fallen on your feet, Mr Hammond,' he said drily.

Perhaps he was joking, Clive thought. But as he had no choice, he set out to be as agreeable as possible. Mr Gresholm actually operated a ship's chandlery, which he stocked with such things as hempen rope, which was in great demand, wooden blocks, iron belaying pins, spare sails, anything which the occasional visiting vessel might require, and which could be made or obtained in Malaya. By far the most important part of his business, however, was the replenishment of the ships which called at Georgetown. For this he acted as factor and general agent, procuring everything from drinking water through rice and fresh vegetables to tubs of lard. In this capacity he even assisted with the restocking of Teng Lee's junk, to which task he appointed Clive as his first duty, 'As you know the damned Chink,' he pointed out. Clive could reflect that at least he had a roof over his head and food in his belly, although both were of a very poor quality.

He found his dissatisfaction, to a certain extent alleviated while in Batavia or on board Teng's ship, growing with every moment he spent in Georgetown. The climate itself was hot and damp, as the monsoon still blew and the mountain barrier behind the town effectively shut out any cooling breezes off the Indian Ocean, and the town was entirely lacking in any spark of architectural or scenic imagination, or even order. The houses, nearly all what the colonials called bungalows — an Indian word — were built as their owners had

82

apparently felt necessary at the time; there were no proper streets, none of the neat order that had been observable in Batavia, and no one had thought to dig the canals necessary to relieve the heavy rains which periodically flooded the town, bringing hordes of ravenous mosquitoes in their wake.

The people were on a par with their surroundings. It seemed logical that every Englishman who travelled east and had an ounce of talent would find himself in Bombay or Calcutta, the central cities of the East India Company's far-flung empire. Those who wound up in Penang were, on the whole, of a much lower calibre. Yet they were determined to maintain not only British superiority over all other races and nations, but even a totally English way of life, the only concessions to the tropical heat being the siesta which most English residents indulged in during the hottest part of the day, between two and three. For the rest, the men wore dark suits and high collars, and sweated profusely; they had already established a club, where they repaired in the early evening to play cards and smoke. Clive was very rapidly informed that membership of this establishment was not extended to factors' assistants.

The ladies, uniformly overweight as they all employed Malay 'boys' to do every household task and therefore had nothing to occupy themselves with save eating, drinking, sleeping and gossiping, wore the corsets and starched petticoats and huge bonnets which were customary in fashionable England. If seldom seen during the heat of the day, they were all out promenading in the early evening, where possible on the arm of a husband who had not yet been permitted to leave for the club, accompanied by Malay servants with parasols and fans. They busily exchanged the latest titbits of news with each other, as if there ever was any news in Penang, or as if they did not already know every detail of each other's business, although the arrival of the survivors

83

from the *Henry Oliver* made a fruitful topic for some time.

The stultifying society and even more stultifying climate only made Clive more sharply aware of the banal existence he, and everyone else, was living. This extended even to the Malays, who, if not slaves, were certainly treated as such by their British masters, who all carried stout bamboo canes which they would use at the slightest excuse on their servants' arms, shoulders or backsides. Mr Gresholm was especially adept with these, and the half-dozen Malays who laboured for him were in a constant state of apprehension. Yet this did not prevent him from taking the sister of one of his servants to his bed – he had left his wife in England – much to Clive's disgust, for the attic room in which he slept on a narrow cot was immediately above the single bedroom in the house, and the floor was not all that well made. In his present ill humour and anxiety over Elizabeth he was in no mood to listen to the girl's giggles and Mr Gresholm's grunts of satisfaction as he 'poked' her, as he was fond of describing the activity.

Additionally, Clive very rapidly came to appreciate that he was the least popular white man in the colony. The dislike the other passengers had conceived for him following their rescue, thanks to his wish to resist the seizure of Elizabeth, and his subsequent friendship with Teng and then with Pieter Hoorn to their exclusion, was quickly spread through the rest of the community, and his pleasantest 'Good day' was rewarded with a cold stare or at best an offhand nod. Even Harriet Phillips, who had been so pleasant to him on board the *Henry Oliver*, now met him with a frosty stare, and worst of all, Stamford Raffles, the Governor's secretary, whom he had considered a very decent fellow at their first meeting, seemed in a hurry to be on his way whenever they encountered one another in the street.

Worst of all was the presence of Edward Blaine. The

ADC could not venture from his bungalow without immediately being surrounded by women apparently desperate to console him in his dreadful misfortune. More than ever Clive felt that Blaine was wallowing in this splendid sympathy, and did not really care whether or not he ever saw Elizabeth again. The contrast with the friendship offered him in Batavia was so marked and depressing that after a week, during which he celebrated his twenty-seventh birthday in lonely frustration, he had just about made up his mind to give Mr Gresholm his resignation, when he received a note from Mrs Thomas Stamford Raffles, inviting him to dine.

Gresholm, as was his way, managed to intercept the invitation and read it himself before passing it to Clive. 'Ha,' he commented, 'you'll want to watch out for that one, young fellow. His head is stuffed full of absurd notions.'

'Indeed, sir?' Clive asked. 'Is he not the Governor's secretary?'

'Oh, he is. Sent here by Minto himself.' Baron Minto was the Governor-General of India and thus supreme commander of every English outpost east of Egypt. 'Can't imagine why, except if it was to get rid of him. I imagine Wilmot feels the same way. Oh, he's bright. Very bright. Speaks Malay, would you believe it? For God's sake, who wants to speak Malay? Teach the Malays to speak English, is my motto. You want to watch him.'

Clive was intrigued, and for all Raffles' stand-offishness in the street, was determined to accept the invitation, which was the first he had received since his arrival. Thus he did his best with his new suit of European clothes, for which he had not yet paid and which was in fact of a most shoddy material, and presented himself at the Raffles' bungalow in the grounds of Government House, at the appointed hour. This was twelve noon, as, in order to fit in the siesta, the English community had

85

adopted the habit of dining very early and never after one.

'My dear fellow.' Raffles himself greeted him on the verandah, dressed as was customary in a black suit and a white stock. 'You haven't met my wife. Flora, this is Mr Hammond of whom I have spoken.'

'Mr Hammond,' Mrs Raffles said, taking his hand. She was considerably smaller than her husband, and spoke with a Scottish accent. She was also somewhat older than her husband, Clive estimated, unless the climate had prematurely aged her. But she was pretty enough, and had lively eyes; to his surprise, she somewhat daringly wore an empire gown, with but a single petticoat and certainly no corset. He warmed to her immediately, for in the climate of Penang that not only indicated an independent outlook, but an intelligent one. 'Your adventures have been the talk of the town,' she told him.

'I am sure you flatter me, ma'am,' Clive mumbled.

'Now, Mr Teng you know, I think,' she said.

Clive paused in the doorway to the drawing room; Teng was apparently the only other guest.

'Mr Hammond,' Teng said, and bowed to him. 'I have to say goodbye. I sail this evening for Rangoon.'

Clive hesitated, then took his hand. 'I apologize for losing my temper last week.'

Teng smiled. 'But you have not yet forgiven me for opposing your plans for leading an assault on Singapura.'

Clive sighed. 'As you said at the time, it was probably a most forlorn idea.' He glanced at Mrs Raffles. 'And it is hardly a subject to inflict upon you, ma'am.' She tinkled a little silver bell to summon a Malay houseboy with a tray and glasses of cool coconut water, to which alcohol had been added. 'Do sit down. Believe me, I am as upset about the fate of that poor girl as you,' she said.

'But I think Teng has a plan for accomplishing her release,' Raffles said. 'Without risking either her life or any others.'

'It is very simply this,' Teng said. 'If Mrs Raffles will permit me to be a little indelicate.' He smiled at her. 'Perak Shah was certainly taken with Mrs Blaine so strongly that there was nothing anyone could have done to secure her release at that moment. But I happen to know that he is a fickle man, who soon grows weary of his wives; he has an inordinate number. I feel sure that were the right approach made to him when he has, shall I say, been in possession of Mrs Blaine for perhaps a month, he can be induced to relinquish her. Again, I apologize for discussing such a matter in your presence, Ma'am.'

Flora Raffles shuddered. 'I feel so sorry for the poor creature. And even if you secure her release . . .' She gazed at him, pink spots in her cheeks.

'When Perak Shah is tired of her,' Clive said in disgust.

'After that, it must be up to her friends and family, and above all, her husband,' Teng said severely, 'to welcome her back into the world she knows, and longs to regain.'

'Quite,' Raffles said hastily. 'But you know, you almost sound as if you intend to ransom the girl. Yet you refused any contribution from the Governor, or Blaine himself, to that end.'

'I do not think that to offer a ransom would be the right approach,' Teng said. 'I will think of something. And now I feel we should speak of happier things.'

Teng proceeded to dominate the conversation throughout the meal, telling them brilliant and amusing stories from Chinese history and legend, obviously determined not to return to the subject of Elizabeth Blaine, or anything to do with Malaya at all. His personality flowed over the other three, and he had them all laughing before the meal was finished, when he took his leave. 'I must catch this afternoon's tide,' he said. 'I will see you early next year, I hope, preferably with Mrs Blaine in my care. Hammond . . .' He hesitated. 'I look forward to seeing you then too.'

87

It was Clive's turn to hesitate. 'I doubt you shall. In fact, Teng, I don't suppose you would care to offer me a passage on your ship?'

Teng's eyes flickered. 'Where would you wish to go?' he asked.

'Anywhere.'

Teng looked at Raffles, who merely raised his eyebrows. 'Because you would like to be with me when I attempt to regain Mrs Blaine?' Teng asked.

Clive flushed. 'Well, I might be able to help.'

'I do not think so. I think your presence will definitely be a danger.'

Clive's face stiffened. 'Well, then . . .'

'I think you should remain here for a while,' Teng told him. 'You can hardly have formed so positive a dislike for the place in a single week. We will discuss the matter further when I return, and if you are still determined to leave, why, then we shall discuss where it is you should go.'

Clive glared at him, again angered by the Chinese attitude of omnipotent judgement in others' affairs.

'Now I must leave,' Teng said. He squeezed Flora Raffles' hand, bowed to Raffles and then to Clive, and hurried down the steps.

'A most remarkable man,' Raffles remarked. 'And a charming one.'

'So calm and collected at all times,' his wife agreed. 'One cannot help but suppose that if the entire earth opened up in front of him, Teng Lee would decorously walk around the chasm to safety, nodding to those who were falling in, but keeping his own balance. Some more coffee, Mr Hammond?'

'I won't, thank you very much,' Clive said. 'It has been a most enjoyable meal. And I must thank you so very much for inviting me. But I think I should also take my leave.'

'Have you then got into the habit of a siesta already?' Raffles asked.

88

'As a matter of fact, no,' Clive said. 'But . . .'

'Then why not stay a while and have a cigar.' He pointed. 'It is starting to rain, in any event; you won't leave in under an hour without getting soaked to the skin.'

Clive glanced at Mrs Raffles.

'Oh, he wants to talk,' Flora said. 'Be careful; he will pick your brains bare, if you let him.' She held out her hand. 'It has been a great pleasure, Mr Hammond. I look forward to our next meeting. Do reconsider your decision to leave Penang.' She smiled. 'At least until after Christmas.'

Raffles had produced a box of Havanas and a pair of clippers, and for a moment was silent as he attended to his cigar, while the rain teemed down only a few feet away at the end of the verandah roof, setting up a dull drumming sound which provided a very real privacy.

'I hope I did not offend you by what I said to Teng,' Clive ventured. 'I really am most grateful for your hospitality. But . . .'

'Penang is not to your taste and you feel that you are not to Penang's taste.'

Clive lit his cigar. 'You are a discerning man.'

'An observant one, at any rate. My opinion arises both from the gossip I hear and from your conversation with Teng.'

'Well, can you really pretend that Penang has anything to offer me?'

'Penang has nothing to offer anyone, Hammond. It is a useless rock, which was seized simply to attempt to have a position *vis-à-vis* the Dutch,' Raffles said. 'And in that capacity would only serve some purpose were it to be the base for a squadron of frigates. As you see, there is one in the harbour, and she leaves in two days' time.'

Clive didn't know what to say. He hadn't expected the Governor's secretary to agree with him so entirely.

'However,' Raffles went on, 'at the present, it is all we

possess with which to combat the spread of Dutch influence, and we must make the best of it.'

'Is Dutch influence then so very dangerous to Great Britain?' Clive asked.

Raffles looked at him through a wreath of smoke. 'That depends on your concept of Great Britain. Do we accept that there are limits on our right to empire? Do we say Penang and no further? There would be a limited horizon. Should we not be thinking in terms of trading with China and Japan, instead of having to depend on the good offices of Teng Lee, splendid fellow that he is? I would estimate that China is the greatest market in the world, and Great Britain lives by marketing. Then what of Australia?'

'There is hardly a market in Australia,' Clive protested.

'It is a vast land. There could be one day.'

'Are the Dutch still interested in it?'

'It matters little whether they are or not. The point is that the trade route to the Pacific, and all the riches that wait for us there, lies through this very Strait of Malacca, a strait which is controlled by the Dutch in Malacca itself, and more importantly in Batavia. A strait which could be closed at any time by a Dutch squadron.'

'Have they shown any sign of doing that?' Clive asked.

'Their record indicates that they would do so, without hesitation, were it considered necessary. Do you know anything of the history of these parts?'

'Only what Teng has told me.'

'Which I would suspect is necessarily from a particular point of view,' Raffles observed. 'From a British point of view, it is a sad tale of missed opportunities, at least during the past twenty years.'

'Teng did say that the Dutch regard us as interlopers, having been here first.'

'As the Portuguese regarded the Dutch as interlopers,' Raffles pointed out. 'Ousting the Portuguese did not give the Hollanders any God-granted rights to rule the East

Indies forever. Unfortunately, our masters in Whitehall, when they think of empire and expanding trade, can see no further than the West Indian sugar islands. They would rather send an entire division of British soldiers to die of yellow fever in Jamaica or Guiana than a single frigate to open up the trade route to China. It does not seem to have occurred to them that now that Bonaparte, to counter the British blockade of Europe, is subsidizing the cultivation of beet with a view to producing beet sugar, cane sugar is going to suffer a great deal of serious, and perhaps fatal, competition. One thing you can be sure of, no matter how this war eventually turns out, those who are now farming beet are going to go on doing so, and if the sugar may not be of so fine a quality, it can be obtained from beet at a fraction of the cost it takes to obtain it from cane.'

Clive listened, suddenly fascinated, at once by this man's grasp of empire, his vision of the future and the lucidity with which he expressed himself.

'There can be no doubt,' Raffles went on, 'in those circumstances, that the future of Britain's prosperity lies in turning away from the Americas and to the east. But no definite step has been taken in this direction by the British Government. Any achievements have been accomplished entirely due to the ambitions of whoever has happened to be Governor-General. Things went ahead in a very positive fashion when Wellesley was in charge. Not only did we expand into India where possible, but the moment the Jacobins overran Holland and forced the Dutch to fly the tricolour, he authorized the seizure of Malacca, down the strait there, as an advanced bastion from which we could at least share the control of the Java Sea. But then, of course, at the Peace of Amiens, those oafs in London handed it back to the Dutch. All that time and effort to no purpose.' He reflected for a moment before continuing. 'Since my arrival here a couple of years ago, I have been trying to persuade the present Governor-General, Minto, who is by way of being a friend of mine, that we simply have to retake Malacca. As we are again at war with France and therefore with Holland, it should be a direct stepping stone on the way to possessing Batavia, and thus ending Dutch power in the Spice Islands once and for all. I'm afraid I have not yet been successful. And Wilmot, of course, is no help at all. All he desires is to be left alone to enjoy a quiet life until it is time for him to retire.'

'It must be nice to have a governor-general as a friend,' Clive murmured.

Raffles shot him a glance. 'Do I detect the voice of an English Jacobin? Perhaps with cause? Teng has been telling me of your misfortunes. Quarrelling with the Prince of Wales, no less.'

Clive wondered what else Teng had told the Governor's secretary; he had no doubt Teng had entirely deduced his relationship with Elizabeth.

'However, if you see in me a scion of that aristocracy which has done you down,' Raffles said, 'well, let us consider the matter. Where were you born?'

Clive frowned; the question had taken him by surprise. 'Why, Hammond Court, in Surrey.'

'That sounds like a family home.'

'It is. My people have lived there for generations.'

'Is your father titled?'

'Heavens, no. He is plain Squire Hammond.'

'Squire Hammond,' Raffles said thoughtfully. 'My father was plain Benjamin Raffles. He was a sea captain. He did not, of course, own his own ship, but he used to take my mother voyaging with him. I was born on that ship, the *Ann*, at sea. Just off Jamaica, as a matter of fact. Fifth July 1781,' he added.

'Why,' Clive cried, 'we are the same age.'

'Are we?' Raffles looked sceptical.

'Well, give or take a few months. I was born third December 1781.'

'My dear fellow, then you have just had a birthday.

Allow me to congratulate you. But would I be right in assuming that you were named after Clive of India? A relative, perhaps?'

'No, no,' Clive protested. 'Father was simply interested in history. You could say that inheriting that interest has landed me here.'

'Yet I hope you will concede that you are far more of an aristocrat than I.'

'Well,' Clive said. 'When you spoke so familiarly of Lord Minto . . .'

'I claimed him as a friend. I think perhaps he is. He is a fine fellow, with a good record of colonial administration. He even managed to bring some of the more vicious West Indian planters to book, I believe he even hanged one of them for torturing his slaves, when he was in the Leeward Islands. And he has an eye for others as energetic and forward looking as himself. May I ask where you were educated?'

'Ah,' Clive said. 'Well, I had a governess, and then a tutor.'

'I left school at fourteen,' Raffles told him. 'My brother had died, and so had my father. He was not a very provident sea captain, I'm afraid, so it was necessary for me to go out to work to support my mother and sisters. In time I obtained an apprenticeship in the John Company and arrived in Calcutta. There I was fortunate enough to attract the eye of Minto — he too had just arrived — and so he found me a post he regarded as more in keeping with my abilities, and sent me here as secretary to the Governor. I can tell you, I was no more happy about it than you are at this moment, but I have always resolved to make the best of my situation and so buckled down to it. I have even learned to speak Malay.' Raffles paused, and stubbed out his cigar. 'Now, I think Lord Minto agrees with me that we shall never again have such opportunity to eliminate Dutch power in the Indies,' he continued. 'The problem is that in his opinion, or rather I should say, in the opinions of his military advisers, we lack the men and ammunition to take Java. I should be interested to hear your opinion on that.'

'I know nothing of military matters,' Clive protested.

'You have been to Java, and you have eyes in your head and also ears, and a brain between them, I'd wager. Teng — ' Raffles made a sudden gesture and his head drooped alarmingly. Clive was completely taken aback and concerned; he had no idea what to do, whether or not he should call for help, but after a moment Raffles raised his head again, somewhat wearily, as if it weighed too much for his neck. He managed a smile. 'Forgive me. I am subject to sudden attacks of what must be migraine, I suppose. The pain is quite paralysing but, fortunately, short-lived. What was I saying? Oh, yes, Teng. He told me you were entertained by no less a man than Pieter Hoorn. I am sure you made certain observations.'

'Well . . .' Clive said hesitantly, still considerably disturbed by his host's strange malady, 'I would have to say that in my opinion Batavia is weakly defended. At the moment, anyway. Most of the Dutch garrison seem to be in the southern part of the island, waging some never-ending war against the Javanese.'

'Is there a fort?'

'Certainly. But not a very formidable one, at least in appearance.'

'So the town can easily be carried by assault.'

'An assault should provide no difficulty. But the approach is across a very wide and open roadstead. Everyone would certainly see an invading fleet coming hours before any men could be landed.'

'And would put themselves in a state of defence,' Raffles mused. 'But would they? Tell me of the attitude of the people.'

'Ah,' Clive said, 'now there you could possibly have an asset, although an uncertain one. I would estimate that the colonists are definitely anti-Bonaparte and resentful

94

of French domination. On the other hand, most of them also loathe us, as they regard us as their principal rivals here in the East. There are exceptions. Mijnheer Hoorn himself, and the commander of the garrison, Captain van Essenling . . .'

'Who are arguably the two most important people in the place,' Raffles put in.

'No doubt. But while they are pro-British, in the sense that they would like to see Great Britain emerge triumphant from this war, I cannot say they would welcome a British army determined to turn Java into a British colony.'

'Not even if we offered Hoorn, at least, security of tenure? It is something to be considered. I wonder . . . would you be prepared to set down your observations on paper, along the lines of what you have just said to me, but in as much detail as you can?'

'To what purpose?'

'I have a notion that a paper such as you may be able to supply would have a very positive effect on Minto's thinking. It is all very well for his army and navy people in Calcutta to tell him how difficult an operation the seizure of Batavia would be, but none of them have actually been there. You have. And, should we get such an operation going, it might well be possible to secure you a position as adviser. Perhaps even a commission.'

Clive had to smile. 'Me, working for the British Government?'

'It would surely be an improvement on working for Gresholm.'

Clive got up and went to the verandah rail. The rain was just about stopping and blue sky was appearing. In another few minutes it would be as hot as ever. 'To war on the Dutch?' he said, half to himself. 'I was shown every kindness in Batavia. And especially by Mijnheer Hoorn. I could almost call him a friend. Certainly he and his family treated me as one.'

'And I have said he would be guaranteed security of tenure,' Raffles reminded him.

'Still. . . .' Clive shook his head. 'I had never thought to take any part in promoting a war.'

Raffles carefully lit another cigar. 'I should add,' he said casually, 'that were we to mount such an expedition against Java, which would necessarily have to consist of a considerable force in men and ships we would, very probably find it expedient to visit this place called Singapura and settle with the pirates there. It would seem to me to make very little sense to expend time, money and men on eliminating the Dutch as a threat to our trade routes, and yet leave this villain Perak Shah able and ready to dash out of his creeks and seize our ships.' He raised his head to gaze at Clive. 'From what Teng has told me, I would think this would be very satisfactory to you. Assuming of course he has managed to rescue Mrs Blaine first.'

CHAPTER FOUR

The Go-Between

It was the business of the women every morning at dawn to go down to the river, both to draw water and to perform their necessaries. This applied even to the women of the harem, together with their children, for Perak Shah's harem was unlike anything Elizabeth Blaine had ever read about or imagined.

His wives were certainly secluded from the other women of the community, and the part of the river they used was reserved for them alone. Within the large bungalow the chieftain called his palace they had their own quarters, a vast dormitory looking out on to the inner courtyard, but there was scant comfort to be found there – no gushing fountains or nodding palm trees, no silk garments or jewelled fingers, such as was the popular conception in England of an oriental harem. Nor did the wives and concubines spend their time in idle luxury, but were required to work as hard as any English housewife, beginning the moment they returned from the river. The preparation of the day's food involved grinding spices for making the sambals and dissecting the chickens as well as the actual cooking, following which the palace had to be cleaned and the washing done.

During all of these chores they were guarded, not by eunuchs, for there were no half-men to be found in Singapura, but by four formidable elderly ladies. Elizabeth gathered these women were actually related to the chieftain, and they were at once fat and muscular, quite capable of wielding either a sword to cut off the head of any male intruder, or a bamboo cane to discipline any of the young women who might have offended her lord. These wardresses, as she came to regard them, accompanied the wives and children down to the water every morning, but as the river was the home of several frightening-looking crocodiles, not one of whom was less than eight feet long, it was also necessary to have male guards in attendance on these occasions.

This made it the least acceptable part of the day to Elizabeth. The absurdity of the garb she was required to wear about the 'palace', which consisted of a sarong and, whenever she left the harem itself, a yashmak, had struck her from the beginning – as had its indecency. The sarong extended from her waist to her ankles, and therefore those two portions of the body most determinedly concealed from prying glances by an English lady, the breasts and the feet, were constantly exposed, while the face, which in England was continually displayed to its best advantage, was concealed. The notion, indeed, that she would ever spend her entire life with her breasts exposed should have been quite as horrific as the idea that she would ever walk along a beaten-earth roadway – or any roadway for that matter – in her bare feet; and yet it wasn't, because she was in the midst of several other women dressed the same and acting in the same way as she was, and because she found herself in an entirely female world, except for the man who controlled their lives. Only on the visits to the river did the concubines see any other man even at a distance, unless they had borne sons; and if Bodaw Shan's mother, Amina, was permitted to spend some time each day with her son, the prince was never allowed into the harem.

The visits to the river were an ordeal, and yet one which daily became more acceptable, because it was acceptable to her companions. The concept, men or no men, that she should bathe in the open air and before a multitude of glances, should have thrown her into a faint. She could not imagine what Harriet Phillips would have made of it. And yet it hadn't, from the very beginning. Indeed, it was a way of life she realized she was almost coming to enjoy.

Her first emotion, on the day that Perak Shah claimed her as his own, had been terrified disbelief. It had not seemed possible that such a thing could happen, in 1808, to a member of the greatest nation on earth. She had screamed and attempted to fight her captors as she was carried into the palace, unable to believe that not one of the other passengers had lifted a finger to help her, save for Mr Hammond, whom she had seen struck to the ground by that treacherous Chinaman.

Once inside the harem, she was submitted to more indignities than she had ever suspected possible, all before she even saw Perak Shah again. She was washed and perfumed, and then . . . shaved. She thought she would die with shame to be handled by other women, and it seemed that the entire harem, children included, took part in the ceremony, fascinated at once by the whiteness of her skin and the gold of her hair. Indeed, they were so anxious to stroke her head she supposed she might be left bald there as well as on her pubes. Then she was washed and perfumed again, and dressed in a sarong and yashmak and escorted to the chieftain's chamber by two of the women guards. It was still only the middle of the afternoon, a time of day she had never previously associated with intercourse, and in addition it was only a few hours after the horrifying events which had so turned her life upside down. When she was shown into Perak Shah's presence, she was able to see, through the jalousies and across the trees, Teng Lee's junk being prepared for sea. Just over there were her friends . . . and Clive Hammond, all of whom would know what was happening to her. And none apparently cared, so long as they could save their own lives, again with the exception, she was sure, of Clive Hammond.

She wanted to vomit with despair and apprehension, and also with sheer physical discomfort, for in addition to her other miseries, she had not eaten all day. And then the guards removed her sarong and yashmak before leaving and closing the door. She was about to be ravaged. That was something you read about; it did not actually happen to you.

She gazed at Perak Shah, who was seated on a divan in front of the window, as a rabbit might gaze at a snake. She even contemplated battle and tried to ascertain where his weapons were, so that she could at least kill herself if she failed to kill him — or even if she succeeded.

He spoke to her, and if she did not understand a word he said, she understood his meaning. He was inviting her to join him on the divan on which he sat fully dressed. She could not, and yet, on the table in front of him there was a bowl of fruit, and another of some kind of sweetmeat, and another of nostril-tingling spiced meat, which he was inviting her to eat.

She sat down as far from him as she could, and took some of the food. Saliva rushed into her mouth so violently she could hardly swallow. But with it flowed strength and courage. She dared to glance at him, and he was smiling and talking and reaching forward to touch her hair. She knew he would not stop there and sat, paralysed, as his hand moved to her shoulder and then down to her breast. Her brain was a kaleidoscope of emotions, thoughts, memories and apprehensions: she had never been naked in the presence of a man, or indeed of a woman either until that day; she had never eaten such delicious food; she had never been so entrancingly warm or felt so entrancingly clean. She had also never been so aware of the presence of the sexual urge in a man, the ambience, the certainty that it would happen; when she had climbed beneath the boat cover with Clive on that unforgettable night she had not really known what she was doing, what to expect. Anticipation had been overlaid with memory, of Blaine's brief caress and quick thrust. Clive had been a marvellous surprise. Desire had come afterwards.

Now the knowledge, the sight, of what lay before her, was creating desire, however much she wished to reject it.

She had never been made love to in daylight, before. Lovemaking had been a matter for the dark, of mutual fumbling. No matter how knowledgeable Clive had been, how stimulating the touch of his fingers, it had employed only some of her available senses. Now she had to look, and not only at Perak Shah as he removed his clothes, but at herself as he came to her. She kept reminding herself that he was utterly repulsive, with his hawklike face, his black eyes, his straggly beard and his strong fingers, which were really like talons . . . but such soft talons at that moment.

Thoughts of resistance, of dying to protect her honour, became peripheral. He seemed to know as well as Clive had done, exactly where his touch would arouse most response, and before she was properly aware of it she was sitting in his lap for him to stroke between her legs while he kissed her face and hair. No doubt, like Clive, he was pleasing himself as much as consciously stimulating her. Oh, Clive, she thought, to be doing this with you! But Clive was not here, and he would never be here again, and this man was making her as hungry for some kind of relief from the building sexual tension within her as her hunger for food and drink had abated. She knew a succession of those dizzying sensations she had first experienced with Clive, each more exquisite than the one before, each threatening more and more to drive her over a precipice at which she might otherwise have baulked, until she was definitely plunging through space into the abyss of total sexual fulfilment.

When he laid her on her face she waited for some more massaging, some new stimulation, and was only vaguely alarmed to receive him in that position. But even then, when she did not know for sure how thoroughly she had been outraged, she felt only the most pleasurable of sensations.

There was no means of knowing the passage of time on the island save by watching the waxing and waning of the moon, and by the coming of the monsoon. Thus when the rains ceased, Elizabeth knew she had been in the harem for over two months. That meant, as it had been early November when the *Henry Oliver* was taken, that it was now after Christmas and actually into a new year. 1809!

The blue sky and hot sun meant that the ground dried quickly, and it was no longer necessary to splash through mud to get to the river. The women travelled in strict order of precedence, and as she was the newest concubine, even if she might have been their master's favourite throughout these two months, she was the very last in line. She waited with her wooden bucket; try as she might, she had not yet mastered the art of balancing it on the top of her head, and therefore had to carry it awkwardly, with water slopping in every direction, on the hike back up to the palace.

The girls around her chattered to each other, and sometimes to her. She had picked up several words of Malay during her sojourn here, but when they were gabbling like this they spoke too quickly for her to understand.

She had actually been more afraid of them than of Perak Shah, after her first day with the chieftain. The thought of sharing one room with so many other women, all of whom were not only of a foreign race and religion, but she assumed would be resentful of this intrusion by a stranger, had been terrifying. In the event, there too her fears had been groundless. The room itself was large enough even to permit some privacy. The ancient wooden structure that was the palace lacked grandeur, but there was an inner court containing palm trees and a pool of water. The communal bedchamber opened on to the court, and the girls spent most of the day there. The inner verandahs were patrolled by formidable-looking women, armed with kris. Their job was less to prevent anyone unauthorised from getting in than to stop any of the wives getting out, but they were mostly ignored as the girls went about their daily routines of washing their clothes, or their hair, preening themselves, chattering to each other, or lying in the sun. Unlike English girls, they paid little attention to their complexions, and Elizabeth soon found herself following their example. Nudity or near nudity was general and caused no comment, and here again she found herself slipping into their ways.

Remarkably, there appeared to be no jealousy amongst Perak Shah's concubines, who were actually an extremely happy group of women. They were all young; even the mothers were not old. The mother of Bodaw Shan, the eldest son of the chieftain, did not appear to be a day over thirty-five; as the young man was about seventeen, Elizabeth estimated that Amina must have been taken into the harem at seventeen years old herself. But all the girls had been selected when young; if they were critical of her at all, she gathered it was because she was somewhat older than any of them had been when first sent to Perak Shah's bed.

Thus where she had expected ill-treatment, perhaps even bodily harm, she had encountered mainly curiosity. It was the responsibility of them all to ensure that the current favourite was always in the peak of physical fitness and beauty. Her diet was studied and planned, her complexion criticized, especially her tendency to freckle wherever the sun reached her, and treated with a variety of creams and unguents, all smelling of coconut oil. They made her roll to and fro on the floor to preserve the slenderness of her hips, and she had to submit to having her breasts massaged and pulled to make them larger;

103

while hours were spent brushing her hair into a constant, ever-smoother sheen. Her beauty concerned them all.

She had supposed she might be pilloried because of her religion. But here again, she soon realized that at the call of the muezzin, when all the girls and even the guards would kneel to bow towards Mecca and remain in contemplation of the west for some minutes, she could do the same and pray to her God in perfect privacy and safety.

Above all, she had expected catastrophe, in some form or another. She was wearing, by European standards, virtually nothing all day, and she slept naked, because the other girls did so. If this was the most delightful freedom she had ever known, it yet did not seem possible for her to avoid the croup, or something far worse – and yet she felt more healthy than ever before in her life. She was eating a variety of strange foods, most of them very hot; she feared she could not avoid a continuing stomach disorder, but after the first few days, during which she had become acclimatized, she began to enjoy her meals and eagerly look forward to them, just as she enjoyed preparing them. She was exposed to assault by a number of insects she had never previously seen, every one of which she was positive could do her some frightful harm, but the guards were always on hand with bowls of unguents they had themselves prepared from herbs found in the forest, to smooth the reddened skin, removing at once the sting and the discolouring, so that she would always be pleasing to their lord and master. Even the fact that she had suddenly ceased to menstruate since arriving in Singapura appeared as part of her new-found health and freedom; she had never in any event been quite sure what menstruation was about. Her mother had only told her it was a curse women had to bear and this she was prepared to accept. Being rid of it was a boon.

To her surprise, when she thought about it, she realized that since that first day she had never contemplated

104

suicide. She had no doubt it could have been accomplished, even if horribly, by throwing herself into the water with the crocodiles. But with every day the thought became more and more absurd. She was living in the midst of a community of wolves, whom she had seen kill several score of men without the slightest compunction, and found them to be an utterly happy, almost childlike people, in the quiet pleasure they took from performing the most simple and even menial tasks. They were brutal in their dealings with those they considered to be their enemies, which on Singapura in fact consisted entirely of animals, but not more so than the average English fox-hunter. And, of course, where the community was built around the personality and strength of a single man, there was virtually no crime in the Five Villages.

For those who did transgress, the consequences were terrible. Elizabeth had not been long on Singapura when there was a fight between two men over a woman, and the husband was killed. The murderer knew his guilt and escaped into the forest, but was pursued by almost the entire male population, shouting and beating drums, while the women, even those of the harem, stayed up all night to await their return.

They were back at dawn, with their victim already bleeding from a dozen wounds. Then both the adulterers, man and woman, were stripped and tied together, all the while mocked and kicked by the entire community, before being suspended from the end of the dock into the deep water where the crocodile lurked. Their screams were heart-rending, and the more so to Elizabeth, who was very conscious that she was as guilty as they. But the crocodile soon came, while the whole village watched, and after several tugs, each accompanied by yet more soul-destroying shrieks of pain and terror, broke the rope and sank into the depths with its victims.

Yet however harsh, Perak Shah was revered by his people. And even by her. If she knew him to be a red-handed murderer, a creature of violent passions and temper, he could arouse in her the most unthinkable desires, simply by toying with her body. He could be personally brutal, and he indulged himself on his wives from time to time, when the female guards would hold one of the girls down while he applied a bamboo cane until the victim bled, or fainted from pain and exhaustion. But he never sought to beat *her*, and he could also be the most gentle of men, while his capacity for enjoying life was even greater than that of his people. She could not help but wonder if an English husband — if, indeed, the Edward Blaine she remembered so vaguely — would be a great improvement. Or as attractive. Or provide her with as comfortable an existence. Her estimation of English marriages had been that after a very brief period they dwindled into mutual neglect and disrespect, in which the wife became a lonely drudge. There was no chance of that where her drudgery was shared with eleven laughing girls.

And she was living in paradise. This only slowly dawned on her with the ending of the monsoon. Even during the rains, Singapura was a beautiful place, once she understood that she was not about to be carried off by either a tiger or a crocodile, that the lizards were harmless, that the magnificent peacocks with their attendant hens were as tame as domestic animals, that she was not about to die of some hideous malady or be executed by an angry tyrant. But with the coming of the good weather, the beauty of the island became even more apparent. Now, on occasion, Perak Shah would visit one of the beaches that studded the west coast of the island, and with him would go the entire harem, until the sand was covered with naked females and their small children, romping with each other and splashing in the shallow water. That Elizabeth Blaine, née Townsend, should ever find herself swimming naked on a tropical beach, in the midst of some dozen other screaming young women, watched by an omnipotent husband, was another situation she could never have imagined.

Was Perak Shah her husband? There had been no ceremony and, in any event, she understood that Muslim law permitted only four wives. She suspected the four harridans might be the actual wives and the rest of them merely his concubines. But it mattered little which she was, for all were treated alike, save for those women like Amina, who had produced sons for their master, and those, like Elizabeth, who were required most often for their master's bed.

To think of having to abandon this physical freedom and re-entering the strict confines of English genteelness, encountering people who would know where she had been and what she had 'suffered', and yet would be able to understand nothing of the truth of it, was increasingly abhorrent. To imagine herself face to face with Edward Blaine, much less sharing a house and a bedroom, or a bed, in his knowledge of what had happened to her, was inconceivable. Or even to imagine herself again face to face with Clive Hammond . . . would even he not be affected by knowing what had happened to her?

The worst thought of all was that she would never be able to persuade anyone that she had managed, from time to time and with growing regularity, to feel happy in these bizarre surroundings; that indeed she would be happy to end her days here, providing nothing changed.

But that was a dream. As she filled her bucket, the last in the line, keeping one eye on the drifting brown water in case a crocodile should suddenly surface, she became aware that two of the women had waited beside her. One was Amina, the lovely Malay who was Bodaw Shan's mother and therefore really the senior concubine; and the other was one of the guards. That they were discussing her was obvious. Then the guard did a remarkable thing: she took the full bucket from Elizabeth's hands and herself carried it up the slope to the palace. Elizabeth stared after her with her mouth open, and Amina smiled and said, as near as Elizabeth could understand, 'You come, Lizbeth. Perak Shah would see you. I have told him and he is pleased. You come.'

Teng Lee stroked his moustache as the junk approached the Dragon's Teeth. He was always happy to have the prow of his ship pointing homeward, however many weary weeks had still to pass before he would be sailing up the Pearl River, the rooftops of Canton in the distance, to the arms of Wu Chang and the laughter of the boy. His month at home between voyages was always the happiest time of his life.

But he was also well satisfied with the results of his voyage thus far. From a business point of view he had done as well as ever, he had a useful store of silver on board as well as having his hold filled with bartered items such as skins for leather, European delicacies, and even a stock of those fine weapons the white men were so adept at making and using. His visit to Rangoon had been informative, as well as lucrative, for there he had learned that the Burmese had finally bowed to the superior military might of the Thais and made peace, at the cost of some territory and concessions. This meant that a great deal might be possible when he reached Bangkok, news which would in turn please Perak Shah and smooth his way in Singapura.

He had found Calcutta depressing, but then he always found Calcutta depressing. It was the furthest point of his voyage from China, and by the time he got there his thoughts were always roving homeward, but in addition he had never felt welcome there, or entirely secure; his junk, so fine and large when lying at anchor off Batavia or Georgetown, was dwarfed by the huge warships flying the Union Jack which were to be found moored in the Hugli.

One of the great charms about Singapura was that it

108

never changed. Standing on the poop of the *Dragon's Wake* as it glided under shortened sail up the river, Teng Lee could admire the same trees he remembered from past visits, and as ever, he could hear the reverberation of the brass gong drumming through the forest; he had been seen and he would be welcomed.

The river opened in front of him into the harbour. He gave his orders in his usual quiet voice, and the sails were brought down on to their wooden flaps, to lie in orderly heaps on the deck at the foot of each mast. The junk lost way and slowly coasted up to the place he always chose to lie, where there was good holding ground, and the main anchor was let go. The ship snubbed the hempen rope cable and came to rest, swinging gently to face the light breeze.

Immediately, the boat was put down and Teng was rowed ashore. There was the usual excited crowd of people to greet him, even if, on his homeward voyage, there was little trading to be done. And there were Perak Shah and Bodaw Shan, as ever, smiling at him as he came ashore, waiting to embrace him and escort him to the palace. Perak Shah had never looked more contented in his life, Teng thought, or more aware of his power. But Bodaw Shan, for all the effusiveness of his greeting, was a man with much on his mind.

'And have you forgiven me, Teng Lee?' Perak Shah asked.

'Who am I to forgive Perak Shah?' Teng asked in turn. 'I thought it a dangerous thing to do. But the English . . . you were right not to fear them. They know they cannot contend with the power of Perak Shah.'

'Ha ha,' Perak Shah laughed. 'Well said. Sometimes you are unduly timorous, old friend,'

'And you remain pleased with the girl?' What he really wanted to ask was whether she was alive and well, but he could not risk revealing any personal interest.

'Oh, very pleased,' Perak Shah said. 'She is more of a delight with every day.'

Teng noted that Bodaw Shan remained silent and frowning, as if he suspected there might be more behind the inquiry than Perak Shah realized. He was a good deal shrewder than his father, Teng reflected, which was something to remember.

They sat on the verandah to eat watched by the usual hungry crowd. 'So what is the news from the north?' Perak Shah asked.

'Much of importance,' Teng told him. 'Peace has been concluded between the empires of Burma and Siam. The Thais have dictated terms.'

Perak Shah raised his eyebrows. 'Then King Rama is disengaged and triumphant.'

'Indeed.' Teng took great care over eating his satay; Perak Shah must not suspect him of lying. 'I spoke with his ambassadors.'

'And what did they say?'

'They spoke of you, Perak Shah, on the instructions of their king. He waits to see me when I leave here, as you know. Now that he has defeated the Vietnamese and settled with the Burmese, he is ready to undertake the next stage of his plan to make the Thai empire secure. To this end he has conveyed to me that he may well find it suitable to conclude the alliance in which you place so many hopes.'

Perak Shah snapped his fingers. 'At last. Now we shall see.'

'All the King requires,' Teng Lee said carefully, 'is a token of your good faith, that once your alliance is joined, you will not abandon him.'

'He can have whatever he requires,' Perak Shah declared. 'Abandon him? He is the source of all my dreams. What does he require?'

Teng finished his satay and carefully placed the skewer on the floor beside his bowl. 'Word has reached King Rama of this wondrous beauty you have secreted in your harem,' he said.

110

Perak Shah frowned. 'The girl, Lizbeth? How could this happen?'

'That I cannot say,' Teng confessed. 'I was more surprised than you. Indeed, I tried to deny it, but the King's ambassadors would not be denied. King Rama would look upon this girl and perhaps take her for himself. He has heard of her beauty, and of her golden hair. He cannot believe there is a woman with hair made of gold. He would see for himself.'

'And take her for himself,' Perak Shah growled. 'By Allah, but he is a lecherous rogue. Does he not have a hundred concubines?'

'He has more than two hundred,' Teng corrected. 'But then, one could say that he is a connoisseur of women. A collector of rare items. And this girl . . . Lizbeth, is it, you call her? A most attractive name. She is undoubtedly a most rare creature.'

'By Allah,' Perak Shah said again. 'It cannot be.'

Teng swallowed more sambal than he had intended and gave a delicate cough. He was more nervous than he would have admitted even to himself. If he could be certain that the King of Siam and a pirate chieftain would never correspond, much less meet, he was yet conscious of his danger should Perak Shah ever even suspect the subterfuge he was practising. But, as he was launched upon the scheme now, he might as well lie even more convincingly. 'It must be, Perak Shah. The King's ambassador said to me, when I demurred, how can King Rama be allied to a man who would deny him such a trifling gift? In return, the King will send you beauty such as you have never seen. It is possible, if the alliance were concluded and proved to be of value to the King, that you might even obtain the hand of a Thai princess to cement your relationship.'

'A Thai princess!' Perak Shah's eyes gleamed.

'But only if the alliance is concluded and proves to be successful,' Teng stressed. 'And in the first instance, that

111

depends on the King obtaining that which he has most set his heart on.'

'I am cursed,' Perak Shah said. 'I would send the girl with you tomorrow, Teng Lee. But . . . it cannot be.'

'You would jeopardize your entire future, and the future of your country, for the sake of a woman?' Teng's voice was severe.

'It cannot be,' Perak Shah repeated miserably. 'The woman is with child. She bears my son.'

CHAPTER FIVE

The King

It occurred to Teng Lee that no man could ever hope to understand the working of Fate. But then he recalled that Fate really did nothing more than raise obstacles to man's progress, and that the wise man, and the resolute one, would overcome those obstacles. Certainly he had no alternative but to do so.

'Are you positive of this?' he asked.

'My women are positive and they are never wrong.' Perak Shah pulled his beard. 'What is to be done? Above all things, I would not like to offend King Rama.'

'You mean, were she not pregnant, you would deliver the yellow-haired woman to the King?'

'Have I an alternative? She is like no other woman I have ever possessed, but if that is the price of Thai support against Johore . . . I would cut off my own finger to secure that.'

'I always knew you were a statesman,' Teng told him. 'Well, then, perhaps the problem is not insuperable. Let me look upon the woman.'

Perak Shah frowned. 'You wish to look upon a woman of my harem?'

'You may leave her face covered, Perak Shah. I need to assure myself that she is as healthy as when I last saw her.'

'I have told you this. Do you doubt my word?'

'We are dealing with kings,' Teng said severely.

Perak Shah considered the matter, then rose. 'I would do this for no other man, and not for you, were the situation not sufficiently grave.' He gave orders, and a few minutes later five women emerged from the interior of the house. It was simple to tell which was the white woman, from the colour of her hair; Teng noted that her skin was not so very different in colour to that of her companions.

The women knelt in a row, Elizabeth Blaine in the centre.

'I am Teng Lee,' Teng said, in English. 'Do you remember me?'

The yashmak inflated and then fell back against the nose and mouth. 'I remember you,' she said.

'I would take you away from here,' Teng said.

'No,' she answered quickly.

Teng frowned. 'I do not understand you.'

'I wish to be left alone,' she said. 'Can you not understand that? Go away and leave me alone.'

'What is it she says?' Perak Shah inquired.

'She praises your greatness,' Teng said thoughtfully. 'You may dismiss her. I am satisfied with her health.' He waited while the women were sent back inside, giving himself time to think. The woman's words were incomprehensible. And in any event, her feelings could not be allowed to interfere with his plans, either to gain the confidence of the British or to settle in Singapura as Perak Shah's friend and adviser. 'You wish this child?' he asked Perak Shah.

'He will be my son,' Perak Shah said proudly. 'He will have the blue eyes and yellow hair of his mother. He will be a man amongst men.'

'No doubt,' Teng agreed, drily. 'Well, then, guard this woman with your greatest care, Perak Shah, and I will represent to King Rama that while you are willing to deliver her to him in accordance with his wishes, you in turn seek some token of his support and that, if he will provide me with such a token, I will escort the woman to Bangkok on my next voyage.'

'That cannot be,' Perak Shah said gloomily. 'She will not yet be delivered.'

'If I do not visit Bangkok on my outward voyage next year,' Teng said, 'but complete my other trading business first, I should return here just about the time she is delivered of her child.'

'Then she will be heavy with milk,' Perak Shah pointed out.

'So you will have the milk sucked out by your wives. If necessary, I will say I have been delayed by bad weather.'

Perak Shah brooded. 'Will King Rama accept this? My demand for a compensatory gift?'

'Should he not deal with you as an equal?' Teng demanded. 'I have never indicated that you are in any way inferior.'

'That is good,' Perak Shah said. 'It is true. But the woman . . .' He was still anxious. 'There may be marks, if the child is large. He will be large,' he added as proudly as before. 'He will be my son.'

'The woman was married before she came to you,' Teng reminded him. 'I have told the King's ambassadors this. If she carries the marks of motherhood, it will be attributed to that. He wants her, regardless of her past. He might even take her pregnant. . . .'

'She bears my son,' Perak Shah said again.

'Indeed. It is not a matter I would press. I am sure I can persuade King Rama that all is well. And my friend, even if he takes one look at her and throws her aside because she is not as he thought, this will not alter the fact that you have kept your word and delivered her to him. There is one matter that concerns me: the woman may not wish to leave her child.'

'It will be your business to see that she does not harm herself once she has left my protection,' Perak Shah said. 'I will fulfil my part of the bargain. This I swear.'

'Then I, too, will fulfil my part,' Teng promised.

'Then are all our dreams come true,' Perak Shah said. 'You are a man of great value, Teng Lee.'

Teng bowed his head. It was his habit when complimented. But at this moment he could not look his friend in the eye.

The Thai capital of Bangkok was situated some twenty-five miles up the delta of the Chao Phraya River, where it had been created some twenty years before by the victorious general, Chakkri, when he replaced his predecessor, King P'ya Taksin, on the throne of Siam.

P'ya Taksin himself had been an usurper. He had been the only general in the armies of King Boromokot capable of withstanding the Burmese armies of the invader Alaungpaya, who had swept across the western border of Siam in a bid to conquer Burma's oldest enemy. And Alaungpaya, a soldier of infinite ability, would have succeeded, but for the daring of P'ya Taksin, who had cut his way through the encircling Burmese force to find safety, abandoned King Boromokot to die, while he raised more armies with which to oppose the invader — and, incidentally, to claim the throne when news of the King's death reached him.

In that war, the ancient capital of Ayutthaya had been all but destroyed, and P'ya Taksin had never had the time to rebuild it, having spent his entire life as King of Siam in fighting the Burmese. The years of struggle had indeed taken their toll, and P'ya Taksin had finally gone mad. *His* chief general, Chakkri, had then deposed him.

Chakkri was of an altogether different stamp to P'ya Taksin, who had been a warrior plain and simple. Chakkri had vision to go with his talents and determination. He did not intend to be recorded in Siamese history as just another usurper in a turbulent era and he had determined to restore the prosperity as well as the greatness of his country. To this end he had concluded peace with Burma, which had itself been feeling the strain

116

of a long war; then Chakkri, now known as Rama I, had set about rebuilding his nation.

He had chosen the site of his capital first. Forty miles down the river from the ancient capital of Ayutthaya, and thus within striking distance of the Gulf of Siam, there had been two settlements facing each other across the Chao Phraya. These had been known as Krung Thep on the east bank, and Thon Buri on the west. Already connected by several bridges, the twin settlements had seemed the natural site for the centre of the new government. Chakkri, with a soldier's eye, had elected to build his stronghold on the eastern bank, for here the river made a deep westward loop and was therefore the more easily defensible. He called his city Bangkok, which means Village of Wild Plums, but as it grew, and canals were dug for drainage and tall temples rose above the swamps, the Thais had preferred to revert to its original name, Krung Thep, the City of Angels.

The city had been founded twenty-six years ago, Teng Lee reflected as his junk glided up the slow flowing water of the river, and had not yet been completed. Perhaps it never would be, as with every year it seemed to spread further beyond the walls. But the outskirts was a shanty town. It was within the walls that Chakkri reached for immortality; he had created the great Wat Po, the grand palace complex which was dominated by the immense, striking, unique pagoda of Wat Ching. The Wat Po was next to the river, and indeed King Rama enjoyed sitting out on the huge balcony overlooking the water, especially on festival days, when he would enjoy mock battles or parades of brilliantly clad Thai women, all singing his praises.

The Wat Po was surrounded by the wall, which was in fact a marvel of architecture even to Chinese eyes, after due allowance had been made for the limited resources of Siam as compared with China, for it was more than four miles long, and no less than ten feet deep and thirteen

117

high, and was protected by fifteen forts, while access to the crowded interior was gained by no less than sixty-three gates.

The wall alone had taken more than twenty years to construct. The Grand Palace was not yet complete, although the wonderful structure of the pagoda roofs and the shimmering gilt of the decorations were clearly visible as the junk brought up on the western side of the river.

This had also thrived during the years of Rama's power. Although unprotected by any walls and ungraced by any magnificent buildings, it had become the commercial quarter of the city, where indeed several other Chinese merchants had set up their warehouses. That of Teng Wong was prominently displayed as it was the largest, and here Teng Lee knew he would find people of his own house awaiting his arrival, eager to assist him in any way. He needed only to hand over the junk for a tallying of the profits of the voyage before taking himself across the bridge to the royal city and an interview with Rama.

The two men had known each other for many years, and like most people with whom Teng dealt, the Thai King had found the Chinese merchant to be a most useful contact and ally. If Teng believed that it was his responsibility simply to make the world a better place for Wu Chang and himself to enjoy, that very goal necessarily meant that he was concerned to please those with whom he conducted business. Rama of Siam was a very important part of that goal, and he had given Teng a status which far transcended his humble station in life. For Rama had not forgotten the Burmese who had so tormented his country in his youth. Once he had restored his country's finances, rearmed his soldiers and raised their morale, he had embarked on a series of campaigns which had completely reversed the situation under P'ya Taksin. He had now finally sent the Burmese, for whom the genius of Alaungpaya was only a memory, tumbling to defeat.

118

In these achievements even Rama had needed assistance, in such commodities as gunpowder, cannon, modern firearms, and the knowledge of how to use such weapons. Teng Lee had not only supplied the guns and the power, but had recruited the gunners from China. For if he prided himself upon being a man of peace, he understood that mankind progresses mainly through war; it only required always to be on the winning side. Thus to Rama he was more than a supplier; he had become a friend.

He intended to be all of those things to Perak Shah, when the alliance between Singapura and Siam was completed, after which he estimated he would hold both the north and the south end of the Malayan peninsula in his commercial grasp.

So now he bowed decorously to the guards on the gate who, for all their protective equipment, left much of their bodies bare in the Siamese heat, and approached the palace, listening to the gong of the brass bells reverberating through a building which in any event contained an inordinate amount of brass. He had taken one of those gongs to Perak Shah as a gift seven years before. He wondered what Perak Shah, with his ramshackle wooden 'palace', would think of this marvellous construction. For he stood at the outer end of a corridor not less than a hundred feet long and wide enough to house his junk, and nearly high enough, as well. The entire room was crowded with guards and court officials, brilliant in their reds and greens and blue; with Buddhist monks, isolated in their saffron robes; with awed suppliants from the country districts, staring at the magnificence with which they were surrounded, at the high ceiling, every inch decorated with scenes from the life of the Buddha; the royal palms which lined the walls, as stiffly correct in their bearings as the soldiers who stood beside them; and at the end of the hall, the huge, ornate, empty throne. Behind the throne waited a crowd of secretaries and

119

major-domos, staring superciliously down the length of the enormous room.

Perak Shah would be struck dumb by such splendour. And he would know that it was a splendour he could never hope to emulate, even in his most heady dreams, simply because the tenets of the Muslim religion forbade such representations of either gods or men. Thus perhaps it would be best if he were never to see it and continue to be satisfied with his own concept of kingliness.

One of the major-domos saw Teng in the crowd and came down from the dais towards him. 'Teng Lee,' he said. 'But it is good to see you.'

'It is good to be back again,' Teng told him. 'But do not tell me his majesty is away campaigning? I understood he had no enemies left to conquer, save the sultanate of Kedah.' And if Rama had begun a war with Kedah without waiting for assistance from Singapura, which he might well have decided was irrelevant, then his plans were in jeopardy.

'Alas,' the major-domo said. 'I wish it were so. But his majesty is ill.'

'Ill?' Teng frowned. That could be more serious than a campaign. Suddenly life had become fi.!:d with unpleasant surprises. 'Is it possible to convey news of my arrival to him? We have important matters to discuss.'

'I will see what can be done,' the major-domo agreed, and drifted off. Teng took his place among the throng, continuing to frown and stroke his moustache. In a changing world, Rama had seemed more permanent than most as, for more than a quarter of a century, he had guided the fate of his country with a steady if stern hand.

The major-domo returned. 'If you will follow me, Teng Lee,' he said.

Teng nodded, and allowed himself to be guided through a doorway on his right and through a succession of corridors hardly less ornately decorated than the reception chamber itself. These were mostly deserted, but

120

after some minutes they arrived before another door, and this had an armed guard in front of it. He stood to attention, however, to allow the two men through an antechamber. There Teng faced a young man hardly half his own age, not tall, as he was a Thai, but with good features and a thin moustache. He was dressed in royal robes, the high, tiered brass hat on his head secured beneath his chin by a strap.

Teng dropped to his knees, as the major-domo already had done. 'Prince Nobhalai,' he said.

The prince extended his hand. 'It is good to see you, Teng Lee,' he said. 'Even if you come upon us at a difficult time. Stand.'

Teng rose. 'Your father. . . ?'

'Is old and tired,' Nobhalai said. 'But he will wish to see his friend.' He gave a brief smile. 'He sees few others.'

The doors were opened and Teng was allowed into a huge bedchamber, in the centre of which Rama I lay on a large divan. Kneeling on the far side of the room were several women, their heads bowed as they intoned prayers together with a Buddhist priest; it was not the Thai way to seclude their women as the Muslims did, although they were no less jealously guarded. Behind them were a score of children. Teng knew these were but a fraction of the enormous harem Rama maintained; no doubt the wives and children took it in turns to kneel by the bedside of their stricken lord.

'You may approach,' Nobhalai told him.

Teng knelt and crawled forward to within four feet of the bed. There he waited, head bowed, until the dying man turned his head to look at him, and after a moment, recognized him. 'Teng Lee,' said the faint voice, which had once been so resonant.

Teng again had to reflect upon the games that Fate plays with all men. Rama had been away campaigning when he visited here in October. The last time he had seen him was the previous spring, and then the Thai warrior

121

had appeared in his prime, a glitter of bronze armour, of waxed moustache, of imperious vision and powerful voice. Now the voice quavered, and the hand which was extended to him was thin and weak; it was difficult to suppose it had ever drawn a sword.

'My heard bleeds, your majesty,' he said.

Rama smiled. 'You are a faithful friend, Teng Lee. You have always been so. Trust my eldest son. He knows my thoughts and thinks with my mind. Trust him, and he will trust you. I give you the prosperity of my kingdom until I am well again.'

'Which will be soon, your majesty,' Teng ventured.

'Soon,' Rama agreed. And sighed. 'Soon.'

Teng crawled back to the door and regained the antechamber. 'You have but to name your requirements, Prince Nobhalai,' he said. 'I can procure the best doctors, the finest medicine.'

'There are no requirements,' Nobhalai said. 'My father is simply worn out by incessant campaigning. If rest cannot cure him, there is no doctor in the world who could do so.'

'His sickness is a catastrophe for his people with his work only half done,' Teng ventured.

Nobhalai glanced at him. 'You are mistaken, Teng Lee. My father's work is all but completed fortunately. He has humbled the Burmese, forced the Vietnamese to make peace. He has ushered in a period of greatness for Siam. I am fortunate that, should it fall to me to rule, I shall inherit so much prosperity. And at least part of it is due to you, old friend,' he added.

Teng bowed. His brain was seething. Yet it was essential to press matters; in the three months before he would return here, a great deal might happen. 'I spoke of your father's lifelong ambition to march upon Kedah, and perhaps make the peninsula his.'

'I doubt he will consider that now,' Nobhalai said. 'His campaigning days are over.'

'Yet would it be the duty of his successor to follow in his footsteps,' Teng said boldly, 'to continue to enhance the greatness of Siam. You will know that King Rama and I have spoken of this, and that, on his behalf' — he could lie as confidently as he conducted most affairs — 'I have undertaken negotiations with the ruling chieftain of the island of Singapura, Perak Shah, who has agreed to launch a campaign against Johore at the moment your armies move against Kedah. This will distract the sultans from helping one another and smooth your path.'

Nobhalai stroked his as yet beardless chin.

'And all this Perak Shah asks of your greatness,' Teng pressed on, scenting victory, 'is the assistance of half a dozen warships of your fleet, and recognition of himself as Sultan of Johore when your victory is complete, in perpetual friendship and alliance with the Empire of Siam.'

'My father has spoken to me of this Perak Shah,' Nobhalai agreed.

Teng waited, heart pounding. It should surely be possible to make this boy walk the path he had selected.

'But my own feelings are that there are more pressing matters to be attended to,' Nobhalai said.

Teng frowned. 'Has Siam other enemies?'

Nobhalai smiled. 'There is China.'

Teng bowed. 'The Manchus are distracted by internal revolution, my lord prince. And the men of Han are your friends.'

'Would that it were always so,' the Prince said drily. 'But so long as the men of Han lie beneath the yoke of the Manchus, there will always be dark clouds in the north. And then there is the west, Teng Lee.'

'Your father has crushed the Burmese, my lord prince.'

'The Burmese are nothing,' Nobhalai declared. 'I speak of the Europeans. You will know that we have received embassies from a man who calls himself the King of Portugal. Do you know of this place?'

123

'I have heard of it,' Teng said. 'It is a small country and weak.'

'Yet once their fleets were powerful in these waters, my councillors tell me,' Nobhalai said.

'Once,' Teng said. 'Now they have been replaced by others.'

'By the English. Then what of these people? The Portuguese who have been here speak of England with awe.'

Teng Lee stroked his moustache. He did not know how much the prince really knew of British power.

The prince continued. 'I have heard tales of great ships, larger than the finest junks, with row upon row of cannon. Of soldiers in red jackets who are invincible. Can these things be true, Teng Lee?'

Teng was making some hasty adjustments to his thinking. Undoubtedly the prince had already arrived at an answer. 'Indeed, the English have great ships, my lord prince,' he agreed. 'And their soldiers are of the highest quality. Fortunately, there are as yet but few of them in India.'

'But there will be more.'

'That is possible,' Teng said. 'But . . . would you go to war on the English?' Then his world would indeed stand on its head, he supposed.

The prince shook his head. 'My business must be to consolidate the great gains my father has made for Siam,' he said. 'If the English would send me ambassadors, I would speak with them, and learn of their intentions, and decide whether they might prove worthy allies. And there is another nation. . . .'

'The Dutch,' Teng Lee said.

'Exactly so. Like the English, the Portuguese ambassadors have told me.'

'But not so strong,' Teng said, without thinking. 'And they are at war with the English, at least in Europe,' he added.

124

'Yet they too must be sought out, supposing the English are arrogant. If they are at war, one side or the other should welcome an alliance with us. It would be good for them, and it would be good for us. Alliance with such a power would do much to deter the Manchus from ever marching south again, even after they have suppressed their rebellions. I consider these matters as more urgent than an invasion of Malaya, Teng Lee. Certainly we cannot undertake another major campaign until they are attended to.'

'Is this the opinion of your royal father, my lord prince?' Teng asked.

The prince sighed. 'No. My father disdains any enemy he cannot see, or any ally. And' – another quick smile – 'even those he can. It is his intention to wage war upon Malaya as soon as he is recovered.'

'Ah,' Teng said. But he is not going to recover, he thought; he had seen the hand of death resting on Rama's brow.

'I but give you my own thoughts on the matter, as I know you are in my father's confidence, and because I also know that you trade with Calcutta, where the English are.'

Teng Lee stroked his moustache, but he was not going to be tempted to undertake any surreptitious mission for Prince Nobhalai at this moment. Even had he not been anxious to get home for his month with Wu Chang, he needed time to consider the changing situation and to discover just how much it was going to change again. 'I am now bound for Canton, my lord prince.'

Nobhalai nodded. 'This I understand. And I have no power to instruct you at this time. My father is still King of Siam. But you will return here, next year?'

'Next year, my lord prince.'

'Perhaps next year we will have much to discuss,' Nobhalai said.

*

When in Bangkok, Teng Lee made a point of lighting a candle to the Buddha in the Wat Ching pagoda. He lit candles to the Lord Buddha wherever he stopped to ensure safe passage for his ship, his men and himself, but never with such pleasure as in the Wat Ching.

There was no building in the world, not even in Peking, that he had ever seen which could compare with the Wat Ching pagoda for size or beauty. The temple towered above the river, visible even from beyond the great bend, as it stood higher than the trees. The towers, the arches, the roofs, were all highly decorated, each piece of ornate carving done by hand over the years, the whole gilded so that in the sunlight the myriad reflections seemed as if the great heavenly orb had itself come to rest in its favourite kingdom. Rama had commenced work on this edifice to thank the Lord Buddha for granting him victory and prosperity, in the very first year of his reign. Like the city, or the palace, it was not yet completed. But equally, like the city and the palace, it had already established a standard of greatness and magnificence which all Indo-China would never equal. Teng had visited Angkor Wat and bowed in awe before the crumbling splendour he had seen there. But the Wat Ching was new and growing, and brilliantly alive. He could understand how the Thais, as they went about their daily business and at every turn had their eyes caught by the splendour rising above them, could believe themselves to be indeed the chosen people of Buddha, the ultimate arbiters of this sub-continent of rice paddies and river deltas.

This morning he was even more thoughtful than usual as he knelt in contemplation, regarding the yellow robe of the priest immediately in front of him. How, he considered, the world had changed since his youth. Twenty years ago, when he first came to Bangkok, it had still been little more than a vast building site. Even then, however, he had not doubted that Rama was all-powerful; it had seemed he would reign forever. But then, twenty years ago, the Emperor Kao Tsung ruled China, and already seemed to have done so forever. The world had been a stable place. The Europeans had already been here, of course. The Dutch had even then been living their orderly lives in Batavia for more than a century, and the British similarly held forts and trading posts in Calcutta and Bombay. But they had then been tradesmen, concerned only with extracting what wealth they could from the Asiatic peoples with whom they were in contact; their wars had been fought either as mercenaries for native princes or against each other, for the possession of some especially valuable market. There had been no sense that here was an empire for the taking; the restless probings of the Dutch in Java and Sumatra, the policy of acquisition of territory undertaken by Richard Wellesley, had not yet begun. And no one had then heard of Bonaparte, the adventurer who was apparently over-running all Europe – which was a country possibly as large as China, he gathered, and whose influence the British seemed to fear would eventually spread even through Asia and the islands.

Now the world was in turmoil. A man must pick his way carefully. Certain facts could be established, like rocks around which the current, and therefore the ship, must swirl. Rama was dying, and it was clear that Nobhalai was not going to follow the policies of his father, however much he might conceal that fact from the old man. Therefore it would be blind folly for Teng Lee to advocate a policy which had no hope of being accepted and could only lower his own esteem in the eyes of the prince. Desirable as Singapura was as a residence, it could not be considered safe as long as it was nothing more than a pirate stronghold, liable at any moment to be destroyed by vengeful Europeans, or even by the Sultan of Johore. It would therefore be necessary to look elsewhere.

Teng had always rejected the idea of moving to Siam itself, because much as he admired and respected Rama, he knew the old warrior to be a tyrant, and knew too that once he abandoned Canton and settled in Rama's country, he would lose much of his value to the King. He had never considered Java, because he abhorred the Dutch system of governing the Javanese, and because he knew he would be treated as an inferior race, that was the European way. The same criticism went for Penang, which in any event was too small and restricted, while Calcutta was unthinkable. And Rangoon, in Burma, was at present an unhappy city, ruled by a half-mad boy who nursed a desire for revenge on Siam. Was his dream, then, unattainable?

He would require the Lord Buddha to show him the way. But it seemed that if he was going to leave China, then Bangkok *was* the only place left to him in which to settle. And if he could earn the gratitude of Prince Nobhalai by acting as an agent between the Thais and the British, and, incidentally, earn the respect of the British at the same time, then he would be foolish indeed not to obey the dictate of Fate.

And Perak Shah? Teng sighed. He did not like the idea of abandoning an old friend. But there was no sense in attempting the impossible. There was, of course, no way in which he would be able to convince Perak Shah of this. Unfortunately, they would become enemies. It might, therefore, be wisest not to call at Singapura again.

But what of the woman, Elizabeth Blaine? Teng stroked his moustache. There too he would need the guidance of Lord Buddha. But it seemed to him that if he was going to preserve the trust of the British, it was more than ever important to regain the white girl before Perak Shah learned of the change in the Thai attitude. And he could do nothing for six months; in that time he could only pray that nothing untoward happened, that the girl was delivered safely and on time, that Perak Shah did not undergo a change of heart. Indeed, he needed not only the guidance but the support of the Lord Buddha.

He rose and turned to leave the temple, and found a man standing at his side. He had seen him at the palace, and knew him to be one of the major-domos there from his brilliant red and green court dress. 'Teng Lee,' the man said. 'There is one would speak with you.'

Teng glanced to his left, and saw an entourage leaving the pagoda by another entrance and pausing there. He knew at a glance that it was the escort of a royal personage, and followed the major-domo, only vaguely interested; this could be any member of Rama's family praying for his recovery.

The party consisted of a dozen guards, an equal number of secretaries and about twenty young women, who were gathered round one of their number. She was of medium height and slender. Her black hair was all but invisible, coiled on her head beneath a broad-brimmed straw hat as the sun was high; it was the sort of hat a peasant woman might have worn, save that it was studded with semi-precious stones. The face thus exposed was exquisite, with a short straight nose and pointed chin, small mouth and high forehead, and wide-set, thoughtful black eyes. The girl was heavily made-up, but that was the Thai way, and in no way diminished the beauty beneath the powder and rouge.

She wore the simple but rich garb of a Thai princess; a brocaded skirt, which might have originated as a sarong many centuries ago, and above it a heavily embroidered tunic, which fitted her snugly although it left her right shoulder exposed and revealed that she possessed a full figure, even if she was clearly still a girl.

'This is the Chinese traveller, Teng Lee,' the major-domo said, dropping to his knees as he approached her.

Teng followed the major-domo's example. He did not consider himself as inferior to any Thai princess, especially one who had achieved her rank by virtue of her father's skill in battle rather than by any pedigree, but he was in no position to risk offending any member of Rama's household.

'Teng Lee,' she said. Her voice was like music. 'My father has spoken of you, of the many lands you have visited. He says you are acquainted with the whole world.'

Teng bowed his head. 'The great King is pleased to compliment me, my lady princess,' he protested.

From the corner of his eye he caught a trace of a smile. 'Truly,' she said. 'You must know him better than I. I would hear of these faraway places, Teng Lee. I would have you speak to me of them. You will attend me this afternoon.'

Teng bowed his head.

She was, he ascertained, the Princess Jalina. As such she was of no great importance, for Rama had well over a hundred children by his innumerable concubines, and only the elder sons truly mattered. But she was one of the eldest of his daughter, although only seventeen years of age, and she was also, he understood, the favourite half-sister of Prince Nobhalai and would undoubtedly be a very powerful influence at the Thai court once the prince succeeded his father on the throne. She was certainly not a young woman to be crossed.

So he attended her suite that afternoon and played the part of a storyteller, standing in the midst of a large group of young women, guards and secretaries, and children, Jalina's brothers and sisters, while he waved his arms and described the wonders he had seen, and spoke of the English and the Dutch, and even attempted to imitate some of their gruff voices. It was a humiliating exercise, but he reflected that it was in a good cause – his own popularity at the Thai court. Certainly his inventive talents pleased the princess, who clapped her hands in delight, gave him a gold medallion and said, 'You will come again tomorrow, Teng Lee, and tell us some more stories. We have had a most enjoyable hour.'

Teng bowed, crawled to the door, regained his feet and wondered at the ways of the Lord Buddha, to give such frivolous creatures so much power, while withholding it from those who both deserved it and could use it to better advantage. He made his way back over the bridge to the west bank, watching the sun setting in a blaze of glory above the forest, its last rays as always reflecting from the Wat Ching, sending brilliant shafts of light across the water. In that light he could see a junk coming up to its mooring, happy to have reached its destination just before darkness fell. He knew the flag, that of the house of Ho Tang, also out of Canton, and a rival, if an inferior one, to the house of Teng Wong. It pleased him to think that Bangkok was becoming a true entrepôt for Chinese merchants, and that Teng Wong retained his pre-eminence amongst them. He had never doubted that of all the people with whom he dealt, the kings and princes and pirates, the chieftains and factors and government officials, the King of Siam was the greatest, the most important. If he truly could make himself invaluable to the next king, and at least interesting to his sister, then equally he did not doubt that he could again control his future and shape it as he wished. In a changing world, a man had always to conform to the different patterns assumed by that world. Only a fool would do otherwise.

He descended the far side of the bridge to the shore and found himself in the midst of commotion. The newly arrived junk had anchored and sent the crew ashore, men who pronounced catastrophe in shrill tones.

'What are you saying?' Teng Lee shouted, pushing into their midst. 'What are you saying?'

'The great thirst,' they told them. 'It is sweeping across South China. Many are dying. It already ravages Canton. The great thirst.'

Teng stepped away from them while he tried to think.

131

The great thirst, known to the Europeans as cholera, but so called by the Chinese because of the total dehydration caused by the disease, was a recurrent and indeed endemic problem throughout the East, but in China more than anywhere else. It seemed to seek out, with malignant fury, the most heavily populated areas, striking down young and old, rich and poor, in a reeking horror of human excrement. There was an outbreak in his youth which had killed many thousands. He and his brothers had only been saved because Teng Wong, who was even then a wealthy man, had placed all his family in one of his junks and sailed them down the Pearl River to the island known as Hong Kong, there to breathe pure air until the noxious vapours dissipated. And now it was back again. And Teng Wong was old and no longer possessed of the powers of decision. Nowadays he would be too frightened that in his absence his warehouses would be looted.

Teng Lee was rowed out to his ship. 'Set sail and raise anchor,' he commanded his mate, Li Yuan. 'We will sail for Canton this night.'

'But we have not completed our business here,' Li Yuan protested.

'It will have to wait on our return,' Teng said. 'Haste, man, haste.'

He had quite forgotten about his appointment with the princess for the following day.

Teng Lee pounded the rail of the junk as the wind eased while they felt their way through the archipelago which clogged the lower reaches of the Pearl River. Behind him now were the Portuguese trading entrepôt of Macao and the islands of Hong Kong. They had made good time out of the Bight of Bangkok with a fair wind, which had driven them all the way down to Cau Mau at the very southern end of Indo-China, where the delta of the huge Mekong River, build up over the centuries, had left a rich alluvial soil to be farmed. Here they had turned north-east, and as if to their aid, the wind had shifted to the west to remain fair. They had been able to stand out from the coast, crossing between the huge island of Hainan to their left, and the reefs and islets of the Paracels on their right, making due north for the landfall of the Lima Islands. All the way the breeze had held steady, and only in these last hours of the voyage, when they were beginning to be sheltered by the land, had it dropped.

Yet there remained enough wind for the junk to make headway coasting against the current; the rooftops and pagodas of Canton were already visible in the distance. Now they sailed between the high embankments which lined the riverside to keep out flood water. Beyond those embankments, the local people farmed, as they had done for centuries. It was the custom that a death was marked by a white flag. Today there were far more white flags than usual, and there was an absence of small children on the levees, to cheer the junk onwards.

'The plague will undoubtedly have spent its force by now,' Li Yuan said reassuringly.

He was probably right, Teng knew, for despite the fair wind it had taken them well over a week to make the passage from Bangkok, and, according to the men from Ho Tang, the plague had already been in Canton when they set sail several weeks before. It had left its mark. In Canton itself, the white flags were even more in evidence, and the pall of smoke still hung across the sky; the only known way to dispose of cholera victims was by total destruction: burning the bodies and anything with which they had come into contact.

The junk eased up to its mooring, and the lines were picked up. The boat was in the water almost before the warps had been made secure; all the crew had their families here. Teng took his place to be rowed ashore, leapt on to the steps and faced his brother, Teng Chiang.

'Lee,' Teng Chiang exclaimed. 'Thank the gods you are back. There has been much sadness here.'

133

'Our father?' Teng snapped.

Teng Chiang bowed. 'He is well. We are the most fortunate of families, Lee.'

'Our mother?'

'Is equally well. The illness was not so severe as the last time, we have been told.'

Teng sighed with relief, and then frowned. His brother was not his usual smiling self.

'And yet, it has been severe enough,' Teng Chiang said.

He was wearing a white mourning band. 'Who has died?' Teng gasped, thinking of all his other brothers, of their wives, of his nephews and nieces.

It was Teng Chiang's turn to sigh. 'The illness struck where it would, according to the will of Fate,' he said. 'My brother. . . .'

Teng seized his arm. 'Wu Chang has been ill?'

Teng Chiang shook his head. 'Your wife is dead, my brother.'

Teng stared at him, then dropped to his knees, only dimly aware of the people who had gathered around him. He took his hat from his head to fan the tears from his eyes. The image of Wu Chang hovered before him, Wu Chang smiling, Wu Chang pretending to be angry, Wu Chang looking sad when he said farewell. That was his last memory of her, and she had looked sadder than ever then, because before he left they had talked of their plans, and dreams, of Singapura, a place she had so wanted to see for herself.

Now she was a pile of ash, blown by the wind.

He stood up, while his men waited sympathetically. 'You all have families of your own,' he told them. 'Leave me, and see to your loved ones. Forgive my weakness, Chiang,' he told his brother.

'You are deeply grieved,' Teng Chiang said quietly. 'Your bereavement is more than a man can be expected to bear.' He was more uneasy than ever, but Teng did not immediately notice.

'I thank you for your words. But Little Chiang must be more grief-stricken than I. Is he with our mother?'

Teng Chiang looked ready to burst into tears himself. 'He is with his mother.'

Teng stared at him, for a moment not comprehending.

'The disease took them both,' Teng Chiang said miserably. 'It happened too quickly for us to save the boy, as we were preoccupied with the mother.'

Teng stared at him for a moment longer, then he uttered a howl of the purest agony, and hurled himself on the ground, rolling to and fro, all his carefully cultivated self-control snapping in a single instant.

Teng Chiang knelt beside him and held his arm to bring him to a stop, waiting while the convulsive despair slowly subsided. 'It can only be the law of the universe, my brother,' he said. 'The law of yin-yang, against which no man can fight. It affects us all.'

PART TWO
The Struggle

CHAPTER SIX

The Mother

It affects us all, Teng thought, as he stood in what had once been his house. He supposed it was still his house, even if these bare walls could not be called a home. Everything had been burned: soft bedding, warm mats, dragon embroidered screens, the pictures he had so carefully accumulated, and worst of all, his books. Because they might have been contaminated. The maid-servants knelt in anxious supplication before their master, afraid of an angry reaction to the unbelievable tragedy which had overtaken him.

It affects us all. But it had never affected Teng Lee before. His first reaction, once the initial paroxysm of grief had faded, had been anger. He had wanted to curse and shout and scream, to take the sword and run amok, slashing off people's heads.

He could not accept that he was suffering from a just application of the law of yin-yang. If he had been fortunate throughout his life, it had been the fortune of hard work, clear thinking, unswerving determination, and the self-confidence born of a knowledge of his own courage. Those were not the gifts of Fate. They had been carefully cultivated assets.

But Fate had still been jealous!

Gradually he became calmer, and could even look at his situation with some degree of objectivity. Fate ruled all things. Even the Lord Buddha could only mitigate Fate – he could not alter it. And if it was difficult to see how even the Lord Buddha was going to soften this particular blow, yet must he believe that it would happen. He realized that he had been punished; not perhaps for his great success in life, but for his complacency, indeed his arrogance, which he had allowed to develop from that success. When he thought of the way he had lectured poor Clive Hammond, dismissed the unhappy woman, Elizabeth Blaine, as of no importance, sought to abandon Perak Shah in the pursuit of his own ambitions . . . it was for those crimes that Fate had punished him. But so cruelly!

And so completely. Perhaps he *was* suffering because of his refusal to practise the virtues of wu-wei. He had never believed in patient inaction himself, however often he had recommended it to others. Patience, yes, but patience designed to bring about a desired result. His life had been a series of planned moves, steps to be taken the moment the time was right, levels to be achieved. But everything he had done, thought, planned, for the past ten years, had been the single aim of abandoning China and the oppressive rule of the Manchus for a country where he would be an honoured rather than a second-class citizen, where there would be peace and he could be prosperous. And therefore happy. But that dream had been built on the vision of Wu Chang and Teng Chiang at his side. What would he do in Singapura, or in Bangkok, with no one but himself?

Teng Wong understood his son's situation, for Teng had never hidden what he intended to do from his father. Teng Wong had never sympathized with Teng Lee's ambitions, because for him there was only one country on earth and that was China, even if it had apparently perpetually to lie beneath the heel of a foreign conqueror. But he knew what an angry void must have been left in his son's life. 'What will you do?' he asked.

'What would you have me do, Father?' Teng replied.

Teng Wong stroked his beard, which was even thinner

than Perak Shah's and was now entirely white. 'No man can truly understand the way of Fate, the meaning of events which affect him,' he said. 'Sometimes those things which seem the most perilous, the most unendurable, turn out to have been for the best.'

'You would have me believe that the death of my wife and son is for the best?' Teng demanded. He reminded himself of Clive Hammond.

'I merely meant that it may be possible, in later years, to understand the meaning of what has happened,' Teng Wong said. 'To spend one's life attempting to solve the riddle of Fate is to waste that life. One can only proceed with one's way, and trust that all things will be revealed to one, before one's own death. But I know your grief. I feel that you cannot stay here, or you will become mad. It is time the *Dragon's Wake* junk was refitted, in any event. I would have you undertake a journey to the north, to Peking, on business for our house. When you return, your ship will again be ready for sea, and you will have recovered your spirits sufficiently to command her. This is what I would have you do, my son.'

Teng understood well enough that his father had already determined the meaning of Fate's blow — he hoped it would end his son's dreams of wandering away from his homeland. Well, Teng did not know if it would do that or not. But he was pleased to leave the deadly confines of Canton and proceed to the north. In so doing he was breaking no promises at the moment, failing no friends; Elizabeth Blaine could not give birth for another five months.

As if his standing with the British or the changing face of Thai politics mattered now! As if anything mattered, save the loss of his wife and son.

But travel was a good way of occupying the mind, and if it was a long and arduous journey, one that he had made but once before in his life, so much the better. It was necessary to go by junk round the coast, in a ship

141

commanded by one of his brothers, to the mouth of the great Yangtse-kiang. That way he avoided having to cross the mountain ranges which lay between Canton and the north. Some forty miles up the river, which was so wide that the junk sailed upon it as upon a sea, he could bid farewell to his brother and join the Grand Canal, cut by the greatest of all emperors, Shih Huang Ti, more than two thousand years before – and there be propelled to Peking in a barge rowed by other employees of his father.

The canal stretched northwards for upwards of a hundred miles, through country which changed from the rice paddies of the south to corn and wheatfields, and even passed between low hills before debouching into the great lake of Weishan Hu. Here the man-made waterway took its path through great beds of reeds before eventually arriving at the Huang Ho, the wide Yellow River, so named from the huge mountains of silk it brought down from the mountains of Tibet and the west. The canal crossed the Yellow River at right angles and then continued north until it reached the Han Ho, just west of the city of Tientsin, the port for Peking. Then it was a matter of ascending this last river by sampan, a slow business as the sweeps were worked against the fast-moving current.

It was a journey which placed his problems in perspective. There was no land as great as China, in size, in contrasts, in population, in industry. China, even under the Manchus, truly was the wonder of the world, he reminded himself. As the journey progressed, he found himself amazed that he had ever wanted to leave it.

And then he came to Peking. The city, he saw immediately, had changed little since his last visit, some ten years before. There was the same huge park of tall pines outside the southern gate, the Yun-ting-men, the same hustle and bustle in the old Chinese city – and the same purple walls surrounding the Tartar City to the

142

north, within which was the Forbidden City where the Ch'ing emperors held their courts. Those purple walls were the limits of the progress of any Chinese who was not a slave or a eunuch, or an especially favoured councillor or soldier – and there were few of those. In there, it was said, were the architectural wonders of the world. But only the Manchus were permitted to admire them. How different from Siam!

Teng had always resented this division of China into Manchus and inferiors. Now he discovered himself more resentful than ever, as he stared at the purple battlements. How attractive Siam suddenly appeared. Of course, he could never hope to do other than crawl across the floor to Rama or his son – or his daughter, for that matter – but he was not barred from their city, their presence; he could still light a candle in the Wat Ching. Even more was this the case in Penang or Batavia. He was treated as an inferior in those places as well, by those colonial officials who considered themselves little lordlings, but there were no parts of the cities from which he was barred, and there were men amongst the rulers, like Stamford Raffles and Pieter Hoorn, who welcomed him as a friend. No Manchu had ever done this.

In such a mood it was easy to denigrate further the Manchu myth. They were the greatest nation, the mightiest warriors on earth, so they thought, and so they had proved, sufficient times. But that was two hundred years ago. Now the famous warriors who had followed Nurhachi and his Eight Banners across Asia to the sack of Peking were dissolute drunkards, inferior men themselves, yet before them the men of Han had to bow their heads in self-abnegation and wear the pigtail as a sign of that humility. That the sons of Teng Wong had received a special dispensation – for services to the Emperor, the document read – merely meant that they paid more taxes than most.

Teng was staring at the wall and brooding upon the

wrong that had been done his people, when there came the clatter of hooves on the cobbles. The people who had been standing by him scattered to left and right, and dropped to their knees. Teng Lee, from lack of practice – for there were few Manchu nobles in the south – turned more slowly, and received a sudden sharp pain on his neck and shoulders as a whip sliced its way into his flesh. He staggered and fell; lying in the gutter, he gazed up at the moustached face above him, the burnished armour, the haughty expression. 'Chinese dog,' the soldier snarled. 'Know your betters.'

He turned his horse and rode after his fellows, who had not stopped. The people raised Teng from the ground. 'You were fortunate,' they said. 'They have cut off a man's head for not kneeling as they ride by. You were very fortunate.'

'To be alive?' Teng asked, almost matching the Manchu soldier's snarl.

He returned to his lodging house in a seething rage as fierce as the searing pain in his neck. If Fate had played him a trick, it had indeed been with a purpose – to demonstrate that ancient laws and philosophies, like that of wu-wei, had merely become instruments by which the strong ruled those they considered weaker than themselves and kept them in subjection. Patient inaction was all very well, but suppose, in the parable he had related to Clive Hammond, the strong man with the sword never did fall asleep? Then the weak man must submit to blows and insults forever. Unless he could devise the means to escape the torment.

One way was to rebel against the strong. But that led to death and destruction for too many, and it did not guarantee success; if the Manchus were degenerates, they were still more skilled and experienced in the use of arms than the Chinese, who had been kept without weapons these two hundred years.

The other way was to escape and seek salvation in

144

other lands, where one's enemies were perhaps not so united. His mind had suddenly hardened and become decided. He would reject the laws of both wu-wei and yin-yang. Lacking a family and any hope of personal happiness, he would seek personal greatness instead, and the power that went with it. These things were not to be had by a man of Han in China. But he would find them elsewhere, because he would pursue them with a ruthless singlemindedness for the rest of his life. And now Fate could no longer harm him, for he had nothing left to lose except his life – and it was welcome to that at any time.

He explained his decision to Teng Wong on his return to Canton, which was well into the summer, and his father listened in sad silence. When Teng was finished, he said, 'I cannot stop you, my son, as you are determined that your destiny lies outside of China. I will conduct an accounting of our affairs, and when you return from this voyage, one seventh of all we possess will be at your disposal. I know you will use it wisely.'

Teng bowed over his father's hand; it was as much as he could have hoped for, even if he understood that Teng Wong's insistence that he *return* from this voyage was in the hope his mood of desperation would have passed by then, and he would have changed his mind. 'As you say, my father, I will use it as my destiny determines.'

It was a feeling of enormous freedom to be once again standing on the poop deck of the *Dragon's Wake*, surging to the south-west, and to the lands he knew so well. Now it was simply a matter of determining the right order in which to conduct his affairs. There could be little question as to his first stop, for whatever he did hinged upon who was now ruling Siam. In fact, he needed to do no more than enter the river and observe the huge white mourning flags which flew from every building, to know that during his long absence King Rama had died. The monarch would have been laid in state upon a golden

145

barge and solemnly rowed up the river to his ancestral home, there to be burned, while the soldiers of his army would have marched along either bank, making sure that everyone knelt in reverence and that all work stopped in honour of the great man.

But Teng Lee was made as welcome as ever, and was taken before Prince Nobhalai, who was now King Rama II, with the reign name Phra Buddha Loes Fa Nobhalai. The young man greeted him as courteously as before, and accepted Teng's condolences with a nod of his head. 'Life must proceed,' he said briefly. He did not, of course, know of Teng's own bereavement, and Teng did not intend to enlighten him. When Rama inquired as to the reason for his delayed return, he explained that there had been family matters to be resolved, which seemed to satisfy the King, who was in any event totally concerned with his own affairs. 'You see me attempting to grasp the oar which steers this ship which is called Siam,' he said sombrely. 'But you will understand,' he continued, 'that I intend to follow the course dictated by my own mind, not the ambitions of my father.'

Teng bowed his head.

'Thus I would seek the way of peace for Siam,' King Rama continued. 'We have nothing to gain by going to war with the Sultanate of Kedah. Of what value to us are limitless acres of impenetrable forest, in which not even rice can be grown? That would be empty glory. Still less have we anything to gain by allying ourselves to a pirate chieftain who seeks to rise above himself. Our principal concerns must be to make ourselves impregnable to attack and increase our trade with other nations. In this regard, I believe that both those objectives can be attained by concluding a treaty of amity, and even of alliance, with the Europeans. I have accepted the Portuguese ambassadors. Now I would do the same with the English. It is a delicate task, as you will understand, Teng Lee. I approach them in no spirit of suppliance. I would have the first overtures come from them. You visit Calcutta regularly, I understand. Would you undertake a mission for me, to sound out the mind of their king, and perhaps obtain a request from him that I should receive his ambassadors, as I have done the Portuguese?' He paused. 'I should esteem highly the man who would accomplish this for me.'

Teng Lee's heart was pounding. Here were his new ambitions falling into his hands at the first opportunity.

'It will be my great honour, your majesty,' he said.

'Then I will give you a private letter, to be used as you see fit. You will not fail me in this, Teng Lee.'

Teng bowed his head. 'Then would I be cutting my own throat, your majesty,' he conceded.

'Then would you arouse my anger,' Rama agreed. 'Now tell me, to whom should this letter be addressed?'

'To the Governor-General of India, your majesty. Lord Minto.'

'A quaint title,' Rama observed. 'But should I not address myself to the king of these people?'

'Their king is many thousands of miles away, your majesty,' Teng explained. 'It would take months, perhaps even years, for me to reach him. This Lord Minto acts for the King of England in India and the East, as the English call this region. He is his appointed deputy, and has plenipotentiary powers.'

'And you know this man?'

Teng hesitated but a moment; there could be no doubt as to the answer Rama required. 'I carry goods for him,' he said. 'As I do every time I visit Calcutta. We take tea together.'

'That is good. But how should I address such a man. Is he not my inferior?'

'Undoubtedly, your majesty. May I suggest that you in fact address the letter to the King of England, but grant me the power to show it to Lord Minto, after I have discovered his intentions, and ask him to remit it to England and to act upon it.'

Rama nodded. 'It seems I must trust you in this most important matter, Teng Lee. I do so because you were recommended to me by my father. Succeed in this, and you shall have whatever reward you desire. Fail me, and my wrath will follow you to the ends of the earth. Now I will have the letter prepared. It will be ready tomorrow, and I wish you to sail immediately.'

'Tomorrow?' Teng was dismayed; he had only been in Bangkok twenty-four hours.

'This is an urgent matter. Besides' – Rama gave one of his brief smiles – 'you are not the most popular person at my court at this moment. Do you not know that you have angered my sister, the Princess Jalina?'

'Angered her, your majesty?'

'I am told you were to recite some stories to her, when last you were here . . .'

Teng clapped his hand to his forehead in dismay. 'How can I apologize, your majesty?'

'It would be useless. One cannot apologize to a woman. The princess thinks you should be seized and bastinadoed.' This time his smile lingered longer as he watched the expression on Teng's face. 'But if you go to Calcutta and return here with satisfactory news, then I will persuade my sister to forgive you.'

Teng bowed his head. 'It shall be as you wish, your majesty.'

Neither Li Yuan nor any of the crew of the *Dragon's Wake* were pleased to be on their way again so soon, not even when Teng told them it was important business. Siam remained now his only true chance of achieving any of his aims, for poor Perak Shah's hopes had definitely come tumbling down. Indeed, Teng would have preferred not to return to Singapura ever again. But he had no option; he had given Rama the impression that he had

148

ready access to Lord Minto, as he had to the King himself. He had never seen Lord Minto, much less met him, and never been treated as other than a minor tradesman in Calcutta. To carry out successfully the mission with which he had been entrusted it would be necessary to obtain an introduction to the Governor-General. And to obtain *that*, he would need to make himself very popular in Penang, and there was only one way it could be accomplished.

So it would be necessary to pay one last visit to Singapura, to deceive Perak Shah for one last time before casting him adrift to find his own way through the reefs that surround those who aspire to greatness. But before then . . . he was in the business of achieving greatness himself, no matter what had to be done to reach that goal. He could afford no enemies who might be in a position to harm him. The Princess Jalina was the King's favourite sister. Even if he were as successful as Rama hoped on this mission, and there was no certainty of that, she might yet be poisoning her brother's ear against him.

He left his men to prepare the junk for sea, and then took himself back across the bridge and into the Wat Po. He knew the men to look for, and soon found one in the crowded reception chamber of the palace.

The secretary was dumbfounded. 'You wish to be introduced to the apartment of the Princess Jalina? Do you not know that she waits for you with powerful anger?'

'I have heard this,' Teng said. 'And I would submit myself to her rage.'

'You are a fool, Teng Lee,' the secretary said. 'She will have the skin from your body.'

'Then you will be rewarded,' Teng pointed out.

The man hesitated, then took him by the side corridors to the princess's suite. Here there were muttered words with other secretaries, and then one of them entered the apartment, leaving Teng outside. He was intensely

149

nervous. It was possible that the princess might be as angry as she pretended – in which case he might within a few minutes find himself spreadeagled on the floor while the hundred strokes were administered. The thought made his skin crawl.

But on the other hand, she might be impressed by his courage and honesty, and he would have secured a most valuable friend.

The secretary returned with two guards. Without a word they seized Teng Lee by the arms and dragged him into the room, throwing him full length upon the floor. He only just got his hands up in time to stop his face hitting the marble, while his hat flew off and rolled into a corner. He let it go, remaining crouching, aware of rather than seeing the people in the room, the maids-in-waiting and the secretaries, all regarding him with the utmost severity.

The princess was seated on her divan. 'Teng Lee,' he said. 'You have the effrontery to wish an audience with me? You have gravely displeased me. Had my brother not required you for affairs of state, I should have had you bastinadoed until not an inch of skin was left on your feet. Are you so insolent that you fail to keep an appointment with the daughter of Rama?'

Teng had already decided on his course of action. There were times when a man must use every weapon he possessed, however abhorrent it was for him to reveal his grief to a stranger. 'I had received news of the gravest importance, my lady princess,' he said humbly.

'What news?'

'I was brought word that my wife and son were dying,' he said, revising the truth to a certain degree.

'You are married?' the princess inquired.

'I was married, my lady princess. By the time I returned to Canton, I was no longer.'

'Your wife has died?'

'And my son, my lady princess. I was so cast down with

grief I lost all sense of time. It has taken me six months to regain my composure. For this I most humbly beg your forgiveness. Command me, and I am yours.'

There was a long silence, broken only by the rustle of the princess's skirt and those of her attendants; a faint breeze was coming off the river and sweeping through the apartment. Teng remained with bowed head, wishing he could know just what expressions were crossing his tormentor's face. But at last she said, her voice softer than before, 'My heart bleeds for you, Teng Lee. But you have regained your composure. I am glad of this. And you have revealed yourself to be a man of courage and sensibility, in coming here to make your peace with me, knowing full well the extent of my anger. I shall indeed command you, when the time is right. But now my brother sends you far away on affairs of state.'

Teng began to regain his confidence; he had dared, and won. 'No further than is my customary route, my lady princess. But on affairs of state, yes, indeed.'

The princess sighed. 'To travel to faraway lands,' she said. 'That is what I dream of doing, Teng Lee. And instead I must wait to hear of them from your lips. Truly Fate is uneven in her distribution of favours.'

Teng wasn't sure what reply to make to that. The idea that a princess would wish to change places with a humble merchant was absurd.

'So, go to your faraway places,' she commanded. 'And return safely. Then come to me and tell me some more of your stories, that I may be happy again.'

'I shall make all haste,' Teng agreed, and crawled from her presence.

Indeed it was a case for all haste. That night the junk slipped down the Chao Phraya, and a week later it was threading its way through the Dragon's Teeth to bring up in Singapura Harbour. Teng arranged his features into an expression of confident happiness and stepped ashore.

151

'Teng Lee!' Perak Shah was on the dock, as always, to greet him. 'You have been gone too long.'

'Family affairs,' Teng said tersely. 'Tell me of the white woman and her child.'

Perak Shah grinned. 'She has delivered me a fine son. And he has blue eyes and yellow hair, as I expected. He will be a man amongst men.'

'The mother?'

'Is well.'

Teng gave a faint sigh of relief.

'And pleased with the child,' Perak Shah went on. 'This is a time of great happiness for me.'

And for me also, Teng thought, as they walked towards the palace, while behind them the Malays swarmed into their boats to assist the Chinese crew in unloading the junk. 'You have heard that King Rama is dead?' Teng asked.

Perak Shah nodded. 'This is what I mean. It is something we must discuss. I am happy because it means I no longer have to send Lizbeth to Siam. But I recognize that there may be a delay in the realization of our plans. Much depends on whether the new king intends to follow in the footsteps of his father.' He glanced at Bodaw Shan, as if to suggest that *his* son would hardly carry out his policies once he was dead. 'But you have just come from Bangkok.'

Teng reminded himself that now was not the moment for weakness. He was gambling for higher stakes than ever before, and friendship could not be allowed to interfere with his plan. 'Where I spoke with the new king,' he said. 'Rama II is like Rama I in all ways. He wishes to emulate his father in all ways.' He gazed at Perak Shah. 'He wishes to *succeed* his father in all things.'

Perak Shah was beginning to frown. 'A boy?'

'Who is anxious to become a man, Perak Shah.'

Perak Shah tugged his beard. 'I had not expected this.'

'Neither had I,' Teng confessed. 'But there it is. I spoke

with Rama I before he died, and in the presence of his son, I promised him the girl with yellow hair. I have now, as you say, just come from Bangkok, and Rama II eagerly awaits her.'

'By Allah,' Perak Shah growled. 'An insolent puppy.'

Teng wondered if this poor man would ever realize the wealth and power of the King of Siam, would ever understand just how absurd it was even to imagine that such a man would be the least concerned over a woman, no matter how beautiful, or would even have the time to think of her. 'He commands the finest army in South-East Asia,' he reminded Perak Shah. 'And also dreams of emulating his father's military glory. With his support, Perak Shah, there is no limit to what you may achieve.'

'By Allah,' Perak Shah said again. 'She will not be pleased.'

Elizabeth Blaine had apparently learned to speak Malay during her pregnancy. She sat on the floor of the inner chamber, with five of the other concubines kneeling about her, and, in the Malay fashion, gave her babe the breast while she looked at the men above the cord of her yashmak. 'Leave Singapura?' she asked. 'I do not understand.'

'Affairs of state,' Perak Shah explained. 'You are to go to the harem of the great king, Rama of Siam.'

Teng held his breath. He would have phrased the matter somewhat differently, and even if it was untrue, there was nothing he could say to this woman until she was safely on board his junk.

Elizabeth Blaine stared at Perak Shah, then looked at Teng. 'Your doing,' she almost spat.

'I am but the messenger of Fate,' he protested. 'But I can promise you that nothing but happiness lies in front of you.'

She looked at Perak Shah. 'You cannot allow this, Perak Shah,' she begged. The yashmak inflated as she breathed, and then settled against her face again. 'You cannot. I am your woman. Your favourite woman. I have borne your child.' She held the babe up. 'Your favourite child. I will bear you others. You cannot send me to another man, like . . . like a letter.'

Perak Shah sighed. 'It is an affair of state,' he repeated. 'Rama desires you, and has named you as the price of an alliance which it is essential to my country to achieve. I am sorry, but there is nothing more to be said.'

Teng was amazed. He had never thought to hear Perak Shah talk so reasonably to anyone, save himself, certainly not to a woman. The old pirate must truly be fond of this girl, he thought. And he was more than ever aware of the despicable role he was playing in deceiving both these people. He almost changed his mind; surely there was another way to gain a letter of introduction to Lord Minto. 'Perhaps,' he said, 'if I were to return to Rama and explain the situation . . .' He could hardly believe that it was himself speaking. Was he going to throw away everything out of pity for a mother? Then he was truly not worthy of that greatness he sought.

But he knew that he would do it, just to see her smile. He spent too much time thinking about wives and mothers and sons.

'Rama would be angry,' Perak Shah announced. 'And I would have broken my word. I am a man of my word; I gave his father that word.' He snapped his fingers, and his guards stepped forward. Teng surmised they must have been instructed beforehand, for without hesitation two seized Elizabeth's arms and pulled her to her feet, while a third plucked the babe away from her before she could attempt to resist them, and handed it to one of the other women.

Elizabeth swung her head left and right, then gazed at the woman beseechingly; the woman stepped back into the shadows. Elizabeth stared at Perak Shah. 'You cannot,' she said. 'You cannot take my child.'

154

'Ali is my son,' Perak Shah told her.

'No,' she said. 'No . . .' Then she changed her mind about what she would say. 'He is mine, equally.'

'Then wait to hear word of him, when he has grown to manhood and Singapura has grown to greatness. One day he may rule this place. I will take good care of him, I promise you. You had best get her on board, Teng Lee.'

Teng stood up.

'Your doing,' Elizabeth spat again. 'I curse you. I curse you. Perak Shah,' she screamed, 'at least let me take my son.'

'I will take care of him,' he promised again. 'Amina will treat him as her own. He will be the brother of Bodaw Shan.'

She still stared at him, her eyes wide, tears dribbling down her cheeks. 'I had thought you honoured me above all other women,' she whispered.

Perak Shah sighed. 'Indeed I do, my Lizbeth. But I must do what is best for my country.'

'Your *country*,' she said. 'I curse you too. I curse you.'

'Take her to your ship,' Perak Shah said again. 'For the sake of the Prophet, take her from my presence.'

Teng had Elizabeth's wrists bound together with a silken cord, and then in turn bound to the thwart on which she was made to sit; he could afford to take no chances on her throwing herself over the side. He expected her to scream and shout, but she was silent; she just stared at the shore with those huge tears streaming down her face and soaking her yashmak. The woman he had 'rescued', he thought sadly. Truly the world has turned upside down.

'He does honour you,' he said gently.

Her head moved, to indicate that she had heard him. But she would neither look at him nor reply.

'I had not supposed Perak Shah capable of such an emotion,' Teng mused. 'Thus it has been a hard decision for him to take. But you . . . he ravaged you from your friends and your husband. And you can wish to stay with him?'

He heard her breathe as her nostrils dilated. 'He honoured me above all other women,' she said. 'And he was the father of my son.'

'There will be other sons.'

'From this . . . this king to whom I am being sent?' She gave a little shudder.

'There will be other sons,' Teng repeated. He could say no more until she was safely out of Singapura. So he had her taken on to the poop deck, and there secured to the mizen mast, while he conned his vessel through the reef. Then he knelt beside her and untied the yashmak. She was even more beautiful then he recalled and, wearing only a sarong and with her hair loose and drifting past her shoulders like a shawl of finespun gold, more desirable as well. He summoned his steward and offered her coconut water to drink and food to eat, as he had done with Clive, but she would not touch it. 'Why do you torture me?' she asked. 'My hands must be untied some time. I will immediately kill myself. It would save us all considerable trouble were you to allow me to do so now.'

Teng signalled for his chair to be brought and sat beside her. 'I regret having to say this, but I was forced to practise a deceit on Perak Shah,' he explained. 'It was the only way I could be certain of persuading him to let you go, to offer him something even more valuable in exchange.'

For a moment his words did not seem to register, then a faint frown appeared between her eyes. But he also noticed a certain hardening about her mouth, and realized that she thought he meant to take her for himself.

He did not immediately correct her misapprehension. 'It was the only way to secure your release,' he repeated. 'However, if you will look at the sun, you will perceive that far from altering course to the east to return to Bangkok, we are still sailing south and will soon bear round to the west and then the north. We are bound for Penang.'

She stared at him, her frown deepening. 'Penang?'

'I am to return you to your husband,' he said.

Her jaw sagged for a moment, then she tugged ineffectively against her bonds. 'You cannot.'

It was Teng's turn to frown. 'You do not wish to return to your husband? To the society of those who loved you and eagerly hope to see you again?'

'Oh, my *God*!' she gasped.

Teng stroked his moustache. He could not understand how, after forty years of proceeding smoothly from point to point, every move based on his judgement of people and situations, his life had suddenly become, over these last twelve months, so bedevilled with unsuspected twists, unforeseen pitfalls. 'Can you mean you found life with Perak Shah more comfortable than with your husband? A man of your own race and religion?'

'I do not *know* my husband,' she said. 'I only know that he will never forgive me, and his friends will never forgive me, my own family will never forgive me, for having spent a year in a harem. Can you not understand that? To them I will be worse than if I had contracted leprosy. Mr Teng, in the name of God, if there is no affair of state involved, and if you have a spark of pity in your heart, take me back to Perak Shah.'

'That will not be possible,' Teng pointed out. 'If Perak Shah discovered that I had attempted to deceive him, he would undoubtedly feed me to that pet crocodile of his.' Only a few months ago he had not cared whether he lived or died. But now success was literally within his grasp.

'Then just set me ashore. I can find my way through the forest.'

Teng thought quickly. 'Perhaps you do not realize Clive Hammond is also in Penang, waiting for you?'

'Waiting for me? Oh, my God,' she repeated. 'It is you who do not realize the truth of the matter, Mr Teng. Do

157

you really suppose my son is Perak Shah's? He has blue eyes and yellow hair.'

'The colouring of his mother,' Teng remarked. But again he was frowning.

'Do you not suppose he would have had at least one Malay characteristic?' she asked.

Teng stroked his moustache. 'You think Clive Hammond is the father?'

'I am sure of it.'

'I see that your life has contained great sadness,' Teng said. But he was reluctant to recommend to her the paths of yin-yang and wu-wei, as he had so totally rejected them himself. Except that yin-yang might provide some comfort for her. 'It therefore follows,' he said, 'that there will be one day a period of great happiness in your life. You must believe this, Mrs Blaine, because it is true. It is the law of the universe. But I do not think you should tell Mr Hammond that the child was his.' Heaven forbid, he thought, unless it really became desirable to destroy Perak Shah once and for all, and that was not something he was prepared to contemplate at the moment; he had already betrayed his friend too greatly.

But it was obviously necessary to make another change of plan. He had not intended to stop in Batavia until his homeward voyage from Penang and thence Calcutta, when he would know whether his scheme was going to be achieved. Now he decided to go there on leaving Singapura, as if on a normal voyage. To take Elizabeth Blaine, who was part of that plan, to Penang before she had properly reconciled herself to her new situation could be disastrous. So he continued to steer to the south-west, and after five days dropped anchor off Batavia.

Elizabeth had somewhat recovered during the voyage, and had been persuaded to eat and drink. He was pleased with her progress; a week in Batavia would complete her

158

rehabilitation, he felt. 'I have friends here,' he told her, as they were rowed between the long twin breakwaters which guarded the inner harbour. 'They will be pleased to meet you.'

He had outfitted her in Chinese robes, which he had brought from Canton especially for the purpose. The Dutch would have been scandalized to see a bare-breasted blonde beauty landing in their community. He had also made her put up her hair beneath a straw hat, as was reasonable in view of the heat and the glare – he did not wish any publicity about her arrival. With her sun-browned skin she could have been anyone, even a Malay or a Chinese, accompanying her master ashore.

Once landed, he took her to the house of Pieter Hoorn, and there allowed her to remove her hat.

Hoorn gazed at her for a moment, and then realized who she had to be. 'By God,' he remarked in Flemish. 'But you have done it, Teng. My congratulations.'

'You will understand that she is in a delicate frame of mind,' Teng replied in the same language.

'Of course.' Hoorn switched to English, and held Elizabeth's hands. 'My dear Mrs Blaine, I cannot tell you how happy I am to see you.'

Elizabeth's gaze was frosty. 'You know of me?'

'I know that Teng Lee has performed a great feat in securing your release from captivity,' Hoorn said tact-fully, then taking her arm, he said encouragingly, 'I would like you to meet my wife and daughters, who are as delighted as I am at your rescue.'

Elizabeth would have hung back, but Hoorn led her into the parlour, where the family was gathered. She accepted the introductions with reluctant gravity, but had to smile when Amalia delivered another of her party pieces: 'I think you are very beautiful,' the Dutch girl said in careful English. Teng gathered that she had been learning the language very hard since Clive Hammond's departure.

But the sight of Elizabeth Blaine smiling was a great relief to him. 'You will stay with the Hoorns,' he told her, 'while I complete my business here. They will make you happy again.'

He had no doubt they would.

Pieter Hoorn thought he had never in his life seen so charming a picture as the two young women walking in his garden, as he looked down on them from his study window on the second floor of his house. They presented a considerable contrast, the English girl tall and slender, awkwardly graceful in her borrowed garments, which had been hastily run up by Juliana Hoorn and her children, her brilliant yellow hair so entrancingly set off by her sun-browned complexion; she was the first European woman he had ever seen whose skin had been exposed to the sun, except fleetingly by accident, and for all the layer of freckles which now covered her face and arms he did not find it unattractive.

Amalia Hoorn, by contrast, was short and inclined to plumpness. Her hair was as black as his had once been, and her complexion was a carefully preserved milky white.

Moreover, the English girl, so fortuitously dropped into the middle of his garden, he decided, could be the answer to his greatest problem.

For Pieter Hoorn had been forced to do a great deal of hard thinking in the year since Clive Hammond had been his guest. It had been a year of increasing disaster, so far as he was concerned. It was not merely that the scarcity of ships getting to and from Holland as the British blockade tightened had meant a considerable diminution of trade in and out of Batavia. If his profits had been halved over the past six years since the European war had started again, there were ways of overcoming even the blockade, at least locally; and thanks to men like Teng Lee he was building quite a trade with China and Siam. Teng even on

160

occasion smuggled goods into Penang and Calcutta for him, simply by not letting anyone know where they had originated. The British had no knowledge of China, no idea whether or not sugar, for instance, could be grown there. In any event, his wealth had been sufficient to allow him to ride even a moderate-sized storm, on the assumption that the storm would end, because storms always did end.

Save for this one, it seemed. It was now apparent that Bonaparte was going to rule France, and Europe, for the foreseeable future. Following France's decisive victory at Wagram, in the summer, Austria had not only surrendered unconditionally, but had agreed that Bonaparte was to divorce the Empress Josephine and marry the Archduchess Marie-Louise. The Habsburgs were giving one of their own daughters to the Corsican corporal. It was undoubtedly the greatest social revolution since Roman times, and it conferred upon Bonaparte, and Bonapartism, the ultimate accolade. He was now legitimate, and his rule had acquired that divinity which kings were wont to believe they possessed.

Even the British had appeared to accept the situation. They at least would not make peace with the conqueror, but they had apparently abandoned any idea of contesting with him for the recovery of Europe, save on the very fringes of the continent, and there, in Spain and Portugal, their armies seemed to be running away whenever a French marshal came in sight. But they were at least still in opposition, and they still commanded the seas, a situation which was daily becoming more important. For now the tentacles of Bonapartism were reaching even to Java.

For the first few years of the Corsican's rule, and during the Consulate, the Spice Islands were too remote to occupy much of his mind. They were a source of riches, and as long as some of that wealth could filter back into Holland, and thence into France, he was content.

In fact, in the last few years, after the Republic of Batavia set up by the Jacobins had become the Kingdom of Holland, ruled by the Emperor's brother Louis Bonaparte, things had even improved. But now that too was changing again, for the worse. New men had come from Holland, men who believed in Bonapartism, to take over the rule of the colony. These men said that Napoleon was disappointed in his brother for failing to squeeze his Dutch subjects hard enough in their contributions to an empire ever short of money. Soon, it was being said, Louis Bonaparte would be sent packing, and Holland would cease to exist, being incorporated into France as a mere province.

The Bonapartists had taken control. Captain van Essenling had been sent home; General Groepner was now in overall command of Dutch forces in the Java Sea, and if he was under orders to continue the 'pacification' of the south of the island, he and the new governor and their aides were also under orders to screw every guilder they could out of the colonists. Taxes had risen, and the yoke of Dutch rule had descended more heavily on those of the Javanese whom it could reach. Pieter Hoorn had little sympathy for the Javanese, but he was very concerned about his own position; and not only because of falling returns and the collapse of land prices. He knew that too harsh a rule might well provoke a native uprising here in the north, and that would spell disaster for the colony. That would matter little to Bonaparte, no doubt; if Java could not produce the returns *he* wanted, then let it revert to the Javanese.

The situation caused concern throughout the colony, but no one was prepared to do anything about it. Most of the colonists were third and fourth generation born in Batavia, thought of Java as their homeland more than Holland and bitterly resented being plundered by upstart republican lackeys with no interest in the island's, or their, future. But they were also fanatically Dutch, and because of their lives in the East Indies, and the lives of their fathers and grandfathers, however much they spoke against Bonapartism, they still regarded the English as their true enemies, since the English had been their only serious rivals for power throughout most of the last hundred years. Perhaps there was even some guilt mixed into their Anglophobia, Hoorn thought; it had been the Dutch who had perpetrated the Massacre of Amboyna, two centuries before, which had turned a trade rivalry into a vicious war of reprisals. That antagonism had just been dwindling, under the influence of the long alliance shared by Holland and Britain in Europe throughout the eighteenth century, when this new war had broken out. And while even down to a year ago the colonists had not truly wanted to see war extending to the Far East, under their new rulers things were very different; he doubted that the survivors of the *Henry Oliver* would be so welcome now. Fortunately, no one outside his own family had any idea who Elizabeth Blaine was, or even that she was in Batavia at all; Teng's junk was a familiar and welcome sight.

But the position was pregnant with catastrophe. Pieter Hoorn reasoned that historical antagonisms were nothing more than that; it was the future which counted. And where he had always hoped for a defeat of Bonapartism and a restoration of the ancient freedom and prosperity of Holland, he had now to face the fact that if that was not going to happen in his lifetime, and Holland and its overseas possessions were simply going to be bled white to support Bonaparte's armies, then it would be far better for Java, and Sumatra, and the whole of the East Indies, to fly the Union Jack. The British at least believed in free trade; their entire wealth was built upon the premise that if their people and their subjects made money, then the Government and the nation must also grow rich.

The question which occupied his mind was how to

bring about such a change for the better. He had no idea how many of his compatriots felt as he did. He suspected there were quite a few, but in an atmosphere in which denunciations for treason were on everyone's lips – it was a way of life to the new administration – he felt the only safe course was to play a lone hand. If he could.

He was aware, because Teng Lee had told him, that there were people in Penang, especially a man called Raffles, who dreamed of expanding British power into the Java Sea. But Raffles was apparently unable to persuade his superiors that such a move was feasible. According to Teng, the British feared becoming embroiled in an endless guerrilla war, with every man's hand, Dutch and Javanese, turned against them; Hoorn suspected Teng had done little to suggest that it would be a simple task, because he did not want a war interfering with his prosperous trade routes.

But if the British *could* be persuaded that there would be support, or, at least, little opposition, for a move into Java ... However uncertain Hoorn was about his compatriots' true feelings, he had no doubt at all that they would not fight for General Groepner and his Bonapartist hangers-on, and that they would accept a British *fait accompli* once they realized it would mean a restoration of their old trading prosperity.

The difficulty lay in communicating with Raffles. He was well aware that his own position, already dangerous, had become more so with the removal of Captain van Essenling and his replacement with more enthusiastically Jacobin officials. He had almost been tempted to use Teng ... but that would mean trusting his prosperity and indeed his life to a man who, however good a friend, was of an alien race. He also had no doubt that Teng's only real interest in this world was Teng himself.

But Teng had always been the sole means of communicating with the British colonies; he was the only regular trader between Batavia and Penang, much less Calcutta.

There had simply been no other way of contacting this man Raffles . . . until now one had suddenly dropped into his lap.

If he dared use her. But she was due to leave Batavia tomorrow, and so far as he could see there was no possibility of her ever returning, or ever meeting any Dutchman again. And if he dared not use her, disaster stared him in the face.

He waited until the two girls had finished their perambulation, and then went downstairs to join them in the parlour. 'Elizabeth,' he said in English. 'I wonder if you and I could have a private conversation about a most important and, indeed, secret matter?'

CHAPTER SEVEN

The Outcast

Teng Lee stood at Elizabeth Blaine's side as the *Dragon's Wake* rounded the north end of Penang Island and altered course into the narrows by the mainland. 'It is small,' he agreed, in reply to her observation.

He was well content with the progress he had made. As he had surmized, the visit to the Hoorns had made a world of difference. The woman had been restored to her own way of life, but in the company of the most friendly family in the world. So far as he knew, no allusion had been made to her year in Singapura, while every day saw a further relaxation of her tension.

For himself, he did not see how he could have done better. He had guaranteed Sir Charles Wilmot that he would return the woman, and he was about to do so. Physically she was unharmed, so far as he could tell, and indeed she was more beautiful than he remembered her from their brief previous acquaintance. Mentally she was at least sane, and no one would expect her to be quite normal after such an ordeal. A certain reward, such as a letter of introduction to Lord Minto, should not be beyond the limits of Sir Charles' gratitude.

As for the possibility of action being taken against Perak Shah, now that the woman was safe this no longer concerned him. He was sorry for his old friend, but he had warned him in the most positive terms that he was making a grave mistake in attacking the *Henry Oliver*; and Singapura no longer held any attraction for him . . .

or for anyone else, he imagined. So he smiled as he stood by Elizabeth's shoulder, and together they looked at Georgetown. 'Soon,' he promised her, 'you will be in the arms of your loved one.'

The boat was put down, and Teng Lee went ashore. He deemed it best for her to remain on board until he had seen Blaine, and she had not argued. Neither of them wished her return to be a matter of publicity until she was safely reunited with her husband – which both viewed as the crux of the whole event, if from widely differing points of view.

So she stood by the rail, gazing across the sparkling blue water at the hills and the houses and the docks. She should have landed here more than a year ago. Now she had no very clear idea of her feelings. She was, in fact, trying to keep her emotions in abeyance at this moment. From terror and resentment a year ago had come acceptance, and then, as she had slowly risen to be the most important of Perak Shah's wives, even contentment. If it was difficult to accept that a man who could order the murder of dozens of people simply because he had no use for them could also be a good husband and a doting father, that was none the less a fact of life. Thus her dream of being returned to her own people had dwindled very rapidly into a nightmare, for as she had told Teng, they would never forgive, or even forget, that she had survived a year in a savage's bed. That was against all the rules of English womanhood, English honour.

And to have given birth to a child . . . In fact, she did not know that the boy, who had been named Bodaw Ali, *was* Clive's son. She desperately wanted him to be; less for the memory of Clive, than to feel that he was entirely hers. She reasoned that he could very well be, as he had been born nine months almost to the day after her night in the lifeboat, so far as she could reckon. On the other hand, the baby could have been a week premature – it

167

had been no longer than that between Clive and Perak Shah. Certainly some time in that week she had been impregnated. The boy was entirely European in appearance, but that was not necessarily conclusive, despite her arguments to Teng. To abandon him had been an unbearable wrench at the time, but she now realized that his presence might well have made her acceptance by her own people out of the question. And she did not consider she had lost him forever. She knew that Perak Shah would take every care of his yellow-haired, blue-eyed son, and Penang was not all that far from Singapura. If she could indeed re-enter English society and play her part as the wife of the Governor's ADC, in time she hoped she might even persuade Edward to mount an expedition to regain Ali.

She was intensely grateful for that week in Batavia, in the down-to-earth company of the Hoorns and their daughters, for the time to think and to understand her best course. Certainly, having survived Perak Shah it would be stupid to collapse now. And the week had had such a strange ending. She had not known what to expect when she was taken into Pieter Hoorn's study. He was such a charming host, and he was a happily married man . . . but she was aware that he had been watching her all the time, and she had become conditioned to expect only desire in men. Yet, as with Teng, she had been proved wrong. He merely gave her a letter, which he said was a matter of life and death, and must be shown to no one save the person to whom it was addressed. She must not even tell anyone she had it, he insisted, not even Teng. Only this Mr Stamford Raffles was to know. The letter made her feel suddenly important, while at the same time she understood nothing of what it might mean, save that Mr Hoorn and Mr Raffles must have opened a correspondence, which had to be clandestine because England and Holland were officially at war. But she intended to deliver the letter, because Mr Raffles, who was appa-

168

rently the Governor's secretary, would also be in a position to help her regain her son.

But first of all she had to meet Edward again. Thus she stood at the rail and fretted, wondering what was taking Teng so long. She was uncomfortable with more than apprehension; the Hoorns had insisted upon fitting her out with some 'proper' clothing, and now she was wearing tight boots and long stockings, secured with garters, drawers and petticoats, and a high-necked blouse, as well as her skirt. She had not worn any of these articles for a year, and she felt unnaturally restricted, while her straw hat seemed to enclose her head in a tight band.

But now at last a boat was returning from the shore. She strained her eyes; Teng had left her his telescope, but she did not want to appear over-anxious. Suppose it contained Clive Hammond? But that was unthinkable. Clive, indeed, remained a cloud on the horizon. A cloud she would very much like to reassure as to her safety, but not one with whom she could ever hope to have relations again.

The boat came in to the side of the junk, and she stepped back from the rail. She had seen Teng Lee, and that was enough. There were two other white men with him, neither of whom she recognized beneath their hats. But one wore a blue uniform, and was fidgeting. He was tall and thin. She twined her fingers together, fidgeting herself, as they came through the gangway, stopped and looked at her. Teng stood to one side, almost apologetically. Then Blaine stepped forward, taking off his bicorne as he did so. 'Elizabeth?' he asked, incredulously.

'Edward?' There seemed nothing else to say.

'But . . . my God . . .' He came closer. 'What have they done to you?'

'Done to me?' Then she realized he was looking at her complexion. 'I'm sorry about the sunburn,' she explained.

'My God,' he said again.

She waited. He was within two feet of her. Presumably he should now sweep her into his arms and kiss her, and she should throw her own arms round his neck. But he didn't move.

'Welcome home, Mrs Blaine,' said the other man, who was somewhat shorter than her husband, although just as thin, and wearing a black suit with a white stock.

'This is Mr Stamford Raffles,' Teng explained. 'Secretary to the Governor of Penang.'

Elizabeth gazed at him: the recipient of her letter. But, as it was confidential, she didn't know if now was the moment. 'I am happy to be home, Mr Raffles,' she said.

'My God,' Blaine said again. 'Elizabeth . . .' He made a somewhat convulsive movement with his arm, and she extended her own hand for him to clutch. 'Elizabeth,' he said a third time as he grasped her fingers. She recalled that he had always been a somewhat inarticulate man, which was probably why he had made so little impression on her three years before.

'I think we should take Mrs Blaine ashore,' Raffles decided. 'We have brought something for you to wear.' He hesitated, holding up a large straw hat, very like the one the Hoorns had given her, but which possessed, drooping from the brim, an almost impenetrable veil. 'My wife uses it for her beekeeping,' he explained, with a sudden smile. 'I am sure you do not want people pestering you until you have had a chance to settle in.'

She liked him. How nice it would be, she thought, were he meeting her instead of Edward. 'Thank you,' she said.

'Well . . . yes, we'd better go ashore,' Blaine said, as if he wasn't at all sure that was the right thing to do.

She shook hands with Teng. 'I must thank you for my deliverance, Mr Teng,' she said.

His eyes were as solemn as hers, but she knew he was smiling behind the mask. 'It was my great pleasure, Mrs Blaine.'

170

'I say, yes, dash it all,' Blaine exclaimed. 'Forgetful of me. I . . . we, never thought you could manage it, Teng Lee. We owe you a great deal.'

Teng bowed.

'Come to see me soon as you can,' Raffles said quietly.

Elizabeth changed her hat and was rowed ashore, sitting on the transom beside her husband. He had by now released her hand, and seemed to be endeavouring not to look at her. Raffles, on the other hand, looked at her all the time, and whenever she looked back, gave her a bright, encouraging smile. He obviously felt she needed it.

They came in to the dock, where there were half a dozen men lounging. One stepped forward with a question, and Blaine brushed him aside. The man gazed at Elizabeth, then at the junk, then turned and ran off up the street.

'That's torn it,' Raffles said. 'That'll be all over the colony by this evening, and in tomorrow's *Gazette*, to be sure.'

'Let's get up the hill,' Blaine said.

Elizabeth was being hurried up the gentle slope to Government House, she realized with a sinking heart. There on the verandah were a stout, quite pleasant-looking couple waiting for her, faces carefully arranged in smiles of welcome.

'My dear!' Lady Wilmot opened her arms, and Elizabeth, pausing to take off the bee-keeper's hat, went forward to be embraced. 'My dear, dear girl. But . . . what have they done to you?'

'They take no care of their complexions, my lady,' Elizabeth explained, stifling an urgent desire to scream.

'You poor, dear child,' Lady Wilmot said.

Sir Charles came forward hesitantly. Elizabeth didn't know whether she was going to be embraced or not, but he contented himself with kissing her hand. 'My dear

171

girl,' he echoed his wife, and looked over Elizabeth's shoulder. 'Raffles, where is Teng Lee?'

'Putting his ship to rights, your excellency,' Raffles replied. 'He'll be ashore this evening.'

'Why don't you take Mrs Blaine to the house, Major,' Lady Wilmot suggested. 'And this evening you will bring her to supper.'

'Yes,' Blaine agreed. 'Yes, of course, m'lady. And thank you. Elizabeth?'

Elizabeth looked at them all, despairingly. But not even Raffles could help her at this moment. 'That would be very nice, my lady,' she said.

To reach Blaine's house it was only a matter of walking across a lawn, for the smaller bungalow was in the Government House grounds. 'The Raffles live over there,' Blaine said, conversationally. 'You'll like Flora Raffles . . . well, you may like her. Raffles himself, well, he's rather an odd fellow.'

'I have a letter for him,' Elizabeth ventured, also conversationally. She knew she had promised Hoorn not to mention the letter to a soul save Raffles himself, but this man was her husband, with whom it was vital to become at least mentally intimate as quickly as possible.

Blaine paused, frowning. 'For Raffles?'

'We stopped in Batavia on our way here, and I spent some time with some friends of Teng Lee's, the Hoorns. Mijnheer Hoorn is apparently also a friend of Mr Raffles, and he gave me a letter to bring to him.'

'Good heavens,' Blaine remarked. 'How very odd. Well, you'd better give it to me.'

'Mr Hoorn insisted I deliver it to Mr Raffles personally,' she said.

Elizabeth realized she had made a mistake. But was the mistake only in mentioning the letter? Yet she was determined neither to be browbeaten nor to break her promise. 'Personally,' she repeated.

172

Blaine gazed at her for a moment, then resumed walking. 'I suppose,' he remarked, 'that you found it necessary to look out for yourself ... amongst the Malays.'

'Isn't it necessary to look out for oneself, no matter who one is amongst?' she countered. And realized that things were going from bad to worse.

'Oh, quite,' he agreed, and showed her up the steps to the verandah, where two Malay houseboys were waiting, and bowing. 'This your missee,' he explained. 'Comee ship from far awayee. You doee what she tellee, eh?'

The boys bowed their heads.

'Do you not speak Malay?' Elizabeth asked.

'Malay? Good lord, no. Why should I?'

'You would be better understood. I am very glad to be here,' she told the boys, in Malay. 'I am sure we will get on very well. Now go about your duties.'

The boys smiled delightedly and hurried off.

'You speak *Malay*?' Blaine was astounded. And annoyed.

'I lived amongst them for a year.' That was something that could not be brushed under the carpet.

'Yes, I suppose you did.'

As he was apparently waiting for her, she went into the bungalow and looked around. It was actually a very comfortable, if small, house, furnished, as was to be expected, in a bachelor style.

'There are two bedrooms,' he explained at her shoulder. 'I suppose .... well ...'

'Thank you,' she said. But even if he was trying to act the perfect gentleman, she suddenly knew that would be the worst situation of all. She was lately unused to English gentlemen, and to English gentility. She could not live in the same house as this man, without being accepted as his wife. By him. She sat down on the settee, hands folded on her lap. 'However, I do not require a separate room.'

'Oh, dash it all, I wouldn't dream of imposing. Until . . . well, until you feel up to it, eh?' He sat opposite her. 'But I really am most happy to have you back.' Clearly he was trying to convince himself.

'But you never supposed it would happen,' she said.

'Well, after all this time, I really didn't have much hope. That you could survive captivity for a year . . . that's quite miraculous.'

She realized he had never really thought about it. But he would have to think about it now, have to understand what was involved. Because, for instance, although in the two weeks which had elapsed since she left Singapura her pubic hair had started to grow, that it had been regularly shaved would be obvious to anyone who saw her in the nude. 'I survived,' she said, as evenly as she could above the thumping of her heart, 'by living. By getting up every morning and walking down to the river to bathe with the other women of the harem, by working with them, by eating and drinking with them, and' – she drew a deep breath – 'by making Perak Shah happy.'

'Perak Shah?'

'The man who kidnapped me.'

'Ah,' he said. 'Good lord. Yes. Do we really have to go into that?'

'Don't we?' she asked.

'Well,' he said. 'The whole thing is unthinkable, of course. But now that you are back . . .'

'It happened,' she shouted. 'I bore him a child.' She had not meant it to come out quite like that, but there is was.

Blaine's head jerked, and his face went red. 'Perak Shah?'

'Well, not actually . . .' She hesitated, unsure of the best way to approach it. She bitterly regretted her outburst.

'*My God!*' he remarked.

'He didn't share me around, if that's what you think,'

174

she snapped, now becoming angry. 'It ... I don't know ...'

'My God,' he said again, more quietly but more vehemently. 'Hammond!'

'What?' she asked, feeling as if she were drowning.

'Hammond!' Blaine repeated. 'People talked ... Phillips ... said the fellow's concern was quite indecent. Didn't know what he meant, really. But you let Hammond have you, and he made you pregnant. You slut!'

'I will not contest a divorce,' she said.

'A ... you are my wife!'

'You cannot seriously want that.' The room was spinning about her. If, in her heart, she had always known that her return would involve catastrophe, she had never expected it to be quite so quick. And yet, in her over-anxiety, she had provoked it.

'You are my *wife*,' he repeated. 'Divorce? Parade our difficulties before Parliament? Yes, you would like that, wouldn't you? You little slut. You utter whore. Sleeping with Malays, sleeping with upstart clerks, sleeping with God alone knows who else ...' He was on his feet again, rearing above her like the cobra she had seen dancing to pipe music in the Five Villages.

'If you hit me,' she said, 'I shall kill you.'

Stamford Raffles hurried up the stairs of his bungalow; across the Government House lawn he could just see the Blaines on their verandah, apparently being greeted by their houseboys. What a splendid woman, he thought. Quite remarkably composed, in view of what she had suffered. And if her complexion was irretrievably ravaged, it somehow enhanced her beauty. 'Has Teng Lee been?' he asked Flora, giving her a hasty kiss.

'No. Is he back?'

'Yes. Is Hammond here?'

'He's in the garden.' She shrugged. 'Practising.'

Raffles walked through the small parlour and dining

175

room, through the kitchen where the Malay houseboys were preparing supper, and stood on the steps, to watch his protégé going through the motions of handling a kris. It was a specialist weapon, the proper use of which depended upon agility as much as swordsmanship; indeed, there was precious little swordsmanship about it. But it was a deadly weapon, when accompanied by the leaps and swift turns that were part of the Malay fighting ethic, which included the use of the feet as an offensive weapon . . . and Clive Hammond had learned fast.

Raffles supposed his energy was as much a result of his frustration as his naturally keen brain. The fellow hated working for Gresholm, that was obvious, but, as he had no choice if he was to remain in Penang – there were no other jobs available – he was prepared to put up with it. Because he was determined to remain in Penang. Easy to say he had no choice here as well: an itinerant European seeking employment would scarcely be welcome in any other domain governed by the East India Company, while the gaol sentence still hung over his head in England. But equally he remained because he dreamed of one day being able to rescue his lady love.

Raffles felt badly about that. He had held out the promise of action against the Malay pirates, because it was a part of his own dream of gaining control of the Spice Islands for Great Britain. Whenever Clive wanted to discuss the project, which was often enough, he pretended a continued enthusiasm. Which was real enough. But he knew that as things were, even if he ever managed to persuade Lord Minto that an expedition against Java was feasible, there would be neither the ships nor the men available for an attack on Singapura, nor could he really afford to stir up a hornets' nest of pirates who might just go and ally themselves with the Dutch. The assault on Singapura would have to wait until after the conquest of Java. That was looking a long way ahead, especially as, despite forwarding to Calcutta Hammond's estimation of the situation in Batavia, he had received no positive response from the Governor-General.

To make up for his deceit, he had taken the young man under his wing, made him a friend, entertained him, indeed, opened his house to him as a second home to the noisome attic at Gresholm's and had found him both a pleasant companion and an apt pupil. Clive had learned Malay, and even a smattering of Flemish, both languages which Raffles had made it worth his own while to speak fluently, as they were important to an understanding of what went on in the region. He had thrown himself even more into the learning of the kris, another art his mentor had deemed it necessary to master. Raffles had no idea what thoughts went through his friend's mind when he leapt and turned, and jabbed the knife forward, cutting the air with such decisive swishes. What faces did he see in front of him, to be destroyed? That of the pirate, Perak Shah? Or that of Edward Blaine?

This was not something they had discussed, since that first day; it was not a matter that gentlemen did discuss. He had no doubt that Clive had fallen in love with Mrs Blaine during the voyage from England. Whether or not the passion had been consummated he had no firm knowledge, but he had too cynical a view of mankind to suppose one could carry so much adoration for so long without having had at least a taste of the reality of it.

Now Clive had to be told, somehow, that she was back, but not to be touched.

'You are getting tired,' he remarked.

Clive stopped, panting. He was stripped to the waist, and his torso gleamed with sweat. But it was a broad, muscular, sun-browned torso now, whereas a year ago it had been hollow-chested and pale, hardly suggestive of a man who might challenge a Malay pirate in his den.

'You move like a cat,' he said, and dropped the kris.

Raffles laughed, and threw him the towel which lay across the banister. 'I have news.'

177

'A letter from Minto?' Clive hurried toward him, vigorously drying himself.

'Ah,' Raffles said. 'No. I —'

'Teng Lee is here,' Flora called.

'Teng!' Raffles hurried back to the house and grasped his friend's hand. 'By God, but you are a man of your word, even if it took you a while. I suspect you have quite a tale to tell.'

'Quite a tale,' Teng agreed, and looked past him at Clive. 'Hammond!'

'Teng!' Clive also shook hands. 'I had thought you dead. Or prevented from returning.'

'There are many things which nibble at a man's plans. But I *have* returned, and . . .' Teng glanced at Raffles.

He gave a quick shake of the head. 'But I think he must be told.'

'Told what?' Flora Raffles inquired.

'Told that Teng has been successful in his mission, as I never doubted he would be,' Raffles said.

There was a moment's silence, while Clive looked from face to face. 'You mean Elizabeth. . . ?'

'Is restored to her husband,' Teng said carefully.

'To . . . my God!' Clive sat down suddenly, as if his legs had given way.

'Oh, lord,' Flora Raffles remarked. It was less a comment on the return of Elizabeth than on the entry of Edward Blaine, who was at that moment stamping up the front steps of the bungalow.

'Is Hammond here?' he demanded. Everyone in Penang knew that Clive spent most evenings with the Raffles.

Clive stood up.

'Now, Blaine,' Raffles said.

Blaine strode across the room and hit Clive across the cheek with the back of his hand.

Taken entirely by surprise, Clive sat down again with a thump.

'Major!' Flora Raffles cried.

'That scoundrel,' Blaine spluttered. 'My wife . . .'

Raffles looked at Teng, who bowed his head.

'By God,' Blaine was shouting. 'I'm calling you out, you — you villain!'

'Your wife?' Clive asked, regaining his feet but still apparently bemused. Then he was looking past Blaine at Elizabeth, who had followed her husband. 'Elizabeth!' he cried.

Blaine stepped backwards and thrust out an arm to prevent her from coming further into the room. 'What the devil are you doing here?' he demanded.

'I have a letter for Mr Raffles,' she said.

'You . . .'

'This is Mrs Blaine, my dear,' Raffles explained to a dumbfounded Flora. 'I think you know everyone else, Mrs Blaine.'

'You harlot,' Blaine bellowed. 'Couldn't wait to see the wretch, could you? Well, by God, you slut, I am going to teach at least one of your lovers a lesson.'

'Major, please, such language,' Flora protested.

Clive continued to stare at Elizabeth, who gazed back at him for a moment longer, while colour flared into her cheeks. Then she said, 'I am sorry to have caused so much trouble. I am sorry to have returned at all.' She placed Hoorn's letter on an occasional table, turned and hurried from the room.

'I'll settle her,' Blaine growled.

'You'll what?' Clive started forward, and was restrained by Raffles' hand.

'And you,' Blaine shouted. 'My second will call, sir. He'll call.' He stamped after his wife.

'I must get over there,' Clive said. 'He'll beat her.'

'He has the right,' Raffles said. 'And if you interfere he'll have the right to kill you without a duel. For God's sake, man, she is his wife.'

Clive glared at him for a moment. 'Then I'll kill the bastard tomorrow morning and make her a widow.'

'Don't be absurd. Blaine is the best pistol shot in Penang.'

'Is there any law says we have to fight with pistols?'

'He'd cut you in two with a sword as well,' Raffles said bluntly.

'He has challenged me,' Clive said. 'I shall choose the kris.'

'You must be mad. That would be murder.'

'If I kill him with a kris, it's murder. What if he kills me with a sword or a pistol?'

'Is duelling not illegal under English law?' Teng asked quietly.

'Why, by God, you're right,' Raffles cried. 'We'll have the Governor put a stop to this.'

'I too would like a word with his excellency,' Teng agreed.

'This is going to be the biggest scandal in the history of Penang,' Flora said sadly.

'Well,' said Raffles, 'we must do the best we can. Clive . . . I want you to stay here with Flora. Give me your word that you will not leave until Teng and I have returned.'

Clive looked as if he would have liked to argue, then he looked across the compound at the Blaines' house, then he sat down. 'I suppose I have no choice.'

'We'll be as quick as we can,' Raffles promised him. He and Teng hurried up the drive to Government House, where they found Colonel Phillips, as he now was, in the Governor's office.

'Teng Lee,' the colonel said. 'My congratulations. I never believed you'd pull it off.'

Teng bowed, and waited for Raffles to speak.

'I'm afraid there has been a slight complication, sir,' Raffles said, and proceeded to outline what had just happened.

'My God!' Sir Charles commented.

'I'd better tell cook supper may be late,' remarked Lady Wilmot, who had come in to listen.

'That little whippersnapper,' Phillips growled. 'I never liked him. Always knew he was a cad.'

'With respect, Colonel, if madam will permit me . . .' Teng bowed toward Lady Wilmot. 'There is no proof that Mr Hammond and Mrs Blaine had ever had a liaison. It is suspicion held by Major Blaine.'

'Suspicion? Ha,' Phillips declared. 'I saw the pair of them, heads together, on the ship. You'll forgive me, m'lady.'

Lady Wilmot was fanning herself. 'Well, I really don't know what to say. Charles . . .'

'We can't have a duel,' Wilmot decided.

'I say let Blaine cut the scoundrel's water off,' Phillips said.

'That is unlikely to happen,' Raffles pointed out. 'Hammond is the challenged party. He has chosen the kris.'

'The . . . good God,' Phillips exploded. 'The man is a thug as well as a cad. That would be murder.'

'It would most certainly be an execution,' Teng observed.

Sir Charles pointed at Phillips. 'I want Hammond locked up.'

'Yes, *sir*,' Phillips agreed happily.

'On what charge?' Raffles protested.

'Ah, protective custody. I know you've befriended the scoundrel, Stamford, but I can't have people running around Georgetown brandishing Malay knives. It'll stir up the natives for a start. I want him locked up and I want him placed on the first ship bound for England. I should have done that with him in the first place. See to it, Colonel.'

Phillips crammed his bicorne on his head, saluted and hurried for the door. 'Sergeant Crawley,' he bawled. 'Stand to, with four men. Armed.'

'I'd better go with him, or there *will* be murder done,' Raffles said. 'Teng . . .'

'I will follow shortly,' Teng said. 'If his excellency will permit me.'

'Of course, my dear fellow. We must talk about your reward. You performed a splendid service.'

Teng bowed his head. 'It warms my heart to hear you say so, your excellency. I made a promise, and I always endeavour to keep my promises.'

'Oh, quite. Most admirable. And I really feel you are entitled to some reward. If I had any idea what it should be. A sum of money . . . well, that would make it seem rather as if that poor woman's misfortune could be paid for.'

'I do not wish money, your excellency,' Teng said. 'But I would appreciate a small token of your appreciation of the time and trouble I have taken to secure the release of Mrs Blaine.'

'Of course, my dear fellow. Of course. Just name it.'

'I would very much like a letter from yourself, Sir Charles, recommending me to Lord Minto.'

Sir Charles stared at him. 'The Governor-General? You wish me to recommend you to him?'

'That is correct, your excellency. He is a man I have always wished to meet.'

'Good lord! I don't think . . . well, I am sure we can think of some other adequate recompense. I mean to say, my dear fellow, the Governor-General of India is like a king. He does not entertain, well . . .'

'Itinerant Chinese merchants?' Teng asked quietly. 'I have been entertained by kings before, your excellency.'

'Hm. Yes, well, I am sure you have. But I am afraid Lord Minto . . . what you ask is really quite impossible.'

Teng sipped his brandy, then stood up and bowed. 'Then I had better leave, your excellency. We clearly have nothing further to discuss.'

*

182

Stamford Raffles sat on the cane settee in his parlour and stretched out his legs; he had just come in and looked hot and bothered. 'What a God-damned mess,' he remarked. 'One almost wishes Teng had left the girl in Singapura.'

Flora gave him a glass of brandy. 'She seemed rather a nice person. To look at, anyway. But she has rather let herself go, hasn't she? Fancy going in the sun without a hat, and apparently without covering her arms. I'm surprised she didn't get sunstroke. I suppose one can never judge by appearances.'

'She *is* rather a nice person,' Raffles said, sipping with great pleasure. 'Far too good for Blaine, in my opinion. And I don't suppose she went into the sun without a hat voluntarily. I feel desperately sorry for her. But more sorry for Hammond.'

'How is he?'

'Bitter, resentful, mistrustful . . . even of me.'

'Do you think he did have a liaison with Mrs Blaine?'

'I have no doubt of it.'

'Well, then.'

'If we seriously started locking people up for adultery, where would we begin, do you think? With the Prince of Wales?'

'Um. Penang really is a little small for that sort of thing.'

'Agreed. Penang is a bit small for every sort of thing. God, this place makes me sick. And now, that poor girl . . . what she is going to suffer – and don't look at me like that. She survived. That is the important thing in life. I hope you would have the courage to do the same.'

'Um,' Flora Raffles said again. 'What do you think about this letter she brought you?'

'My God, I'd forgotten all about it.' He got up, fetched it from the table where she had left it, slit the envelope with his thumb and began reading.

Flora watched him for a moment, then turned to the

door as there were footsteps on the verandah. 'Mr Teng,' she said. 'You'll stay to supper.'

'Thank you, no,' Teng said. 'I will return to my ship. I sail tomorrow morning.'

'But you've only just arrived,' she protested.

'Good lord,' Raffles remarked, still reading.

Teng and Flora both looked at him. 'I really cannot stay,' Teng said.

Flora frowned. 'You're angry.' She had never seen Teng angry before.

'Yes,' Teng acknowledged. 'I am angry. I shall not be returning to Penang again.'

'But. . . .'

'Great Scott!' Raffles, exclaimed, having finished the letter, and folded it shut. 'That is just what I have been waiting for. Teng, how good to see you. You'll stay to supper.'

'He is just leaving,' Flora explained.

'Leaving?'

'I have been rejected by your governor,' Teng told him, and when Raffles looked totally mystified, related his conversation with Sir Charles.

'Hm,' Raffles commented. 'Well, he is right. Governors-general do have an exalted idea of their position. I suppose they have to. Is it very important that you meet Minto?'

'It is very important to me,' Teng said.

'Hm,' Raffles commented again, and half opened the letter, then let it fall shut again. 'You would, in the normal course of events, be going to Calcutta after leaving here.'

'I would,' Teng agreed.

'Hm,' Raffles said a third time. 'Supposing I offered you an introduction to Minto.'

'You? Can you do it?'

'I think so. He and I are by way of being friends. But I would require something from you in return.'

184

Teng reflected only for an instant that he had already done something for Raffles, and for the whole British community in Penang, he assumed, by returning Elizabeth Blaine to them. His sole purpose in life was to obtain that interview with Lord Minto which he had assured King Rama he could do without difficulty. He sat down. 'Name it.'

Raffles smiled. 'Let me get you a glass of brandy,' he said. Then he too sat down, and began to talk.

'How is she?' Clive demanded. 'Have you heard?'

Raffles looked around the small cell, the baked-mud walls and felt the heat pounding on the mud roof. The prison was removed some distance from the town itself, but as it had never been intended to house Europeans, it was in one of the less salubrious parts of the island, close by a swamp. As, in addition to Clive, it contained several Malay prisoners, it smelt like a sewer. Nor did Clive smell much more wholesome, although he did have this cell to himself. 'How are they treating you?'

'Like a dog. But I have had a visitor.'

'Indeed? Who.'

Clive's smile was bitter. 'Who do you suppose? Gresholm, to inform me that my services are no longer required by his establishment, and further, that all the back pay he owes me will be charged to my account, payable in respect of board and lodging. I would have strangled the scoundrel with my bare hands had that lout of a gaoler not interfered.'

Raffles nodded. 'They do like to kick a fellow when he's down.'

Clive seized his hand. 'Raffles . . . have you seen her?'

'Yes. I see her, from time to time.' Raffles sat on the slender cot which was the only furniture in the room. 'She appears quite well. I would not pretend that I thought her happy, but then, circumstances have been against that, and she is the centre of a certain amount of gossip.

185

There's an understatement. Phillips knows the whole story, of course, and therefore so does his wife, and that means the whole of Penang. But apparently, despite all, he means her to remain as his wife.'

'God . . .' Clive's fingers curled into fists. 'While I am to be deported for disturbing the peace.'

'Indeed you are. By the first available ship.'

'God!' Clive repeated. 'If only . . .'

'Forget if onlys. The first available ship happens to be the *Dragon's Wake*. Teng was going to leave sooner, but I persuaded him to wait.'

Clive, prowling restlessly to and fro across the cell, paused to look at him.

'Teng is willing to give you a passage,' Raffles repeated.

'Back to England?' Clive's tone was now both bitter and incredulous.

'Out of Penang. First of all to Calcutta, which is his normal next port of call, after Rangoon. Then to Batavia.'

Clive had now stopped perambulating and stood still, staring at him.

'What I have to say is of great importance,' Raffles told him. 'And of great secrecy. You told me that when you visited Batavia, you made the acquaintance of a man named Pieter Hoorn.'

'Pieter Hoorn. Yes, I did.'

'And he is one of the leading factors there?'

'Just about the leading factor, so far as I could gather.'

'Did he discuss politics with you?'

'Not in so many words.'

'Did you obtain the impression that he was pro-British?'

'Oh, indeed I did. I told you so when I got here. But what has this man Hoorn got to do with my predicament?'

'I will explain it to you,' Raffles said. 'Hoorn has written me a letter, sent in the care of your lady love,

186

would you believe it, suggesting that if the British were to attack Java, we would find the burghers there at least indifferent, at best on our side. He would be on our side, certainly.' Raffles leaned forward. 'Don't you see, Hammond, this is the ammunition I have been waiting for. Minto has made no positive response to the opinions you gave on Batavia, because they were only opinions. But if he can be assured there is a section of the Batavian citizenry which would support us, or at least not oppose us, then the assault becomes a much more practical proposition. This letter must be shown to Minto, but frankly, knowing what an old ditherer Wilmot is, I dare not reveal it to him and send it through normal channels. It must be conveyed in secret to the Governor-General. And more than that, as it involves Hoorn's life – for were it to get into the wrong hands it could involve his execution and the end of all our hopes – it must be delivered personally by a trustworthy courier.'

'You mean Teng Lee?'

'No, you dunderhead, I mean you. Teng, in fact, must not know the contents of this letter; much as I like the chap, and indeed trust him, I am by no means certain he would support a move by us into Java. But he has agreed to take you to Calcutta, in return for a letter of introduction to Minto. This I have given him, again privately – apparently Wilmot would not do so. I have no idea why he wants it; I suppose it is to impress his friends back in Canton, but I don't see what harm can come of that, especially as he is being so cooperative to us. I may point out that your being the agent I have selected to deliver Hoorn's letter to Minto cannot help but be of use to you.'

'Hm,' Clive commented.

'Teng will then take you on to Batavia,' Raffles repeated, watching him carefully. 'In this instance, of course, we will have to trust him absolutely. But I believe

187

he is genuinely fond of you, and would never dream of betraying you.'

'That I don't understand at all. Why am I going to Batavia, if the British are getting set to take the place?'

'Because I need you there, for a while. There is every reason for you to go there right now. You are about to be deported from Penang back to England, where you face a gaol sentence. Does it not make sense for you to prefer to escape from us here with your old friend Teng, and persuade him to take you to your only other friend in the world, Pieter Hoorn, who once before offered you a position with him?'

Clive gazed at him.

'That is, I am sure, how the Dutch will consider the matter. They may be a little suspicious of you at first, but Teng will back your story, and they can check it out, if they wish. They will find it to be the truth in all the details that matter.'

'And you say you require me in Batavia. What for?'

'I need you to find out if Hoorn's estimation of the situation there is an accurate one. As I say, I know you have already supplied me, and Minto, with a report on the situation there, which I certainly then thought was promising, but that was a year ago, and I happen to know there have been some substantial changes in their establishment, especially in the military command, which suggest a stiffening of their attitude. Now, this may have antagonised the colonists, as Hoorn suggests – but it also may just have sent Hoorn into despair and caused him to build castles in the air. Although I am sure Minto will wish to act upon this letter, he will also be anxious to know that it is neither a trap nor a case of wishful thinking. So you will be a fugitive from British justice, make yourself popular with the mijnheers, take up that position Hoorn offered you, and observe, while Teng goes about his business. When Teng returns from his next voyage, you will give him a message for me.'

'Do I confide my true role to Hoorn?'

'That is up to you. But I would say, yes. You are liable to get more done with him firmly on your side.'

'And this message: does that not involve trusting Teng, after all?'

'It does, to a certain extent. But the message need be nothing he could understand. Simply, you will ask him to tell me whether you are happy or unhappy. If you are happy, I will know that Hoorn's estimate is correct, and I can promise you that the invasion will be prepared immediately.'

'And if I am unhappy?'

'I suggest in that case you make your own decision. Remain there, if in actual fact you are finding it worthwhile, or leave with Teng, and try to make a home for yourself somewhere else.'

'You are asking me to act the spy, you know.'

'Well, perhaps that is one way of putting it. I am giving you an opportunity entirely to rehabilitate yourself. If we are successful in this, and I believe we will be, your every crime will be forgiven. I can promise you that.'

'Supposing the Dutch do not shoot me first.'

'That is entirely up to you. But if you are careful, and are prepared to trust Teng, then who can betray you, except Hoorn? And he would be betraying himself at the same time.'

Clive took another turn up and down the cell. 'And Elizabeth?' he asked, when next he paused.

'What about her?'

'I love her, Raffles. God, you must realize that.'

'I am trying not to. She happens to be another man's wife, Hammond. And she is going to stay that way. You don't even have any proof that she loves you. But that is irrelevant. If this were England and you had money and position, you might just be able to swing an elopement. There is no hope of that here, and it would be ruinous of you to try. The only place you could go is into the jungles

189

of Kedah, and if the natives didn't cut your throats in five minutes, you'd have fever. You'd be damned forever in the East, as well as in England. Your only course is to forget her, and try to make something of your life at least.'

'Easy to say.' Clive sat on the cot himself, causing it to sag dangerously.

Raffles studied him. He simply had to have this young man's cooperation — oddly enough, although they were virtually the same age, he felt old enough to be Clive's father — because there was no one else who so naturally fitted the role in which he had to be employed. Hoorn's credentials, his ability to estimate a situation, had to be checked out before Minto would dream of committing a large part of his scanty resources to such an exercise. Clive was the only person who could do so and yet, because of his background, remain outside Dutch suspicion. Of course he would be risking his life, but Raffles was quite prepared to risk his own life in the pursuit of his dream of turning the East Indies into a British-controlled lake. And it would be better than spending several years in gaol.

And Clive obviously realized all of those things. Therefore just the slightest encouragement would win his agreement. What immediately came to mind as the final inducement would involve a certain risk to Raffles' own reputation, and perhaps even to his position here in Penang, were it ever to become known. But he had no fear of taking risks where the possible gains were so great, and he was confident that Minto, who, he knew, felt as frustrated as himself at having to deal through bumbling place-men like Charles Wilmot, would never let him down. As for the woman, if she had to become even a tiny part of the great game he was determined to win, then she would at least have done something worthwhile with her shattered life.

So he would be once again twisting and manipulating

people and things. He had never shirked from that before, when his objective was involved.

'I could, perhaps,' he said, again speaking very carefully, 'arrange a last meeting between you.'

Clive's head jerked.

Raffles held up his finger. 'It would be brief. And it must contain not a thought of that elopement, because if you try it, I will arrest you myself. It will be farewell, and it must be farewell forever. And you must promise me to go through with the Batavian proposal.'

Clive was on his feet, his eyes dancing. 'Arrange that for me, Raffles, and I am your man.'

His heart pounded and his throat felt dry. Having spent a further three days in gaol for form's sake, and while Raffles wove his spells, he had been released into his friend's custody this very evening, in time to be conducted on board Teng's junk, most publicly, there to remain until it sailed at dawn the following morning. Once on board, he had been able to have a bath and get rid of his filthy gaol clothing, and begin to feel almost human again. And now the moment of which he had dreamed for over a year was finally at hand.

The plan was an elaborate one, but then, all of Raffles' plans were elaborate; he had something of the gambler in him, although his risks were always carefully calculated and his manoeuvres carried out with disciplined precision. Thus after dark Clive had been returned ashore, lying at the bottom of Teng's boat, and taken not to the dock, but to one of the Malay fishing platforms to one side of the town. From there he had made his way through the darkened streets to the Government House grounds, and thence to Raffles' bungalow. It was a route he knew well, as in his year in Penang he had come to know the whole island well, and Teng had outfitted him with Chinese clothing, so that if he encountered anyone they were not likely to pay him too much attention – as with Bangkok and Batavia, a sizeable Chinese colony was building in Georgetown as well.

The window to Raffles' own bedroom had been left open for him, and it had proved a simple matter to creep in and secrete himself by the wardrobe, trying to control his breathing, listening to the clatter of cutlery from next door, where Mr and Mrs Raffles were entertaining Major and Mrs Blaine to supper. They were, no doubt, celebrating the departure of the trouble-maker.

But now . . . the meal was finished and the men would be lighting their cigars and enjoying their port. He could hear footsteps in the corridor leading to the bedrooms, and a moment later the door opened. Flora Raffles entered first, carrying the candle, and this she placed on the high chest of drawers, before turning to Elizabeth, who was closing the door. 'My dear,' she said. 'I'm afraid that I have a surprise for you. I beg you not to scream, as it would place my husband and myself in a most embarrassing situation. You have but to say, and the vision will fade away forever.'

'I don't understand . . .' Elizabeth caught her breath as she saw the shadow of the man.

'I wished to say goodbye,' he said. 'And Mr and Mrs Raffles very nobly agreed to help me.'

Elizabeth looked at him, then at Flora.

'Do you wish him to leave now?' Flora asked.

'I . . .' Elizabeth bit her lip. 'No, please,' she said. 'Do not send him away.'

'Very well,' Flora agreed. 'I will step into the next room. I will be gone five minutes. No longer.' She opened the door and went through, closing it again behind herself.

Elizabeth gazed at Clive.

'Has it been very bad?' he asked.

'I survived Perak Shah. And you?'

He smiled. 'I survived gaol. But not for so long.'

192

'And now they are sending you away.'

'Yes. I . . .' He longed to tell her that he would not be so very far away, and that there was even a chance they might one day meet again, especially if Raffles' plans came to fruition, Java fell to the British, and he was, as his friend had promised, fully rehabilitated. But part of the bargain he had struck with Raffles was that no one save Minto and Teng Lee were to know his destination. To the rest of the Georgetown community he was being taken to Calcutta to be put on a ship for England. 'I doubt I shall return.'

'I think that is probably best,' she agreed.

He searched for words. How he wanted to ask her what she had suffered in Singapura, what she was suffering now at the hands of Blaine, whether *she* had any hopes for the future . . . but he had only five minutes, and those questions were too intimate to be rushed, after a whole year. 'I love you,' he said.

Her chin came up. 'After one —' She bit her lip again.

'After a year of dreams. And memories.'

'Are you not afraid I have changed? You must be the only person in Penang who has not commented on my ruined complexion.'

'I think it makes you more beautiful than ever. Elizabeth, I love you. I know I can never have you. But we have only these minutes. . . .'

He was never sure whether she had moved or not, or whether he had actually reached for her. But she did not resist him, was in his arms and kissing him as passionately as she had done that night in the life-boat, while he felt her against him, so desirable — and so unattainable.

She gasped for breath. 'Oh, Clive. I must —'

'I love you,' he said. 'Love you, love you, love you. I shall always love you.'

'Clive . . .' She moved her head back as if she would tell

193

him something. Then she said softly, 'I could love you too.'

CHAPTER EIGHT

The Princess

Gilbert Elliot-Murray-Kynynmound, Baron Minto, the East India Company's Governor-General of all its vast Indian Empire, was fifty-eight years old. He had a fine face, long nose, wide-set eyes, a firm chin, and a high forehead, made higher by his receding hairline. His face was expressionless as, having invited Clive to sit down, he read first of all Raffles' covering letter, then Hoorn's, and then the despatches from Sir Charles Wilmot. The large, airy office was silent save for the whirring of the fan swaying above their heads, operated by a punkah wallah in the corridor outside. The secretary who had accompanied Clive into the room stood motionless to one side.

Clive endeavoured to calm his nerves by looking through the open window at the town, listening to the sounds and inhaling the odours of this oldest of British Indian settlements.

India was a place he had often read about, and yet it exceeded both his expectations and his apprehensions. The approach to the low-lying coast, where the myriad mouths of the great Ganges had created a delta of swamp and mudflat, had itself been startling. The sudden appearance of the River Hugli, westernmost of the exits, streaming out to sea past Sagar Island, had come as a surprise; it was apparently the only navigable channel for ships of any size. Even then it had been a long beat up against the current to reach the town of Calcutta, which the pilot Teng had prudently taken aboard – despite the many times he had previously been here – still referred to as 'the fort', and whenever the wind died the junk was hastily anchored so as not to lose ground.

'The fort' itself was very nearly a hundred miles from the sea, at least by river, for the Hugli coiled back and forth like a snake. But gradually the vessels at anchor, several of them warships of considerable size, had come into view, and then the actual fort. Teeming close-packed houses surrounded it, although at a distance, for the land immediately about the fort had been cleared – no doubt originally for defence, but now that Bengal was largely British-controlled, it had been turned into an attractive park.

Which was more than could be said for the native town behind it. The place had a miasma which could be seen and smelt at some distance, accentuated by the swamp extending to either side of the river. Here the Indians had crowded both for work – areas of the native city were still divided up into quarters named after the principal occupation of their inhabitants, such as potters or conchshell workers – and also for protection from the excesses of their natives rulers. Never had Clive seen as many people assembled in so small a space, and he had been appalled by the beggars of both sexes – and, on occasion, their children – many with open sores, who held up their arms to him.

'They are a sad people,' Teng had observed. 'They would sell you the babe from their breast for a few rupees.'

The English had apparently soon understood that to live by the river was to die of fever, and had moved themselves to the high ground beyond. Here was a different world, of flower gardens, and smooth-cut lawns, of Indian ayahs and laughing children, and above all, of magnificent houses, some of them mansions which could easily have graced an English country estate. 'They call Calcutta the city of palaces,' Teng had told him. 'One

196

presumes they accept that every palace must contain a dung heap in its backyard.' He spoke reflectively rather than critically, but that he did not like the place was evident. Well, Clive thought, I do not like the place either. He wished his lordship would make haste, and let him get on with his mission.

At last Minto raised his head and gazed at Clive for several seconds. 'You seem to have led an adventurous life,' he remarked.

'Yes, my lord,' Clive acknowledged.

'And it was your report on Batavia that Raffles forwarded to me last year?'

'Yes, my lord.'

'It showed good observation,' Minto commented. 'And now he wants you to return to Batavia as a spy. You are aware of the danger?'

'If I am detected, yes.'

Minto nodded. 'His Excellency Sir Charles Wilmot requests me to place you on a ship and send you home in disgrace. Does Raffles really expect me to deceive one of my own governors?'

'The business of spying, my lord, surely involves deceiving everyone, as I understand it.'

Minto raised his eyebrows, then half smiled. 'Of course, you are a writer. You can play with words. You are also something of a scoundrel, I would say.'

'For falling in love, my lord?'

'With another man's wife, Mr Hammond. Now what of this Chinaman you have outside?'

'Teng Lee is a *Chinese* merchant of great standing, my lord,' Clive said carefully.

'And he too has impressed Raffles?'

'He is privy to our plan, at least in part. He knows nothing of Hoorn's involvement; he believes that Raffles is sending me to Java on my own, as it were. He is willing to cooperate in establishing me there by supporting my story.'

197

'And what happens should he change his mind?' Minto inquired. 'To my mind, trusting a foreigner, and an oriental, is the most dangerous part of the whole scheme. He could betray you, and us, whenever he feels like it.'

'Teng Lee will never betray me, my lord.'

Once again the Governor-General regarded him for several seconds. 'Why is he so anxious to see me in person?'

'I do not know, my lord. But it was a part of the bargain we struck. That is, he and Mr Raffles struck.'

Minto considered. 'If I permit you to go to Batavia, Hammond,' he said, 'you must be very clear about two things. Firstly, interesting as are Hoorn's proposals, the man is playing the traitor to his country and must therefore be regarded as intrinsically unreliable. Thus I have no intention of attempting any invasion of so large an island unless I am positive that such an invasion will be a rapid success. Your report to Raffles will obviously be of prime importance in enabling me to arrive at a decision.'

'I understand that, my lord.'

'And secondly, should you therefore feel tempted to paint your report in unrealistically bright colours so as to encourage me to come to your rescue, and I find the situation to be less promising than you suggest, I will denounce you to the Dutch; or, if you happen to fall back into my hands, I will have you shot as a traitor, as you will have fled from British to enemy territory in time of war. Do you understand that?'

'Yes, my lord.'

'Very good. Now show your Chinese friend in.'

Clive got up, went to the door and opened it. Teng was sitting very straight in his chair, a small satchel on his lap. The two men had entirely renewed their friendship during the voyage, and Teng had shown no curiosity concerning Clive's real motives in returning to Batavia, or Raffles' in sending him there, although Clive had no

198

doubt he was interested. Certainly he had willingly agreed to support the tale Raffles wanted the Dutch to be told, and he had proved as enjoyable and interesting a companion as ever. He had shown Clive the wonders of Rangoon when they put in there, and had told him of the splendours of Bangkok, where he confessed he was thinking of making his home. It was in fact the first time he had ever spoken of his personal life, and then very briefly. Clive had not wanted to probe, but he assumed Teng had a family; as to why he should wish to leave China he could not say. But as they approached Calcutta, he had become aware that Teng was nervous, and this had surprised him, as it was not a state of mind he would ever have associated with his friend. Obviously this meeting with Minto was very important to him.

'His excellency will see you now, Teng,' he said.

Teng got up without a word, entered the office and bowed. Minto was clearly surprised; he had not expected anyone quite so elegant. 'This is a great honour, your excellency,' Teng said.

Minto looked even more surprised, as he had not anticipated such perfect English, either. 'It is my pleasure, Mr Teng,' he said. 'Did you have a request to make of me?'

'That I may speak with you alone,' Teng said.

Minto raised his eyebrows.

The secretary gave a warning cough. 'The . . . ah, gentleman has not been searched, my lord,' he said.

'I will vouch for Teng Lee with my life,' Clive declared.

Teng bowed. 'What I have to say to you is of great importance, your excellency.'

Minto regarded him for several seconds, then nodded. 'Leave us, Jason,' he said. 'You too, Hammond.'

The secretary hesitated, but Clive was already at the door, and he followed reluctantly. Minto opened his desk drawer and took out a pistol, which he placed in front of him. 'It is primed and loaded,' he said.

Teng bowed again. 'I expected nothing less,' he said enigmatically. 'Is it permitted to sit?'

'Why, yes, if you wish.'

Teng sat down. 'I am on a most secret mission from His Majesty King Rama II of Siam,' he said.

'A mission to me?' Minto asked.

'That is correct, your excellency.'

Minto leaned back in his chair. 'Then I would be interested to hear what his majesty wishes.'

Teng told him.

'You have credentials to support you?' Minto asked, when he was finished.

Teng gave him the King's letter. 'Should you feel that your king will not be interested,' he said, 'I am to take the letter back.'

Minto glanced at the letter, which was of course in Thai. But there was no mistaking the seal.

Minto hid his elation. If he could arrive at a treaty of friendship with Siam, the strongest power in the area, both to keep her neighbours under control and to ensure that the Thais would not seek any profit for themselves in a British war with the Dutch in Java, then all things were possible.

'I will have this translated,' he said, 'and I will give you a letter to take back to King Rama, written under *my* official seal, in which I will beg him to receive a duly accredited ambassador from the Court of St James. Would it be worth my while to send such an ambassador with you now?'

'No, your excellency,' Teng said. 'I assume you do not wish to appear over-anxious either.'

Minto smiled. 'I think you and I understand each other very well, Mr Teng. I am most heartily glad to make your acquaintance. I shall look forward to your return to Calcutta with interest.'

Teng Lee bowed his head.

*

200

'Teng Lee,' said Rama II. 'I am pleased with you.'

Teng Lee remained kneeling, head bowed. Indeed, he felt it might be dangerous to look up, even were he permitted to do so, because then he might reveal the triumph in his expression. He was pleased with himself.

It just went to show, he thought, how a man could spend his entire life worrying about the working of Fate, the inscrutability of his destiny, when all that was required were a few bold strokes and an equal measure of determination, then he could make his own destiny and snap his fingers at Fate.

He had, in the past few months, achieved far more than he had ever expected. Even the rejection of his request for a letter to Lord Minto by Sir Charles Wilmot had turned out to his advantage, because it had driven him into the arms of Raffles. Or Raffles into his arms. Now, in addition to being the agent between Lord Minto and King Rama, he was even privy to the British intentions concerning Java. If he had not been told so in as many words, there could be no other reason for sending Clive Hammond there.

Now that he considered a daring and dangerous enterprise; the undertaking of it had increased his respect for his young friend. And it remained dangerous, so far as he could judge. That there had been no difficulty in landing Clive Hammond in Batavia, was neither here nor there. Teng had supported his story, as he had promised to do, and Pieter Hoorn had appeared, after an initial suggestion of concern, pleased to see him.

Teng was not only now in the confidence of the two most powerful men in the Far East south of China, but also privy to the secret plans of two entire governments. His position was unassailable.

Of course the British were not as important as the Thais. Even if any British possession could compare with Bangkok as a future home, he would not care to put himself in their power, aware as they certainly were of his

201

knowledge. Stamford Raffles was a good friend, but also an utterly ruthless man, Teng knew. But once he was suitably accredited by Rama and could travel as the representative of the Thai government, then his safety and his power were assured – especially as he would warn Rama when the British were intending to expand into Java, and thus still further enhance his reputation.

And only a few months ago he had been a downcast wreck, thinking only of suicide.

'To serve your majesty is all I desire,' he said.

'And serve me you shall,' Rama declared. 'As of this moment you are one of my most trusted councillors, and you will learn that I know how to reward those I trust. Now I will have another letter prepared, officially informing this Minto that I will accept his ambassadors.'

Teng bowed his head.

'When you return with the news that they are on their way,' Rama continued, 'you will have a house near my palace, and be always at my side. Teng Lee, I am well pleased.'

Indeed, he was clearly delighted. Teng had to force himself to make another decorous bow, when all he wanted to do was shout and scream with joy.

'Now you can perform another small service for me,' Rama said. 'Visit my sister, and make her laugh with your stories. She is unhappy.'

It was difficult to envisage the Princess Jalina as unhappy. Angry, yes. Arrogant, often. Beautiful, always. But unhappy. . . ? Yet there were tear stains on her cheeks, which were in themselves a clue to her misery, and her determination to make it public, and her attendants were restless and apprehensive.

Additionally, he observed, her hair was loose, hanging in a huge black cloud to either side of her face; a most unusual sight for any Thai lady – they were the neatest of people – much less a princess.

'Teng Lee,' she said. 'How I have looked forward to your return.'

'My heart bleeds to see you unwell, my lady princess.'

'I am not unwell, Teng Lee. Only in the mind. There I am the most miserable of women. Would you hear of my unhappiness?'

'Your highness,' protested one of the older of her women warningly.

'Bah,' Jalina said. 'Will it not be common knowledge soon enough? And Teng Lee is my friend. But if you do not wish to hear what I shall say to him, leave me.' She clapped her hands. 'All of you.'

'Your highness, it is quite impossible to leave you alone with this –' she gave Teng Lee a scornful glance – 'peddler.'

'I will have you flogged,' Jalina said coldly. 'What, do you suppose I am going to lie on the floor with a man old enough to be my father? Leave me, I say. Go to the far end of the room where you may watch, if you are so concerned. But I do not wish you to hear what I am going to say.'

The women exchanged glances, but they knew the princess was quite capable of carrying out her threat. They also knew that this Chinese upstart was high in the favour of the King, at least at the moment – and so it might be no use to go carrying tales.

'As you command, your highness,' the woman said, and signalled the ladies-in-waiting to withdraw across the large room, until they stood in a group by the window, watching their mistress with a series of frowns.

'Come closer,' Jalina said.

'Your highness?' Teng asked nervously.

'I am not going to bite you. I wish to speak with you alone.'

He hesitated, then crawled to where he could inhale her scent.

'I am to marry,' she announced.

'And this makes you sad, my lady princess?'

'You do not know the truth of it. I am being sent to some Vietnamese robber chieftain who calls himself a king. Me, the eldest daughter of the great Rama! It is part of my miserable brother's scheme to ally himself with all his neighbours. As if we have to fear any neighbours. My father will be turning in his grave.'

By all the gods, Teng thought, had it been possible to persevere with the Singapura alliance, this gorgeously fragile creature might well have been sent to Perak Shah. There would have been the crime of the century.

'I am sure the Vietnamese prince will bring you great happiness,' he said.

'I would rather kill myself.'

Teng couldn't decide what reply to make to that.

'Tell me where you have been on this last voyage, Teng Lee,' she said. 'The places you have visited, the people you have met. Enable at least my spirit to soar like a bird through that window.'

Teng obliged. He enjoyed telling the stories of his travels to those who wished to listen, especially when they were as beautiful and eager as the princess – and if he embroidered them a little, why should he not, if it made his listener the happier? So he told her of his visit to Calcutta, and of dining with his good friend Lord Minto, making her eyes widen as he described – drawing on his experiences at the Raffles' and the Hoorns' – the crockery and cutlery, and the quaint habits of the Europeans, while he also told her of the sights and sounds of India. She listened enraptured, and sighed when he was finished. 'I wish you would take me there, Teng Lee,' she said.

'Your highness?'

'Take me from this place on your junk to Calcutta, and Penang, and Batavia – and let me live, and know of the world, and be free.'

204

'And have my head cut off by your brother, the King?' Teng pointed out.

She gazed at him, her face serious. 'Yes,' she said. 'He would do that, would he not? Then we would have to make sure he never captured you, would we not?'

'We would become fugitives for ever. My Dutch friends tell of such a legend, of a sea captain who angered the gods and was forced to spend the rest of eternity sailing the seas, unable ever to make port or to die.' Teng found her little verbal game amusing, and was quite willing to indulge her.

'I can think of nothing finer,' she declared.

Teng allowed himself a deprecating smile. 'You would exchange all of this for my poor hospitality, your highness? These marble floors for the wooden deck of my junk? Those silks and satins for rough-spun Chinese cloth? Gold for porcelain?'

'Am I not being forced to exchange all of those things for a Vietnamese hovel?' she demanded. 'But I would certainly exchange everything I have to be free.'

'Your highness,' Teng said uneasily, beginning to wonder if she *was* playing a game, after all.

'What do you suppose my brother would do to me,' she asked, 'if I were to sail away with you, and he managed to capture us?'

'I cannot think, my lady princess.'

'I have heard of one of the ladies of the old king,' she said, 'before my father's time, who attempted to run away from court. She was shut in her room and starved to death. I suppose Rama would execute me too. He would suppose you had seduced me, Teng Lee.'

Teng bowed his head.

'Would it not please you to seduce me, Teng Lee? Even if you should lose your head for it?'

Teng raised his head again in alarm. This conversation was taking a direction he did not like at all. Almost it sounded as if she was considering odds. 'My lady princess . . .'

'A woman likes to know what a man thinks of her,' she said.

'My lady princess, you are the most beautiful woman I have ever beheld. I gaze at you in wonder, as I do upon the moon. But like the moon, I know you are forever out of my reach. I must remember always the fate of Li Po, the greatest of Chinese poets.'

'I have read Li Po's poems,' she said, and smiled. 'I remember: he fell from his boat one night, while seeking to embrace the moon, and was drowned. But was he not drunk at the time?'

'So it is said, your highness. It is said that Li Po was always drunk, or he could not have written such exquisite verse. Or aspired to things beyond his reach.'

'Had he been sober,' she remarked, 'who knows what he might have achieved. You have always struck me as a sober man, Teng Lee. Go now, and come again tomorrow, and tell me some more of your tales. But wait. That ring you wear. What is the stone?'

She pointed at the ring on his forefinger, his only jewellery. 'It is but jade, your highness.'

'I think it is very beautiful,' Jalina said. 'Will you not present it to me?'

Teng gazed at her in bewilderment; there were several rings on her fingers, mainly set with rubies; each one was worth several times more than his.

'I should like that,' she said.

Teng drew off the ring and gave it to her. One did not refuse a princess.

Jalina smiled at his expression. 'It will be a keepsake, to remind me of the pleasure you have given me. Do not fret, Teng Lee. I will study to find a gift of greater value to return to you.'

Another unhappy woman, Teng thought. But then, surely all princesses were unhappy women, because they were at the disposal of the state. That went with the enjoyment of the wealth and power they possessed. But still, to think of all that beauty in the arms of some Vietnamese savage was as disturbing as it was titillating. To think of possessing it for himself, as she had suggested, in return for her freedom, as she called it, was breathtaking. But he had no intention of repeating the folly of Li Po, drunk or sober.

He returned each of the remaining four nights of his stay in Bangkok, while his cargo was unloaded and traded, and the royal letter was prepared. When this was ready, Rama instructed him to depart immediately for Calcutta, to set the process of exchanging ambassadors in motion. So he would not this time be returning to Canton. That would have to wait until after this special voyage had been completed, when he would be ready to move himself and his share of Teng Wong's fortune to Bangkok, and set about making a new life for himself. It would be a shame, he thought, that the princess would no longer be there, but if she was starting to have odd ideas it might be a good thing.

He attended her, as usual, on the afternoon immediately before his departure — the tide down the river would be best in another hour — and was surprised and concerned to be told that she was ill. Immediately he thought that she had attempted to implement her threat to kill herself rather than be sent to Vietnam, but a friendly secretary told him that it was apparently just a chill; her highness had confined herself to bed and did not wish to be disturbed.

Just like a woman, and a princess, Teng thought; she was not even going to bother to say goodbye. Nor had she given him the gift she had promised in return for his ring. But in fact he was relieved, as he had been afraid his departure might have sent her into a tantrum. He returned across the bridge to his ship, and gave the orders to have the anchor raised.

The sails were set and the junk glided down the river under the light of the moon. It was close to midnight before she was clear of the shoals and islands and safely into the Bight of Bangkok, and with a fair north-easterly wind could set a course south for Singapura and the Java Sea. Teng handed over command to Li Yuan and went below, to a supper prepared by his steward Chou Tao. He had hardly seen Chou since coming on board, as he had gone straight on to the poop to make ready for sea. Now it occurred to him that the cook was somewhat nervous; as he placed the bowls of rice and sweet and sour pork and bamboo shoots and the little jug of sake on the table, the crockery clattered together — equally he seemed to have prepared far too much food.

'What is your trouble?' Teng inquired.

Chou Tao did not reply, but rolled his eyes and looked above his master's head. Then Teng, bending his head to pick up the first piece of pork between his two foodsticks, suddenly inhaled a most delicious perfume. He raised his head sharply, stared at the steward and then turned, to look at the Princess Jalina.

For a moment Teng's heart stood quite still. He had never seen anything quite like her before, for she wore the blouse and trousers of a Chinese peasant — the red contrasting strongly with her milky complexion — over soft boots. She had removed her hat, and her hair was confined in the required pigtail of one of the lower Chinese orders. Had he not known her to be a princess and remembered her in all the splendour of her cloth-of-gold skirt and tunic, her jewels, her attendants, he would have supposed her indeed to be nothing more than a runaway Chinese schoolgirl. Yet she remained the most beautiful woman he had ever seen.

'You see I keep my word, Teng Lee,' she said.

Teng swallowed, and looked at Chou Tao.

'Have I done wrong, master?' Chou asked.

'Wrong?' Teng wanted to scream. 'Wrong!' He pushed his bowl away and got up.

'Where are you going?' Jalina inquired.

'On deck, to turn this ship about, your highness. You must be returned to Bangkok before you are missed.'

'I am already missed,' she informed him. 'I instructed one of my secretaries to deliver, within one hour of your junk raising anchor, a letter I have written to my brother, to the effect that I am leaving Siam for ever, with you. I should think there are already warships sailing behind us. But I do not suppose they can overtake so fine a vessel as this.'

Teng dashed up the ladder to the poop, seized his telescope and studied the northern horizon. Perhaps he could make out sails there; he could not be sure.

Jalina had followed him. 'I did say that we would be returning to China,' she said. 'To make our home there. It is there that he will send to look for us. So it is unlikely they will come to the south.'

Teng groaned, and pounded his forehead with his fist.

'But I do not want to live in China,' the princess explained. 'I want to sail around the world with you.'

He turned to face her. 'Do you realize what you have done, your highness?'

'I have decided to live my own life.'

'And have thus ruined mine. Do you not understand that all my wealth is in China? You have made it impossible for me to return there. I was going to make my home in Bangkok. Your brother was going to give me a house close to the palace, and I was to have been one of his most trusted councillors. You have made that impossible, too. You have turned me into a fugitive, a man without a country, a man with nothing!' He wanted to weep. Everything had lain in his hand, every single thing he had aimed at since the death of Wu Chang. And this little chit of a girl had kicked it all away; he knew he dared not take her back to Bangkok. Even if she were

209

proved to be still a virgin — and he wasn't at all sure that the little hoyden *would* stand up to such an examination — he would still be regarded as the man who had abducted her, would stand accused of having been alone with her, whatever his protestations of never having touched her. He would be bastinadoed until on the point of death, then he would be castrated, then they would cut off his head and mount it on a pole.

He felt sick. Almost he wanted to dive over the side and consign himself to the deep, there and then; at least he would go to his ancestors whole.

It was Fate's doing, of course. He had thought he could laugh at Fate, because he could no longer be harmed, once the goddess had taken his wife and child. But no man could laugh at Fate. And now his arrogance was to be punished in the most terrible way.

'I had thought we would seek refuge with your friend Lord Minto,' Jalina remarked. 'You have told me that he is nearly as powerful as my brother.'

Teng raised his head in anguish. He had forgotten the exaggerated tales he had told her. Once again he was being punished, this time for his mendacity. 'That is impossible,' he groaned. 'Lord Minto is also a friend of your brother's. I am totally ruined.'

'Are you, Teng Lee?' the princess asked softly. 'In return for what you have lost, am I not giving you myself?'

He turned to face her, slowly. 'You are demented, your highness. Me? I am a Chinese merchant. I have no royal blood.'

'It is my royal blood that I am trying to get rid of,' she told him.

'I am old enough to be your father.'

'I am glad you are not my father. You are good, and kind, and honest. My brother has told me this, and I have observed it for myself. You are also healthy and strong, because this too I have observed for myself. I would

210

rather be wed to you than a Vietnamese robber and live in a mud hut.'

Teng stared at her.

'I am also very hungry,' she said. 'I have been confined in that laundry basket for several hours, with nothing to eat.' She went to the companionway. 'I instructed Chou Tao to prepare enough food for two. Will you not join me?'

Teng followed her as if in a dream. 'A laundry basket?' he asked. 'I do not understand.'

'It is very simple.' Jalina ate sweet and sour pork with great animation; the sauce dribbled down her chin. 'When I decided to leave Bangkok, I arranged to become ill. It was not difficult. I told my attendants you were becoming tiresome . . . my dear Teng,' she rested one superbly manicured hand on his for a moment, 'and that therefore I did not wish to see you again, a decision that they heartily applauded, I can tell you. But I also explained that, as you were such a favourite of my brother's, I could not just send you away. So I retired, insisting that I be left alone. I then changed into the Chinese clothes which I had worn for a masque at my father's birthday two years ago, made my way from the palace by the secret corridors I know, and crossed the bridge to Thon Buri. I hid in a ditch to pigtail my hair, and then sought out your steward. This too was not difficult, because everyone in Thon Buri knew of Teng Lee, and of his steward, Chou Tao. I found him in the act of retrieving your laundry, and explained to him that I was your woman, whom you were intending to take from Bangkok . . .'

Teng swung to face Chou Tao. 'And you believed her?'

'She gave me this, master,' Chou Tai said, and held up Teng's jade ring. 'And said you had given it to her to present to me, that I might understand she came on board at your command.'

Teng turned back to the princess, realizing that she must have planned this flight from the first time he had called on her this visit, when she had asked for the jewel – if indeed she had not planned it even before he returned to Bangkok. 'Have you no scruples, your highness?'

'Highness?' Chou Tao muttered, rolling his eyes again.

'I wished to be with you,' she said.

'To our joint ruination.'

He gazed at her, and she returned his gaze. 'Why do you not send the servant away,' she suggested.

Teng waved his hand without thinking, and Chou Tao left the cabin.

'He is suspicious anyway,' Jalina observed. 'But I do not suppose it is important. Now we can get to know each other.' She wiped her fingers on her napkin, stood up and lifted the blouse over her head. She wore nothing underneath, save for a small silk bag, which was suspended round her neck by a cord and nestled between the velvet skin of her breasts. She now lifted the cord over her head – the bag was obviously very heavy as there was a red line on her neck – and proceeded to empty the contents on to the table in front of him. Out spilled an assortment of rings, necklaces, brooches and unset stones, each worth at least as much as the entire junk, Teng knew at a glance. 'I told you I would replace your gift to me with something of greater value,' she said. 'And I do not even speak of myself.'

Teng was struck dumb, equally by the beauty and the wealth being thrust at him. Then he said, 'Your highness . . .'

'You cannot possibly continue calling me "your highness",' Jalina pointed out. 'Now I have something else to give you.' She released her waistband.

'Sit down!' Teng shouted in panic.

She raised her exquisite eyebrows, but obeyed him. Her breasts seemed to rest on the table. Thai girls had small breasts, for which he was truly thankful, or he did not think he would be able to restrain himself. He was not sure he would be able to do so anyway, especially as he was going to lose his head whether he touched her or not. But that someone as young and lovely as the princess could possibly wish to give herself to him was too overwhelming to accept. Of course, he could reason that if the choice truly lay between him and a Vietnamese lout, she had made the obvious decision; but he felt he simply had to protest, even if the deed was in effect already done — she could now offer herself to no one else.

And he objected to the feeling that he was being bought. That was surely the man's prerogative.

'Jalina,' he said. 'You have exchanged a life of luxury for one of toil and danger. Increasing toil and danger,' he added feelingly. 'You have fallen in love with an idea of travel and faraway places.'

'And with you,' she put in.

'With me? What can I offer a girl like you? I am more than twice your age, a humble Chinese merchant, and you are —'

'If you say that again, I shall strike you.'

He did not doubt she would do it. 'But please, can you not see this must surely be an idle infatuation, based on the stories I have told you . . . many of them lies.'

'You are a fool, Teng Lee,' she said. 'Do you suppose a woman is like a man, and seeks only physical beauty or worldly wealth? A woman knows to look deeper than the skin for her happiness. I have studied you, and I have chosen to love you. I shall not cease to do so. Is there some impediment in the way of your returning my love? You told me you had been widowed.'

'That is true.'

'Then do you not require a wife?'

'That is true, too.'

'And do you not like me? Perhaps I am not beautiful enough for you.' She stood up again, stepped away from

213

the table and released her trousers; she had already unfastened the waistband.

As with the blouse, she wore nothing underneath. Teng Lee watched the garment slide past her hips, then down her thighs, hesitate at her knees and gather in a rumple round her ankles.

'Once you told me I was beautiful,' Jalina continued. 'Now I think that was merely to flatter a princess.'

'I did not know how beautiful you were.' He held out his hands, and she stepped out of the trousers to come to him, but he caught her hands to stop her as she would have rubbed herself against his face. 'Jalina, you are committing suicide.'

'I have already done that.'

'But . . . me?'

'I beg you never to say that again. I have explained to you how a woman's heart seeks love. You are the only man I have ever met I have wholly admired, and envied.'

'Am I permitted to say that you have not met many men, Jalina? Only your father and brothers, your secretaries and your slaves. In this new life you have chosen there will be no slaves. Chou Tao is my only servant. There will be no one to manicure your hands or dress your hair. There will be no more jewels, and there will be constant fear that your brother's agents may catch up with us.'

'I will be free, until the moment they do, when I shall die,' she said. 'And I will be with a man I love, instead of one I hate. Will you not love me, Teng Lee?'

Teng sighed. But it would now be quite impossible to resist the demands of his own manhood, as he suspected she could see. 'Have you ever been with a man before, Jalina, my princess?'

She shook her head. 'But I have been taught what to expect, what to do, by my ladies. I have been prepared for marriage. I will not disappoint you, Teng.'

Teng released her hands and got up. 'Then unfasten that pigtail, and I shall try not to disappoint you.'

CHAPTER NINE

The Spy

The music stopped, and the whirling dancers also ceased their gyrations, most with relief, some with reluctance. Clive Hammond smiled down into the face of Amalia Hoorn. In her pale pink décolleté Empire gown, with her bare arms and her wealth of white flesh, her even whiter breasts straining against the thin muslin, and her fashionably upswept hair, she was as attractive as — he would have said in a London drawing room — she was indecent.

But she was part of the company, and she was very pleasant company indeed. He had seen a great deal of her during the fortnight since his arrival, because, as she was now eighteen years old, she no longer attended the classes conducted by the governess of her two younger sisters. She acted as a deputy for her mother in social affairs, and had set herself, or been set by her father, to entertain him. In addition, she now spoke English quite well — while his Flemish was still halting. Thus they were enabled to carry on private conversations, as long as they were out of earshot of her father. Not that she in any way suspected why he was in Batavia; she subscribed to the popular belief that he was a fugitive from English justice.

But he *was* here, and he had been accepted into this febrile society — even as he tucked her arm under his to go in search of some rum punch they were approached by Major Wrinteler, commander of the garrison of Batavia in the absence of General Groepner, who was up-country

216

conducting the never-ending campaign against the native princes. Wrinteler had interrogated him upon his arrival, with Teng faithfully at his shoulder, supporting his every claim. The major was a short, bow-legged man — a cavalry officer — who was near-sighted and therefore no longer considered suitable for field service. His pince-nez sat awkwardly on his nose, seeming to belittle the various medal ribbons on his chest and the gleaming epaulettes on the shoulders of his pale blue uniform. With the yellow stripe down his breeches and the gold braid on his jacket, together with his highly polished black boots, he might have been a hussar, his uniform designed by Murat himself. But he was, in fact, a representative of the new Holland, which was so closely united to the greatness of Bonaparte. This ball in Government House was equally representative of the new French spirit sweeping Europe, and now penetrating to the colonies: a world of indecent waltzes, and even more indecent gowns, of flirtations and fluttering fans, of brilliantly uniformed men and seductively smiling women. What the Dutch burghers, and even more their wives, most of whom had never left Batavia in their lives, thought of it all was impossible to say. They were all part of the very positive information Clive was assembling, with the aid of Pieter Hoorn, and if they made a compelling picture and a delightful society, he did not consider any of them were of the stuff to go down in blood defending their city for Bonaparte. While if the soldiers might be prepared to do so, he doubted their ability, if Wrinteler was an example.

Or their judgement, as they had accepted into their midst a scoundrel expelled from the very limited society of Penang. They had, moreover, made him the most popular young man in Batavia within a couple of weeks, because he was tall and dark and handsome, because he was a fugitive from the British — and because Major Wrinteler liked him. Major Wrinteler, indeed, regarded Clive as his own very special protégé. True, everyone

217

knew he was an acquaintance of Pieter Hoorn, and that he had fled to Batavia simply because, having been deported from Penang, he could think of nowhere else to go. The story of his unhappy clash with Major Blaine over an unfounded allegation of his amour with Mrs Blaine had been thoroughly publicized, by Wrinteler more than anyone – because Clive was naturally full of information about the British which Wrinteler found both valuable and reassuring. The young fugitive had not only spent a year in Penang, which he described as a half-asleep mud-hole run by incompetents, but had also touched at Calcutta before coming to Batavia. Calcutta too was lifeless and heavily occupied with threats from the Indian princes and the rampant Burmese, Clive had told him. Certainly he had seen neither the men nor the ships to indicate that the British could attempt any expansion into the Java Sea, even had they been so inclined.

Major Wrinteler had taken Clive to meet the Governor-General, Herman Daendals, also a confirmed Bonapartist, who, if not quite so easily taken in as the major, still could find nothing to fault in Clive's story, or anything to regard as dangerous in the presence in Batavia of a runaway English factor's assistant. He had instructed Wrinteler to forward a report of what Clive had to say to General Groepner – who worried more about what the British were doing than the Javanese he was fighting – and offered the major congratulations. Wrinteler, indeed, was prepared to take all the credit, if not for bringing Clive to Batavia, certainly for recognizing him as what he was: an angry young man who had turned against his own countrymen – there were few more valuable agents, in his opinion. Now he smiled and bowed to Amalia, clicking his heels as he did so. 'A splendid occasion, is it not, Mejnffrouw? Mijnheer Hammond, do you not enjoy our social occasions?'

'I have never known anything like them in my life,'

Clive admitted truthfully – the London balls and tea parties he had attended while enjoying the status of a successful author were totally ersatz compared with this.

'Ah, we have been taught how to live by our French masters. Mijnheer Hoorn.' He clicked his heels again as Pieter Hoorn came up to them.

Pieter Hoorn seldom let Clive out of earshot for very long. He had in fact been most suspicious and alarmed when Clive appeared two weeks before, and had taken some convincing that he was actually an emissary from Raffles. Even once he had accepted that, he was a very worried man, astounded at the boldness with which Raffles had pressed ahead, and for several days was able to envisage only his own imminent ruin, and that of his family. Gradually he had relaxed, but whenever Clive was in Wrinteler's company, he clearly still felt uneasy that he might make a slip. But Clive caught his eye and raised his eyebrows reassuringly.

'Your daughter grows prettier every time I see her,' Wrinteler remarked. 'Soon you will be finding a husband for her, eh?'

He laughed at Amalia's blushes, and she hastily released Clive's arm.

'Soon indeed, Major,' Pieter agreed. 'But it is late, and Mr Hammond and I start work very early in the morning. So I think we should be taking our leave. Your mother is waiting for you, Amalia,' he said meaningfully.

Amalia curtsied and hurried across the floor, while Clive bade the major good night and accompanied Hoorn more slowly towards the exit.

'What did he want?' Hoorn asked in a low voice.

'Nothing at all, save to flirt with Amalia. I really feel we have nothing to fear there.'

'Hm. Well, I have news for you. One of my people has reported seeing a junk he reckons to be the *Dragon's Wake* standing towards the roadstead this evening.'

Clive frowned. 'Already?'

219

'Exactly. Are you ready to give your friend the signal yet?'

'Well, I hadn't expected to have to come to a decision this quickly. But . . . yes, I think I am.'

'The sooner it is done, the better,' Hoorn said, wiping his neck with a silk handkerchief. 'I am too old for this business. And what do you suppose brings Teng back so soon? Something has miscarried, I'll be bound.'

'Possibly it has something to do with that storm last week,' Clive said soothingly. 'His ship may have suffered some damage. Anyway, I am certain he will be ashore to tell us, first thing tomorrow.'

He was on the dock to meet his friend. There was nothing unusual in this; Pieter Hoorn had appointed him to the position of dockmaster for the Hoorn products, pre-ferring to have him there than in the town office, or away on one of the plantations; it was on the dock that he could most easily note the comings and goings of ships, the arrivals and departures of men, under the guise of taking delivery of all goods incoming for Hoorn and Company or being shipped from their warehouses. So he waited, pad and pencil in hand, as if to take an early inventory of whatever Teng had brought for his employer, while the junk's boat was rowed between the breakwaters. The junk itself, he was relieved to observe, appeared quite undamaged, if it had encountered the storm.

The boat came alongside, and Teng hurried up the steps, moving much faster than was normal with him. His grasp was also tighter, as he shook hands. 'Clive! Is it well with you?'

'Indeed,' Clive acknowledged. But he frowned. He had never known Teng like this, a strange mixture of anxiety and elation. 'But what brings you back so soon? That storm last week?'

'That, certainly,' Teng agreed. 'But not perhaps for the

reason you suppose. Fate has sought to play me a trick. Is there somewhere we can speak in private?'

'Well, of course. Come into the warehouse. None of the Javanese understand English.'

Teng nodded, and turned back to look down at the boat. 'You can come up,' he said in Thai.

Clive did not understand the instruction, but he watched in surprise as a quite extraordinarily handsome Chinese youth rose from the transom, where he had sat beside Teng on the way in from the ship, and came up the steps. 'Your son?' he asked.

'Ah, no,' Teng said. 'But I would like him to accompany us, if you do not object. He is not feeling very well.'

Clive could see that, as the boy nearly fell on reaching the dock, and Teng had to grasp his arm. He did not look ill, and Clive surmised that he was suffering from the after-effects of seasickness.

'Of course you must bring him along,' he agreed. 'I have some arrack in the office. A shot might do him some good.' He led the two Chinese into the warehouse, through the piled bags of sugar and rice, the boxes of nutmeg and cloves and other spices, and the jars of coconut oil, which all combined to made a most heady scent. The office was to one side, and he closed the door on the three of them, before sitting behind his desk. There was only one other chair in the little room, and Teng offered this to the young man, remaining standing himself.

Clive opened one of his drawers, took out the bottle of arrack and a small glass, filled the glass and held it out.

The boy gazed at him with solemn eyes, then looked at Teng, who nodded. 'You can drink it,' he said in Thai. 'Sip it, like sake.'

The boy obeyed, gave a little shiver, took another sip and looked slightly more cheerful.

'Now take off your hat,' Teng commanded. 'And loose your hair.'

221

Jalina again obeyed, laying the broad-brimmed straw hat on the floor beside her, then releasing the pigtail. Clive gazed at her in consternation, then looked at Teng.

Teng bowed. 'She is a very high-born Thai lady,' he explained. 'Who has determined to share her life with me.'

Clive opened the drawer again and took out two more glasses, which he filled. The last of Jalina's hair was now free; he thought he had never seen anything more exquisite in his life than the piquant features shrouded in the silky black mass. 'I can only offer my congratulations,' he said. 'But . . . I think you owe me at least a little explanation.'

'Oh, certainly,' Teng agreed, sipping arrack. 'You should know that my wife has died.'

'My dear fellow, I am so sorry.'

'It was the hand of Fate,' Teng said. 'With her went my son. I was cast adrift in an emotional wilderness, from which Jalina has rescued me.'

'Jalina,' Clive said thoughtfully. He knew Teng well enough by now to be sure his friend was carefully selecting what aspects of the situation he should relate. As Teng himself had said often enough, words are there to be used to convey ideas — they have no intrinsic value in themselves.

'Unfortunately,' Teng went on, 'Jalina's family did not approve of our match, and so we have had to elope.'

Clive gazed at the girl, and she gazed back. She had now finished the arrack, and there was even colour in her cheeks. Her face remained solemn but quite unafraid, even though she had no idea what the two men were saying about her.

'Yes,' he agreed. 'I can see their point. She *is* a little young.'

'She is seventeen years of age,' Teng said.

'And you are . . .?'

'I am forty-two,' Teng agreed.

Clive had to resist an enormous temptation to smile. That Teng Lee, so completely master of his destiny, should have been so absurd as to elope with a girl less than half his age, almost restored his faith in human nature.

'The question is, what is to be done now?' Teng said.

'You are asking my advice?'

'No man can live for ever, however sage he may be, without from time to time requiring the counsel of others,' Teng pointed out. 'My life has been utterly destroyed.'

'Oh, come now,' Clive said. 'You have lost a market. And even that is not irreparable. Marry the girl, make her a mother and then go and patch up your differences with her family. You told me once you were on good terms with the King of Siam. Surely he would intercede for you, rather than have you never visit Bangkok again.'

Teng considered the matter for several seconds, then came to a decision. 'I think you should know,' he said carefully. 'That the Princess Jalina is King Rama's sister.'

'The Princess . . .' Clive looked at the girl, who had recognised her name and gave him a bright smile. 'You're not serious?'

'Unfortunately, I am.'

'Good God!' Clive remarked. 'When you decide to stir the pot, old friend, you use a mighty big spoon.'

'It is doubly sad,' Teng went on, 'because I had achieved a position of some standing with Rama. As you know, I was acting as his agent in his negotiations with Lord Minto . . .'

'I didn't know that,' Clive said. 'You never told me.'

'But now that is finished,' Teng continued. 'In fact, my life has been utterly destroyed. I cannot return to China, as Rama will certainly send to the Manchus for my head. I cannot return to Siam. There would appear to be nowhere that I can go. I have brought disgrace upon my family, and like you, I am friendless in the world.'

'Oh, you can count on me,' Clive said. 'In so far as I can help you at all. May I ask what King Rama and Lord Minto are negotiating about?'

'Why, an alliance, or at least, a treaty of friendship, between Great Britain and Siam. In fact, I have on board the letter from King Rama inviting Lord Minto to send an ambassador to Bangkok, in order that such a treaty may be concluded.'

Clive's brain was racing because he was suddenly beginning to understand the true situation. Minto did mean to invade Java, but he could not do so until he had closed all his back doors. Hence the necessity for a pact with Siam. Thus he would be waiting for Teng's return with the news he wanted. He would not act before he had received the necessary assurance from Rama, no matter what report Clive might send. And if he never got that assurance, he might never act at all. Nor would be, if he learned that Rama was vowing vengeance on his emissary.

So Teng *had* to deliver that letter, and before any other news from Bangkok reached Calcutta. But he could not let Teng understand the urgency of the matter. He would have to be as devious as the Chinese himself. The idea rather appealed to him.

'I see,' he remarked. 'But obviously it is the question of the princess that is most pressing. Do you wish to get rid of her?'

'Heaven forbid,' Teng said, squeezing Jalina's shoulder; she put up her hand to grasp his. 'She loves me. And I love her. She is all I have left in the world.'

'Except for your junk.'

'Except, as you say, for my ship,' Teng agreed. He had no intention of divulging that on board the *Dragon's Wake* at this moment were more riches than he had ever dreamed of possessing, even after obtaining a seventh share of his father's wealth.

224

'But I would be right in assuming that the princess does not wish to make a home on your ship?' Clive asked.

'Alas, that is now true. It is what she most urgently desired, before the storm. We were to sail the world together. But when the storm came, she was most terribly ill. It made my heart bleed to watch her vomit. I was afraid she would die. That is why we are here.'

'Quite,' Clive said. 'May I ask if you are married?'

'There has been no opportunity for a ceremony,' Teng explained. 'But I consider her as my wife.'

Clive decided to take the plunge. 'Then my advice to you is to mend what bridges you can. Leave Jalina here, to stay with the Hoorns, and then continue your journey to Calcutta with all haste. You say you have King Rama's letter with you?'

'Indeed.'

'Then why not deliver it, requesting Lord Minto to instruct his ambassador to be sure to make it perfectly plain, when he reaches Bangkok, that he is there in response to an invitation extended by *you* in the King's name.'

'You think that will earn my forgiveness from Rama, after I have run off with his sister?' Teng shook his head.

'You are sad, my Lee,' Jalina said.

Clive thought he had never heard a more liquid voice. And she certainly could made Teng smile. 'No, no, my sweet,' he replied in Thai. 'But it is difficult to see our way.' He squared his shoulders. 'I will do as you recommend, Clive. Do you really think Hoorn will accept Jalina as a guest, until I can find a home for us?'

'I am sure he will,' Clive assured him. Because he will have no choice, he thought.

Pieter Hoorn was actually even more taken aback to have Teng's mistress — she was carefully not introduced as a Thai princess — brought to his house than he had been at the arrival of Clive.

225

'They have eloped from Canton,' Clive explained, now thoroughly enjoying his new role of manipulator in the middle, whereas for so long he had needed to clutch at the strength provided by Teng and Raffles. 'As she suffers from seasickness whenever the weather is rough, he has nowhere for her to live. And he must continue his voyage, as he is on a most important mission for King Rama of Siam. A mission which vitally affects us as well. It will only be for a short while.'

'Having a Chinese girl in the house,' Hoorn grumbled. 'It will make people look at us. And ask questions.'

'Why? They all know that Teng is your friend, who visits you every time he is in Batavia. Why should his wife not come to stay with you for a while?'

'We live in a suspicious age,' Hoorn remarked.

'Dear friend,' Clive reminded him. 'You must accept her, because we have no choice in the matter: Teng knows what I am doing here.'

That made up Hoorn's mind, of course, and he was greatly relieved at the reception Jalina received when she was introduced into his household. The girls were delighted with her, as was Mevrouw Hoorn. 'Oh, what a charmer she is,' she declared. 'What a charmer. Teng Lee, you are a very lucky man. I hope you are going to treat her properly.'

'She is my wife,' Teng declared.

'That is as it should be. But is she properly your wife?'

'She will be. We have not yet had time to make our vows.'

'What a pity there is no active Buddhist temple here in Batavia,' Juliana Hoorn said. 'I don't suppose you would marry her in a Christian church?'

Teng glanced at Clive.

'That is something to be considered after he returns from Calcutta,' Clive told her, 'where he has the most urgent business.'

226

'Hm,' Juliana remarked. 'Well, until then, she can share Amalia's bedroom. They look about the same age.'

Teng looked at Clive again, who shrugged. 'You will be leaving tomorrow, in any event,' he pointed out.

Teng held Jalina's hand. The princess had been looking about her, taking in the Delft china and the chintz curtains and cushions, and even more the hair-styles and gowns of the sisters, with enormous interest, while she stared at the Negro serving maids with her mouth open; at least, he thought, everything was as he had described it to her. Now he sat her in an armchair and knelt beside her. 'You will stay with these people until I return,' he said.

'Without you?' she cried. 'We are to be together always, my Lee.'

'It will only be for a little while, my sweet,' he promised her. 'I do this to save you having to risk another storm at sea. Here you will be safe.'

'But if anything should happen to you . . .'

'Then you must trust this gentleman in everything.' He indicated Clive, and she gazed at him most solemnly. 'He is my friend,' Teng told her. 'He will never betray you. But nothing will happen to me, anyway. I have sailed this route forty times before without mishap. I will soon return.'

Jalina bit her lip and looked about to cry. Amalia immediately ran forward. 'Come with me,' she cried, holding Jalina's other hand. 'I will show you to our room. We are going to have such fun. I will teach you how to speak Flemish, and how to dress, and . . . everything.'

Jalina allowed herself to be drawn to her feet, reluctantly, but still obviously gaining confidence from the Dutch girl's warmth. Teng smiled at her in turn, and she allowed herself to be taken to the stairs.

'Well,' Pieter Hoorn said. 'I think this calls for a glass of good geneva, eh, Teng? We shall celebrate your new

227

happiness. And drink to all our fortunes,' he added meaningfully, looking at Clive.

Jalina was more amazed than ever at the meal to which they sat down that evening, and the sisters laughed happily as they taught her how to use a knife and fork, at which she was most unsuccessful, and as she sipped the geneva which Hoorn insisted upon giving her, and gave a shudder of distaste. But she was responding to the laughter and merriment about her, and even laughed herself, although she naturally only understood those exchanges Teng translated for her. By the end of the meal she was totally relaxed, and also slightly tipsy, and wept only a little when Teng said goodbye. 'I shall not sleep until you return, my Lee,' she promised, falling asleep as she spoke.

'I will take her upstairs,' Pieter Hoorn volunteered, and lifted her into his arms. 'Come along, Amalia, you will have to put her to bed.'

Clive walked down to the dock with Teng. 'I wish I could explain to you how I feel,' Teng said. 'On the one hand, my heart is filled with despair, and even anger, that all I have worked for, and all I thought I had achieved, has been set at nought. On the other hand, every time I look at the princess, much less touch her, I am overwhelmed with joy and cannot help but regard myself as the most fortunate of men to have been granted possession of such a jewel.'

'I understand entirely how you feel,' Clive said. 'Had Elizabeth been prepared to run away with me, had it ever been possible, I would have felt the same.'

Teng brooded at the dark water, across which the lanterns on the junk twinkled at them. 'I have often thought about that. Do you think I made a mistake in returning Mrs Blaine to Penang? Suppose I had kept her on board my ship and merely sent word to you that I had her there, would you have come and sailed with me?'

228

'Without hesitation,' Clive said. 'But . . . did she ever give any indication that that was what she wanted?'

'I do not think so,' Teng said carefully, and realised that this man's life was far more tortured than his own. As Hammond had pointed out, he at least had possession of *his* love. But there was more. Clearly Hammond still did not know that it was his son abandoned in Singapura. Would he have been able to enjoy Elizabeth knowing that? Or would he have thrown his life away in some futile effort to regain the boy?

Teng had no answer to those things. And anyway, in even suggesting that he might have kept the woman on board his ship, he was deceiving his friend; he had needed Elizabeth Blaine, he had supposed, to make the Governor of Penang give him that precious introduction to Lord Minto. If only he had known that Raffles was equally able to provide him with that . . . He sighed. 'I am sure, by the laws of yin-yang,' he said, 'that your life, which up to now has seen so much frustration and sadness, will one day soon become one of great happiness.'

'Even if I believed in yin-yang, I would have to doubt that,' Clive said. 'However, Teng, I would ask you to do something for me on this voyage. Do you intend to stop at Penang?'

'I had not intended to, as there is so much reason for haste. But I can do so if you wish.'

'Briefly. I would like you to tell Raffles that I am happy here. Very happy.'

Teng frowned at him in the darkness, obviously reflecting on what they had just been discussing.

'I know he worries about me,' Clive said. 'He is a true friend. I would like to reassure him.'

'Then I shall do that,' Teng promised solemnly. 'I shall tell him that you are happy here.' His face relaxed almost into a smile. 'And that you long to share your happiness with him, perhaps?'

'Pigue-nique,' Amalia Hoorn said, trying French as Flemish had had no effect. 'You savvy? Pique-nique?'

The Princess Jalina smiled politely but uncomprehendingly.

'Try her in English,' Amalia suggested to Clive.

'It is the same word in English. Well, virtually. Picnic. I am sure she will enjoy it. Why do we not just go?'

'Yes, let's,' said Louisa Hoorn.

Irene, the youngest sister, clapped her hands.

'Come along then.' Amalia held Jalina's hand and led her to the waiting trap, where the Negro slaves were already loading the hampers.

Jalina moved cautiously, as she was still unused to the buttoned boots and the stockings, the Dutch clothing into which the girls had fitted her, with as much glee, Clive suspected, judging by the peals of laughter coming from Amalia's bedroom, as if they had been playing with a life-size doll.

Presumably to them she was a doll; they had not the slightest idea that she was a real-life Thai princess – he had still not confided that fact even to Hoorn himself. But he wondered what Jalina really thought of it all. In the fortnight since Teng's departure – he should be back any day now, Clive reflected, his blood tingling at the thought of it – she had picked up one or two words of Flemish, and she had tried hard to learn to live like her hostesses. She appeared to enjoy doing so, for she seemed to be blessed with an inexhaustible curiosity, which made her anxious to try anything new at least once. She had even attended church with the Hoorns, but had clearly been able to make little of the very plain Dutch Calvinist service, the absence of any large numbers of robed priests, of incense, of chanting, and above all, of an enormous statue of the god these strange people were supposed to be worshipping – all so different to the splendours of the Wat Ching. When the congregation joined in singing one of the psalms, the high voices of the

230

women winging across the town and the road-stead, she had looked positively alarmed.

She was the gayest of companions, when in company. But Clive had observed that when not laughing, her face was unnaturally solemn, and at times even sad. Of course he knew she missed Teng. But even more, she was totally adrift in an entirely alien civilization; she still stared at the black people in amazement, and had no understanding of things like chamberpots and their usages – again to the amusement of the Hoorn sisters. They were astonished at her utter ignorance of the most elementary domestic matters. It was rapidly apparent, for instance, that she had never entered a kitchen in her life, nor did she show the slightest interest in picking up any of her clothes, which she let lie wherever they happened to fall when she discarded them. 'I do declare,' Amalia remarked, 'if this is how they live in China, I do not see how they have survived.'

Jalina had naturally aroused a considerable amount of interest amongst the burghers and their wives. Most of it had been hostile, as the Dutch did not believe in treating the native population as anything better than a work-force, and this included the small group of Chinese merchants who had set up their godowns in Batavia. Jalina was represented as being Chinese, of course – as indeed the Hoorns believed her to be – and it was regarded as definitely beneath Pieter Hoorn's dignity to have taken her into his house as a guest, even if she was the betrothed of his friend Teng Lee – but, then, his friendship with Teng had always been frowned upon as well, by the more strait-laced members of the community.

That there could be anything suspicious about this sudden influx of foreigners into the Hoorn household never seemed to cross anyone's mind. Major Wrinteler came to call the moment he was informed of the girl's presence, but Clive surmised it was more to inspect

231

someone who had been represented as remarkably lovely than for any reason of state. He had, of course, to make sure that she was in no way lowering the moral tone of the Hoorn household, and this obviously bothered him, for after he had sat and goggled at her for some time, he wagged his finger at Pieter Hoorn and warned him that he would be watching events with great interest, clearly presuming that the tale of her being Teng's intended was all subterfuge, and that the factor, no doubt with the permission of his wife, had simply imported a Chinese mistress under the guise of a house guest and playmate for his daughters. Clive felt that the major was actually more jealous than censorious.

So life had returned to normal. As it was again the monsoon season, there was less business than usual, and in addition society was rather dull, as the long hours of incessant rain limited all the more popular outdoor activities. Hoorn fretted, but Clive gathered from Juliana that he always fretted during the wet season. He could not tell whether Hoorn had confided his treachery to his wife, nor did he feel he could ask so delicate a question, but he felt called upon to attempt to calm his employer's nerves by reminding him that it would have to be at least a fortnight before Teng could make Calcutta and back, especially with a stop at Penang thrown in, and in unsettled weather. And even if Teng came back with positive news – which was unlikely, as neither Minto nor Raffles would actually wish to confide their plans to him – it would still be several months before an invasion fleet could be assembled. Hoorn's nerves were in fact the principal danger to the whole enterprise, so far as he could see; the Dutch had apparently become so convinced that the British really wished to maintain the status quo in the Far East, Clive felt quite sure that when the invasion fleet did appear, it would be welcomed and presumed to be seeking water and provisions.

From his point of view, life had never been so

comfortable. He was well paid, had a pleasant room in the Hoorn house, was tremendously popular with the burghers, as he went out of his way to ensure, and had really only half the work he had had to do at Gresholm's in Penang. He knew that if he could bring himself to forget about Elizabeth, he could actually be happy, for the first time in his life. Certainly, never had he been surrounded by such delightful companions. The three sisters, seeming to grow in womanhood with every day, even little thirteen-year-old Irene, adored him, and were quite immodest in their relations with him, bursting into his room as they felt like it, playing games and flirting with him, hugging and kissing him at the slightest opportunity. Juliana, indeed, had to lecture them from time to time, reminding them that if they thought of Clive as a brother, he was *not* their brother, and if they were not careful, at least in public, they would receive a visit from the morals committee, which had the power to order floggings for indecency. In fact, one of the most reassuring aspects of the society which he had infiltrated — at least from the point of view of a British spy recommending invasion — was the widening gulf between the mainly French-oriented adminstration, with its accent on the romantically frilly side of life, and the old colonial burgher class, desperately attempting to preserve the iron principles in which they and their fathers had been brought up.

Certainly the Hoorn girls were determined to be as French as possible, and as this morning the sun was actually shining, Amalia had decided on a picnic. Amalia usually got her way, and although her father shook his head and forecast that it would almost certainly rain again by afternoon, she persisted, and permission was granted for Clive to leave his office and accompany them, both to drive the trap and to make sure they were not upset by any sneaking Javanese or inquisitive snake. It was felt that the four girls would be sufficient to chaperon each other.

'Where are we going?' Clive asked, as he sat on the driving seat and grasped the reins.

'To an old Hindu temple I know of,' Amalia told him. 'It is not very far from town. Father took me there once, and I have always wanted to go back. It is a very special place. Louisa and Irene have never been there before. And I want to show it to Jalina too.'

The sun was very hot, but the trap had a roof, and the girls sat and laughed and chattered and drank lemonade as they trotted along. Clive wore a broad-brimmed straw hat and actually enjoyed the sun beating down on his back and shoulders, especially as he agreed with Hoorn that it would not last; heavy dark clouds were gathering over the mountains to the south-west.

'Hindu,' Amalia told Jalina. 'You know, Hindu?'

Jalina merely looked mystified, but she understood when she saw the ruined temple, nestling in a grove of high bamboos and hardly visible from the road, at the end of a two-hour drive from Batavia.

'Hindu,' Amalia explained again. 'Very old. Hundreds and hundreds of years.'

Clive helped the girls down and told them to stay by the trap while he went ahead of them into the temple. He knew that all manner of things lurked in abandoned Hindu temples, from runaway slaves to sleepy pythons. He was armed, of course, with both sword and pistols, but he would have preferred to have his trusty Malay kris with him as well. Yet as his feet echoed in the huge empty vault – the roof had fallen in long ago and was lying in clumps of shattered masonry on every side – he saw and heard nothing.

Except the spectacularly carved stone walls, and the beautiful mosiacs of the floor, which still showed a trace of the original colours. He could not help but pause in some concern, because they possessed all the delicate earthiness of the Hindu concept of life and love, overlaid with the eroticism of the islanders who had adopted it

234

centuries ago, before they were caught up in the strict puritanism of Mohammedanism. Even then, they had only accepted what truly interested them: few Javanese women, for instance, went veiled.

But what on earth could Amalia have had in mind, he wondered, bringing them to a place like this, especially as she knew what it contained? Her mother was going to be furious when she found out.

'Aren't those carvings superb,' remarked Louisa, coming up behind him.

'If only we knew what they were doing,' Irene grumbled.

'Oh, you know, they are, well . . .' Louisa looked at Amalia, who had led Jalina into the chamber and was also regarding the multi-limbed figures which were intertwined in a variety of postures.

'Making love,' Amalia said.

'Are they really?' Irene was intrigued. 'But what's that thing?'

'Ah . . . that's what the Hindus call a lingam.'

'A what? What does it do?'

Amalia looked at Clive, her cheeks pink.

'Nothing much,' he said. 'Do you want to explore further?'

Jalina clapped her hands and said something, presumably in Thai, which no one could understand, then followed Amalia and the other girls into the interior. Clive decided to hang back and unpack the picnic hampers; he had no doubt it would be a mistake to allow himself to become too interested in erotic art when in the company of four very nubile young women.

He carried the various boxes through the doorway and set them close to the outer wall, having checked again to make sure there were no snakes in the immediate vicinity.

Amelia came back to him. 'They want to swim,' she said.

'Swim?' he asked in alarm. 'Swim where?'

235

'In the sacred pool,' she explained. 'It is at the back of the temple. I'm afraid you will have to stay here.'

'You must be joking. Is it safe? What about alligators and things like that?'

'There are no alligators in Java,' she said severely. 'Only crocodiles.'

'That is very reassuring. Crocodiles are bigger.'

'And there are none in the sacred pool,' she went on patiently. 'You cannot come; they have already started to undress.'

'Oh. Well, if you're absolutely sure. . . .'

'Stay here and rest,' she recommended, and went off.

Clive lay down with his hands beneath his head and looked through the roof at the sky. It was intensely hot, and intensely pleasant . . . and intensely suggestive that four lovely young women were splashing about nude not more than a few feet away – he could hear them laughing and shouting – while the eroticism was enhanced by the sculpture surrounding him.

He dozed off and dreamed of Elizabeth . . . and was awakened by a stinging drop of water on his face, followed by a host of others as the rain teemed down, flooding through the broken roof to gather in pools on the temple courtyard. Hastily he moved the hampers to a dry place, while listening to louder than ever screams from the girls. He didn't know what to do; however tempting it was to see if they needed rescuing, he remained kneeling by the hampers. Amalia came back towards him, down the steps from the inner chamber which bordered the pool. She wore only her shift, which was very wet and clung to her like a second skin as she stumbled across the broken stone in her bare feet.

'It's torrential,' she said. 'Father was right.'

Clive forbore to remind her that he also had been right. 'What's to be done?'

'There is nothing we can do, now. They are all wet. Our clothes are all wet. Is the pony all right?'

236

'My God, I'd forgotten him. I'd better check.'

He ran to the doorway and looked out into the bamboos. The pony stood patiently in the rain, occasionally snorting; water was pouring out of the trap itself.

'What a mess,' Amalia said at his elbow; her hair was now plastered to her head. 'Well, we may as well eat. I will take food in for the others.'

'Can you manage?'

'No,' she agreed. 'You can lift the hampers. If you promise not to look.'

'If I don't look, at least where I am putting my feet,' he pointed out, 'I will very probably break my neck.'

'Oh . . .' She picked up the smallest of the hampers and hurried ahead of him. 'Into the pool,' she shouted. 'Quickly, now. Clive is coming.'

They gave squeals of delight, and he heard a succession of splashes. By the time he emerged on to the stone surround only their wet heads were showing, while the rain drops sizzled off the water around them.

'Oh, Clive,' Irene shouted. 'You're all wet.'

'You'll catch your death,' Louisa cried.

Jalina made a remark, punctuated by pearls of laughter.

'Just set it down here,' Amalia instructed. 'I will bring you something to eat in a moment. Now off you go.'

'Oh let him stay,' Louise begged.

Clive gave her a wave and went back through the inner chamber. He sat on a stone which was somewhat protected from the downpour and took off his shirt, wondering when the rain was going to stop. The wind had now risen, and the trees were bending and soughing. It was a thoroughly miserable afternoon.

'Here we are.' Amalia returned with the smaller hamper. 'I have brought enough for us both.'

For a moment her intention did not register, as he was too entranced with her attractiveness, revealed by her shift which clung to every curve and every valley of her body.

She knelt beside him to open the box. 'I don't think you should stay here,' he said.

She uncorked the wine and poured them each a cup. 'I cannot leave you alone.'

She gave him his cup and raised her own. They drank, staring at each other, and then they both moved their faces forward together, and their lips brushed. He was aware of utter confusion, his mind a strange mingle of animal desire and concern that this girl, all of them, were in his charge. But Amalia had planned this, it was clear. He knew she had been attracted to him from the beginning, but as she was so obviously a young girl and his heart was engaged elsewhere, she had seemed quite irrelevant to either his problems or his needs. Since returning here over a month ago, he had thrown himself into squiring her with all the enthusiasm at his command – she was his employer's daughter and her presence added to his ready-to-hand reasons for coming back to Batavia; the new government in Java, being French oriented, was most certainly romantic in concept.

But here she was in his arms, a delightful bundle of extremely voluptuous and anxious femininity, squirming against him as his lips caressed hers. They were both sopping wet, which made their scanty clothing no more than an outer skin. Then his hands were dragging the rain-wet cloth over her legs and thighs, scooping it to her waist, as she lay on his chest and played games with his tongue.

'Amalia,' he tried to protest.

'Do you not believe in Fate?' she asked. 'The Javanese do. Fate brought you to me. You resisted Fate, fought against it, I know, and went away. But Fate cannot be resisted. It brought you back again.' She rose to her knees and shrugged the wet garment over her head.

Clive realized that he had never held a naked woman in

238

his arms before, had indeed never even seen one. His London liaisons, no less than that unforgettable night in the lifeboat, had been conducted at once in the dark and in a whirl of silk and satin. But here, in this temple to the erotic worship of the human form, was total woman-hood, his to look at and his to possess. Her breasts were large and her thighs were wide, waiting. She was at once compelling and loving.

He was into her before he could stop himself, her virginity proving no obstacle to his passion. He caressed her nakedness, drawing murmurs of delight as she responded to his thrusts. When he finally came, she lay gasping on his chest. 'Oh, Clive,' she said. 'I am so happy. So very happy.'

She was still lying on his chest, fifteen minutes later, when they heard footsteps, and Clive watched the other three girls, appearing through the gloom, peering at them.

Irene gave a faint exclamation of alarm. Louisa just stared in consternation. Jalina clapped her hands in delight.

'Oh Christ,' he said, and attempted to sit up, having to roll Amalia off himself to do so, and hastily grabbing a sodden shirt to replace her.

'*That*'s a lingam,' Irene announced. 'Oh, Clive, I never knew you had one. I think I'm going to faint.'

She didn't, and Amalia lay on her back, sleepily blinking at her younger sisters. 'Well, gooses,' she remarked. 'Have you never seen a naked man before?' She gave a peal of laughter. 'Of course you haven't. Well, do not look any more. Clive is my lover.'

They shrieked their approbation, surrounded him with hugs and kisses, so much so that, as they were wearing very little and that was wet, he thought he could have any of the three of them, had he truly wished – and been able. Suddenly they had achieved intimacy on a vast scale, revealed themselves to him – dressed in front of him,

239

hugged and kissed him again as they climbed into the sodden trap together and began the journey back to town.

It was still drizzling, but Amalia sat on the driving seat with him and held his arm. 'I am so happy, Clive,' she said. 'So very happy. I always knew this day would come, and yet . . . one is never sure, until it happens, is that not right?'

Fate, he thought, and wondered what Teng Lee would make of it. But Teng Lee would heartily approve. So would Raffles. Oh, Raffles, certainly. There could be no better cover than for him to marry Pieter Hoorn's daughter — that would clinch his reasons for being in Batavia. Both Teng and Raffles would be sure that to forget Elizabeth Blaine and marry a girl at once loving, and free, and perfectly lovable, was the best course for him to take. And were they not right in that?

And if he did not, could never, love her as he loved Elizabeth? Forever was a very long time, as Teng had told him, especially when applied in a negative sense. Amalia Hoorn was everything a man could desire in a wife, providing his heart were not occupied elsewhere . . . and if that elsewhere were impossible to achieve, then he would indeed be a fool to tie himself up in dreams, forever.

'My Clive,' Amalia said, squeezing his arm. 'You are pensive.'

'I am thinking that I must talk with your father, as soon as I get back,' he said. 'And ask for your hand in marriage.'

'Oh, Clive, will you do that?' she cried, kissing his cheek.

'Well, I think I should . . . if that is what you wish.'

Was he still hoping for a way out, a rejection, perhaps, even if she had given herself to him?

She gave a scream of delight. 'Clive and I are betrothed,' she shouted, twisting in her seat. 'We are to be married.'

240

Louisa clapped her hands.

Irene said, 'I guessed it!'

'Married,' Amalia explained to Jalina. 'Married. Like you and Teng. Why, we could be married together.'

'She's a Buddhist,' Irene pointed out.

'Well . . . we could have a joint reception. We *shall* have a joint reception. Oh, I wish she could understand.'

Clive looked over his shoulder at the Thai princess. 'Teng, and you,' he pointed at her, 'and Amalia and I,' he pointed at himself. 'Marry.'

Jalina clapped her hands again, and said something in Thai.

'I love you,' Amalia said, squeezing his arm again. 'I loved you from the moment I first saw you. We are going to be so happy together.'

Strangely, he believed her.

'Hm,' Pieter Hoorn said. 'I do not know what to say.'

'We love each other,' Clive said earnestly. He could not actually tell his future father-in-law that he had anticipated the marriage. But Hoorn obviously was beginning to realize that; he was frowning.

'You have taken advantage of my daughter?'

'Let us say that we have mutually taken advantage of each other,' Clive suggested.

'Do you realize that you are a scoundrel, who has shamelessly betrayed my hospitality, and my trust, in allowing you to escort my daughters without a proper chaperon? Do you understand that I can have you locked up, and flogged, for fornication?'

'I realize that I am your partner in a very serious enterprise,' Clive told him, evenly. 'I trust we will bring it to a successful conclusion. But it must fail if we quarrel. I also know that Amalia is in love with me, and has been for some time, and that I am in love with her, and that we shall make each other very happy. I am also certain that, whatever we may have done to consummate our love, I

241

have done the honest thing in approaching you immediately on the matter and asking for your daughter's hand, instead of just trading upon our mutual necessity to remain friends.'

Hoorn gazed at him for a moment, then grinned and held out his hand. 'Forgive me, Clive. You are right, and I could wish no one better than you as a son-in-law. I am delighted. It is just that I lie awake at night, wondering if I have acted properly, what the outcome will be, if we will be found out before your friends arrive . . .'

'I think you have done the only thing you could do, having regard to your circumstances,' Clive assured him. 'I had not realized how stagnant affairs were here, until I saw your books. To have Great Britain in overall command of the entire East Indies must be to the benefit of every merchant in the area. Your countrymen will certainly applaud you, once the conquest has been successfully brought to a conclusion. As for being found out, who can betray us? Apart from ourselves, there are only three men in the world who know what we are about.'

'And one has to trust your Lord Minto, and your friend Raffles. Men I have never met,' Hoorn observed, gloomily.

'You have at least met Teng Lee, and know his worth.'

'Teng Lee,' Hoorn said with a shudder. 'He is the one I most fear.'

'Why? He will certainly never betray us now. You have his future wife in your keeping.'

'Is she really his future wife? I must confess I wonder about it. My God, Clive, sometimes I wish I had never started this terrible thing. To bring warfare to Java, European-style warefare — ships of the line, cannon — I sometimes suppose I have been an agent of the devil. When one thinks of the destruction . . .'

'We can hope it will be done so quickly there will be little destruction,' Clive said.

242

'Even a little destruction is too much,' Hoorn groaned. 'God, how I wish Teng would return with news of what is happening.'

Teng returned a week later. Both Clive and Hoorn were on the dock the moment the *Dragon's Wake* was sighted, waiting to welcome him ashore and hurry him into the privacy of the warehouse office. 'What news?' Hoorn demanded, speaking English. 'What news?'

'Did you see Minto?' Clive asked.

Teng bowed. 'His lordship is well pleased with me.'

'And Raffles?'

'Oh, indeed. Raffles asked me to give you a message in answer to yours. It is: "Your happiness in Batavia makes me glad. I have no doubt that when the monsoon ends, the sky will be bright with hope." '

'Next year,' Clive said. 'They will be here in the spring.'

CHAPTER TEN

The Conqueror

'Bless my soul,' remarked Sir Charles Wilmot. He looked from the sheet of paper lying on the desk in front of him, to the captain of the frigate who had brought the message from the Governor-General, to Raffles, who – having received a private communication from Minto which told him everything that was in the official letter of instruction – could hardly stand still he was so excited, and then at Blaine and Colonel Phillips. 'Bless my soul,' the Governor repeated. 'Why was I not informed of this venture before?'

'I think his lordship wished to make sure everything was in readiness for the campaign to begin, your excellency,' Captain Dawson suggested. 'Even we were not informed of our purpose until just before sailing. But you will observe that he now commands your total co-operation, and all haste, in this matter.'

'An assault upon Malacca,' Wilmot said. 'My word. That will stir things up.'

'Malacca is to be just a stepping stone on the way to Batavia,' Dawson explained.

'Oh, quite. That is what the letter says. Good Lord, what an undertaking. But haste. Yes, of course, haste. We are commanded to supply a contingent, Colonel. How many men are fit for duty?'

'I had two hundred and three on parade yesterday morning, sir,' Phillips told him. 'But there are some thirty in sick-bay who will soon be on their feet again, God willing.'

244

'Well, we must keep ourselves adequately garrisoned.' Wilmot declared. 'I mean, with Siam just across the water, waiting to attack us. . . .'

'But that is the whole point, your excellency.' Raffles could contain himself no longer. 'Lord Minto has just concluded an alliance with Siam, which frees us from any threat to the north. I think we should send every man we can spare.'

'And you are to accompany the troops,' Wilmot remarked, peering at the letter again. 'As administrator of the conquered territory. I must say, I find that the most remarkable thing of all. But I suppose it is a promotion. Yes, indeed. I congratulate you, Stamford. Now, Colonel, I suppose we could send a hundred and fifty.'

They settled down to haggle over figures, and Raffles accompanied the frigate captain outside. 'I gathered from his lordship that you are to act very much as his deputy until his arrival,' Dawson said, somewhat disapprovingly; he was several years older than the pale young secretary. 'Have you any military experience? Or naval?'

'None, sir,' Raffles confessed. 'I shall not interfere with your arrangements, you may be sure of that. I am to organize the victory, pending, as you say, the arrival of Lord Minto himself. I take it there will be a victory?'

'Oh, I could take Malacca with one ship, much less two, providing I have an adequate landing force.'

'I am sure you can,' Raffles agreed. 'But would it not have been better to assault Batavia directly? I mean, taking Malacca first will but alert the Hollanders in Java as to our intention. While once Batavia has fallen, Malacca will be isolated, and can be taken even more easily.'

Dawson smiled condescendingly. 'There you show your lack of strategic appreciation, Mr Raffles. We could not possibly undertake an invasion of Java while a Dutch outpost lay behind us.'

'Even one as weakly held as Malacca?'

'It is the principle,' Dawson told him. 'In fact, my instructions are not only to seize Malacca, but also the island of Bencoolen, just across the strait, so that we have the entire bottle-neck in our power, so to speak. In any event, as you can see, the main force for the taking of Java has not yet arrived. I believe the assault force, which will be commanded by Brigadier Gillespie, will be assembled very shortly, but the rest of the army, under the overall command of General Sir Samuel Auchmuty, is still being raised. And, of course, Lord Minto intends to accompany the expedition personally. The entire armament will sail to Malacca once I inform them that the city is in our hands, and from there will launch the attack on Batavia. I assure you that it has all been most carefully planned. Well, sir, Mr Raffles, I look forward to entertaining you on board the *Lion* as soon as you can have your gear made ready.' He hurried down the steps.

'One would almost think you had had a hand in organizing this venture,' Blaine remarked. He had followed them from the office.

'Yes,' Raffles agreed. 'One would. Do you mind if I call on your wife? I believe Flora is taking tea there this afternoon, and I must inform her right away that I am leaving.'

'Of course. I will come with you. I am sure all the ladies will be interested.'

They walked across the lawn together. Raffles' brain was quite swinging with excitement; all his hopes seemed about to be realized. He had waited for so long he had never really expected this day to arrive; certainly he had never anticipated being given an executive role in the campaign. It was like a dream come true. His elation was tempered only by his fears for Hammond and Hoorn, especially Hammond, as a result of this new plan of campaign.

'Do *you* consider it necessary to seize Malacca, and this

place, Bencoolen, before assaulting Batavia?' he asked Blaine. 'Bencoolen, as I understand it, is a virtually uninhabited island of the Sumatran coast, quite lacking in any kind of harbour, and a pestilential hole into the bargain. And Malacca has never been restored to its old importance since we gave it back to the Dutch.'

'Well, as for pestilence, a few cases of fever are synonymous with campaigning in the tropics,' Blaine pointed out. 'And I am sure there are sound strategic reasons for securing our bases. Why are you so concerned at the decision to seize them? I had understood it was your dream to have all the Dutch possessions in the Far East flying the Union Jack. Batavia will certainly fall.'

'I have no doubt about that,' Raffles said. 'It is merely that I happen to know that the Governor-General has some agents in Batavia, from whose information I would estimate he had formed his plans for the attack. Once the Dutch know that we mean to make a war of it in these waters, I wonder what their position will be.'

Blaine shrugged. 'Spies, like soldiers, must accept the risks they run. If they are found out, I imagine they will be shot, or hanged. All we can do is avenge them. Ah, my dear, Raffles has the most tremendous news,' he announced, as they went up the stairs to the verandah.

There were six ladies enjoying afternoon tea and gossip on the Blaines' verandah, served by the attentive Malay houseboys, and without doubt they were dominated by the blonde beauty of Mrs Blaine. Raffles felt that he had to take off his hat to her for the way she had fought her way to acceptance by Georgetown society. She had not in fact been rejected by that society, even in the beginning, when the scandal over her husband's challenge to Clive Hammond was on every lip. The general feeling had been that, whatever crime she and Hammond might have committed, she was to be pitied for her experiences with Perak Shah. And if everyone had agreed that she should have killed herself rather than submit to the embraces of a heathen savage, yet as she *had* survived those embraces, she was the most interesting arrival in Penang for many a year. Not that she had ever told of them, so far as Flora Raffles, at any rate, was able to ascertain. Instead she had sat out the innumerable tea parties and dinner parties and coffee parties, at which she had been the recipient of sidelong glances and loaded questions, until her presence began to appear perfectly normal.

Her looks and her suggestion of an erotic past had from the beginning made her a great favourite with the men, although there again, so far as Raffles was aware, she had permitted not even the slightest flirtation. That would have been disastrous for her, as Blaine watched her very carefully. Their private relations Raffles did not like to consider. At least in public, and however withdrawn her expression and her mind seemed sometimes to be, she never revealed a trace of the misery he felt sure she was experiencing, day in and day out.

Thank God, he thought, that she had no idea Hammond was in Batavia, waiting for their arrival . . . or for the executioner's rope, which had so suddenly become likely.

'Do you mean you wish to trade these?' Pieter Hoorn scratched his head and looked at the jewels Teng had spread before him. 'But this is a fortune.' He looked up at his friend suspiciously. 'How did you come by them?'

'They are my wife's dowry,' Teng explained.

'Good Lord!' Hoorn picked up one of the ruby brooches, fingered it, then passed it on to Clive for his appreciation. 'Quite exquisite.'

'You are a sly old devil, Teng,' Clive remarked. 'I had supposed you destitute.'

'A man does not wear all his wealth on his sleeve, or spit it forth from his mouth,' Teng pointed out. 'Yes, Hoorn, the stones are very fine. But they are of no value to me, as jewels. I need the capital to recommence my business, and I know that most traders would seek to rob a humble Chinese sea captain.'

'Oh, indeed,' Hoorn aid. 'But I am afraid I do not command sufficient funds to pay you for these.'

'I do not require to be paid in silver. At least, not for the main part. Let us arrive at a valuation of the stones, and I will give you a certain number of them in return for goods of an equal value, that I may recommence trading. We can continue to deal from that basis, as I make some profit.'

'Hm,' Hoorn said. 'You know, of course, that things in Batavia are going from bad to worse. The British blockade of Europe means there are no markets there any longer. My business dwindles every day. Ask Clive how many ships have cleared the port in the past month, while he has been here.'

'Five,' Clive said. 'Including the *Dragon's Wake*.'

'In brief, my only hope of avoiding bankruptcy in short order is to pray for something to happen to improve the situation' – he gave Clive a sideways glance – 'or to find new markets here in the East. In fact, I was hoping to expand my business with China; there is nowhere else I can sell my sugar in bulk. But you say you cannot return to China. This is catastrophic news.'

'I think it is possible, that were I to go as far as the Philippines, with which my brothers trade regularly, I should be able to make contact with them, and through them recommence a certain trade between Canton and the Java Sea, which would provide an outlet for your produce. It will take longer than before, of course, and thus be an added expense because of the extra transhipment, and I will have to see if I can secure warehousing rights in Manila. My own trade too will suffer, as Bangkok is now closed to me, as well as one or two other places. However, with the aid of my friends, I can see new markets possibly opening up in the course of time. What I must have is a headquarters where I know my

249

warehouses will be protected, my goods and my people safe during voyages.'

'And this cannot be in Manila?'

'Ah, no,' Teng said. 'That will have to be a transhipment base only. The Spanish are an untrustworthy people, and an agreement made today can be undone tomorrow at the behest of some priest who tells them that a pact signed with a non-Christian is not necessarily to be honoured.'

'With a non-Catholic, you mean,' Hoorn growled. 'And you also need a home for your young lady.'

'A headquarters,' Teng repeated. 'With a house for myself, to be sure. But also with adequate, safe, warehousing facilities. The question is, where is this to be found? My instincts are for Batavia.'

'Of course,' Hoorn agreed. 'It is the most populous city this side of Calcutta.'

'Indeed. But what assurances do I have that my goods and my new home will not be destroyed or confiscated in the near future?'

Hoorn and Clive exchanged glances. 'Why should that happen, Lee?' the Dutchman asked.

'Do you really suppose I am that innocent, Pieter?' Teng replied.

Hoorn and Clive exchanged glances, and Clive shrugged. 'Well, I suppose we cannot guarantee that, at this moment,' Clive said. 'But in view of your services, Teng, and your loyalty to our cause, I think I *can* guarantee you preferred treatment and total protection once Java becomes a British colony.'

'Which will be when?'

'I expect to see a fleet appear on the horizon at any moment, now that the rains have gone. Certainly by the time you return from your next voyage.'

Teng nodded. 'That will be satisfactory.' He swept the precious stones back into his bag.

'Do you realize that scoundrel has virtually held us to blackmail?' Hoorn remarked, as they stood on the dock, together with Amalia and Jalina, to watch the *Dragon's Wake* sailing away from Batavia.

'I doubt he thinks of it that way,' Clive suggested. But Teng had certainly had a very good week in Batavia, with the Hoorns going out of their way to humour him, so that Jalina had been allowed to go out to the junk every day, in the company of the three sisters and Clive, of course. The arrangement had suited everyone, even Juliana, who was perfectly sure they were behaving in a most seemly manner – naturally no one had told her that Clive and Amalia had already consummated their love. Once on board, Amalia and Jalina were each given a separate cabin, while Louisa and Irene, to their great joy, were allowed on deck to play at *go* with Li Yuan, who equally thoroughly enjoyed the company of two pretty girls, even if he could not understand a word they said. Below decks Clive and Teng were able to enter a wondrously private world, where there was not the slightest risk of interruption. After a lazy afternoon, all six of them would gather in the main cabin of the junk for some of the Cantonese cuisine so deliciously prepared by Chou Tao, which they washed down with cups of heady sake. Of course the two younger girls knew exactly what was going on, but they were delighted to be included in the conspiracy, both to outwit their mother and the good burghers of Batavia, and also to assist the happiness of Amalia and Jalina.

It was thus an even happier week for Clive. Never before had he been the object of so much adoration. Amalia was so loving that he could not help but respond, and his very last doubts and hesitations were swept away. That he had been her beau ideal since their first meeting was very obvious, and she confessed she had spent the entire year of their separation dreaming about him – his return seemed like a gift from heaven, which was why she

251

had hardly hesitated before plunging into letting him know her feelings. Her love, and her dreams, left her as far removed from her mother's strict concept of correct moral behaviour as could be imagined, at least where Clive was concerned. She wanted only to be in his arms, naked whenever possible, which of course was never within the Hoorn household.

Thus the junk was for them both an escape into paradise, while sharing such stolen moments brought Teng and himself closer together than ever before.

'Well,' Hoorn remarked, as they turned away. 'Now we can but wait on events. It cannot happen too soon for me, I can tell you that.'

He continued, in Clive's opinion, to be the weakest element in the entire situation, with such careless remarks in front of his daughters; but Amalia did not seem to have heard him, as she remained looking out to sea. 'There is a ship standing in.'

'A ship?' Hoorn spun round again. 'Only one?'

'For God's sake control yourself,' Clive snapped. 'People are watching you.' He stood beside Amalia to stare out to sea; Teng's junk was now almost lost to sight, but the other vessel was approaching every moment. 'I can see only one.'

'By God, but I thought the moment had arrived,' Hoorn said in a lower tone. 'One ship. And standing down from the north. That hardly makes it seem as if the British are holding the strait, eh? I shall go home. You'll accompany me, if you please, Amalia, Jalina.'

'I'd better stay until she reports,' Clive said, and squeezed Amalia's hand. 'I'll be back in an hour.'

In fact he was at least as interested in the new arrival as he was disappointed that she was obviously not the advance guard of a British fleet; her rig was definitely European, which meant there was the possibility that she had slipped through the blockade and come down from

252

Holland. In which case, even if she had no goods to be traded, she would have news, of which they had been sadly starved these past few weeks. As she came closer, however, he saw that she was too small to have undertaken so long a voyage, although she was certainly flying the Dutch flag. Therefore she had to be out of Malacca, which was the only Dutch port to the north of them, and would hardly be carrying anything of interest to Hoorn and Company.

But as she came closer yet, he began to frown. She seemed to have been in a battle. His first impression was that she must have encountered Perak Shah's pirates . . . but if she had, then the Singapuran had got hold of some cannon; there were shot marks on her hull, her bulwarks were holed in several places and her canvas was torn. She was also in a great hurry, for she sailed nearly up to the breakwater before dropping anchor; and before she had even brought up, her boat was swung out and into the water, and was pulling for the shore.

Her appearance and unusual behaviour had been observed from the fort, and men were hurrying to greet her. Clive went with them. He was only a few feet from Wrinteler when the Dutch captain leapt ashore. 'The British,' he gasped. 'They have seized Malacca. Two frigates, soldiers . . . they suddenly appeared, bombarded their way into the harbour, put men ashore. . . . When I realized what was happening, I up-anchored and escaped. They fired into me, as you can see. And at least five ships were taken at anchor.'

'My God!' Wrinteler shouted. 'And the city? What of the city?'

'It has fallen, I would say. The firing had stopped before we were out of earshot, and the British frigates were still in the harbour.'

'By God,' Wrinteler said again. 'General Janssens must know of this.' Janssens had recently been promoted to supersede the incompetent Groepner as commander of

253

the Dutch forces, and was already down in the south-west conducting operations.

And Mijnheer Hoorn as well, Clive thought, hurrying in the other direction. He could not imagine what Raffles thought he was doing. The whole concept, as he understood it, had been based on a direct assault on Batavia, when the surprise appearance of a British fleet would cause those elements in the colony hostile to Bonapartism to hesitate and be overwhelmed before the Francophiles could rally them. Malacca had no part to play in the plan; even if the Dutch there had seen the British squadron sailing past them, they could not have sent word to Batavia in time. Nor were there any sizeable Dutch ships in the harbour to dash out upon the British flanks; the place was simply too small. Now Batavia was alerted, and there would be time for Janssens to bring his men back from the south to the defence of the capital, and make sure that the burghers knew which side they had to be on – under pain of death, most likely.

Hoorn listened to what he had to say in equal dismay. 'These friends of yours are either incompetent, or they are playing us false,' he growled. 'What can we do?'

'Nothing, but sit it out,' Clive told him.

The girls and Juliana were also highly agitated, while Jalina looked from one to the other in bewilderment, unable to understand what was happening.

'Who would have thought it of the British?' Juliana complained. 'It is years, more than ten years, since they fought us out here. Everything was going so well. . . .' She looked reproachfully at Clive.

'Things were not going that well,' Hoorn told her. 'So perhaps it will all turn out for the best. Certainly there is no need to be alarmed by the situation.' His own expression, and his sweat, belied his words, and when there came the sudden jingle of harness on the street outside, followed by the tramp of booted feet on the garden path and a heavy thump on the front door, he looked ready to faint. 'Open it, you black devil,' he bellowed at his butler.

The man hurried to the door, and admitted a lieutenant in the regular army, dressed in his white jacket and breeches, with yellow facings and epaulettes, his black shako with its huge yellow plume tucked beneath his arm, while his sword slapped his black boots. Six troopers remained at the door.

The lieutenant saluted, his face very serious. 'There is a summons to arms of every able-bodied man in Batavia, Mijnheer Hoorn,' he explained, trying to ignore the excited girls. 'You are requested to report immediately to the fort for weapons and instructions.'

'My God,' Hoorn said. 'Well, I suppose I must go, even at my age.' He looked at Clive.

'Oh, Clive cannot be expected to go,' Amalia declared. 'He is English himself.'

'Indeed he is, Mejnffrouw,' the lieutenant agreed. 'I have a warrant here for his arrest. You will accompany me, please, Mijnheer Hammond.'

'Arrest?' Clive demanded. 'On what charge?'

'On the charge of being an enemy alien. The order is signed by Mijnheer Daendals himself.'

Amalia Hoorn fainted.

'This is a catastrophic situation.' Pieter Hoorn stood in the middle of the tiny cell, one of several situated down in the dungeons of the fort. He inhaled the foetid air, looked at the damp walls and the crawling insects and listened to the slurping water only a few feet away. The fortress had been built on the very edge of the sea, close to the breakwaters which enclosed the harbour; and the surrounding land was swampy. It was about the most unhealthy place in the colony.

'I have been in a cell before,' Clive reminded him. 'Although, and I hate to say this, the cell in Georgetown was far superior. Nor did I have to stay there very long. I am hoping my acquaintance with this pest-hole will be similarly brief.'

Hoorn peered at his future son-in-law. Clive actually looked quite well and healthy – but, then, he had only been here two days. 'How are they treating you?'

'Very well. They seem rather apologetic about the whole thing. And what you have brought me' – he looked at the hamper of food and the parcel of clean clothing – 'will of course make things much better. You must thank Mevrouw Hoorn most warmly for me. Now tell me, how is Amalia?'

'Oh, she has recovered – her strength if not her spirits. She moans and wails, and is sure that she will never see you again. I do what I can to reassure her. But I was talking about the whole situation. You realize that the entire colony has been called to arms?'

'And very smart you look too,' Clive assured him. Hoorn was wearing the tight blue jacket of the militia infantry, with red collar and cuffs and sash, and dark grey trousers. As a lieutenant he was permitted only a single epaulette, on his right shoulder, and the hat might have been an ordinary beaver but for the high white plume and the huge badge situated immediately above the brim. His only weapon was a straight sword. 'Do you think your comrades will fight?'

'I have no idea. But I must go along with them, at least until the last possible moment. Otherwise . . .'

Clive shook his head warningly. He was not sure whether there was some means of overhearing what was said in the cell, and Hoorn had a booming voice. 'Of course you must defend your country to the last possible moment,' he said, equally loudly. And then dropped his voice to a whisper. 'But you must also endeavour to weaken your friends' resolve by convincing them that resistance is useless.'

Hoorn appeared not to understand him. 'It would be

too horrifying were I to be shot down defending this place just before the British conquered it.'

'One cannot possibly suppose the British could take Batavia,' Clive said, again in a loud voice. 'I am only sorry I am on the wrong side in this quarrel. You know my feelings. I fled here to avoid British justice. I cannot imagine my fate were they to find me here. Now you must convince Wrinteler and Daendals of that, and secure my release as soon as possible. And then, why, I shall join you on the battlements of this very fort.'

He pushed Hoorn, a sadly confused man, through the doorway, and then sat on the cot and fanned himself, a prey to the most lively apprehensions. For however confident he felt it necessary to appear to Hoorn, he was well aware that he was in a most dangerous situation, and one in which he was quite helpless to influence the course of events; his survival seemed to rest on Hoorn keeping his head, which was becoming daily less probable, and on Raffles arriving here quickly.

That also daily seemed less likely to happen in time. His anxiety increased as the weeks went by and nothing happened, at least in a positive sense for his rescue or release. He did not know if Hoorn had approached the Governor-General — the visits became less frequent as Hoorn's duties increased; and too often the door had to be left ajar, with the guard standing immediately outside making it impossible to discuss anything of importance. Not that there was anything to discuss, for the garrison of Batavia knew as little about what was happening as he did in his cell. He gathered that ships had been sent north in an attempt to reconnoitre the British position, but they brought back no information other than that a British force had landed on one of the islands off Sumatra, called Bencoolen, and were apparently fortifying that — why, no one could imagine.

He longed for Teng to return, because Teng would surely have news. But Teng did not appear, and the cell grew daily more noisome, while not even Juliana's efforts could keep his clothes wholesome or his food edible – although he shuddered to imagine his fate without her. She also sent him books to read, but the cell had but a single small grating set high in the outer wall, and the light was poor, and besides, his mind was too consumed with worry. Spring was almost over, and once summer arrived, the next monsoon season was also in sight. There could be no British fleet in these waters come the monsoon.

Summer brought a new complication. Amalia was not allowed to visit him, for which he was in fact grateful, as he did not know how he would cope with either her grief or her remonstrations, but there came the day when Hoorn came in and sat on the cot without a word for several seconds.

'Whatever is the matter?' Clive asked at last.

Hoorn sighed, and humped his shoulders, and stared at the wall. After several seconds, he said, 'Amalia is pregnant.'

'My God!' Clive sat beside him.

'It is your child,' Hoorn announced.

'Well, I sincerely hope so. How splendid. Oh, I wish I could see her.'

'My God, you can just say that. She is five months gone, she thinks. And she, and her sisters, and that Chinese girl, have concealed the fact from us all this time. I cannot believe it. Do you understand the implications?'

'There will be talk,' Clive agreed. 'Well, you will just have to arrange for us to be married immediately. Surely there can be no objection to that? In England, I believe it is a popular pastime marrying prisoners, especially if they happen to be condemned. Instant widowhood and that sort of thing, which can be useful.'

'It pleases you to joke about everything,' Hoorn grumbled. 'This is not England, my friend, and sexual excesses are regarded more seriously here than under

258

your regency, eh? If I go to the courts and ask for a marriage licence in such haste as to permit Amalia to marry you while you are in prison, they will ask why. If I tell them, they will accuse my daughter of fornication and lewd behaviour. Why, she could be sentenced to a flogging.'

'Not until after she has had the child,' Clive pointed out.

'Juliana is quite distraught. She has taken to her bed and does not wish to hear your name spoken again. The disgrace of it,' Hoorn said, holding his head in his hands as he wandered from the cell, leaving the guard to bang the door. 'My daughter is in disgrace.'

Clive realized his life was hanging even more by a thread while his future father-in-law was in so depressed a mood. During the next week he was nearly out of his mind with despair and misery, for the clean laundry and extra food suddenly stopped coming. Then without warning there was a most tremendous trample and bustle above his head, punctuated by bugle calls. He could not see out, as there were no windows in his cell, only the single grating above his head, but he gathered from the various shouts he could hear – and the gunfire that soon commenced, causing the old stone walls to shake in a most alarming fashion – that the British fleet had at last appeared off the breakwater.

His initial reaction was to shout for joy, but as he listened to the unceasing cannonade, he realized that these next few hours would be vital to his existence. Obviously, if the resistance was going to be as determined as it appeared, Minto might well decide that his reports had been over-optimistic and sail away, implementing the threats he had made in Calcutta. That evening the noise died away, and he feared the worst. He hardly slept, and was rudely disturbed just after dawn when the door of his cell was thrown open. An officer and four men stood there, together with a parson, and beyond them,

Pieter Hoorn, looking very serious indeed. Amalia, weeping her head off, rested on Jalina's arm, her sisters supporting her other side.

'My God!' He scrambled up. 'You are ill, my love.'

'We will allow you one minute with your betrothed, Mijnheer Hammond,' the lieutenant said, 'and then three minutes with Reverend Kuyper. Then we must be about our business. Time is short.'

'One minute? Three minutes? What are you talking about?' Clive demanded.

Amalia gave a shriek of the purest misery.

'Yesterday you were tried and condemned by a military tribunal, as a spy against Holland,' the lieutenant said.

'Tried, and condemned? That is impossible. I was not even informed that I was accused,' Clive declared.

'A deposition was made,' the lieutenant said. 'And in time of war, with the enemy knocking at our gates, that is sufficient.'

'Sufficient?' Clive shouted. 'Accused? By whom?' He glared at Pieter Hoorn, who gave his head a brief, helpless shake. 'Have I not the right to face my accuser?'

'There was no time,' the lieutenant told him. 'Nor is there time now. General Janssens has implemented his decision that Batavia is not defensible, and has ordered the evacuation of the fort by all military personnel. The general considered that you should be hanged from the battlements as a warning to all those who would seek to betray our cause in the coming struggle. Now, Mijnheer, you either take advantage of my offer, or I must ask you to accompany me immediately to the gallows.'

'But . . .' Clive looked at the parson, then at Hoorn again. 'Is this justice?'

'It is justice as practised by our masters,' Hoorn said, 'who have learned it from the Jacobins. As they have learned their strategy. I am being asked to abandon my family and my warehouses for a campaign in the jungle. I

260

have endeavoured to persuade this good fellow to wait ... the city is about to fall ... British troops have been landed north and south of us. ...'

'You are speaking out of turn, Lieutenant Hoorn,' the lieutenant said severely.

'But you are about to murder my betrothed,' Amalia wailed, half falling through the doorway to reach Clive's arms. 'The father of my child.'

'Mejnffrouw, you are behaving in a most unseemly manner,' the officer remarked, clearly at once embarrassed and annoyed by the way things were getting out of hand. 'And, indeed, condemning yourself. When your case comes before the courts next week, I will have to report this virtual admission of your guilt.'

'Next week,' Amalia sneered. 'Next week you will all be in the jungle, fighting the crocodiles. Do you think I care whether you consider me guilty or not? Yes, I am pregnant. Yes, Mijnheer Hammond is the father. Yes, I have fornicated with him. Time and time again. So flog me through the streets if you can spare the time before the British throw you out. You have no right to deprive a woman of her future husband, or a child of his father.'

The Reverend Kuyper gasped at such impudent impropriety. The officer was equally taken aback, and looked at Hoorn. 'I suggest you remove the young lady, Mijnheer Hoorn,' he said.

But as he spoke there was a fresh outbreak of firing from quite close, and this was musketry rather than cannon fire. The sound, added to Amalia's desperate defiance of the authority under which she had lived her life, galvanized Clive into action. He had never actually fought anyone in his life before, not even with his fists, but he had spent sufficient time in Raffles' back garden practising to do so, and if he lacked a kris, he had no doubt that he and Hoorn could win the day against these fellows, who were obviously in a great hurry to be off.

'Together, Hoorn,' he bellowed, as he thrust Amalia

261

behind him, reached for the parson, seized him by his cassock, picked him up and threw him into the arms of the soldiers. They instinctively brought their weapons up, but were not prepared to bayonet a man of God, and stumbled backwards in disarray, two of them even dropping their weapons as they endeavoured to catch the helpless man.

As Hoorn continued to hesitate, Clive whipped his sword from its scabbard – and just in time, for the Dutch lieutenant had sidestepped the flying parson and drawn his own weapon. But Clive was ahead of him, and ran him through with a single thrust. He gave a groan and fell to his knees, blood staining his white jacket, while Amalia gave a gasp and withdrew against the wall, to be joined by her father; the girls were still in the corridor.

The parson was now on the floor beside the wounded officer, and the four soldiers had recovered their wits, the two who remained armed raising their muskets, but still hesitating to shoot because of Amalia behind Clive. Then Jalina, who was behind them, uttered a most blood-curdling shriek and slammed the cell door. The last of the soldiers was actually in the doorway, and he was propelled into the midst of his fellows, once again throwing them off balance. For a moment there was the wildest pandemonium; two of the muskets were discharged, filling the small room with powder and the stench of cordite, but not actually hitting anyone.

'Come on, Hoorn,' Clive shouted again, and the Dutchman bestirred himself to grab one of the discarded muskets and swing it, catching the nearest soldier across the head and tumbling him senseless to the floor. Clive lanced another, and Jalina, having reopened the door, also picked up a dropped musket, encouraged by tremendous shouts from Louisa and Irene.

The smoke cleared, and the two remaining soldiers stood against the wall, their hands in the air, staring in alarm at the girls from whom had come so unexpected an assault.

The parson was already kneeling beside the officer, endeavouring to staunch the flow of blood – with some success. 'He is badly wounded,' he said. 'By heavens, Pieter Hoorn, but you will hang for this.'

Hoorn looked at Clive, obviously agreeing. 'They will have heard the noise and be here to arrest us all at any moment.'

'I doubt they will,' Clive said. The noise above and around them was tremendous: the cracking of musketry, the shrieks of men, the clash of steel, the drumming of feet. 'Our people are carrying the town by assault. We had better try to get up to them.' He put his arm round Amalia. 'Are you all right, my love?'

She gasped, and sniffed, and nodded. 'Are we all going to die?'

'Not if I can help it. You stay close to Jalina. Louisa and Irene, come behind us.' He smiled at the Thai princess. 'I think I owe you my life,' he said, and kissed her on the forehead.

She gave him a delighted hug, and waved the musket she obviously did not intend to relinquish.

Clive handed Hoorn his sword, picked up another of the muskets and reprimed it. Then he pushed the remaining two soldiers against the wall, got the girls outside, and closed and bolted the door. 'You know the way out of here? I hardly remember it.'

'There is no way out,' Hoorn told him. 'This corridor leads to a staircase into the courtyard, which is over-looked from all sides.'

'There must be a way off it.' Musket and bayonet thrust forward, heart pounding with exertion, and elation at having fought and won, he led the way. Hoorn, at his elbow, also carried a loaded musket, his sword now sheathed. The girls came behind, both Jalina and Louisa now armed. They reached the staircase without encountering anyone, climbed to another corridor, at the end of which they could see an open door – and daylight.

Clive went towards it, reached a transverse passageway and checked at a shout from his right. He turned towards the sound and saw two soldiers running at them, carrying flaring torches.

'What news?' Clive demanded.

The men clearly did not recognize him as the prisoner. They goggled at the girls for a moment, then saw Hoorn, whom they certainly did recognize. 'You must leave this place, Mijnheer,' one of them gasped. 'And quickly. The fort has fallen and we are to fire the magazine.' He pointed past them to the other arm of the transverse corridor, where a waiting powder train led away from them and under a heavy wooden door some feet beyond.

'Oh, God in heaven,' Hoorn muttered.

Amalia gave a moan.

'Make for the central courtyard,' the other man suggested. 'And lie down. There will be an enormous blast.'

'No.' Clive brought up his weapon. 'Go back whence you came, and surrender. Leave those torches.'

They stared at him; their own weapons were slung on the backs. Then they realized who he was. 'It is the Englishman,' one muttered.

'And I will shoot whichever of you attempts to light that train,' Clive said.

They hesitated, weighing their chances, knowing that they would certainly die unless they obeyed. But while they hesitated, there were more shouts, and the clatter of boots and weapons.

'Redcoats,' Hoorn snapped.

'Hallelujah!'

'Drop those weapons. Drop them, I say, or we will fire,' a British officer shouted.

Clive laid his musket on the ground, and Hoorn did likewise. 'Welcome, gentlemen,' Clive said in English. 'I am most heartily glad to see you.'

They were taken up on to the battlements, to gaze at the tremendous sight before them. Off the breakwaters there lay a fleet of war: three ships of the line, six frigates and some sloops. These were a-flutter with flags and humming with activity, as boats pulled to and fro, more men were landed and the guns continued to oversee the town.

That they had fired into it with effect was obvious at a glance. The fort was badly knocked about, and some of the balls had inevitably penetrated the city itself; there were two or three fires burning, and an enormous hubbub as the citizens tried to put them out. The small garrison which had been left to defend the fort to the last had been herded into the courtyard below them and disarmed, while sentries had been placed over them and over the magazine. Major Wrinteler, who had apparently been left in command by General Janssens, was the very picture of angry discomfiture, especially when he saw Clive and Hoorn. 'By God, gentlemen,' he said. 'If you had a hand in this I hope you rot in hell.'

'The fortunes of war, Major,' Clive told him.

'You will understand that you have to remain here until Sir Samuel Auchmuty comes ashore with the Governor-General,' said the brigadier who had led the assault. Rollo Gillespie was at once remarkably youthful-looking and remarkably small, hardly more than five feet tall, but his sword was bloodied, as was his uniform, suggesting that he had been in the thick of the fighting. 'I have only your word for it that you have been British agents, although I must thank you for preventing the firing of the magazine, which would have made a pretty mess of us all.'

'We understand your requirements, sir,' Hoorn agreed. 'But you must keep us apart from those fellows. And I would like my daughters returned to their home, under an escort.'

'Of course, Mijnheer Hoorn,' Gillespie agreed, and gave the necessary orders.

'I would rather stay with you,' Amalia begged.

'Yes, we'd rather stay here too,' Louisa and Irene chorused.

'You must go home,' Clive said. 'And remain there until we come. There is nothing to worry about, now. Oh, my dear girl.' He held Amalia tight. 'My dear girl, it is all over. We do not ever have to fear again.'

'I don't know whether to laugh or cry,' she sobbed, giving him a last hug.

'Nothing to worry about,' Hoorn grumbled, as the girls were led off. He was looking down on the Dutch soldiers sprawled on the grass of the courtyard and watched by the victorious redcoats. Most of the captured men wore the uniform of the militia and were people they met on the streets every day. 'They will not forget,' he said. 'Nor will they forget those.' He indicated other British soldiers, assisted by bluejackets from the ships, who were carrying dead men down from the battlements and laying them in orderly rows, while wails and moans arose from the wounded who were already undergoing surgery.

'It is a sad business,' Clive agreed. 'Let's just be happy that we are on the winning side.' He preferred to look at the fleet. He could hardly contain his elation, for all his acceptance of the horror of the war and his own recent brush with death. He felt sorry for the burghers, who had been commanded to fight whether they would or not — and had then clearly been abandoned by the regulars, or the British could not have succeeded so easily in taking the town. But he could feel no real sympathy for the people who had condemned him to death simply for being an enemy alien — and who would have flogged Amalia for becoming pregnant out of wedlock. Besides, to see the great warships riding to anchor, so exemplifying Great Britain's power, made the blood surge in his veins. And he had played his part in bringing them here. Seeing them quite dissipated any resentment he might

266

have felt at their long delay, which had caused the nearness of his being executed.

He watched as more boats rowed ashore flying huge Union Jacks from their stems, full of officers in brilliant uniforms with plumes nodding from their cocked hats . . . and with them, a slight figure in a black suit. Raffles, he thought. Raffles! Here in Java. 'There is the architect of our victory,' he told Hoorn, pointing. 'And my very good friend.'

The general officers came up to the battlements, escorted by Brigadier Gillespie, to oversee their victory and survey their conquest. They were headed by Lord Minto himself, who advanced to Clive and shook his hand. 'Mr Hammond,' he said. 'A great venture, brought to a most splendid success. You told us the Dutch would not stand and fight, and by God, they did not. I have also been told how you prevented them from blowing up their magazine. A sterling feat, sir, sterling. But then, your whole performance has been up to the mark.'

Clive decided against pointing out that he had had no part in Janssens' decision to abandon the town, or that the British delay had really negated all his advice and information. 'May I present Mijnheer Pieter Hoorn, my lord,' he said.

Minto hesitated for a moment before shaking hands. 'My pleasure, Mijnheer,' he remarked. 'I trust you are satisfied with this day's work?' Clearly he was not prepared to compliment a traitor. He turned to the officer at his side. 'Sir Samuel Auchmuty, Clive Hammond, of whom I have spoken. And Mijnheer Hoorn. They have been my agents here this last year.'

Clive shook hands with the commanding officer, who was now in his fifty-fifth year and had had a very distinguished career in the British Army, fighting all over the world. Clive knew he had begun life as the son of an American loyalist who had lost everything in the War of the Revolution, having risen since then entirely by his own talents and exertions.

'And, of course, Mr Stamford Raffles,' Minto said, with a twinkle in his eye. 'Whom I understand you have already met.'

'Raffles!' Clive clasped his friend's hand. 'This is Pieter Hoorn.'

'At last, Mijnheer Hoorn,' Raffles shook hands with the Dutchman. 'I appreciate your initiative, believe me. I am only sorry it took so long to come to fruition.'

'Well, your excellency,' Lord Minto said, now smiling broadly, 'you will have to tell us what you wish done. I am sure Sir Samuel is in a hurry to be off after the Dutch army.'

'The sooner the better,' Auchmuty growled.

'Your excellency?' Clive asked in wonderment.

Now Minto laughed out loud. 'Ah, you did not know, did you, Hammond? Well, I have appointed Mr Raffles Lieutenant-Governor of the new British colony of Java. Can you imagine a more appropriate choice?'

PART THREE
The Pearl

CHAPTER ELEVEN

The Administrator

'Raffles!' Clive shook his friend's hand again and again. 'I can hardly believe it.'

The Governor-General and Auchmuty had already left to accept the formal surrender of the burgomaster – Governor-General Daendals having fled the city with General Janssens – and then to hold a hasty inspection of the victorious troops. Clive had remained with the new Lieutenant-Governor, while Hoorn had hurried home to prepare his family for the great good fortune that had overtaken them. He too had had all his dreams realized.

'But you, Raffles . . . Lieutenant-Governor?'

'From secretary to command at a single leap. I suspect Minto had long had this in mind, but I will confess I can hardly believe it myself.' Raffles stood on the battlements and looked out across the fires, now all under control, at the great plain and, in the distance, the mountains glowing in the afternoon sunlight. In the distance, too, they could make out the Dutch army retreating towards more defensible grounds; behind them a column of redcoats was already toiling in pursuit. Had Minto been able to provide a regiment of cavalry, Clive thought, this war might have ended in very short order.

'A dream come true,' Raffles said. 'Do you realize that this island is virtually the same size as England?'

Clive nodded. 'But not all of it is Dutch held.'

'It is all of it going to be British held,' Raffles declared. 'Just as soon as we can manage it.'

'Oh, make no mistake about that,' Brigadier Gillespie agreed. He had been appointed garrison commander, while Auchmuty was to lead the field force against the Dutch. 'That is my prime responsibility.'

'I am sure, Brigadier,' Raffles agreed. 'But I think we should attempt peaceful negotiations first. I certainly propose to try it before I send you and your good fellows off into the jungle to die of fever.' He gave one of his singularly winning smiles and clapped the brigadier on the shoulder. 'I do assure you that we shall discuss the matter thoroughly before any decision is taken. Now, Hammond, you promised me some real Dutch cooking, I believe.'

He was delighted with the Hoorns, and especially with Amalia. When he learned of Amalia's pregnancy, he declared, 'Then the wedding shall be held immediately, and if you will permit me, Hammond, I shall be your best man. That should silence the critical tongues, eh?' He gazed at the young Negress who was presenting a tray at his elbow. 'You seem to have a good number of these people about the place, Mijnheer. Are they slaves?'

'But of course, your excellency,' Hoorn agreed.

'Ah,' Raffles said, nodding thoughtfully.

'I can see I shall have to hurry slowly,' he remarked to Clive after supper, as they walked the garden together. 'I see much that I do not like.'

'If you are thinking of slavery, it is found all over the tropics. All over the world, according to Teng Lee,' Clive pointed out. 'Including those very West Indies where you were born.'

'Indeed,' Raffles agreed. 'But it is still not an admirable institution, and there is a growing sentiment against it in England. Of course, not even my friend Wilberforce, or Clarkson, will be able to do much in general until this interminable war is concluded. But still, it may be possible to take some steps against it locally. Providing I do not at the same time upset these good people, who will have to remain the backbone of our colony for the foreseeable future. In this I will need your help.'

'Mine!'

'You have lived with them, and know them. I am appointing you my secretary, as of this moment.' He grinned. 'You at least know how to hold a pen.'

'Secretary to the Governor? My God,' Clive said.

'Will you accept the position?'

'I am absolutely overwhelmed, Raffles. But I think I should warn you that I doubt I am terribly popular with the Dutch at this moment.'

'Do they know you have been my agent here these last few months?'

'They don't *know* it. But at least one of them suspected it. I was in prison when you so happily arrived, on a charge of being an English spy.'

'That has been a fairly common Jacobin reaction to invasion these last twenty years.'

'Agreed. But this was an actual accusation.'

'Made by whom?'

'Now that I do not know as yet.'

'Hm. Well I do not think we will press an investigation too closely for a while, if you do not mind. Our business is reconciling these people to their fate, and they cannot harm you now. Besides, you will be married to one of them, and the father of a half-Dutch child.' He clasped Clive's hand. 'I cannot tell you how happy your situation makes me.' For a moment his face was serious. 'Would that I could rival you.'

'Has your wife never conceived?'

'Oh, indeed. Three times, and three miscarriages. She is not strong, that is the trouble, and does not do well in that terrible climate in Penang. I can hardly wait to bring her down here. But that is enough of private matters. We have great things to attend to here, and great problems. One of which is our friend Rollo Gillespie.'

'Indeed? I thought him a most dashing officer.'

'Certainly he is. And there is his trouble. His whole life has been one long dash, and he is now quite unable to stop himself from continuing that headlong career. Do you know, he is only forty-five years old, and has crammed sufficient excitement and misadventure into the past twenty-five years to last several men all of their lives: an elopment when he was twenty; a duel which all but had him convicted of murder; fighting the blacks in Hispaniola; a bout of yellow fever; accused of peculation in Jamaica; and then earning glory fighting against the Mughals.'

'My God,' Clive commented. 'As you say, an eventful life.'

'Now he is determined to earn himself more glory and distinction, and of course, promotion, by taking over this senseless war against the Javanese. Naturally, he will have to be handled with great tact. I foresee hard times ahead, indeed I do.' He clapped Clive on the shoulder. 'But you and I, together, will cope.'

'I look forward to it,' Clive agreed. 'Raffles . . .' Clive hesitated. 'How is Elizabeth?'

Raffles gave him a searching look. 'She would appear to be perfectly happy in her new life, and perfectly reconciled with Blaine. You have done wisely to make a new life without her.' He smiled and slapped Clive on the back. 'Now, we have a great deal to do tomorrow, so let us get to bed and prepare ourselves with a good night's sleep.'

It was indeed a period of intense activity. Clive had never worked so hard in his life, and had little time to brood on who might have denounced him. In fact he was happy to take Raffles' advice and forget the matter, content that no one could harm him, or Amalia, while they enjoyed the new Governor's favour. Raffles liked to be up and doing at dawn, and immediately commenced seeing the burghers, reassuring them that their property and wealth would be untouched, save by a proper taxation, and that it was his earnest desire to restore the life and the trade of the colony as rapidly as possible. He rode out to the plantations, Clive and Hoorn at his side, and sat and watched the acres of waving cane, the huge rice paddies, and the forced labour which produced the wealth.

'That has got to stop,' he told Clive. 'I know all the arguments; that the Javanese do not understand the value or the use of money, that they will not labour unless forced to it – but to my mind that is nonsense. It must be part of our duty to teach them the value of work and of recompense for labour and raise their dignity as human beings, just as it must also be part of our duty to put an end to the tyrannous authority of their princes, both for our good and theirs.'

The process of defeating the small Dutch army took much longer than anyone had expected. Clive was relieved that Janssens had decided to evacuate Batavia, for he doubted that Minto would have undertaken the invasion if he had known what lay ahead. But even knowing that there was no prospect of aid from Holland or France, the general determined to fight to the end. He retired to a strongly fortified position at Cornelis in the foothills, and it was here that Auchmuty had to assault him, in the broiling heat of a Javanese August. Gillespie, fire-eating as ever, by a most daring flanking manoeuvre got behind the Dutch and forced their retreat. Janssens withdrew to the east and coast, and it was not until 8 September, at Semarang, that the gallant defenders at last laid down their arms, and the Dutch-held part of Java became a British dominion.

Throughout these anxious weeks, Minto remained in Batavia, giving Raffles his support in all his rulings. His intention was also, Clive soon discerned, to apply a slight brake on some of his young protégé's more extreme ideas. The pair had lengthy discussions, at which Clive was usually present. While Minto fully agreed with Raffles' intention to abolish the corvée and deal directly with the Javanese rather than through their princes, he insisted that restoring the prosperity of the colony must come first. While also entirely agreeing that if possible a peaceful accommodation should be reached with those princes who had not yet surrendered to the Dutch, he stipulated that no European, and especially British, lives were to be lost, and the army must be used where necessary to ensure this.

In all these conferences, to Clive's concerned amusement, nothing was said about endeavouring to find out how the Javanese themselves would most prefer to be governed. It was simply taken for granted that they *would* be governed, and that was that. Certainly Minto's presence did much to ease the minds of the burghers in Batavia.

No one could now doubt that Clive Hammond *had* been an agent for the Governor-General – his swift promotion from factor's clerk to Raffles' secretary indicated that. It was suspected that Pieter Hoorn had also been implicated – *his* preferential treatment by the new British administration seemed to confirm that. But the Dutch rapidly realized that they had to make the best of their situation, and indeed soon began to turn to Hoorn whenever they required any intercession with permits from the Lieutenant-Governor, as he usually did.

'Mark my words,' Hoorn said to Clive with a delighted grin, having quite recovered his spirits, 'if I am not careful I will be elected burgomaster. That was not an honour they would ever have considered before for an upstart factor.'

But for the Hoorns the great event of the summer was Amalia's marriage to Clive, for she was evidently soon to give birth.

Not that this mattered as much under Stamford

Raffles' benevolent dictatorship as it would have done had the colony still been Dutch ruled.

The burghers' wives might whisper to each other behind their fans, but when they discovered that Lord Minto intended to attend the ceremony, and that the Lieutenant-Governor himself was acting as best man, they all accepted their invitations, as, to Clive's great joy, did Teng Lee, who had returned from his prolonged visit to Manila just in time.

Teng was a happy man, for he had at last made contact with his brothers, and if, as he had suspected, he had been pronounced an outlaw in China as well as Siam, he and his family had yet been able to set up a delivery system, using Manila for the time being, by which he would be able to ship goods from the Spice Islands into China, and obtain silk and jade in return. But of course the British conquest of Java made this largely unnecessary, to his great relief; with Great Britain now controlling all the Far Eastern seas, there would be sufficient carrying trade just between the various colonies to make a man at once busy and rich.

Teng's only reservation was the unceasing pirate activities in the South China Sea; he had had a brush with several Malay prahus as he approached too close to Singapura on his return voyage, the first time that a ship flying the flag of the house of Teng Wong had been attacked since his rescue of Perak Shah twenty-three years before. It disturbed Teng to think that such an implacable enemy as Perak Shah now undoubtedly was, could be sitting athwart his route to Manila.

'It would be doing a service to mankind were you to deal with that scoundrel once and for all,' he told Raffles.

The Lieutenant-Governor could not resist a smile. 'You are speaking of your old friend Perak Shah?'

'He is my enemy now,' Teng declared. 'I would have acted properly had I left him to drown, so many years ago.' He had no doubt himself that his act had been a delusion, as had his dream of making his home in Singapura.

'His turn will come,' Raffles agreed. 'But Java has to come first. I think even Hammond agrees with that.'

Clive saw no reason not to, even if Teng gave him a long look; to Teng, Perak Shah had to be as hateful to Clive as to himself, because of the rape of Elizabeth.

But Teng allowed himself to be mollified, because Batavia had suddenly become a very pleasant place in which to live. He was given permission to build himself a large warehouse, and even more important, to build himself a house as well, and install Jalina, even if he had not yet got around to marrying her. Although Clive suspected that problem might soon resolve itself. Jalina was one of Amalia's attendants at her wedding, and was fascinated by the magnificent gown she had been given to wear, and by the awesome simplicity of the service. Clive felt she was becoming increasingly interested in the Christian religion, at least as it applied to festive occasions.

Clive himself still had occasional difficulty in believing that he was out of prison, that all the tensions of the past year were behind him, that he was married to Amalia. He counted this year of 1811 the most memorable of his life. And then to become a father of a chubby baby boy was the crowning joy. The birth of her first grandchild in October even reconciled Juliana Hoorn to the situation. She had been distinctly hostile to him, or perhaps, he thought, even afraid of him, since his release from prison, obviously resenting the disgrace he had brought on her daughter. But now that they were married, and more, that Clive, as secretary to the Governor, was one of the most important men in the entire colony, she was prepared to be friends again.

Clive was also happy. Once Amalia was delivered of baby Pieter, named after her father at Clive's request, she was as passionately adoring as before. Motherhood, as was to be expected, made her bloom, and she soon regained her figure, which had always been intensely voluptuous. So when he sometimes lay awake and thought about Elizabeth with her slender body and quiet voice, he hated himself for a rogue, and threw himself harder than ever into the work that needed doing.

There was a great deal of this, for the problems facing the new British administration were severe, and the workload was increased by Raffles' enormous enthusiasm for everything. In his few spare moments, he turned to botany. Clive knew he had kept a small laboratory of specimens in Georgetown, but here in Java was a whole new world to be explored and appreciated, each new plant to be potted and tabulated, notes made of its progress and its variations.

With the surrender of General Janssens, Sir Samuel Auchmuty regarded the colony as pacified, at least *vis-à-vis* the Dutch and British. He therefore relinquished his command to Gillespie and took himself back to India. With him went Lord Minto, who had spent long enough away from Calcutta. He held a dinner at Government House immediately before leaving, at which he formally handed over the keys to Raffles, amidst the careful applause of the burghers and their wives. It was naturally a somewhat muted occasion, although splendid enough, with the officers in their uniforms, the glowing candelabra, the best silver that the fleeing Dutch had not carried away with them. The meal itself, a rijstafel, or rice table, consisted of no less than twenty-two separate dishes for each cover — everything from the bowls of rice which gave the menu its name, through various assorted fish and meat dishes, served with the very hot sambal sauce, to sliced bananas and pineapples which, to the amazement of those of the British new to the area, were supposed to be eaten with the meat.

But, of course, there were no Englishwomen present,

and the mevrouws were for the most part intensely nervous, and though unaware that high society in Regency England was doing its best to leave the excesses of the Empire far behind, had opted for the dowdiest and most correct of dresses. Amalia, having only just been delivered of her son, was unable to attend, but Pieter and Juliana were there, enjoying the reflected glory of their son-in-law and his friend. Major Wrinteler was also present. He had been especially requested by Raffles to remain in Batavia as head of the police, because he was so well acquainted with the local population. Wrinteler was enormously gratified – and, Clive suspected, relieved – by this, and went out of his way to shake hands with Pieter Hoorn and Clive, both of whom he had avoided since the British conquest, and assure them of his entire co-operation in the restoration of the colony under the British flag. Teng Lee and Jalina was also invited, despite the sideways glances of the burghers and their wives.

The next day, Minto received Raffles in the Governor-General's office, where he formally vacated the great desk to his protégé, who as usual had Clive at his side. 'I need hardly remind you that I look for great things from Java under your rule, Stamford,' Minto said.

'I need hardly promise you, my lord, that I shall give you the very last drop of blood in my veins to achieve that success,' Raffles replied.

'I never doubted that. You will understand by now that a successful administration never lacks for enemies. Remember, I will support you against petty complaints, and even more serious representations, should there be any, provided I remain convinced that you are following the principles in which we both believe. But remember also that my term of office in the East is limited. Your future depends upon making Java into a model and, above all, prosperous colony.' He gave a grim smile. 'We can never afford to forget that our masters in Whitehall regard the pound sign as more holy than the cross.' He held out his hand. 'God speed you, Stamford, and all who march with you.'

He shook hands with Clive in turn, and then they accompanied him down to the dock, where a guard of honour of the North British Fusiliers, wearing their traditional grey trousers beneath scarlet jackets, and their high black shakos, was drawn up to be inspected by Auchmuty and himself, watched by a large crowd of Dutch and Javanese. These were the men who had won the colony for Great Britain – with the aid of the fleet. Anchored in the roadstead were four frigates surrounding the seventy-four-gun line-of-battle ship which would carry the Governor-General and his commander-in-chief back to Calcutta. Merely a squadron, yet in their high varnished topsides, their rows of black gunports, their myriad flags – for they were dressed overall – their white canvas waiting to be unfurled, with their blue-jacketed seamen and red-coat marines, and above all the startling efficiency with which sheet and halliard, boat and gun, were handled, they represented the true power of the British navy.

Clive, watching the boats pulling for the ships, heard a quiet snap of the fingers beside him, and glanced at his friend.

Raffles' face was alight. 'Now, then, Clive, would you not say that I am my own master?'

'I would say so, your excellency,' Clive replied.

Raffles regarded him somewhat quizzically for a moment, then laughed. 'Why, so I am. Let us take charge of our kingdom.'

For the time being it was impossible to do that, however. The monsoon arrived within the week, and for the next few months it was not practical to venture too far from Batavia. Which was probably just as well, for the task of remodelling the administration was far from complete. Apart from investigating and taking control of the financial system of the colony, and appraising the tax returns as well as the trade figures, Raffles was also determined to undertake a revision of the laws. These had become a confusion of old Dutch and new, French-inspired usage, which he intended to clear away as rapidly as possible and replace with English custom. All of this meant much reading and transcribing, most of which fell to Clive, and even more conferring with those Dutch civil servants who had elected to remain and serve their new masters.

Clive, indeed, remembering Raffles' bouts of debilitating headaches, began to worry for his health, but Raffles seemed to have taken on a new lease of energy, only ever irritated by the frustration of waiting for the rains to cease.

The weather was unfailingly bad, which meant there was little movement even by sea. In fact, it was the worst monsoon for years, and Teng was confined to port by the unceasing high winds. For Raffles it was increasingly aggravating as, unlike his friends, he was separated from *his* wife.

'Teng Lee,' he said, one night at a supper party soon after Christmas, 'I have a charge for you.'

Teng bowed.

'The very moment it is possible, I would have you sail for Penang, and there pick up my wife, and my library, and my specimens, and bring them here to Batavia. Can I put that in your charge?'

Teng bowed again. 'I am honoured. And flattered, your excellency.'

'I suspect Flora will be happier in your junk than in any ordinary ship,' Raffles said, 'as she is a poor sailor. And I know she will be in good hands.' He smiled at Jalina. 'Your good lady will not mind this?'

'Jalina knows that I make my living by seafaring, your excellency. I shall sail the moment the winds abate,' Teng promised.

With the end of the monsoon in sight, Raffles began to consider his more extensive plans. 'Now, General Gillespie,' he said. 'I think it is time we had a conference.'

Gillespie, who had been given brevet major-general rank by Minto as he was in command of all the considerable forces left in Java pending the arrival of a senior officer to replace Auchmuty, had also been waiting impatiently for the weather to improve. Now he invited Raffles and Clive up to the fort, which had been restored into a proper state of defence, and showed them into a large map room, where a huge table contained an equally large map of Java covered in variegated coloured pins. 'Now here is the situation at the present time, your excellency,' he said. 'There you see the actual limits of our effective control. You will observe that it is a large area, and we really do not have the men adequately to defend it against dissension both within and without. Within, I must leave to you and your civil administrators, and' – he gave Clive a somewhat contemptuous glance – 'your advisers. I am informed by the Dutch that the people are largely quiescent, having been accustomed to more than a century of Dutch rule, which has been stern.'

Raffles nodded. 'What are those pins away in the east?'

'They are actually at Semarang, where I have had my people take over the old Dutch fortifications. It may be regarded as the furthest limits of the territory we have actually taken from the Dutch. Beyond it is the land held by the confederacy of those native princes who are still resisting European rule. One of the reasons why I have garrisoned Semarang is to apprise those gentlemen that we have no intention of giving up any of the prerogatives, or the land, we have taken by reason of our success against the Dutch. With this in mind, I have also drawn up a plan of campaign against this place called D'joejocarta, which is apparently the headquarters of the confederacy. It will require a reconnaissance in force before the details of the campaign can be made final, but I intend to conduct this myself as soon as the rains cease. I can assure you that I do not mean to commit our scanty resources to a long, wasting war, such as has handicapped the Dutch these past ten years. But I have no doubt that a single bold stroke will terrify the native chieftains into accepting our rule throughout the island.'

He paused, his chest stuck out like a pouter pigeon's, waiting for the Governor's approbation of all the hard work he had put in.

'You have undertaken all of this without conferring with me?' Raffles asked.

'I was informed,' Gillespie said stiffly, 'that military matters were to be strictly my concern.'

'Within the framework of the dispositions I have made for the government of the colony, sir,' Raffles said. 'I have also been informed that you were merely to hold the command here pending the arrival of Sir Miles Nightingall, your superior officer. I am certain that any offensive action against the Javanese should wait on that, if it should prove necessary at all. Assault D'joejocarta? Have you any conception of the strength of this place? Mijnheer Hoorn tells me it is held by thirty thousand men and thirty guns. I am sorry, General Gillespie, but I must forbid such a rash expedition at this time.'

'You, sir?' Gillespie seemed about to choke.

'As Lieutenant-Governor I am the ultimate commander here,' Raffles told him.

Gillespie attempted to stare him down, but quickly realized that the young Governor – Raffles, like Clive, was still only just thirty years old – was not going to be browbeaten. 'Then may I ask just what *are* your instructions, your excellency?' he inquired.

'That you remain in command here, while I conduct a tour of inspection of the interior of the colony. I propose to visit Semarang myself, to make contact with these native princes.' He smiled. 'You may consider that I will be carrying out your reconnaissance for you.'

284

'You? And I suppose you will require the entire garrison as your escort.'

'I shall not require an escort at all, in the sense you mean, General. I think that would be a mistake. I shall take Mr Hammond, my secretary, and Mijnheer Hoorn, as interpreter and guide. And Lieutenant Morton, my aide-de-camp. And some servants, of course. That is all.'

'You will be committing suicide,' Gillespie declared.

Raffles continued to smile at him. 'Then you would be in command of the colony, pending the appointment of a new governor, General. I am sure that is a responsibility you will not shirk.'

Amalia was appalled at the idea that her husband was taking himself off into the jungle so soon after their marriage and the birth of their child, and on such an apparently dangerous mission. 'I am barely a wife and you will make me a widow,' she complained.

'But I am going to return,' he promised.

'But will you be back for Easter?'

'I believe I shall. I certainly mean to try.'

He suspected that Raffles was as apprehensive as either Hoorn or himself, but the three of them set off in high spirits, accompanied by Evan Morton, the ADC, and by six of Hoorn's black slaves as bearers.

Morton, a captain in the army, was a fresh-faced, heavy-shouldered young man who clearly regarded this as the adventure of his life, and insisted on wearing his scarlet tunic at all times, despite the heat and the way in which he stood out amongst the more sombre jackets of the others.

The white men were mounted, of course, while the bearers walked behind, and for the first week they made deliberately slow progress, through territory which had been Dutch for generations. They followed the coast, with the tumbling rollers of the sea always on their left and the high mountains ranging always on their right, at some distance. Between the two was a mainly level grassy plain, intersected by several fast-running streams, one or two of which could be called small rivers, all hurrying to debouch into the ocean. There was little game because there was a remarkable number of people. Almost every few miles there was a village, and the travellers were immediately surrounded by a horde of inquisitive children, who presented a fascinating pot-pourri of racial backgrounds, as did their parents. The broad face of the Malay was strengthened by the more aquiline features of the Indian, the whole somewhat incongruously clothed in the intensity of the Muslim – although here, as in Singapura, the women went unveiled, and too often revealed almost toothless mouths in their invariable grins; the result, Hoorn suggested, of too much sugar in their diets.

They were all friendly, as they had lived under Dutch rule for some two hundred years and saw little immediate difference between Raffles' party and his immediate predecessors. There was a great deal of evidence of the Dutch presence, in the houses of factors and merchants, and the occasional fort erected to control a strategic river crossing, and now abandoned.

At each village Raffles sat down with the headman, each of whom called himself a prince and kept some state, again reminiscent, Clive thought, of Perak Shah's regime in Singapura.

Certainly Raffles knew how to charm the Javanese, listening courteously as Hoorn translated their problems and complaints, and having Clive make copious notes. Instead of rudely informing them he wished the corvée system to be abolished, he discussed with them the benefits of other systems and almost appeared to ask for their advice on how to improve the lot of everyone in Java. At least one of the princes' complaints regarded the acquisition of land by the Dutch, which was generally felt to have been on an unfair scale. As Hoorn translated this,

286

and watched Raffles nodding thoughtfully and sympathetically, his face grew longer and longer.

'You must realize that these fellows are out for everything they can get,' he pointed out over dinner.

'Agreed. But then, aren't we all? But these people are virtually slaves to their princes. The result of the system is that they obey their princes slavishly in everything. We must make them obey *us* in everything. Otherwise you certainly have a recipe for disaster; there are too many of them, and too few of us. We will only make ourselves secure here by giving everyone a share in the prosperity I intend to achieve and equally important, by giving everyone the same justice, rather than leaving the majority of the population at the mercy of our excesses or their chieftains' moods. Believe me, Hoorn, I mean us all to benefit, yourself most of all. You have survived now for nine years of blockade and shrinking markets. Now we have opened the whole world save for continental Europe to your goods, protected by the Royal Navy. I do not think you are going to suffer. And if I ask you to return some of your peripheral lands to the Javanese, lands which you hardly make full use of, again you will not suffer. The Javanese will wish to better their lot and trade with you, and you will then have yet another market, here on our doorstep.'

'That is supposing they have the money, or the goods, with which *to* trade,' Hoorn argued. 'Suppose they simply refuse to work when all compulsion is removed?'

'I think they will work, because they will soon see the additional advantages of improving their own standards of living, and of having one law for them all, prince as well as peasant, which will be administered without fear or favour.'

'What do you think the princes will make of all that?'

Raffles shrugged. 'I would hope they will make the best of it, because that is how it is going to be.'

287

'And you propose to tell this to these hostile chieftains we are seeking?'

Raffles smiled. 'No, I do not propose to tell it to anyone, until we have the whole island firmly under our control. But I certainly intend to start implementing it as rapidly as possible.'

They continued their journey along the low coastal plain, Raffles in a daily ecstasy at the wild flowers — varying from pale-shaded daisies to huge purple and white orchids — which surrounded them. He gazed in awe at the huge teak trees — 'Imagine,' he said, 'a fleet built of teak. Why, they would be impervious to cannon-balls. Now that is something I must put in my report' — and at the groves of giant bamboo which had so fascinated Clive on his first acquaintance with them. But he was at least as interested in the mountains which now soared to their right, some of them clearly reaching the ten-thousand-foot mark. 'Have you ever been up there, Hoorn?' he asked.

'I do not think anyone has,' Hoorn replied.

'But think of it, man. Think of what we might find on those peaks. That is something I must do, when I have the time. Will you accompany me, Hammond? It would be the adventure of a lifetime.'

'I suspect we are already embarked on the adventure of a lifetime,' Clive told him. 'But I will certainly come with you, supposing we do not get blown up by a volcano.'

Several of the peaks were smoking. 'Are there ever eruptions?' Raffles wanted to know.

'From time to time,' Hoorn said. 'We even hear them down on the coast, distant rumbles like continuous thunder, but out of a clear sky. They are too far away to trouble us. I am sure no Javanese would complain if you announced *that* land to be British. They have no use for it.'

'It already is British,' Raffles replied.

He was equally delighted with the amount of game they saw, but would permit no shooting except for food, which left Hoorn speechless when one morning, at dawn, they found themselves being inspected, from a cautious distance, by one of the very rare rhinoceroses which remained on the island. 'I have only ever seen one before,' he whispered, fingering his musket.

'Just looking at the noble fellow is the prize of a lifetime,' Raffles insisted. 'And he may well be here when next we pass this way.'

Having thus expressed his sentiments, he was furious when they came upon a small Dutch settlement, a considerable distance from Batavia, where there were tiger skins and even some crocodile hides pegged out to dry in the sun. 'I have never been able to understand man's weakness for making war on unarmed animals,' he remarked. 'I would have supposed that they were sufficiently occupied in making war on each other.'

'Would you say these tigers are unarmed, sir?' Morton asked. 'Or the crocodiles we have seen?'

'They are being forced to pit their teeth against musketry, and that gives them no odds at all.'

'Still,' Clive put in, 'I suspect these fellows earn their living by securing and selling these hides.'

'Hm,' Raffles said thoughtfully, and made no further comment.

The Dutch in the settlements knew of the colony's surrender, having witnessed, from the safety of the bush, the withdrawal of Janssens and the pursuit of Auchmuty. They appeared quite contented with the situation; Clive rather felt that they did not much care who made the laws down in Batavia, as long as there was no interference with their lives in the bush. Most appeared to have native wives, and were surrounded by happy half-caste children, and seemed to have made a very satisfactory life for themselves, far from civilization.

A week later they arrived at Semarang, which they

discovered to be a sizeable village, protected by a stout wooden stockade, above which the Union Jack fluttered proudly in the breeze. It was indeed a pretty spot, hard by a stream which bubbled across a white sand beach to dissipate itself in sparkling blue water, and laid out with all the meticulous care the Dutch invariably applied to their settlements: straight streets, a square, a church and a town hall, and steep-roofed gabled houses. There was also a considerable Javanese village outside the town proper. The inhabitants worked for their Dutch masters, who were growing sugar as well as spices, and harvesting timber.

'A paradise,' Raffles exclaimed with pleasure.

The commander of the fort, Major Clarke, was astonished to be visited by the Lieutenant-Governor, and took great pride in turning out his garrison for a guard of honour. He showed Raffles and his companions around the town, and then took them to the stream itself, which he explained was the official boundary of the Dutch advance. The land beyond, and inland, was in the hands of the Javanese. In fact, the entire island seemed to change shape at this point. The coast, which had inclined in a generally south-easterly direction since they had left Batavia, now abruptly turned to the north, while the mountains inland were higher and more formidable-looking than ever.

'Have you seen any of these independent people?' Raffles asked.

'From a distance,' Clarke told him. 'They have undoubtedly been reconnoitring our position, but I think they are uncertain who we are, as our uniforms are different to those of the Dutch. Obviously they know that we have forced the Dutch here to surrender, and thus we must be the stronger nation, which I consider is to our advantage. Certainly they have offered us no hostility as yet.'

'And the local inhabitants?'

'Ah, well, they regard us with some suspicion, I would say, your excellency. They don't seem convinced we are not going to start looting them at any moment.'

'I must meet their leaders,' Raffles decided, and the next day sat down to dinner with the burgomaster and several of the leading men of the community. As usual, he listened with grave courtesy to all their complaints and recommendations, having Clive write them down as Hoorn translated. In fact they, like the hunters they had met, or indeed, the people of Batavia itself, wished only to be left in peace to pursue their livelihoods without excessive interference from the government, and this Raffles was happy to promise them. They did, however, have an additional cause for concern: the proximity of the independent and, in their eyes, hostile Javanese in the mountains and to the east.

Raffles told them, 'It is my intention to open negotiations with these people immediately.'

'Negotiations?' The burgomaster was astounded.

'Negotiations should always take pride of place over bullets, Mijnheer,' Raffles reminded him gently.

'They will never negotiate, your excellency,' he declared. 'We only ever see them when they come to raid our fields or our flocks.'

'This I understand. Thus I intend to go and seek them.'

The burgomaster scratched his head, 'You intend to cross the mountains to D'joejocarta?'

'If I can find a reliable guide. Have you such a man to recommend?'

The Dutch conferred amongst themselves. Clearly they were under the impression that a madman had been sent to rule over them, but they also seemed to feel that he should be humoured, and that if he was truly bent on committing suicide, that was no business of theirs.

'I can take you into the mountains,' one of them said at last, a heavy, black-bearded man. 'I have been up there several times.'

'And you know where this armed camp they are supposed to maintain is situated?'

'I have seen it, your excellency. It does exist. It is over the mountains, almost due south of here.'

'Is it difficult of approach?'

'It is simply a matter of walking through some paddy fields. By the same token, you cannot *hide* your approach; they will be able to see you coming.'

'Well, then they won't be surprised,' Raffles said with one of his easy smiles. 'Will you guide us to this place, Mijnheer Roose?'

Roose looked at Hoorn, who shrugged. 'It is what his excellency wishes.'

They left the next morning, walking their horses into the hills. They were the same party as before, Raffles having declined Major Clarke's offer of a military escort. 'If there really are thirty thousand men over there,' he pointed out, 'then nothing you can provide would be in the least adequate for our protection. Besides, it must be our first intention to prove to them that we are on a peaceful mission.'

To Clive's relief it was not necessary to climb right over the mountains, as there were sufficient passes through the range, but it was still like entering a world he had not supposed to exist. Now they left the extreme heat and damp of the coast for a dryer, cooler climate – they awoke in the mornings shivering. But it was no less active and interesting a world. Their route took them close to a smoking volcano, where occasional rumbles would make the ground tremble beneath their feet and cause the black bearers to look at each other in alarm. They saw eagles swooping overhead, and an even greater variety of monkey than down by the coast, including some of enormous size, fully as large as a man. From a distance they might very well have been mistaken for human beings, as they walked upright. 'The natives call them orang-utans,' Roose explained.

There were tigers in these hills as well, who prowled around their campfires at night, but the mountain streams were free of crocodiles and could be used for bathing without risk. All the time they were aware of being watched. But no overt move was made against them, as Raffles insisted that their two flags, the Union Jack and the white flag, should be flown. They crossed the mountain range without difficulty, and looked down on the south coast, which appeared even more lush than the north, and upon the armed camp of the Javanese princes.

Clive caught his breath, because this was indeed a fortress, of wooden palisades rather than stone battlements, to be sure, and with a single ditch rather than a glacis and counterscarp; but none the less sufficiently formidable in appearance, and certainly defensible against all but the most determined assault.

'That is what our soldiers have been up against these last fifteen years,' Hoorn remarked. 'D'joejocarta is only the strongest of the Javanese strongholds; there are several in this area, I have been told.'

Raffles studied their position through his glass, then turned his attention to the surrounding countryside. 'I take leave to doubt the strength of this one,' he commented at last. 'There are a considerable number of men concentrated behind those palisades. Accumulating and then maintaining such numbers is a difficult business. I suspect they would be as happy as we to arrive at a peaceful settlement. Those fields are sadly undercultivated. And keeping men from the fields, and under arms, is costly, even if they do not use money. Shall we approach, gentlemen?'

Roose shook his head. 'I have done my duty, your excellency, in bringing you here. I can contribute nothing further to your expedition, except to wait here to guide you out. I will confess that I have no stomach for a spear between the shoulder-blades.'

'Will you then remain here with our bearers until we return?'

'Of course. But if you do not return?'

'If we are not back within forty-eight hours, then I wish you to return to Major Clarke and ask him to put his garrison in a state of defence, and to communicate as rapidly as possible with Major-General Gillespie and tell him that he must do as he thinks best.' Raffles smiled. 'But I have no doubt that we shall return in time, Mijnheer.'

Clive wished he could be as confident. He carried the Union Jack, and Moreton the white flag, as the four of them descended from the hills on foot, as Raffles had decided would be best. They carried sufficient rations in their knapsacks for two days, but Raffles had made them leave their weapons behind; he pointed out that their swords and pistols would be as inadequate as half a dozen soldiers, and he wanted to leave the Javanese in no doubt that they *were* on a peaceful mission.

They paused for luncheon by a stream where there were some poinsettia trees for shade, and here, amidst the brilliant red blooms, they ate their food and watched the people around them. For now there were a considerable number, emerging from the rice paddies and the various groves, women as well as men. The women were unveiled, Clive noted, although presumably they were all Muslims. Both sexes wore the sarong, and the men were armed, some with the kris, most with either wooden spears or somewhat rusty muskets, undoubtedly taken from the Dutch.

'I think we should speak with these people, Hoorn,' Raffles said, delicately patting his lips with a linen napkin. Up to now, none of the white men had even turned their heads, for all the pounding of their hearts and the sweat gathering beneath their shirts. 'If you would be so good as to pack up, Hammond, Moreton,' he said, and stood up. 'That looks a likely fellow, Hoorn. Tell him that I am the new ruler of this land, that I represent the great king from across the waters, the master of limitless resources, of the huge ships he must have seen sailing past these shores. Tell him all this and ask him if he has not heard the sound of the big guns from Batavia. Tell him my people are more powerful than the Dutch, and that we have replaced them in power here in Java. But tell him also that, unlike the Dutch, we come in peace to speak with his prince.'

Hoorn nodded, and somewhat uncertainly approached the man Raffles had indicated, who looked distinctly alarmed to be singled out, even as he observed that the Dutchman was unarmed. But he listened to what Hoorn had to say, then replied. 'He says he will lead us into the fortress,' Hoorn translated. 'You do not suppose we may be marching to our deaths?'

'If they decide to kill us,' Raffles pointed out, 'they could do it now. In fact, they could have done it at any time in the past four days. Shall we go, gentlemen?'

He marched ahead of them, with the guide, and they followed with their flags and knapsacks. It was impossible to believe he was as confident as he appeared, or as careless of death. What he possessed, Clive realized, was a sublime dedication to what he considered his duty, and that was the prosperity and expansion of the British Empire by every means in his power. So that if his power failed him, and he died by the wayside, he would yet be content.

They were taken aback by the strength of the fortress, on closer examination: by the numbers of cannon — closer to a hundred than the thirty which had been reported — old enough, but still serviceable, by the rank upon rank of armed men who waited to greet them, and by the princes. Some five chieftains, decorated with gold

295

jewellery and feathered turbans, carelessly lolled upon cushions on the verandah of their apparently common palace, regarding the visitors with a mixture of hostility and curiosity.

Raffles, with equal aplomb, pointed at a cushion occupied by an obviously lesser individual. After a moment's hesitation, and a quick nod from one of the senior princes, the cushion was abandoned, whereupon Raffles sat down and proceeded to talk, through Hoorn, while the Javanese listened. His approach was the same as that he had used both to the subject Javanese outside Batavia, and to the Dutch themselves. He told them that he intended equal justice for all, that British rule would be beneficial for all, and that the Royal Navy would protect them from any outside threats. He painted grandiose pictures of British achievements, playing down the name of Bonaparte, of which they had certainly heard, and harping instead upon the achievements of Lord Clive, of whom they had also heard, and more immediately.

The three elder princes seemed impressed, the two younger ones less so. But the Europeans were invited to eat with them, which Raffles told his companions was at least a sign that their lives were safe, as no Muslim would kill a man with whom he had broken bread. The meal was eaten on the same verandah on which they had been received, and watched by the assembled army and their women, much as Clive recalled Teng Lee's tales of eating with Perak Shah. It was disturbing to eat with the fingers, to be aware of so much naked flesh, and even more, of so much naked power, even if it was displayed in an essentially primitive fashion.

Raffles told the chiefs that he would be erecting a European fort in this area, and therefore he required them to dismantle their defences, as they would no longer be necessary, and to disband their army. He projected his plan for the colonists to expand into the east, but with full protection of Javanese rights. He talked and they

296

listened, exchanging glances and occasional grunts. Then he invited them or their representative to Batavia for a conference at which they would discuss their problems with the Dutch and his own administration. The senior of the princes, Sukulor Ali, nodded gravely and agreed to this, whereupon Raffles shook him by the hand.

That night they were entertained to another huge feast, at which four girls provided the entertainment, dancing a *serimpi*, or stylized combat between the two pairs. All four were utterly lovely, and their sinuous movements, the way in which they came together and parted again, seemed to twine themselves round each other in their mock combat, was at once fascinating and erotic.

They were followed by a *wayang kulit*, or puppet show, in which famous heroes and heroines of Javanese history, and from the *Ramayana*, the great Hindu epic, fluttered to and fro in wooden splendour, expertly manipulated by the hands reaching over the white screen, to the accompaniment of fearsome noises off, from screams and groans to the simulated booming of cannon.

It was the small hours of the morning before this display ended, and Clive wondered what Roose made of it all, perched up on his hillside overlooking the fort, and certainly able to see the huge fire which blazed in the centre of the palace courtyard.

But the visitors were not yet allowed to retire. They were now presented with gifts, first sarongs decorated in the famous age-old *batik* manner, in which the cloth is printed by hand with a wax and dye method, to produce a scintillating variety of colours which are almost indestructible. Then Sukulor Ali clapped his hands, and his guards came forward with four ceremonial kris, one for each of the Europeans. They were quite the finest weapons Clive had ever seen, alike in the magnificence of their hilts, which were studded with semi-precious stones, the perfect symmetry of the waves of the blades — seven on each side, as Sukulor Ali told them there had always to be an uneven number – and in the temper of the metal itself, which was as hard as steel. In fact, they learned that it was virtually steel, because the finest kris are forged from two different kinds of iron, one of which is meteoric, with a high nickel content. Clive, wrapping his hand around the hilt as he would have held a pistol, for the kris is essentially a thrusting weapon, felt almost reverent as he tested the balance and appreciated the destructive capacity of the short sword.

Next day they returned to Roose to tell him of their experiences. Raffles was elated. 'I knew they would listen,' he said. 'They are sensible men.'

'It costs nothing to listen,' Hoorn commented. 'Or to give expensive gifts, where they own everything.'

'Do you not think they will send people to Batavia?'

'They may well do that. As to whether they were totally convinced . . . I would say we have left them some hard wrangling amongst themselves. It all depends on who has the better of that argument. The two younger men did not seem as accommodating as their elders.'

'Which is common enough in all societies,' Raffles agreed. 'Well, we shall have to wait and see. I put my faith in old Sukulor Ali. Certainly I intend to move ahead with my plans to expand into this part of the country, and to move colonists out here. Gillespie can provide us with an adequate escort for that, and I imagine he will be pleased to do so. But I will wager that we manage it without fighting a single battle.'

They returned to Semarang four days later, to the great relief of Major Clarke, and not only because he had begun to worry about their safety. A message had come down from Batavia, and Raffles pounded his head as he read it. It was from Gillespie, to the effect that there had been an attack upon Europeans in the Sultanate of Palembang, just across the water in Symatra; it had always been accepted as part of the Java colony, and had indeed been included in the general surrender agreed by

Mijnheer Daendals and General Janssens. Gillespie had therefore taken it upon himself to embark an expedition of one thousand men, requisitioning every vessel he could find in the harbour, and had gone to restore order.

'Restore order, by God,' Raffles groaned. 'Haste. We must make haste.'

They rode as many as twelve hours a day, stopping only when Raffles was afflicted by one of his searing headaches, which had been so conspicuously absent in the exhilaration of the journey out.

In a fortnight they were back at Batavia, Raffles galloping into the courtyard of Government House and shouting for Gillespie.

'He has not yet returned from Sumatra, your excellency,' explained Colonel Williams, acting commander of the garrison, who was waiting for him with an anxious face.

'Not yet, by God? But he has suffered losses.' Raffles pointed at the flag, which drooped at half-mast above the building.

'Ah,' Williams said, and turned toward the doorway, where Teng Lee waited for them, his shoulders bowed.

'Teng,' Raffles cried, hurrying towards him. 'It is good to see you back. And Flora . . . where is she?'

Teng seemed to bow lower yet. 'It is my misfortune, your excellency, to be the bearer of ill news. Your wife . . .'

Raffles stared at him, his face ashen. 'Where is she?'

'She died before I ever regained Penang,' Teng said miserably. 'And is buried in the cemetery in Georgetown.'

CHAPTER TWELVE

The Lonely Man

'You've been to the cemetery again,' Edward Blaine accused.

Elizabeth came up the steps of the bungalow, folding her parasol as she did so; the sun blazed down on Penang with its usual intensity. 'Why, yes,' she said. 'So I have.'

'Your interest in that unfortunate woman is positively macabre,' her husband commented.

'She was my friend,' Elizabeth said. 'I think she was my only friend in this misbegotten place.'

She went into the bedroom, stripping off her sodden gloves as she did so. She was a mass of sticky sweat, as ever at this time of year; often she found herself remembering the delightful freedom of dress she had enjoyed in Singapura — but then, with every day, she thought more and more of Singapura, and little Ali. He would be getting on for three years old now. And she did not even know what he looked like.

As she unbuttoned her blouse and draped it over the clothes horse which was so essential in the tropics for airing discarded garments, she heard the door open behind her, and checked herself, watchfully. He was a man of unpredictable moods. There were times when he could be forebearing and almost sympathetic. But there were others, more regular, when he brooded on what had happened to his life, tied by the requirements of his caste to a woman he could never love, and often enough found it difficult not to hate. It was a situation she too could only endure, with increasing despair. Enduring meant at least remaining in this part of the world, breathing the same air as her son, praying for the miracle which might restore him to her. But with the departure, first of Clive, and then of Raffles himself, that dream had become even more remote.

Raffles, in his new role, might have been more than a hope – but that had rested mainly on her friendship with Flora. Neither had known of little Ali, but she had been working herself up to confide in her friend, in the hope that Flora might in turn plead with her husband for an expedition against Singapura. Now that too had fallen into the realms of unrealizable dreams.

'Your only friend,' Blaine remarked. 'Yes, I can believe that, at least amongst women. It may interest you to know that his excellency has just received despatches reporting in full the conquest of Java. Stamford Raffles is quite the hero of the hour.'

'Poor man,' Elizabeth said, and sat down on the bed to unlace her boots, half-turned away from him. 'To suffer such a blow in the moment of his triumph.'

'But he did not achieve his triumph without help,' Blaine went on. 'Do you know who helped him most, it appears?'

'I have no idea.'

'Clive Hammond.'

Elizabeth's head turned involuntarily.

'Ha,' Blaine said. 'Oh, indeed. Sending him back to gaol in England was all a lie apparently. He was sent instead – with the connivance of Minto, would you believe it – to Batavia, to sniff out the lie of the land. That upstart little whippersnapper, acting the spy for Britain.'

Elizabeth realized she had been holding her breath, and let it out in a rush.

Her husband heard the sigh. 'That pleases you, does it?'

Her shoulders rose and fell. 'I am happy the venture

301

was a success,' she said. 'Yes, it pleases me that Clive should have been able to do something worthwhile with his life.' Her brain was racing. Clive was still in the Indies, only a few hundred miles away! And much closer than that to Singapura. If only she had gone against Teng's advice and told him about his son.

'Apart from fucking you,' Blaine suddenly shouted.

Elizabeth stood up, her boot in her hand. Blaine was not in the habit of using obscenity, at least in her presence. She gazed at his red face and could see the veins pumping in his neck.

'Do you expect me to reply to that?' she asked quietly.

He came round the bed to stand before her. 'You still dream of him.' It was not a question.

'I dream of many things,' she said, trying to control the pounding of her own heart, which she knew was driving blood into her cheeks.

'The father of your child,' Blaine sneered. 'You have never managed to conceive for me.'

'No,' she agreed. 'I have not. Perhaps it is necessary to love in order to conceive.'

'Love,' Blaine commented. 'Well, I will tell you about your love. Hammond is married. Married, do you hear? To some Dutch girl, and is the father of another son. So why do you not dream of that?'

Amalia Hoorn, she thought instinctively. Amalia had made no secret of her admiration for Clive, two years ago. So now she had achieved her goal. O, lucky Amalia. And lucky Clive, to have found happiness as well as glory. Even if it meant that he had forgotten her, meant the end of that brief resurgence of hope.

'Have you nothing to say?' Blaine bellowed.

'I will write him a note of congratulations,' she said. 'Now I know where to find him. Do you think you could leave me alone, now?'

She sat down to remove her other boot, and he grasped her shoulder and threw her across the bed. She lay there,

302

gasping for breath, again totally surprised. Even on the dreadful night when he challenged Clive, he had not used violence towards her. Perhaps it was her threat to kill him if he did, but she rather supposed it was his breeding, his sense of gentility, his determination always to do, and to be seen to do, the 'right' thing, that had protected her, then and ever since. Then he had merely sat in a chair in the corner and glowered at her, and when she ostentatiously went into the master bedroom and undressed, sending her Malay maid away so that he could come in if he chose, he had used the spare room, and indeed stayed there for the next week.

Ironically, he had first repossessed her on the night she had seen Clive for the last time. Perhaps she had been softer, more accommodating to him in the light of that stolen meeting. Or perhaps he had himself been more relaxed in the knowledge that the one rival he knew personally was at last gone from their lives, as he supposed, for ever. But when he came to her it had been in the half-embarrassed, more gentle than passionate manner she remembered from the early days of their marriage. He had not paid the slightest attention to satisfying her, of course. He clearly did not comprehend that women could obtain any satisfaction, much less ecstasy, from making love. But he had not hurt her. Since then their relations had been almost painfully regular, every Sunday night and every Wednesday night. She was able to set her mental clock by his desires, to know, and to count on, those other five days when he would leave her alone and hardly come to bed until he felt sure she was asleep. For the rest, they had hardly spoken save to exchange the most trivial of commonplaces over the dinner table.

If it was no more than an existence, it was tolerable, and surviving it, she had been able to make her own way in the community, well aware of the whispers behind her back, well aware that there was not a man on the island who did not have a mental image of her cowering naked before a rampant savage, as they imagined had been the case.

If the poor fools could only know, she thought often enough. The same went for their wives, who had probably never been allowed to feel the faintest stirrings of feminine passion throughout their lives, who accepted their husbands as she was now forced to accept hers, as necessary evils in a masculine world.

What a swathe Perak Shah would have cut through the middle of them!

When she tried to sit up, he threw her down again and slapped her twice across the face, so hard her brain seemed to have been dislodged. She realized that this was what he had wanted to do to her since the first night of her return, that now at last he was allowing his true feelings to come to the surface. When she tried to ease herself away from his reach he seized her ankle and dragged her towards him, so forcefully she came right off the bed and fell heavily on the floor. She heard anxious voices in the corridors; the Malay servants, the house-boys and her maid, with whom she had become a great favourite, had been summoned by the noise.

'Go away, you yellow bastards!' Blaine shouted. 'Go away, or I will take my sword to you.'

The voices died, and she hoped they might have gone for help. But where was help to be found, when a man was beating his wife? Was there a soul in Georgetown who would say that Blaine did not have that right, with such a wife?

He was undressing. She tried to roll under the bed and was dragged back, her skirt torn off and with it her drawers. Now anger got the better of fear and bewilderment, and she struck at him, scratching his face; but earning in reply a blow to the stomach which again knocked her, curled and helpless, to the floor. Every muscle seeming to be bruised. Lying there, she watched

304

him kneel between her legs, his face distorted with angry hatred, and then felt him plunge into her, while she wept as he held her shoulders flat with his hands and breathed his lust into her face.

Stamford Raffles sat at his desk with his head between his hands as Clive entered. 'Is Gillespie here?' he asked.

'He is waiting, your excellency.'

'Then I will see him now.' Raffles sat straight, and looked up as the general entered. 'Will you report?' he asked quietly.

'Indeed I will,' Gillespie agreed. 'Word having been received that the Sultan of Palembang had murdered a European in his palace, and knowing that Palembang had been tributary to the government in Batavia and had therefore become ours when Batavia surrendered, I immediately proceeded to Sumatra with a force of one thousand men, entered Palembang, dispersed the troops who would oppose me, deposed the Sultan and set his brother on the throne in his place. I learned that the Sultan had in fact determined to renounce any allegiance to Great Britain, as he did not consider himself bound by the terms of the Dutch surrender at Semarang. His brother, however, is well disposed towards the British, and has willingly accepted the idea of being our vassal. I also took the opportunity, while in Sumatra, of annexing the island of Banca to the crown, and then returned here.'

'You abandoned your command in Batavia,' Raffles said, 'in my absence, to go chasing glory in Sumatra.'

'In your absence, your excellency, I *was* in command here, and therefore acted as I thought best. A European had been murdered. It matters not the man's character, or the reason behind the crime. It remains a crime against our sovereignty. There is only one way to deal with these fellows, and that is by the use of superior force, and to remind them time and again that we possess such force.'

Raffles sighed wearily. 'I should be obliged if you

305

would give me a full written report of your exploits, General Gillespie, that I can forward it to Lord Minto. Thank you.'

Gillespie remained standing before the desk. 'I would like to offer my condolences upon your bereavement.'

'Thank you, again.'

'And also to welcome you back. I imagine you found it impossible to approach D'joejocarta in safety.'

'On the contrary, General, I dined in D'joejocarta.'

'Good Lord,' Gillespie remarked. 'Then I must congratulate you, your excellency, on having returned at all. No doubt you will give me the benefit of your observations in due course.'

'In due course, General.'

Gillespie hesitated, glanced at Clive, realized he was going to obtain nothing further, saluted and left the office.

Clive closed the door. 'If there was a murder of a European. . . .'

'The murderer should have been brought to justice, agreed. But by due process of law. How can I preach equal justice for all when Gillespie takes it upon himself to depose a sultan and launch an invasion of a tributary state, without reference to any higher authority? And his thinking is entirely that of the majority of people in the colonies: one set of values for anyone with a white skin, and another for anyone with a brown one. Unfortunately, there are too many people with those ideas in London, as well. I have no certainty his action will be disavowed. But I wish to God Nightingall would get here so that we could be rid of Gillespie. And I tell you this, Clive, if he steps out of line again I will dismiss him whether Nightingall is here or not, and defend my actions to the company.' He sighed. 'How I wish. . . .' His voice trailed away, and he stared at his desk, his head drooped. 'Leave me, Clive,' he said. 'I have a migraine coming on.'

Raffles was actually less stricken by Flora's death than Clive had feared would be the case. No doubt he had long anticipated some such misfortune in his life, as his wife had never been strong. It was, of course, distressing for him not to have been present at her death, and for him to be unable even to visit her grave, for the present. But he knew that in the climate prevailing in Penang, and in Java for that matter, she would have had to be interred within twelve hours, and there could be no question of him leaving his post.

After Flora's death, Raffles threw himself more vigorously than ever into his work, but it was noticeable, as Clive observed with concern, that his headaches now returned more regularly, and more intensely, than before; often he was incapacitated for several hours at a time with the raking pains, which were quite incapable of relief save with the strongest drugs. Yet physical misfortune allied to his bereavement did not weaken the energy with which he approached his work, or interfere with the clarity of his thinking. He tried bhang, which the Javanese recommended as the universal panacea for pain, either in the mind or in the body, but he very rapidly abandoned it, despite the relief it brought him, because it also dulled the senses.

Yet it seemed that his splendid triumph in masterminding the British conquest of Java was to be offset by repeated misfortune, for when he sent emissaries back to D'joejocarta to renew contact with the independent princes and renew his invitation to Batavia, they were fired upon, and this was followed by an assault on Semarang itself. The garrison repulsed the onslaught easily enough, but some civilians were killed, and the citizens of Batavia were highly alarmed when the news reached them.

Gillespie was delighted, naturally enough. 'It is simply essential that we show ourselves to be in sufficient force, your excellency,' he insisted. 'I have no doubt at all that

307

some of the chieftains, as you have claimed, would be willing to come to terms with us, but clearly they have not yet been able to persuade all their people of the wisdom of this. I think a demonstration of the kind of power we can put into the field would be very useful.'

'What sort of demonstration?' Raffles asked wearily. He was in fact much more depressed by this breakdown in his efforts to achieve a peaceful settlement with the Javanese than by his personal tragedy.

'I would propose to march the better part of my establishment to Semarang and invite the independent princes to have a look at *them*,' Gillespie declared. 'That should make them think again. I calculate I can take fifteen hundred men with me, and still leave the city adequately defended.'

Raffles sighed again. 'I suppose you are right, General,' he said. 'You will need someone with you who knows the terrain and has spoken with these people before. Clive, will you accompany the army as my representative?'

'Willingly, your excellency,' Clive agreed.

Amalia was horrified. 'What, are you now become a soldier?' she demanded. 'You will again wander off into the bush, to get knifed by some savage?'

'I am going with fifteen hundred soldiers,' Clive explained patiently. 'And thus will be better protected than the last time. And we are not going to fight anyone, just let them see the power they are meddling with.'

That seemed to satisfy her. The army actually marched out within the week, Gillespie, of course, having long before drawn up plans for such an enterprise, and made good time along the coast. They were a most impressive sight, as Gillespie no doubt intended. The long line of redcoats marched with fixed bayonets glittering in the sun, their black shakos nodding in time to the band which led the way, the dust rising from the two batteries which brought up the rear, the colours proudly displayed at the head of each regiment. When the army camped, the

308

changing of the guard and the bugle calls displayed the marvellous discipline and cohesion of the force. Certainly those Javanese they passed on the way were suitably impressed, and turned out in their thousands to watch and clap their hands at the military display.

On the march, Clive got to know Gillespie well as they ate every meal together. The general was a great talker, and his conversation concerned only military matters. His knowledge of the campaigns of the past was profound – and not only of British military experts such as the Duke of Marlborough, but such other masters of the art of war as Frederick the Great and Prince Eugene, Gustavus Adolphus and Wallenstein, and even the great figures of antiquity, such as Casesar and Alexander. If he was undoubtedly bitter at having been so often passed over for command by younger and, in his opinion, less competent men, for he would not accept that his failure to obtain a rank commensurate with his talents had anything to do with his tempestuous youth and his over-aggression, he yet hoped to achieve immortality. Clive suspected he would succeed. It only seemed a pity that his abilities were being focussed out here, where there was no real call for them, and where he was bound to remain at loggerheads with the Lieutenant-Governor.

The citizens of Semarang were also delighted to see such a large army arriving on their doorstep, and Major Clarke turned out a guard of honour to welcome the general. 'Now, sir,' Gillespie said, having dispensed with the formalities of his arrival as rapidly as possible, 'a situation report, if you please.'

'Well, actually,' Clarke explained, spreading the map, 'the Javanese, having made their demonstration, have withdrawn over the mountains again to the south coast. My patrols encounter occasional parties of them, but they generally retire at the first exchange. I really feel the

309

crisis may be over; they have made their point, so to speak.'

'The crisis has only just begun, Major,' Gillespie informed him. 'Those savages will consider that they have gained a great victory, and will invade our territory again just as soon as they feel like it.'

'I accept that is possible, sir,' Clarke agreed. 'But it is difficult to know how to stop them. The Dutch maintained a sizeable force up here for some years and engaged in constant skirmishing, quite without checking the Javanese incursions, which took place, as you have said, whenever the savages felt like it.'

'Exactly,' Gillespie said. 'So what we want to do is put an end to this business once and for all. I take it you were with the Governor when he crossed the mountains and entered D'joejocarta, Hammond?'

'I was,' Clive said.

'Then you can lead us the same way.'

'You propose to march this army across those mountains? With their guns?'

'It will not be difficult. We will recruit local labour.'

'You mean you will enslave a few hundred friendly Javanese.'

'If you consider any Javanese innocent, in the light of recent events, you too are an innocent, Hammond. I intend to *requisition* native labour, certainly.'

'In order to undertake a campaign without the agreement of the Governor,' Clive pointed out. 'Indeed, in direct contradiction to the plan you outlined to his excellency.'

'I would argue that point,' Gillespie replied. 'I proposed to Mr Raffles that we let the native princes take a close look at the power we command, and that is exactly what I intend to do. With his agreement.'

'He certainly foresaw no campaign being undertaken,' Clive said. 'I am sorry, General, but I must respectfully

310

decline to have anything to do with your enterprise, until we have received a clear directive from Mr Raffles.'

'Which could take another month, at least,' Gillespie snapped. 'I am in command here, Hammond. As of this moment I decree that the district of Semarang is under martial law. Have that proclaimed immediately, Major Clarke. And assemble me the labour I require to drag those guns over the mountains. Hammond, I am requisitioning you as well, as guide. If you refuse, by God, sir, I will have you shot for mutiny.'

'Very good, General,' Clive acknowledged. 'But I would like you to put that order in writing.'

In fact, he was more than a little excited at the prospect of taking part in a campaign, even if he knew that Raffles would heartily disapprove. And even if he had his doubts as to what Gillespie would achieve against the fortifications of D'joejocarta, manned by thirty thousand men. But then, if the general suffered a defeat, supposing he did not actually manage to lose his entire army, Raffles would have the reasons he so urgently wanted for dismissing him.

Yet whatever his reasons for opposing the general, he could not fault Gillespie's mastery of the art of war in all its phases. The march was naturally far more arduous for nearly two thousand men than it had been for Raffles' small party, but the general looked after his people — including the hapless Javanese dragging the guns — with solicitous care, determined not to lose a man if he could help it.

The daily march was from four in the morning until ten, when the sun became too hot to continue. Skirmishers always preceded the main force, usually accompanied by the general himself, with his staff — and Clive — mounted, to look out the lie of the land, select the camp sites and seek any signs of the enemy, as Gillespie relentlessly called them. A site chosen, an ADC would be sent galloping back to the main body to summon up the sappers to dig latrines and pitch tents, and the cooks to prepare dinner. The soldiers themselves had nothing to do when they arrived but stack their muskets, brew canteens of tea and enjoy their meal and siesta. The result of this was that morale was kept very high, and the only grumbling resulted from their inability to come to grips with their enemies. Clad as they were in red and blue serge, with high stiff collars, several cases of heat stroke were reported every day despite the general's care, but after a few hours in litters carried by Javanese bearers, most were soon ready for duty again. It was an exhilarating experience to march in the midst of so much martial ardour, and Clive's heart pounded in anticipation as they topped the last rise and looked down on the southern plain and the fortress of D'joejocarta.

Although they had seen almost no one while passing the mountains, their coming was obviously expected. In place of the women working in the paddy-fields that Clive remembered from his last visit, or the men gathered beneath the trees to smoke their bhang or chew their betel nuts, the landscape beneath them was deserted. But there were a large number of flags — some red, some green, most black — flying from above the fort itself, and even without their glasses they could make out the cannon peering through the embrasures.

Gillespie immediately called a conference of his three lieutenant-colonels and his battery major, and gave them their instructions. The infantry were to deploy in their battalions on a fairly extended front across the north side of the fort; the exact order in which they would attack, Gillespie kept to himself for the time being. The artillery were to take up a position in the centre of the British line.

'But do you mean to attack without any parley at all?' Clive demanded.

'I do not consider a parley necessary, as they attacked Semarang first,' Gillespie pointed out. 'But if you are concerned that we should be in no doubt about what those fellows intend, why, let's put it to the test.'

He rode forward, with just one of his ADCs and Clive. Slowly they walked their horses along the roadway between the water-filled paddies, watching as they did so a great sort of seething from amongst the men behind the earthworks. 'What is your estimate of their strength, Hammond?' the general asked.

'I would say not less than thirty thousand.'

'That is twenty of them to each one of ours. Well, I would call those fair odds. And we can see quite a few cannon, eh? That's the spirit.'

For even as he spoke the first of the guns belched smoke, and a round shot plunged into the rice stalks some hundred feet away.

'Excellent shooting,' Gillespie remarked sarcastically. 'I assume they were aiming at us.'

Several more of the cannon exploded, and then the firing became general, but all the shots were well wide.

'I think we have proved our point, gentlemen,' Gillespie said. 'Shall we return and plan our advance?'

His coolness under fire was quite remarkable, as was his almost prescient anticipation of the enemy's weaknesses. They trotted back to the lines, while the guns behind them fell silent, having discharged their cartridges.

Gillespie stood his horse in front of his men, watch in hand, until the Javanese had reloaded and fired again, churning up the paddy-fields with great plumes of water but again doing no damage. He nodded his satisfaction. 'It takes them twelve minutes to reload,' he remarked.

'Now, gentlemen,' he told his officers, who were again gathered round him, 'the situation is simply this. We will carry that earthwork by frontal assault. You will advance your battalions at a steady pace. Two companies will incline to the left, and two to the right, leaving the other ten companies in the centre, but in the same extended order as you are at present. As the smoke of the guns is

313

seen, you will command your men to fall flat. It matters little whether they do so in a rice paddy or not; the vital work will be done with the bayonet, in any event. The enemy will take at least twelve minutes to reload their pieces, so that as their shot is passed, you will recommence your advance until the next smoke is seen. You should be able to advance a hundred yards between each volley. All of this time, our batteries, Major Henry, will continue to play on them with all the power you command. I want accuracy, above all else. This will drive their gunners from their cannon and seriously distract their riflemen. As the breastwork is neared, the flanking companies will incline towards the centre, so that we shall hit them with a solid wedge. They are a rabble who will not stand up to a concerted effort. Bayonets will be the main weapon. I expect the fortification to fall to our first assault, if everyone does his duty and obeys my orders. Any questions?'

No one spoke.

'Then take your positions, gentlemen, and I will wish you good fortune.'

The officers marched off to their respective posts.

'And what part do we play in this, General?' Clive asked.

Gillespie gave a brief smile. 'You and I, Mr Hammond, will conduct the advance from the front; did not his excellency instruct you to remain at my side always, and oversee what I am doing?'

It was at once exhilarating and terrifying. Clive had never been under fire before, except for that brief moment in the cabin of the *Henry Oliver*, when it had been difficult to decide what was happening, and the equally confusing few seconds in the cell beneath the fort in Batavia. Now he was required to walk his horse forward as if he were on parade, while Major Henry's battery opened fire to their left, and they could watch the shot plunging amongst the

314

Javanese defenders, causing consternation. The Javanese themselves replied hotly but with even less accuracy than before, which disappeared altogether as the line of redcoats rose up out of the paddy-fields and surged forward during the interval while the guns were reloading. The moment the smoke was seen again, the superbly trained soldiers fell to the ground, often up to their necks in water, firing not a shot in reply, as they could not, their powder being wet. But the cannon continued to boom, not altogether without effect; to Clive's horror one of the aides-de-camp, riding not six feet away from him, suddenly gave a peculiar little cough and tumbled from his saddle, blood gushing from his mouth. Gillespie spared him only a glance before walking on, while the line of steel and scarlet, glittering in the afternoon sunlight, approached closer and closer.

Now the Javanese fire became even more ragged than before. The shot, which might have been expected to concentrate on the general and his staff, conspicuous at once by their horses and the gleam of their accoutrements, grew ever wilder. Gillespie nonchalantly rode his horse up to within a hundred yards of the breastworks, and then waved his cocked hat into the air, the pre-arranged signal for the British cannon to cease firing. 'Now, then, lads,' the general called. 'Disperse those fellows, if you will.'

The redcoats rose in a rush, screaming their battle-cries as they charged forward behind their bayonets and the swords of their officers.

'Now, gentlemen,' Gillespie remarked, 'we may not be a squadron of cavalry, but I have never *followed* my infantry into battle.' He drew his sword and pointed it at the earthworks in front of him. His staff gave a halloo and followed him, and Clive could not but do likewise, drawing the sword he had been commanded to wear – incongruous with his civilian clothes – and waving it wildly as they charged the barricades, leapt over them in the best fox-hunting style and crashed into the terrified Javanese beyond.

The Javanese had been sufficiently distracted by the sight of the advancing bayonets of the infantry, only a few yards behind the horsemen. Now they broke and fled, as the redcoats, uttering terrifying yells and oaths, rushed at them with their hideous steel prongs. For a moment it was cut and thrust and slash, and then suddenly there were no more enemies, and Clive could look down on his bloodstained hand and wrist and sleeve, and realize that the battle had been won, in the shortest possible order. 'By God, sir, General Gillespie,' he said. 'But I must congratulate you.'

Gillespie smiled. 'Against your will, I think, Mr Hammond. Against your will. But was it not a pretty sight? You'll not see a better. By God, sir, show me an enemy, and I would conquer the world for this old England.'

CHAPTER THIRTEEN

The Governor

Raffles rested his head in his hands as he listened to the account of the campaign. When Gillespie was finished, he at last looked up, at Clive. 'And you did nothing to prevent this murderous assault?'

Gillespie replied before Clive could speak. 'I wish it to be clearly understood, your excellency, that Mr Hammond, acting as I imagine he believed you would require, did his utmost to dissuade me from undertaking the assault, and rode with me only because I commanded him to under threat of arrest. I must also add that he behaved with the utmost gallantry on the field. Having said which, your excellency, I must take exception to your use of the words "murderous assault". There were some thirty thousand savages in that fortification, determined to oppose us, as they proved by firing upon us. I consider it a highly successful operation, to have been able to disperse them with but thirty casualties on our side, at a cost of several hundred of theirs, and to have burned and uprooted their earthworks, rendered their cannon useless and, in general, made them rue the day they sought to oppose his majesty's army.'

'I will record your opinions, General Gillespie,' Raffles said. 'And my own, that the differences between us are too great to be bridged, even in phraseology. Where you speak of thirty thousand savages determined to oppose us, I think of thirty thousand Javanese determined to defend their homes. Our only common ground is a desire to see all of Java British. But as I am the one who has to govern this island, when that happy day is reached, and therefore rule the people on the island, I intend that they should be persuaded to accept our jurisdiction because of the benefits it will bring, rather than be bullied and murdered into doing so. I must now set about rebuilding the confidence I believe I was instilling in the independent princes, and repairing the damage you have done.' He pointed. 'As our position here is still precarious, I shall refrain from making our differences public unless I am forced to. But should you undertake any further military adventures in your time here, except on my express instructions, I shall place you under arrest.'

'*You* will arrest me?' Gillespie spluttered.

'I am the King's representative on this island, sir, and I have the right to arrest any person who in my opinion is a danger to the public peace. You, sir, in my opinion, do constitute such a danger. I shall obviously press for your replacement at the earliest possible moment. However, as the deed is done, and as you have told me that our troops behaved with exemplary gallantry, as I have no doubt you did yourself, I think it would be correct for me to inspect them and publicly congratulate them. Please arrange that immediately, General.'

Gillespie stared at him for several seconds, then saluted and left the room.

'Poor man,' Raffles said. 'He knows only one way to live. But then, so do I. And if I do not believe that my way is the only way, then I am unfit for this position.' He looked at Clive. 'Did you enjoy your first battle?'

'I was terrified,' Clive confessed. 'But it was the grandest thing I ever saw. And whatever his faults, Rollo Gillespie is surely the finest fighting soldier in the British Army.'

'I am certain you're right. I only wish they had sent him to some place where there is actually a war, rather than leaving him to start one here.'

318

Clive stood to attention. 'You shall have my resignation within the hour,' he said.

Raffles turned his weary eyes on him. 'Why, for God's sake? Have Gillespie's gallantries so bewitched you that you have no more time for me?'

'Quite the contrary. Much as I admire his ability and his courage, I do not agree with his point of view in the least. But I feel that I have quite failed you, in not refusing to fight with him.'

'No one can blame you for that. The blame, in fact, is entirely mine. Had I not been suffering so dreadfully from depression, to which no man should submit, I would have refused him permission to undertake that senseless demonstration, and returned to D'joejocarta myself. There you have the truth of the matter. No, no, Clive, I would like you to stay at my side. God knows, I am lonely enough without losing my closest friend. And besides, I need you. Would you not now agree that we must work harder than ever?'

Sir Miles Nightingall arrived a few months later, and General Gillespie was returned to Calcutta. Relations between the general and the Governor had not improved during the final days of Gillespie's stay, and Raffles could be under no doubt that he had made an enemy. As it proved, for Minto wrote to say that Gillespie had submitted a lengthy report charging the Governor with everything he could think of, from interfering in military affairs to incompetence. He brought up the matter of the alienation of Dutch-held land, some of which Raffles had already returned to the Javanese in the interests of peace, and of the Governor's choice of subordinates and associates, by which he undoubtedly meant Clive and Pieter Hoorn and Teng Lee. Minto's letter was as reassuring as possible, but he pointed out that charges of this nature had to be submitted to the board of the East India Company itself, and although he would defend his

319

appointment to the last, he could not guarantee the outcome.

'At least,' Raffles commented, 'if they take as long over impeaching me as they did poor Warren Hastings, I shall be retired before I am brought to book.'

Yet he had to regard it as a personal affront when news was received that Gillespie had been knighted for service to the crown — no such honour was bestowed on the Lieutenant-Governor.

In fact, conditions in the colony improved immediately Gillespie had departed. Nightingall was no less distinguished a soldier, having campaigned all over the world. But, although a couple of years younger than Gillespie, he had managed to do better in his profession in terms of promotion, having avoided the scrapes and misadventures in which Gillespie's temper had kept him embroiled throughout his life. Nightingall had indeed only recently been wounded in the Spanish Peninsular War, in which, commanding the Highland Brigade under Wellesley, he had earned distinction at such famous battles as Vimeiro. He was a man of singular charm and shared many points of view with Raffles, the most important being that it was preferable to rule by peaceful persuasion, wherever possible, rather than by armed might.

He accompanied Raffles, together with Clive, Hoorn and Morton, back to D'joejocarta, where the princes were ready to meet them again. There could be no doubt, however much Raffles hated to admit it, that Gillespie's bold assault, which had been as successful as it had been reprehensible, had frightened the Javanese. They had encountered nothing like that from the Dutch, who had always been keenly aware of their limited resources, and they were now ready to accept British sovereignty. Raffles was therefore enabled to make a triumphal progress the entire length of the country, until he could look across the strait at the neighbouring island of Bali, like Singapura a nest of pirates, and write to Minto to tell him that the whole of Java was now pacified beneath the Union Jack — which he felt to be the best possible answer to his detractors.

The next three years were extraordinarily happy and successful ones, at least for those who served Raffles and shared his dreams. They should have been happy for the Governor as well, as they were certainly successful — in that short space of time he virtually re-created the colony along his own lines, ensuring more prosperity both for the Javanese and for the Dutch, in a manner which men like Daendals had been quite unable to achieve. There were frustrations. Minto felt obliged to refuse his proposal to free the black slaves and ship them back to Africa — the movement towards emancipation in England had temporarily come to a halt under the repressive laws the Government had felt it necessary to pass in its life-and-death struggle with Bonapartism. And there were many Dutch who grumbled anyway at the concept of giving the Javanese more freedom and returning to them some of their land, or at being governed by the British, sure that somehow they were being cheated.

These things Raffles took in his stride. But he could not overcome either the deadening burden of personal loneliness, which not even the company of Clive and Amalia and their children could alleviate, or the recurrent bouts of debilitating headaches. Clive felt sure these headaches and his widowerhood were connected, the one being a result of the depression engendered by the other. It made him bitterly angry that he could do almost nothing to help his friend and benefactor.

It was the more sad because *his* life and those of his other friends were indeed happier than ever before. Amalia soon became pregnant again, and this time was delivered of a daughter, named Margaret after Clive's mother, and then, at the beginning of 1815, she bore another son, who was called John after Clive's father.

One of the additional causes for happiness was being able at last to correspond with his parents, and reveal to them that their son had after all embarked upon a successful and honourable career, which could one day bring him high reward.

Equally pleasurable for both of them was the decision of Evan Morton and Louisa Hoorn to marry, which enabled Amalia and her sister to be closer than ever.

Pieter Hoorn was no less pleased with the way things were going. Apart from marrying two of his daughters into the British establishment — Irene preferred to remain single for the time being, apparently — he was, as the Lieutenant-Governor's closest Dutch associate, naturally the most important member of the Dutch community, and as he had expected, he was elected burgomaster for 1814. Better than that, however, his affairs now took an upturn, as more and more British ships began to use Batavia as a port of call. He was able to send his spices half-way around the world — even if a mainly naval war between Great Britain and the United States once again put merchantmen at risk, unless sailing in convoy.

The new war did not bother Teng Lee, who, while spending several months at sea as always, also found the time to become a father again of two boys by his beautiful Thai princess. And the end of the senseless struggle in Europe was definitely in sight. In the very year of Gillespie's great triumph at D'joejocarta and his subsequent quarrel with the Governor, Bonaparte entered upon *his* fatal campaign against Russia. The following year it seemed all Europe was in arms against France, and in 1814 the Emperor was forced to abdicate. By the time the news reached Batavia, he had already embarked upon his last throw for power, the Hundred Days, and was failing.

These great events abroad were bound to have some repercussions in the colonies, everyone knew, although no one knew quite what. More importantly, from the point of view of Raffles and Clive, news arrived of the death of Gillespie, leading his men into battle, in an assault on the Gurkha stronghold of Kalaunga, in Nepal. He was apparently shot through the heart while conducting one of those frontal attacks so dear to him.

'A strange waste,' Raffles commented, 'of a man of remarkable talent, as you have claimed, Clive. Had he lived a more regular life, and thus been employed in Europe instead of on the fringes of civilization, what a name he might have made for himself.'

It was at this time, also, that Minto's term of office came to an end, and he departed for England. He was succeeded by Lord Hastings, who had been a soldier himself: as Sir Francis Rawdon, he had earned great distinction fighting against the Americans in the War of Independence. Minto apparently left warm comments regarding Raffles with the new Governor-General, for Hastings wrote in a most friendly style, congratulating him upon the success of the Java administration – but his letter contained a most disturbing remark. 'It would be a great pity,' he wrote, 'if, as our masters may well dictate, all of your work and your achievements should be handed away on a platter, one might say.'

Raffles read the letter in silence, then handed it to Clive and leaned back to stare at the ceiling.

'What does he mean?' Clive asked. 'Surely not. . . ?'

'They are redrawing the map of Europe, the map of the world, at Vienna,' Raffles said. 'I know it is impossible for us to contemplate, but . . . they gave everything we had gained in these waters back to Holland once before, in 1802.'

'My God!' Clive remarked. 'But that would be the most awful stab in the back a man could possibly imagine. Not only for you, but for Gillespie, and Minto, and Auchmuty . . . and all those brave fellows who died to secure Java for us.'

'Put not your trust in princes,' Raffles said. 'And even

323

less in duly elected governments, it appears.' He seemed to have shrunk in size.

'What will you do?'

'Write to Hastings, to begin with, and implore him both to understand the situation himself, and to convince those oafs in London that Java is already more secure than India, and of possibly greater importance to the future of the British Empire. Here, I shall dictate it now. And in the meantime, Clive, not a word to anyone that this is even a possibility.'

Clive was actually more taken aback by the contents of Hastings' letter than Raffles. For Raffles it meant the end of the dream he had held ever since he first came to the East Indies, but the dream had been an abstract, a concept of the British Empire spreading ever farther and more splendidly. He had no personal stake in the land, or the future, of Java. But Clive had not contemplated making a home anywhere else ever again. He was married to a Javanese girl, to all intents and purposes – Amalia had been born in Batavia – as indeed was Evan Morton. His father-in-law's whole life was bound up in the colony. So was Teng Lee's, now that he had rebuilt his trading empire, based on Batavia. And they were all identified with the British regime.

He found it very difficult to contemplate the next few months until further news was heard from Hastings. He tried to keep smiling and to be his usual cheerful and confident self, but did not altogether succeed.

The news, when it came early in 1816, was shattering. Hastings wrote:

It has been agreed at Vienna that the Dutch colonies in the East Indies should be returned to their rightful owners as soon as possible. Those in Guiana, the colonies of Demerara, Berbice and Essequibo, are being retained by us, because of their immense sugar-producing capacity, as is the Cape of Good

324

Hope, as a staging post on the sea route to India. But it is felt that it would be unjust to the restoration of the Netherlands as a viable political entity to deprive her of all overseas possessions, as the loss of these possessions was occasioned through the action of Bonaparte rather than the Dutch people themselves.

Raffles threw the sheet of paper across the desk. 'My God,' he said. 'The world is gone mad. With the price of sugar falling every day, with emancipation of slavery surely just around the corner – without which the West Indian sugar plantations would not earn a penny – they have elected to exchange Java for *Guiana*. They must be utterly without sense.' He picked up the next sheet.

The necessary commissioners will be on their way as soon as possible, but it will obviously be some time before they reach you, and the hand-over can be completed. Until then you will, of course, continue the British administration as you have done so successfully for the past four years. However, it is the requirement of His Majesty's Government that you immediately take steps to prepare the Dutch colonists, and such local officials as you have been employing, for the resumption of their duties under the laws of Holland. This should not be interpreted to mean that any laws which you have introduced, and which you may feel are beneficial to the community as a whole, should be rescinded. Those are decisions for the Dutch administration to make when they are again in control of the island.

Another sheet was hurled across the desk to a silent, aghast Clive.

Now, you will naturally be interested to learn of our plans for your future. Although it has been decided to return to Holland Java and all its appendages, in the islands and on the mainland of Sumatra, as well as Malacca, it is still felt desirable for Great Britain to retain some station in the straits area, as this remains an uncertain world. To this effect you are commanded, once

325

you have handed over your Javanese responsibilities, to proceed to the island of Bencoolen, where there has been a British establishment for the past five years, and where you will take up residence as Lieutenant-Governor. It is understood that this will entail considerably fewer responsibilities and, indeed, scope for action, than your present command, but His Majesty's Government is confident that you will apply yourself to your new duties with all the diligence and energy that you have shown in the Java area.

The Governor-General had added a note in his own hand:

I know how you will feel about this, Raffles, and I can but ask you to be patient. The fact is that the representations made against you by Major-General Gillespie have been largely accepted by the board of the company, and they were seeking your dismissal from all responsibility with a view to bringing charges against you for maladministration. Your friends, and I beg you to believe that you have many – amongst whom I number myself, even if we have not yet met – could not contemplate this proposal, and by having your name accepted by the Foreign Secretary as Lieutenant-Governor for Bencoolen, we have managed to postpone any action against you for at least the period of your office there, which can hardly be for less than five years. By that time the political climate may have greatly changed, and it may be possible to find you a position more in keeping with your talents. I must therefore beg you to accept this apparent demotion with good grace, and sit out the coming period with patience. You are yet a very young man to have accomplished so much and, with perseverance and determination, I have no doubt that you will yet scale the heights.

Raffles handed the personal note, too, to Clive. 'Bencoolen,' he remarked. 'From eighty thousand square

326

miles to perhaps five hundred. There is a depressing change of fortune.'

'I do not even know where it is,' Clive confessed.

'You have sailed by it often enough. It is an island off the coast of Sumatra, virtually opposite Malacca. The Dutch had a small fortress there, and so we seized it at the same time as we took Malacca, to hold both sides of the strait. It really is a misbegotten spot, damp and feverish, and with no harbour to speak of.'

'And they would send you there, after what you have accomplished here? The gratitude of governments is truly incomprehensible. What will you do?'

'Oh, I will accept the appointment,' Raffles said. 'Beggars really cannot be choosers. Besides, as his lordship points out, if I decline and resign, not only will I be destitute, but I will then become a target for every charge that can be brought against me – instigated by a dead man.' He got up, suddenly a bundle of energy. 'Which is not to say that I shall not fight the decision to abandon Java. I will go to Calcutta and see Hastings personally. He has never been here, never had an opportunity to see what we have done, how we have remodelled the colony. Yes. you will arrange me a passage on Teng Lee's junk, Clive. This is really is urgent.' He had been walking about the room; now he stopped. 'But you?'

'I suppose I can always go back to working for Pieter,' Clive said.

'Certainly you cannot. It would be too dangerous.'

Clive frowned. 'Dangerous?'

'Do not suppose these Dutch commissioners are going to arrive here in any very Christian frame of mind,' Raffles told him. 'Or that the burghers – many of whom still resent our intrusion, no matter what benefits it has brought them – will have forgotten that you came here as an apparent fugitive, were welcomed into their society and then turned out to be an English spy, and therefore

327

were at least partly responsible for our invasion. No, no, you cannot remain here if the island is to be handed back.' He snapped his fingers. 'I have the perfect solution. Will you continue working for me?'

'Of course, if there is a place for me.'

'There will always be a place for you, Clive. I intend to accept the appointment to the governorship of Bencoolen. But I cannot go there immediately, as I must have a go at changing Hastings' mind, and thus getting him to change the minds of those oafs in London. So, as my secretary, I will send you to Bencoolen now. You will take possession of the island in my name, set up an administration, and remain there in perfect safety until either I win my point, and we shall all return to Java, or I join you there. Will you do that? You will, of course, take Amalia and the children with you, and I will appoint Evan there as well, with Louisa.'

'Of course I will do it, Stam,' Clive said. 'But . . . my God, if you think I may be endangered by a Dutch return, what of Pieter?'

'Was he ever denounced as a traitor?'

'Not to my knowledge. But I do not think many people in Batavia have any doubts where his sympathies lay. Or lie.'

'Hm. Well, all we can do is put the situation to him. And to Teng, I suppose. We promised him safety and security for his business here, under our protection. They will have to know the facts, before anyone else.'

He held a supper party for his intimates, and there broke the news to them all. The reactions were uniformly horror-stricken.

'My God,' Nightingall commented. 'Just as the whole island is at peace, for the first time that anyone can recall. If the Mijnheers – with respect, Hoorn – start to treat the Javanese as slaves again, the whole business could start up once more.'

328

'Bencoolen,' Amalia said, and shuddered. 'It will be like living in a jungle.'

'It is terrible, terrible,' Juliana moaned. 'I do not know what we shall do.' She indeed seemed more alarmed even than her husband.

Louisa just looked at Evan Morton with huge, anxious eyes.

Irene said nothing, but looked at her father.

Hoorn seemed struck dumb by the catastrophe. He kept opening his mouth as if he would say something, and then closing it again.

And Jalina, who still only understood a few words of English, looked at Teng Lee.

Teng said, 'It is a great misfortune, for us all. I think you are quite right, Stamford, to protest most strongly against such an act of folly, and the *Dragon's Wake* is at your disposal to sail for Calcutta the moment you are ready. As for myself, however your mission turns out. . . .' He shrugged. 'I have no choice but to remain here. All my warehouses, my goods, my home, are here. Besides, I am Batavia's principal trading link with the Philippines, and thus China. I do not wish you to imagine that I am turning my back upon any of you – I shall never do that – but I think I will have to come to terms with my new masters. Certainly there is no way in which I can move my warehouses to a place like Bencoolen.'

'You're right there,' Raffles agreed. 'Well, old friend, I will be ready to board your ship at dawn tomorrow.' He had already arranged that Nightingall would govern the colony until his return. 'And if the worst comes to the worst, you will at least be able to keep us informed of what is going on here.'

'I, too, will stay,' Pieter Hoorn decided.

'But, Father,' Amalia protested. She now knew the inside story of Clive's arrival in Batavia and his employment, and thus of her father's involvement, even if she did not know of his original letter to Raffles – or of Clive's

329

relations with Elizabeth Blaine and the aborted duel. 'Suppose. . . .'

'Amalia is right,' Juliana declared. 'You — we, cannot stay.'

'Of course we can stay,' Hoorn said. 'People can suspect what they like. They can prove nothing against me. So I have come to terms with the British occupation. That was the act of a sensible man. People have accepted my place, as their leader, these past four years. Why, I have been burgomaster.'

'Yet they hate you,' Irene said quietly. 'For your success as much as for being pro-British.'

'What do you expect me to do?' her father complained. 'Pick up my plantations, my house, my goods, my accounts, and magically move them elsewhere? To leave Batavia would bankrupt me. I am not about to do that to myself. I have no doubt at all that our new masters will regard me as what I am: the most important merchant and planter in the colony.' He gazed around the table, as if daring anyone to argue with his self-assessment.

'Let us pray to God that you are right,' Raffles commented.

Juliana burst into tears.

Raffles had decided not to publicize the news of the projected return of Java to the Dutch until he had had an opportunity to confer with Hastings, and thus the departure of Clive and Morton, with their families, was prepared under the guise of a holiday. As Raffles was in great haste, Teng volunteered to transport the others on his return from Calcutta, which would give them the time to pack up their belongings. He and Raffles sailed at dawn the following morning.

It was the first time that Raffles had sailed on board Teng's ship, and Teng was delighted to show him the great comfort and safety in which he travelled. The *Dragon's Wake* was now fifteen years old, but she remained in prime condition, from the care which Teng and Li Yuan bestowed upon her. Now it was a pleasure to surprise Raffles with his mastery both of seamanship and navigation, arts in which the British considered themselves to be the best in the world, but which, Teng could not help but point out, had been practised in China when the British were still painting themselves blue and attempting to discover how to paddle their coracles in better than aimless circles.

Raffles laughed good-naturedly at the comparison. 'Believe me, Lee, I have often wished I could have followed in my father's footsteps and spent my life at sea. I think it must be the most relaxing life in the world, providing one does master the art of it.'

'The art, yes. But one never masters the sea,' Teng said wisely. 'It is like playing cards with a goddess, who may let you win a few rounds, but who you know will scoop the pot when she is in the mood. Yet truly, spending most of one's time upon the water, far away from the pettiness and absurdities of landsmen, enlarges the spirit. Indeed, although the concept frightened me at the time, had Jalina been able to stand the motion, I would have done as she wished and sailed the seas for ever.'

'What do you really think of it all, Lee?' Raffles asked. 'Behind that unchanging façade you maintain?'

'Many things?' Teng replied. 'My heart bleeds for you in this great disappointment you are enduring. But I believe you will succeed in life. You have the aura of success about you.'

'You are a skilful flatterer. And Clive?'

'Clive will support you to the end, as he has always supported me. He is the most loyal of men.'

'I will say amen to that. Although what you are really telling me is that his success depends upon mine, and that therefore I had *better* succeed.'

'It is to you — wisely, in my opinion — that he has hitched his star.'

331

'It is still quite a responsibility. And Hoorn?'

'Ah,' Teng said gravely. 'Now there I will confess I am unhappy. We must hope that he is right about the esteem in which he is held by his countrymen. Had you been left in command at Batavia for ten years, then I think he would have had nothing to fear. Five years is not long enough. There are still mothers grieving over those of their sons killed by British shot when the city fell. If any of them believe Hoorn had anything to do with that assault, then it could go hard with him.'

Raffles studied him for several minutes, obviously debating in his mind just how much Teng knew about that business. But he decided against pursuing the matter. 'And Teng Lee?' he asked.

Teng bowed. 'Oh, my heart bleeds for me, too. All my life I have sought but a single goal; a home for myself and my loved ones, free of the Manchu tyranny, where I could pursue my life and my business in peace and prosperity. I had twice thought I had found such a place, before coming to Batavia. And each time Fate ordained otherwise. Indeed, when my wife and child were taken from me, I had almost abandoned the whole concept and prepared myself to live as a slave for the rest of my life. Then my happiness was so dramatically restored to me, and I began the search again. Successfully, as I thought. In Batavia, under your aegis, I truly felt I had come home. Which is why I am reluctant to leave there. Under Dutch rule, I suspect that I shall again be treated as an inferior. But so long as they do not interfere with my personal or my business life, I shall endeavour not to mind. Anyway, where would you have me go? Can you seriously contemplate I would set up my godowns in Bencoolen?'

'No,' Raffles agreed. 'No, I cannot. Believe me, my heart bleeds too, that I should have been forced to let you down like this. But you, Lee, you also have the aura of success about you. You will prosper.'

'I certainly intend to try,' Teng agreed.

332

'Where will you go, from Calcutta?' Raffles asked.

'Oh, back to Batavia. Clive and Mr Morton will be ready to depart by then, and will be waiting for me to transport them. Besides, I will confess that I am curious to see your new empire.'

Raffles' smile was twisted. 'I wonder if I could ask you to do something for me on your return journey?'

'Of course.'

'It will not take you very far out of your way to call at Penang.'

'Not very far,' Teng agreed.

'And there, perhaps, you could visit my wife's grave. I went there myself as soon as I could spare the time, three years ago, and attended to the erection of a headstone, but I would like to know it is being cared for. Perhaps you could place a flower on it. And even shed a tear, for me.'

Teng clasped his hand. 'I can take you there.'

'I must get to Hastings as quickly as possible. Besides, I doubt I could stand it, in my present frame of mind. But just to know that it is being tended. . . .'

'It will be my charge,' Teng promised. 'You may depend upon it, old friend.'

He had not intended to return to Georgetown, ever again. As with Batavia, it had been a place where he had been sure of a welcome, as long as the Raffles had been there. Now he was again an alien. He seemed doomed to be an alien, in every society he encountered, for the rest of his life.

He was, in fact, far more downcast by the situation than he had allowed himself to appear to Raffles or to anyone else. Not even Jalina had any idea of how crushing a blow the British decision to abandon Java had been to him. For however lightly he pretended to treat the matter, financial prosperity and even domestic bliss – and he possessed both in abundance – were, for him, nothing if they could not be accompanied by social equality. Had that not been his dream, he might as well have remained in Canton and grown into a second Teng Wong, a most respected and indeed revered figure in the Chinese community, but still forced to bend to the ground whenever a Manchu bannerman rode by.

In Batavia, as a friend of the Governor's, he had achieved his dream. There would be no hope of maintaining that position with the stiff-necked Dutch, so certain of their own superiority over all other races. Why, they might even decide that his house was too close to their residences and require him to leave it. What would he do then? What could he do, save bow his head and accept their decree. The future seemed as dark as it had been when he fled Bangkok. And this time, with even his English friends in disarray, there was no saving solution that he could see. He could only fall back upon the principle of wu-wei, which he had once resolved to abandon, and hope.

As he had suspected would be the case, there were customs officers and port officials waiting to board his ship and examine it thoroughly, to frown disbelievingly when he explained that he was simply carrying out a mission for an old friend and had no goods to trade. It took him several hours to gain permission to go ashore and visit the cemetery, and even there he knew he was being watched by a Malayan spy for the military, as if they thought he might intend to blow the place up.

But the grave was in almost perfect condition, the grass around it clipped, the simple, beautifully carved headstone gleaming white, while there were already fresh flowers in the pot beneath the little cross. Raffles will be pleased, he thought, and I must have misjudged these people, in their respect for him.

He stood there in contemplation, until he heard a stone turn behind him, and looked at Elizabeth Blaine. It was the first time they had seen each other since he stood in this same place to watch Flora Raffles being lowered into

334

the ground, four years before. Now he wondered if they both thought the same thing — how little the other had changed physically. But she too had shadows behind her eyes, visible even in the greater shadow of her wide-brimmed straw hat, although she smiled graciously enough. 'Teng Lee,' she remarked. 'What a pleasant surprise. I saw your ship in the harbour and could not believe my eyes.'

Teng bowed.

'And you have come to visit your old friend?'

'I have come at Raffles' request,' he told her. 'He worried, but needlessly, I see, that the grave might have been neglected.'

'I come here every day.'

'I should have guessed. He will be grateful to you, because be sure that I will tell him of this.' He hesitated, but of course she could not, and should not, know of the great setback Raffles had just received. 'Well, I stopped here for no other purpose. And I no longer feel welcome here. I will take my leave.'

'Please,' she said.

He glanced at her in surprise.

'For a moment,' she begged.

Teng bowed.

The woman hesitated in turn, and he knew that she was trying to recapture that brief but intense intimacy they had shared on board the junk when he took her from Perak Shah. She was a woman with much on her mind, and she was turning to him for help.

'May I ask when last you were in Singapura?'

'I have not been in Singapura for five years now, Mrs Blaine.'

'Oh. I . . . I had hoped for some news of my son.'

'Alas, I have none,' he said. And waited, because that had been only her opening gambit, he knew.

'You see,' she said. 'I, too, do not feel welcome in Penang.'

335

Teng Lee said nothing.

'I . . .' She bit her lip. 'I have tried,' she said, 'in many ways. I knew it would be difficult. You knew it would be difficult, too.'

Teng bowed again. But he was aware of a most unhappy sensation. He knew what she was about to ask him to do.

'I . . .' This time she licked her lips. 'It was just bearable in the beginning, while Flora lived, while Edward was . . . forbearing. While he thought Clive Hammond had been banished from our lives forever. Since learning that he is still in the East, and prospering, my husband has become. . . .' She drew a long breath. 'A vicious beast. Mr Teng, I am exposed to an almost nightly assault. I dare not show you the bruises he has inflicted upon me. Once I swore I would kill him, if he ever struck me. Now he has discovered I have not the resolution to do that, he throws my threat in my face.'

She paused for breath, and Teng's heart went out to her. She must have suffered a great deal to bring herself to confide such a personal catastrophe to him. Or had the sight of his junk anchored in the harbour after so long a time seemed to her like a last chance?

'If . . . if I could feel that my misery, my humiliation, was private to my own house,' she said. 'I could stand it, perhaps. But it is known throughout the island. People stare at me, and whisper as they smile behind their fans or their hands. I am totally without friends here. I am in hell, Mr Teng. I can stand it no longer.'

'I am deeply sorry for your misfortune,' Teng said.

'Take me away, Teng,' she gasped. 'Rescue me as you did from Singapura, so mistakenly.'

Teng raised his eyebrows. 'Where would you go?' he asked cautiously.

'Back to Singapura.'

'Back to . . . you cannot be serious.'

Her chin came up. 'Why not? Do you think I would be

336

sacrificing anything? Perak Shah is a *man*. He never beat me, or ill-treated me in any way. He made me his favourite concubine. And he has my son. My son. . . .' Her voice trailed away as she gazed at him.

Teng Lee considered the situation, as he attempted to consider every situation, save occasionally his own, seriously and carefully, and dispassionately. He had supposed she might wish to flee to Clive. But she had not suggested that; clearly she knew of Clive's marriage, perhaps even that he was a father, and did not wish to bring any unhappiness on him. But to take her to Perak Shah — even supposing that were possible without involving his own destruction . . . how could he return a European woman, and Elizabeth Blaine above all others, to the hands of a murdering pirate, and not have it known? However carefully he and his crew might keep the secret, it would come out eventually. And he would be damned, by the Dutch no less than by the British; he could not afford, in his own currently precarious position, to do anything which might offend either of the European nations.

Besides, would not such an act estrange him from his friend Clive, and cause Clive still greater unhappiness?

And incidentally, by ruining Clive's life, this woman would be making herself unhappier than ever.

He thought she was a most unhappy woman. Her life had apparently been doomed to disaster by the gods and, being doomed, she cast a spell of unhappiness over all those with whom she came into contact. Had Clive ever been happy, even for a moment, between meeting her and finally forgetting her in favour of Amalia? Now she would, inadvertently as always, insert her unhappiness into a group of people who, whatever the ups and downs of their lives, were doing their best to make successes of themselves, to enjoy the peace and tranquillity which is surely the goal of everyone.

It would have been better if he had been able to leave her with Perak Shah. He could never take her back.

Elizabeth had been watching his unchanging expression with increasing anxiety. 'I . . . I have some money,' she said. 'A little jewellery.'

'I cannot take you back to Singapura,' he said.

She gazed at him and he hurried on.

'It is almost certain that by now Perak Shah knows that you were not taken from him for the harem of Rama. He will never forget or forgive that deception.'

'He will not punish me,' she said. 'I was his favourite.'

'Five years ago.'

'I will be his favourite again,' she insisted. 'I know it. And I do not care if he kills me, if I can just see my son again, for a moment. I have nothing else, Mr Teng.'

Teng Lee bowed in compassion.

'I. . . .' Her lips were slightly parted. 'I would grant you anything you wished,' she said.

She was so desperate she was offering herself to him. Almost he capitulated. Not to the offer, of course; it would never have occurred to him to betray Jalina, even with the Moon Goddess, but in his sheer sympathy for here. Then he remembered that he had almost succumbed to her tragic appeal once before; she had that quality. Only good sense would rule here.

'I cannot take you back to Singapura,' he repeated, his voice harsh.

She fell to her knees. Whether she intended to beg him, or whether her strength had just given way, he did not know.

'I cannot,' he said, more gently. 'I have told you, Perak Shah knows by now that I have deceived him. He might just accept you back, although I doubt that he will, but he would certainly execute me, were he to discover me in his territory.'

She raised her head. 'There is no need for him ever to do that. Set me ashore on an empty beach. In a swamp.

338

Drop me in the water close by the shore. I will be able to reach the Five Villages. Just set me ashore on Singapura.'

Her anguish was pitiable. Therefore his mind must be inflexible. 'I cannot take you back to Singapura,' he said a third time, and turned away from her.

He walked to the gate of the cemetery, and there paused to look back. She had remained kneeling beside the grave, and even from a distance, he could tell that she was weeping.

CHAPTER FOURTEEN

The Diplomat

The anchor rope hissed through the hawspipe; the sails had already been dropped, and the *Dragon's Wake* slowly came to a halt. Clive, standing beside Teng on the quarterdeck, inspected the land through his glass.

They had come round the island from the strait – after sailing past Singapura in the night – and were now in a narrow and, from the pale green colour of the water, shallow and therefore not very navigable smaller strait between Bencoolen and the mainland of Sumatra. To their left now lay the island, deeply wooded, low-lying, and dank even from a distance. To their right lay the huge mass of Sumatra itself, also low-lying and dank on the coast, but soon rising into hills, while in the distance was that lofty range of mountains which had so attracted Clive's attention when he first saw them.

But Sumatra – except in those places where either Dutch, or now the British, had secured a foothold – was a world of its own, entirely unexplored and, according to legend, so thickly forested as to be impenetrable even to the natives, much less to Europeans. In any event, it was no concern of his. He could only be interested in Bencoolen and its possibilities.

Supposing there were any.

'There is no harbour,' Morton commented. 'You could hardly bring anything with a deeper draft than this junk into here.'

'Nor would I like to lie here when there is a gale

blowing,' Teng remarked. 'There is no real shelter, and I think the holding ground for my anchor is very poor.'

'It looks horrible,' Amalia commented, holding little Johnnie in her arms.

'Island, island, island,' shouted five-year-old Pieter, jumping up and down.

Margaret, who was in her aunt Louisa's arms, just stared at the shore.

'Well, I see people there, at any rate,' Clive said, as reassuringly as he could, while he continued his scrutiny through his glass. 'Quite a few of them. And the British flag flies above the fort. You'd better put us ashore, Lee, and be off again before the weather changes.'

'Yes,' Teng agreed, to Clive's surprise; Teng was usually the most curious of people, and he had several times in the past expressed his interest in Bencoolen. But, in fact, he had been in an odd mood since his return from taking Raffles to Calcutta — if Teng Lee ever got into so European a state as a 'mood'. Yet he had entirely lacked gaiety, had seemed to be overborne by some enormous weight on his mind. No doubt what he had seen and heard in Calcutta made him less than ever happy about the future. But Clive knew better than to press him. When Teng wished to speak of his troubles, he would do so; until then, nothing could be extracted from him.

The boat was put down, and the two families were embarked, with their boxes, to be rowed to the wooden dock. Red-jacketed soldiers were there to greet them, and a captain saluted as they came ashore. 'Captain Runsley, commanding officer,' he announced. 'May I ask you to state your business here?'

'I have a letter for you,' Clive told you. 'You are aware that Mr Stamford Raffles is appointed Governor here?'

'I was so informed,' Runsley acknowledged. 'From Calcutta. If you are he, sir, I apologize.'

'I am his deputy,' Clive said, and handed over Raffles' letter. 'Do you mind if we disembark?'

341

'Please do.' Runsley slit the envelope and rapidly scanned the contents. 'Well, sir, I must say welcome. But. . . .' He looked at the women and children somewhat uncertainly.

Clive introduced them and Morton, and Runsley shook his head. 'This is a bad place for fever, sir. I worry for your good ladies. As for the children. . . .'

'Are those not women and children over there?' Amalia inquired. For quite a crowd had gathered to receive them.

'Oh, indeed, there was a Dutch settlement before we came,' Runsley explained. 'And most of them have opted to remain. Then there are quite a few Sumatrans, as well as the blacks.'

'Black people? You have African slaves here?' Clive demanded.

'Well, sir, *we* do not. But the Dutch use them, yes. Perhaps I had better find some accommodation for you.'

He took them to the town – or, rather, village, Clive supposed. Even the Hollanders had not been able quite to create one of their superbly neat communities on Bencoolen, principally because the land was too low-lying to allow reasonable canals to be dug. They had, however, in the best Dutch tradition, erected a stone sea wall along the eastern side of the town, to keep out the seas which in a storm must come boiling up out of the Strait of Malacca. Behind this wall the houses and the church, and the town hall, nestled in comparative safety, sheltered also by the stout little stone fort on the northern side. With its cannon, the fort could command both sides of the island, although, as Clive knew, it had not been able to withstand an attack from a British frigate. To the south there were thick forests, stretching for most of the fifty odd miles of the island, but some of the land had been cleared, and the Dutch had planted their crops and were gathering nutmeg and cloves. 'It really is quite a prosperous little place, Mr Hammond,' said Mijnheer Schooten, the burgomaster. 'But for the fever.'

'I have buried seven men this last year,' Runsley put in gloomily. 'And supposing it had a harbour, of course.'

He himself had built quite a respectable white-painted house close by the fort, and in this he installed the Hammonds and the Mortons, pending the building of houses of their own – he moved into the fort for the time being.

'What a terrible place,' Amalia remarked, looking out of the window at Teng Lee's junk, which was already standing past the headland on its way back to Java. 'How I wish I were going with him.' There were tears in her eyes.

It was, fortunately, the dry season when they arrived, and the malarial miasmas seemed temporarily abated. When the rains came, Runsley told them with his invariable gloom, they would also have to contend with hordes of mosquitoes rising up out of the swamp which composed so much of the island. But in Clive's opinion a far greater problem was going to be boredom. The small Dutch population, having become accustomed to British rule, were prepared to welcome their new administrator, and especially his Dutch wife, and they were also prepared to welcome Louisa and Morton. But their only amusements seemed to be eating, drinking and gossiping; it was like Penang reduced to a minuscule scale, and suffered by comparison. The men were coarse and overweight, red-faced from drinking too much home-made arrack, and pompously depressing. The women were coarse and overweight, red-faced from wearing too tight corsets and far too many clothes in general for the climate, and ponderously depressing. The children were very like their parents.

There was little outdoor activity to be enjoyed, where the sun was so hot, and the island itself was so unexciting.

There was a kind of rough track – it could hardly be called a road – which led out to the plantations and beyond. Clive and Morton followed it through the trees, in company with Runsley, right to the southern end of the island, some fifty miles from the town. There they could again look at the Strait of Malacca, beyond an empty mangrove beach.

They camped for the night before beginning their return journey. 'Should we not mount a post here?' Clive asked, as they sat around the fire. 'Anyone could put a considerable force ashore on that beach and be on us before we knew they existed.'

'Oh, indeed they could,' Runsley agreed. 'But why should anyone wish to do that, Mr Hammond?'

Lying awake that night, slapping mosquitoes and sand flies, or walking his horse back through the overhanging trees the next morning, listening to the ground squelching beneath the hooves, the cicadas whistling in the swamp to either side, Clive had to agree with him.

Administration consisted entirely of finding out who was sick every morning, and who was again fit for duty. And who was clearly dying. The numbers were few when they first arrived, but the dying season would soon be upon them, Runsley said, with gloomy cheerfulness.

Soon even the interest of building houses for the new arrivals was over; the Negro slaves, employed by the Dutch, quickly attended to that. Amalia and Louisa were at least happy to have found homes of their own, but the furniture, hand-made by the local carpenter, was primitive in the extreme, as were living conditions. They soon tired of the aimless prattle of their compatriots, and took to spending almost their entire days together, mending – which was a very important occupation where clothes could not be replaced – playing with the children and reminiscing about the good times in Batavia.

'I suppose we are all going to wind up going mad,' Clive told Morton, as the two men fenced every morning in the cool of the dawn. It was at least a form of exercise.

'It'll be different when Mr Raffles gets here,' Morton suggested. 'He'll stir things up.'

But three weeks later they discovered that Raffles was not going to get there for some time, as a sloop of war – their only link with Calcutta – came down with supplies, money for the garrison's pay and letters. One letter was from Raffles himself:

My meeting with Hastings has left me in a much more positive frame of mind. He is a fine, determined man, who knows where he is going. He entirely agrees with me that the policies of the present Government are madness, and that it will be a crime to hand back everything we have gained, and accomplished, to the Dutch. However, he can do nothing by himself, and has suggested that my best course is to proceed myself to England, and lay my case before the Foreign Secretary in person. This I am resolved to do, and I leave on *HMS Renown* the day after tomorrow. Alas, this means I shall not see you again for some months, but be sure that I intend to carry our battle to the very limits, if I have to. Meanwhile, I know that you are holding down the situation in Bencoolen with your usual splendid efficiency, and I beg you to give my best regards to Amalia, and Louisa and Evan, of course Teng Lee when next you see him. I shall be writing in similar vein to Nightingall.

'He sounds very optimistic,' Amalia remarked. 'I think we may well soon be going home.'

Clive thought *she* was being very optimistic, although it was simple indeed to be pessimistic in the surroundings of Bencoolen. He longed for Teng Lee to stop by, but the junk never appeared. Of course, there was no material reason for him to visit Bencoolen, but after they had shared so much together, he was disappointed that Teng should have so abandoned them.

The arrival of the monsoon brought torrential rain for

345

two months, and the entire settlement turned into a quagmire. It was impossible to do anything but huddle indoors and attempt to repel the snakes which came crawling out of the swamps seeking shelter anywhere to avoid drowning; with them came hordes of ants, spiders and scorpions, all of which needed to be trampled on as quickly as possible. As Runsley had prophesied, the rain also brought a plague of mosquitoes, which invaded the house and attacked everything that breathed, it seemed; the children were a mass of bites and often lay awake at night screaming their misery, while Amalia, herself covered in huge red bumps, endeavoured to comfort them.

Then came the malaria, another apparently invariable accompaniment of the rain. Soon half the population of the island were prostrated with high temperatures, and several died – this seemed to be regarded as inevitable. To the alarm of Clive and Amalia, Pieter was taken ill, but after a couple of nights of tossing and turning, the fever broke and he made a speedy recovery.

Through all of this continuing crisis Amalia remained amazingly cheerful and confident, although she had to say, 'Truly, we have been sent to the ends of the earth.' But then, soon after the monsoon ended, a frigate dropped anchor off the island, and Miles Nightingall came ashore for a brief visit . . . on his way back to Calcutta.

'But who is in charge in Batavia?' Clive asked.

'Mijnheer Daendals is back,' Nightingall explained. 'Restored as Governor-General.'

'You mean the Dutch have taken over after all? But what of Raffles' mission to England?'

'Now that I cannot say. It seems obvious that the Dutch despatched their people the moment they heard the decision of the Congress of Vienna, and long before Raffles could ever get to London. They arrived on this very British warship, would you believe it? But with them

346

was a letter, signed by Castlereagh himself, requiring Raffles to hand over his authority, and another, from the Horse Guards, summoning me to a new posting in India. I could not afford to ignore such clear instructions, either as a serving soldier or as Raffles' deputy. So there it is.'

'What is the atmosphere in Batavia?' Morton asked.

'Grim,' Nightingall told him. 'The burghers are confused, some of them; saddened, a few of them; and savage, most of them. Daendals was welcomed back with acclamation. Well, you cannot blame them. They have not universally approved our methods of government. No doubt it will all work out.'

'No doubt,' Clive said gloomily. But three months after Nightingall's departure, the *Dragon's Wake* dropped anchor once again off Bencoolen.

Clive was on the dock, with Runsley, Morton, Amalia, and Louisa, to greet Teng. They had been so starved of news for the past weeks they would have welcomed anyone. But Teng . . . and with him, Jalina and the two boys? Jalina had clearly not enjoyed the short voyage up from Batavia, and had to be helped ashore, while Teng's shoulders were bowed, and he looked much older than his forty-eight years.

'Whatever is the matter?' Clive asked him.

Teng turned and pointed at his ship. 'Is she not a fine vessel, Clive?'

'Indeed she is,' Clive agreed, mystified.

'Look well upon her. She is all I possess.'

'All . . .' He scratched his head. 'You'd best come up to the house and tell me what has happened.'

Jalina was hugged reassuringly by Amalia as Teng told their tale. 'I was accused of being a friend of the British, of having taken messages to and from Calcutta, of conspiring with that scoundrel Raffles and that spy Hammond, for that is how they speak of you in Batavia, Clive.'

'And so they punished you,' Clive said bitterly. 'As I have escaped.'

'Alas, that it were. . . .' Teng checked himself. 'They sequestrated my godowns, my house, and everything in them, as payment for the disasters I had helped to bring them, they said. And gave me permission only to take my junk and my family and depart, for ever more.'

'My dear friend.' Clive shook his hand. 'To think that you have suffered so much, for us. What will you do?'

'Seek shelter with you, for a start.'

'You have it.'

'If you will give it to me when you hear what I have to say.'

Clive frowned. 'There is more?'

'There is too much more. Mijnheer Daendals immediately introduced an investigation into the reasons for the defeat and capture of the colony. At least, Colonel Wrinteler did. The moment the last British soldier had embarked, he professed his loyalty to the Dutch, and said that he had only cooperated with Raffles and yourself because there was nothing else to do. You were immediately tried in your absence, and the original evidence called into court against you. It was a sad business, I can tell you.'

'The original evidence?' Amalia cried. 'Who supplied that?'

Teng sighed, and bowed his head. 'Your own mother.'

'My. . . ?'

'I cannot accept that,' Clive shouted.

'She admitted as much. It seems that when she discovered that Amalia was pregnant – dishonoured as she called it – she was so ashamed and angry that she went to Wrinteler and told him how she had never believed your story of why you came to Batavia, and how she had crept outside her husband's office door to listen to the two of you conferring.'

'She accused Father?' Louisa was aghast.

348

'She endeavoured not to, it seems,' Teng said. 'Her claim was that both Clive and I had tried to suborn Pieter into betraying the city, and were refused, but that Pieter would not denounce either of us – me because of our long friendship, and you because you were betrothed to his daughter. Juliana declared in her secret deposition, which Wrinteler read to the court, that she would rather have her daughter flogged through the streets of Batavia as a whore than married to a treacherous spy.'

'Oh, my God,' Amalia gasped. 'Oh, my God.'

'But how could she accuse you, Lee?' Clive demanded. 'You were not a part of it.'

'I think I was known to be your friend, and that was sufficient. After all, looking at the event from their point of view, I was the one who first introduced you to Batavia, and I was the one who brought you back again a year later. I think I was fortunate to escape with my head. I presume executing a Chinese was beneath their dignity. But, as I said, you have been condemned to death, in your absence.'

'Well, that's nothing new,' Clive said. 'But tell me, how did poor Pieter take this?'

Teng sighed. With his innate reluctance to break truly bad news, he had put off this moment as long as he could. He could think of no way to soften the blow. 'Pieter is dead,' he said.

Amalia gave a shriek and appeared to faint. Louisa and Jalina patted her cheeks. Clive fetched her a glass of water. 'How the devil did that happen?' he asked Teng.

Teng sighed again. 'Women should never meddle in men's affairs, Clive. In her anger, Juliana thought she could destroy you, and in her innocence thought that she could do so without also destroying her husband. But Wrinteler claims to have seen through her deception and to have guessed the truth from the start. He did not place Pieter under arrest during the last days of Dutch rule, because he was seeking additional evidence, he told the

349

court. Then he was overtaken by events when the British appeared and launched their assault. But now, of course, he could produce all the evidence — that Raffles had immediately stayed with the Hoorns, that Pieter had received most favourable treatment from the British — to indicate almost certainly that Pieter was in British pay.'

'He could have had no proof,' Evan Morton objected. 'Only supposition. And circumstantial evidence.'

'Nothing more was needed, with the mood of the people at this moment.'

'So that's why Wrinteler behaved so oddly after the surrender,' Clive mused. 'Anger, then trying to avoid us, and then almost cloying friendship. He is a little scoundrel. And that's why Juliana seemed afraid of me. I remember thinking so at the time. My God . . . Amalia.'

Amalia was sitting up. There were tear-stains on her cheeks. 'What can I say, Clive? My own mother . . . but to condemn Father to . . .' she looked at Teng.

Teng bowed his head. 'Your father was arrested, charged, condemned and hanged. There was nothing anyone could do to save him. Trial, sentence and execution took place in a week.'

'And Mother wanted that?' Louisa could not believe it.

'No. Of course she did not. As I said, she had no idea that Wrinteler had prepared a case against Pieter. Your mother was crushed by what she had set in motion. She is now a bedridden wreck, cared for by your sister, while the Hoorn plantations are overgrown and dwindling.'

'I must go to her,' Amalia said.

'How can you?' Louisa snapped. 'They'd probably arrest you too. Oh, we must be the most miserable of families.'

'Things will improve,' Clive said. 'I know they will, as soon as Raffles returns. Even if we are not able to return to Batavia as its rightful rulers, he will secure safeguards for us to go for your mother and Irene.'

'You *want* to care for my mother?' Amalia asked. 'After what she did?'

'She acted as perhaps many a mother would have done. I did dishonour you.'

She squeezed his hand. 'At my begging. Oh, Clive, I am so happy we escaped. But Father, oh poor Father . . .' She burst into tears again.

'Leave her with me,' Louisa said. 'We will pray together.'

Jalina also stayed, and Clive went outside with Teng and Morton. 'So there you see the quality of the news I have brought you,' Teng said. 'In some societies you would cut off my head.'

'It is news I think we all suspected might happen,' Clive told him. 'I am only sorry that you have been involved in our catastrophe.'

'But what I have said has destroyed your family.'

'Of course it has not. I am terribly sorry about poor Pieter, but Amalia and Louisa will recover. I wish there was something we could do to get Irene out of there – but we really can do nothing until Raffles returns – just as I wish there was something we could offer you . . .'

Teng bowed. 'You are too generous. I have certain monies in my possession, and I am still the son of Teng Wong. If Jalina can remain here with you for a while, I will go to Manila and contact my brothers. It will be possible for me to start up again, at least in a small way. But to find a home . . . that I have been seeking all my life.'

'Can you not return to Singapura?'

Teng shook his head. 'Perak Shah now hates me. As I am hated in Siam, and China and Java. And even in Penang.' For a moment Clive thought he might be going to say something more, but he checked himself and was silent for a few minutes before continuing. 'The world is shrinking about me.'

'I think it is shrinking about all of us,' Clive agreed.

351

'But when Raffles returns, things will improve. I am sure of it.'

It became the most important thing in any of their lives, waiting and knowing that the man who was now the acknowledged leader of them all was coming back to them. If indeed he was. As month after month passed, even Clive began to wonder, and Amalia grew quite fretful, as she too was counting upon Raffles' return to be able, somehow, to regain contact with her sister and mother. From Batavia there was no news at all.

Their only reason for optimism was that, if there was no news of Raffles when the sloop came from Calcutta, as it did every three months, there was no news of some other appointment to Bencoolen either, and the captain was quite happy to deal with Clive as Raffles' agent. But they were getting ready for the next monsoon, with its attendant miseries, when an even greater catastrophe than the news from Java overtook them; the earth shook.

It happened just after dawn, and could not have lasted more than five seconds. Clive and Morton were as usual squaring off with their rapiers; the guard had just been changed at the fort, and the Union Jack had fluttered in the gentle breeze; the slaves were drawing water from the town well, waiting in patient line; the fishermen were launching their boats for their daily trawls up and down the passage between the island and the mainland; and various interesting smells were coming from the houses as the mevrouws prepared the morning meal. Then there was an immense shudder. Clive found himself lying on the ground, staring at the sky, quite unable to tell how he had got there. The rapier was still in his hand, but he wasn't even sure for a moment what he had been going to use it for.

He was aware of an immense silence, the most profound he had ever heard; the birds had stopped singing, and even the cicadas had ceased their interminable slither. Then suddenly there was too much noise. A tremendous roaring filled the morning, drowning the equally sudden chorus of cries and screams, the belch of flame and smoke from the town. He scrambed to his feet, dropping the sword, and took in the scene in a single horrified glance. The outer wall of the fort had fallen, and the flagpole had collapsed. The town had almost disappeared into dust and rubble, from which flames were already rising as the various cooking fires ignited the crumbled wood. Trees were down, and great gullies had opened in the ground and across the rough track they called the road. The dock had disappeared, and the fishing boats were overturned, their crews struggling in a uniquely turbulent sea.

But that was on the shallow side of the island. The real noise was coming from behind him, and he turned round to see that the sea wall had also crumbled, and that the water in the strait seemed to be boiling and gathering itself as it rolled towards them. That was the roaring sound which had obliterated all others.

He shouted to Morton, who was just regaining his feet, and they ran across the torn earth, leaping over sudden holes and ravines, plunging into the debris of the town. Their houses, fortunately, had been built a little away from the rest, but they too were on fire. People were screaming and shouting for help, but Clive had eyes and ears only for his own at that moment. He tossed fallen timbers right and left as he sought his family; he found the two elder children first, huddling in their collapsed bedroom with Jalina and her sons, eyes stark with horror. 'Over there,' he shouted. 'Get to the fort. For God's sake, hurry.' The fort was at least on slightly higher ground than the rest of the island.

'Amalia,' Jalina gasped.

'I will find her,' Clive told her, and gave her a push in the direction he wanted her to go. 'Get the children to the fort.'

Evan had managed to find Louisa; like the others, she wore only her nightdress and was too dazed to be frightened, yet. He escorted them towards the fort, while Clive turned his attention back to the heaped timber which had been his house. The house had been built with a single upstairs chamber – their bedroom – and before leaving that morning he had, as he usually did, placed Baby Johnnie in his mother's arms. Now he panted as he picked at the wood, finding a child's doll here, a discarded garment there, shouting, 'Amalia! Amalia!'

And at last getting a reply. 'Clive,' she screamed. 'Oh, Clive.'

He could smell smoke and, indeed, hear the crackle of flames from close at hand. More frightening, the roaring of the sea was now also very close. But at last he could see her, pinned by a collapsed beam, saved from being crushed by the fact that the bed had somehow fallen half on top of her and was itself supporting the weight above her. Johnnie was in her arms.

'Is he alive?' he asked.

She nodded, and held out the child. He clasped him close, then extended his hand to her. She hesitated. 'It may come down,' she whispered.

'If you do not come now you will be drowned,' he told her.

She held out her hand in turn, and he grasped her wrist, took a deep breath and pulled with all his strength. She screamed in pain but then was in his arms. Holding her hand and ignoring her moans as she put down her left foot and discovered that she had a sprained ankle, he turned towards the fort, and watched the wall of water bursting over the beach and racing at him.

Stamford Raffles stood on the deck of His Majesty's Sloop *Gryphon* and studied the island of Bencoolen through his glass. It was six years since he had been here, yet he remembered it well. At least, he had thought he

354

remembered it well. But now he saw nothing that could possibly reawaken any images in his mind. 'When last were you here?' he asked Captain Collins.

'Three months ago, Sir Thomas,' the captain said.

'And all was well then?'

'Indeed it was, sir.'

'Let me see, Stam,' said the tall, slender young woman at his side.

He gave her the glass. 'There has been some catastrophe, my dear,' he said. 'It almost looks as if it has been razed to the ground. By God . . . pirates?' He looked at the captain.

Who was also studying the shore. 'There is the Union Jack flying from a flagpole,' he said. 'At least, from what looks like the branch of a tree stuck into the ground.'

'Haste, man, haste,' Raffles said. 'I must get ashore.'

The anchor plunged into the shallow water, and the boats were put down. 'You'll wait for my signal, until I ascertain it is safe for you, Sophia,' Raffles told the woman, and took his place in the gig. He stared at the shore as he approached; now the full measure of the destruction could be seen, the tumbled wreckage of the houses, the half-destroyed fort, the broken timbers of what once had been a dock. But there were people there to greet him, redcoats, and . . . 'Clive!' he shouted, leaping over the bow into the shallow water as the boat grounded. 'By God, but it is good to see you. Are you all right, man?'

There was more to the question than the state of the colony, or politeness. Clive's face was gaunt, he was unshaven, and his clothes were in rags. So were those of the men around him, even the soldiers. 'I am alive,' he said, and clasped his friend's hand. 'Thank God you have come.'

Raffles shook hands with Morton and Captain Runsley. He looked up the slight slope from the beach at the women and children, and made out Louisa and Jalina . . . 'When did this happen?'

'Ten days ago,' Morton told him. 'The tremor was followed by fire and then a tidal wave. There were seventy dead, all told.'

'It was quite terrible,' Runsley said. 'We in the fort were safe, because of its elevation, and so were those who managed to reach us. But those who were swept away ...' His voice tailed away. Raffles realized that Runsley had glanced at Clive as he spoke, and that he had not yet seen Amalia.

'Tell me,' he said.

Clive's shoulders rose and fell. 'I got her and Johnnie out of the building, but the sea was already upon us ...'

'Amalia *and* Johnnie?'

Clive nodded.

'Oh, my dear friend,' Raffles said, and clasped his hand. 'Oh, my dear, dear friend. But you. . . ?'

'Oh, I am alive, as I have said,' Clive said bitterly.

'We watched,' Morton said. 'All of us. They were seized by the water and swept away, with so many others. But Clive ...'

'I managed to grab hold of a tree,' Clive said, 'which miraculously withstood the water, although it swirled around my neck. I did not let them go, Stam. You will still find Amalia's nail marks on my flesh. We were still there when the wave passed on. But they were dead.' His shoulders bowed.

Raffles stared into his eyes. 'I sent you to this,' he said. 'And arrived myself too late.' For a moment he seemed almost bowed down himself by the tragedy he had so narrowly avoided. Then he squared his shoulders. 'She would not have us surrender to Fate.'

'I know that,' Clive agreed. 'The fact is, we have all been so cast down by what happened – but to see you ...' He realized that he had never seen his friend looking so well, or so ebullient, for all the terrible news with which he had been greeted.

'The sooner we get to work the better,' Raffles

356

declared. 'We have a town to build.' He turned to the lieutenant who had brought him from the sloop. 'You'll fetch my family and my gear, Mr Pomfret.'

'Aye, aye, Sir Thomas,' Pomfret said.

'*Sir* Thomas?' Clive cried.

'Family?' Morton inquired.

Raffles' smile was twisted. 'Aye, well, I have prospered, in a sense, since last we met. While you have suffered. There is much to tell you. And much to be done, as well.'

'And Batavia?' Clive asked.

Raffles frowned for a moment. 'I could make no impression there. But still, the situation is not without hope. We shall have to see what we can do. But first . . .' He turned to face the sea and the boats pulling for the shore, then waded back in the water to lift Sophia into his arms and set her ashore. 'My wife, Sophia. Mr Clive Hammond, my dear, and Mr Evan Morton. I am sorry they currently look like castaways, but that is what they are at the moment. There has been a great tragedy here.'

'Stamford has told me so much about you,' she said, shaking their hands. Clive was again astonished. Sophia Raffles was as great a contrast to Flora as it was possible to imagine, being tall and willowy – rather on the lines of Elizabeth Blaine, he realized, except that she was dark. 'But . . . tragedy?' she asked.

'There has been an earthquake, which has killed seventy people. Including Amalia Hammond and Clive's younger son.'

'Oh, my *God*!' she cried, and threw both arms round Clive's neck, to kiss him on the cheek. 'I am so terribly sorry. Oh, Stam . . .' She released Clive and looked at her husband.

'I have had time to recover, Lady Raffles,' Clive told her. 'At least to a certain extent. Perhaps I am fortunate in having two other children. But you . . .' He was looking past her as the next boat approached the shore; Raffles was already dashing back into the water to reach into the gig and remove an infant from the arms of the distinctly apprehensive-looking English nursemaid who was carrying him.

'Allow me to present Stamford Raffles junior,' he said. 'I wish it were a happier occasion.'

'My dear fellow,' Clive shouted, well aware of how long Raffles had wanted a son of his own. 'Allow me to congratulate you.'

'You should congratulate Sophia,' Raffles said. 'And there will be another within a few months.'

Lady Raffles blushed prettily. 'Stamford,' she protested.

'These people are my friends,' Raffles said. 'My oldest and dearest friends, whom I have shamefully abandoned for fifteen months.' The nurse having been ferried ashore, he returned his son to her arms. 'Now come along,' he said. 'There is much to be done.'

He was once again the bundle of energy Clive remembered from the early days in Java. He wasted no time before meeting the surviving members of the Dutch community, and left them in no doubt that their town would be rebuilt, commencing immediately. He inspected the ruined site, insisted on being introduced to the Sumatran head man and frowned at the slaves. He stood in silence at the sudden proliferation of graves in the little cemetery, and knelt beside the mound containing the bodies of Amalia Hammond and her son. He kissed and hugged Louisa and Jalina and the children, introduced Sophia to everyone, read Clive's report, had a long conversation with Captain Runsley and listened with a grave face to the descriptions of the earthquake. 'Does this happen often?' he inquired.

Mijnheer Schooten shook his head. 'No, thank God, your excellency. None of us remember anything like it before.'

'Well, then, we may trust that it will not recur in the

358

immediate future. Certainly we must act on the assumption that it will not. Tomorrow, gentlemen' – he looked around their faces – 'every able-bodied man in the colony will commence cutting timber, and building; I wish this colony to be totally rebuilt within six months at the very outside.'

'The monsoon will soon be here,' someone murmured.

'What, sir?' Raffles demanded. 'Are you afraid of a little rain? Would you live your life in a tent? Tomorrow, sir, this colony commences rebuilding.'

That night he sat with his friends round the camp fire, Sophia leaning against his shoulder, and talked. 'It is remarkable how little we know,' he said, 'of what is going on in the world around us. I will confess that when I left Batavia, I was thoroughly downcast and could see only that my life's work had gone for naught. Not even Hastings' encouragement, no matter how hard I tried to pretend, could allow me to see my way. Yet many things happened on my journey to make me realize that God moves in a mysterious way. We touched at St Helena, you know, for water, and there I was introduced to the Emperor. I cannot tell you how gratified I was when he shook my hand, and said, "Raffles. I have heard the name. Ah . . . you masterminded the capture of Java, with but a handful of men." To think that so great a man should have heard of me. And he made me relate the entire operation. Do you know, he showed as much interest in my law reforms as in the campaigns themselves?'

He paused in thought, while Clive and the others waited; this was a man who had rubbed shoulders with greatness.

'Then London,' Raffles said. 'Would you believe that I found myself the hero of the hour? *The Times* had my coming prominently displayed. There were gentlemen wishing to speak with me, and not only on political matters; there were ladies wishing to entertain me. My fame as a naturalist was equally spread abroad. By Minto, of course. He had not been idle. Why, we are to form a society, to which the Regent has graciously agreed to give his patronage. It will be called the Royal Zoological Society, or some such name. And I will be counted as a founder member. I was overwhelmed. But then came the meeting with His Royal Highness himself. "Raffles," he said to me, "without men like you the empire would surely have crumbled away by now." '

'And he knighted you,' Clive said.

'Oh, indeed, he did. "We cannot neglect our heroes," he said.'

'It's a pity he did not think of that sooner.'

'Well, perhaps he thought of it just in time. As you may imagine, all of this adulation did not sit well on the brows of those members of the board of the company, and I gather they are quite a few, who regard me as nothing more than an upstart clerk who is bent on causing as much disturbance as he can here in the Far East. But, of course, at the present time they cannot harm me, which is a very comforting thought. And then I met Sophia . . .' He smiled at his wife and squeezed her hand, and she smiled back. That they were very much in love was obvious. 'And when I asked the silly girl to marry me, she said Yes.'

'But they would not budge on Java,' remarked Evan Morton, always a tactless young man.

'No, they would not,' Raffles said, again serious. 'The spirit in this moment is one of burying Bonapartism – and Jacobinism, and all the revolutionary fervour which has caused so much redrawing of maps these last twenty years – as deep as is possible. The only idea of the Congress of Vienna was to restore the Europe of 1789, including the political map. Well, one has to say this is a laudable aim. However, as you know, our masters in Whitehall were determined to receive some compensa-

360

tion for the immense effort and expenditure they put forth to defeat Bonaparte, and while willing to restore most of the Dutch Empire, they reserved certain portions of it to themselves. We may suppose they made the wrong choice, but it was done, and they would stand by their decision. However, gentlemen' – he looked around at their faces – 'they are not quite such dolts as they sometimes appear. They listened to my case and they recognize that we must obtain a substantial position vis-à-vis the Dutch in these waters.

'The goal now is not so much the trade in spices. They are available from other sources, and perhaps are not so necessary to improve the taste of our meals as they were a quarter of a century ago, thanks to the various improvements in storage and maintenance of live animals – table meat is so much more palatable than it used to be. But they have at last become aware, in London, of the immense possibilities of the China trade; there is even talk of despatching an ambassador to Peking! In any event, they are determined that British merchants shall have the right to penetrate the South China Sea, if they wish, and the Yellow Sea, and they understand that should the Dutch retain total control of the Strait of Malacca, and also become interested in China – as they most certainly already are – then we may well find ourselves altogether excluded from the markets of Canton, save by attempting the most devious and dangerous passages between the islands further to the south. I have therefore' – he leaned back in his chair and smiled at them – 'been authorized to turn Bencoolen into a naval and commercial base which will be able to compete with anything the Dutch may set against us in these waters, even Batavia itself.'

'Bencoolen?' Clive cried.

'There is no harbour,' Morton pointed out.

'I lose a dozen men every year to malaria,' Runsley murmured.

Once again Raffles searched their faces. 'I know it is not ideal.'

'Ideal!' Clive exclaimed. 'It is the very farthest place on earth.'

'This is something we must discuss, obviously,' Raffles said. 'Although I suspect that recent events have somewhat coloured your point of view. They suggested Bencoolen because it is the only place we possess in a position to control the strait, and obviously they understand none of its drawbacks. Neither did I, at the time, and I was enthusiastic for the idea, naturally – I just wanted them to do *something*. But my instructions do say – I can quote them from memory – "Bencoolen, or any other convenient place", with the proviso, and this was very strongly made, that I should, under no circumstances, attempt to appropriate any territory held by the Dutch or any other European power, or belonging to any well-established sultanate. Great Britain must stand forth as the champion of law and order, from here on. And I agreed with that in principle. But who knows, there may be another site in Sumatra. It is a vast island, with only a few sultanates, and the Dutch have only nibbled at the southern end, even if they do occasionally lay claim to the entire country. I think we could dispute that, where they have not actually hoisted their flag. When we have set this place to rights, we will investigate the possibilities there. But until we find somewhere better, we will act on the assumption that Bencoolen is all we have, and we will work to make it into the sort of base in which a dozen three-deckers can lie at anchor in complete security, and twenty thousand people can live and trade, and prosper, in equal security. For I tell you this, gentlemen, I will make my city into a metropolis which will leave Batavia no more than a village.'

There was no point in arguing with him, in pointing out the absurdity of supposing a single frigate could ever lie securely at anchor in these waters, much less a three-decker, or in supposing that any sensible man would wish to establish himself in such an unwholesome and benighted spot. Nor did Clive wish to. To have a rejuvenated, once again confident Raffles back was all he really desired.

For Amalia's death, quite apart from the shock of it, the nearness of the whole colony to destruction, the horrifying minutes he had spent clinging to the tree supporting two people he already knew to be dead, had affected him more deeply than he suspected at the time. Indeed, with every passing day he was only beginning to understand how deeply it had bitten into his soul, his spirit. Perhaps he had never been as passionately in love with her as he would like to have been. But she had loved him, and he had responded with a deep-seated affection. Now, as he thought of her faithful support, of the tragedy of her family, and of her fight for life, he was again afflicted by a furious anger such as had overcome him as he helplessly watched Raffles' illness in Java a few years before. He knew now that he was never fated to achieve that happiness Teng Lee had assured him would one day be his, by the natural order of things. He was a doomed creature. But he could yet support a great man as he sought his goal.

And immediately the colony began to surge with Raffles' transmitted energy. Even Teng Lee, returning just before the onset of the monsoon, was amazed and delighted with the hustle and bustle, as the trees were cut down, the sea wall rebuilt, the houses reconstructed. He was horrified to learn of the earthquake, and of the deaths of Amalia and Johnnie Hammond, but once reassured that Jalina and the boys had survived, threw himself into the project with an equal will, having had a successful voyage to Manila.

It was of course impossible to commence any work on constructing a harbour until after the monsoon, and indeed, even rebuilding the town was hampered by the strong winds and the persistently heavy rain, for all Raffles' determination that the work should not be impeded by the weather. Teng was forced to carry out six anchors in an attempt to make sure his ship did not drag, and strand on the beach – which she did in one extra-strong gale, despite his precautions, and all the men in the community had to turn out to secure additional warps, working in torrential rain and often up to their waists in water, to prevent her becoming a total wreck. But she did not, and what might have been the ultimate catastrophe for Teng – for without his ship he was nothing – was averted; the junk was holed in two places, but nothing that could not be repaired the moment the winds dropped.

Still the work went on, everyone driven to it by the Lieutenant-Governor's persistent energy and enthusiasm, supported by the gracious encouragement of his wife. Her stamina and fortitude were amazing, Clive thought. Her maiden name was Hull, and her father was a wealthy man. She had been brought up in luxury, and could have been considered a romantically empty-headed girl for having fallen head over heels in love with a penniless adventurer from the ends of the earth who happened to be the toast of London for a season. Yet her support, and tha of her money – she had a private income left to her by her grandfather – had given Raffles the confidence he needed to assert himself more than ever before. Far more important, she was now revealing herself to be very much a woman to whom pioneering was, and remained, a vast adventure, no matter what the physical discomforts or indeed the dangers with which she was surrounded. She was some four months pregnant, it turned out, when they landed, and by the end of the monsoon was obviously so. She had to do most of the caring for her first-born herself, as the nurse she had brought with her from England was definitely *not* a pioneering woman, and spent most of her time prostrated by heat and having hysterics at every new sight or smell or sound.

But not even her domestic distractions could prevent Sophia from taking her full part in the rebuilding and remodelling of the community. Aghast to discover that there was no school on the island, she immediately persuaded her husband to place the building of one high on the list of priorities, and made him promise to send to Calcutta for a master as soon as the weather abated. Until then she proposed to conduct classes herself, but was immediately joined by Louisa Morton, who was as busy and energetic as anyone, as she had taken over the upbringing of Clive's remaining children, Pieter and Margaret. That she had been bitterly disappointed at the impossibility of regaining contact with her mother and sister, or even discovering if they were alive, was obvious. But she was revealing herself to be a much stronger character than Amalia, and if this was to be her life, then she was determined to make the best of it.

Her example inspired some of the other Dutch women, however askance they were at Lady Raffles' insistence that the school be open to all, whether British, Dutch, Sumatran or Negro. Soon there were classes every day, at least in religious instruction.

The monsoon lasted a month longer than was usual, and, of course, for this period the colony was entirely cut off from the outside world, so much so that they were completely out of imported food or wine by the end of it. The rain made the mosquitoes worse than ever, while the swamps were more extensive and evil-smelling than usual. While the rain still teemed down the first case of malaria appeared, and soon, as usual, half the population of the island was ill, trembling with agues, twisting in convulsive fits, vomiting black bile and being rendered totally incapable. All work on building had to cease, as everyone who could keep his or her feet had to become a nurse.

Then the sick began to die.

'My God,' Raffles said. 'I feel I am going out of my mind.' He stood in the rain by the open grave into which three soldiers of the garrison had just been lowered, the prayers having been read by the Dutch pastor. 'How can we possibly attempt to make a colony in these conditions? Is there no cure for this plague?'

'None has ever been found,' Mijnheer Schooten said. 'It is the scourge of the tropics. Of the world.'

'Wherever there is marshy land,' Teng observed. He was desperately worried for Jalina and his sons, and would have taken them to sea, whatever the weather and however great Jalina's distaste for shipboard life, had his junk been repaired.

'I suppose one answer would be to drain the marsh,' Morton suggested.

Clive gave a brief laugh. 'That would be to drain the island.'

'I am sure there must be a simpler solution than that,' Raffles said, adding, 'damned brute,' as he slapped a mosquito on his arms, dissolving it into a slodge of blood. 'If only we could see it.'

The dying continued. And then Stamford Raffles junior became ill. Louisa and Sophia – now very pregnant indeed – stared at the babe in horror as his skin became hot to the touch and clammy with sweat, and he moaned and tossed and uttered little cries, while every so often he would go quite rigid as his muscles were seized with a fit.

'We cannot just watch him die,' Sophia wailed, for the first time revealing that she was, after all, a human being.

'The only hope is to bring the temperature down,' Jalina said in her still halting English. 'This is what they do in Siam. Immerse him in a cold bath.'

They stared at her in consternation.

'It is worth a try,' Raffles said. 'Anything is worth a

try.' He concealed his own distress with his usual determination, although Clive could tell, having known him for so long, that he was suffering from one of his headaches.

'We have no ice,' Morton said miserably. Stamford junior had been like a child of the entire community.

'Well, even ordinary water is better than nothing,' Raffles insisted.

They filled a tub with water, and Louisa and Jalina held the baby in it. For a few hours it was possible to feel they were winning the fight for his life; his temperature went down and he became less restless. He was dried and put back into his cot, but that night the fever got hold of him again. They all stayed by his side, listening to the rain drumming on the lean-to shelter which was all they could provide, feeling the earth squelch beneath their feet every time they moved as the entire site turned into a vast bog, feeling their own clothes sodden with the accumulation of sweat and damp, watching a child die.

A huge pall of gloom settled over the community with the death of Raffles' child, to which was added tension, as Sophia was close to delivery. But she bore her tragic misfortune with the same fortitude as she had borne everything else, and was safely delivered of another son. It was after contemplating his newborn baby that Raffles left his house and walked to the sea wall to gaze at the strait, summoning Clive to keep him company with a jerk of the head.

'It goes hard to accept failure,' he said.

'I have never known you to do so,' Clive replied.

'Yet what have I here? I did not choose this benighted spot. Indeed, I would have settled for almost anywhere else in the East Indies. We can never create a successful economy here. As for making it a naval base, an entrepôt for China and the Far East ... that is an impractical dream. Only a most desperate man would wish to make his home here, to see his loved ones die of fever. Only a fool would bring his ship into these shallows to watch it stranded and wrecked. It is an impossible situation. And I must write and tell Hastings the truth of it.'

Clive stood with bowed shoulders. If he had long felt this, he had never once contemplated giving up, even in the despair which had followed the death of Amalia and Johnnie. It had been Raffles' dream, and his whole life had become devoted to supporting that dream – without it, he had no reason for living at all. But if Raffles had himself lost his dream. . . ? 'And then what?' he asked.

'And then . . . God knows. I shall be a governor without a colony. Impeached by the directors of the company, no doubt; I have heard they are still after my blood, presumably for involving them in that Javanese adventure in the first place. And yet . .' He squared his shoulders. 'We'll not go down without a fight, by God. There must be somewhere we can hoist the British flag, in safety and convenience. And in power, too.'

'Where do you suppose, that does not already belong to somebody else?' Clive asked.

'Well . . . perhaps in Sumatra. Clive, you and I have some exploring to do. Certain it is that we do no good here.'

Raffles' true reason for leaving the colony, Clive knew, was a desire to escape, to lose himself in action; to sit and contemplate the grave of his first-born son, would have driven him to madness – as sitting and watching the grave of Amalia was doing to him. Sophia gave them their blessing; she might even have inspired the expedition, Clive felt, as she had no more desire than they to spend another monsoon season in Bencoolen. And Louisa was happy to continue nursemaiding her nephew and niece, for the first time perhaps relieved that she had none of her own. Teng, the moment the junk was again seaworthy, put to sea for Manila, in search of trade, of course – but

368

no one could doubt that he had also resumed his search for some place on earth where Jalina and his sons would be truly safe.

Meanwhile, Raffles and Clive plunged into the wilds of Sumatra, in one of the open fishing boats used by the community, taking with them only half a dozen Negroes – who all volunteered to accompany them – and leaving the colony in the joint hands of Schooten, Morton and Runsley.

To begin with, they followed the coast to the north, finding it to be unchangingly low, swampy and unhealthy. The same went for the various islands they came across and explored. There was not one of them which was any improvement on Bencoolen, and most were a great deal worse. After a week of steady progress, in which Clive estimated they must have covered over a hundred miles, they had to face the fact that there was simply no possible site for a colony on the coast of even this huge island. The Sumatrans clearly felt the same, for they found only occasional fishing villages where they were made welcome – and also the object of a great deal of curiosity. The Malays – they were the same stock as the people of the peninsula – had never seen either white or black men before.

But always they were within sight of the great mountains of the interior. 'I should deem the expedition a total failure were I to return to Bencoolen, not only empty-handed as regards a fresh site, but without at least having looked down on this land from the top of one of those,' Raffles said.

'That is not possible,' said the head man of the village at which they were staying. 'No man has ever reached those mountains; they are the homes of the gods.'

'Well, perhaps the gods will look with favour upon two white men who mean them nothing but good,' Raffles told him, and two days later they set off, travelling in a generally north-western direction, towards the very highest peak they could see in the distance, without any clear idea of how far off it was.

It was actually a hundred and fifty miles away. The first part of their journey was intensely difficult, for it took them through the same swampy and unhealthy country as lay along the entire coast, and they stumbled onwards, often up to their waists in water, attacked by every living creature from leeches to crocodiles.

But Raffles was in his element. Clive recalled how he had always wanted to explore the interior of Java, and had never found sufficient time – he had had to content himself with ordering the restoration of one or two of the more famous and dramatic Hindu temples, such as the one at Borubudur. But here, in this constant endeavour, far away from the daily responsibilities of government, never knowing what the next day might bring, he was exorcizing all the unfortunate memories of the past few years, including even the most tragic of all.

It was a renewal, too, of their friendship. They had now known each other for some seven years, and in every way had slowly gained in respect and trust and understanding for one another. Now they talked about every subject under the sun, from wu-wei and yin-yang to the Western concept of the future, from whether a man can possibly make his own destiny or whether he is a fool to do anything more than sit back and allow life to flow around him, carrying it with him from time to time.

'You have to admit that all the men who have attempted to seize time by the forelock, as the poets would have it,' Clive said, 'have lived miserably unhappy lives, or come to most untimely deaths.'

'And you would number me amongst Caesar and Alexander, Nelson and Don Juan? I wish I were deserving of such honour. And what of Washington, who died in his bed, and Bonaparte, who still lives? He may be a prisoner, and given more to complaining about his health than to planning campaigns, but who is to say that will

370

last for ever? But I would have you consider this: has not the world only progressed simply by the efforts of those men who have made themselves — and no doubt others — miserable in their efforts, but have yet achieved so much.'

'Agreed. I would simply wonder if they had any right to inflict such torment on their loved ones, and if, at the end, they thought it was worth it, any of them.'

'That surely depends on how much is actually accomplished in the lifetime, and how much is not apparent. Believe me, Clive, I am well aware that I have a twisting knife inside me. And believe me, too, I explained as much to Sophia when asking her to marry me. She is a magnificent woman. She will support me through thick and thin. It is when I think of the risk that she is exposed to there in that pest-hole that I really become angry and feel like throwing the whole thing up.' He clasped Clive's hand. 'Do not worry. I shall not abandon you. Let us complete this safari together, and then, by God, I *will* find the place I seek. I know it is there.'

Eventually they left the swamps and came to grassland. Far from being impenetrable to man, it was the most delightful country, roamed by tiger and wild boar, but its principal attraction was mile after mile of rolling savannah, with the mountains always in the distance. 'By God, if it were possible to make a colony up here,' Raffles exclaimed. 'If only we could do without ships.'

'But we cannot,' Clive reminded him.

Raffles nodded despondently. But next day he was overwhelmed with pleasure and excitement when they came across a quite remarkable flower, no less than three feet across and weighing fifteen pounds, Raffles estimated, which quite lacked a stem or surrounding leaves, but emerged from a sort of vine growing out of a giant fungus, which he identified as the *Cissus augustifolia*. Even Clive, who knew absolutely nothing about botany, was taken aback by the sheer size of the thing, quite apart from the beauty of the huge brown and white petals gathered around a red and yellow stamen.

'We must take that back,' Raffles said. 'By God, to have that established in London would make a man famous for ever.'

'It will never survive the journey,' Clive told him. 'But look, here are some seed pods. Do you imagine they come from the flower?'

Raffles dropped to his knees. 'We will take them with us and find out. If not, we will have to return here. For I will have that in England.'

His interest in further exploration ceased, although they encountered Sumatran natives, like those on the coast more curious than hostile, who told them there were even lakes up there in the mountains. But his sole idea was to return to Bencoolen with his prize.

And this they did, to the amazement of the colony, who had almost abandoned them. Teng Lee had just returned from Manila, and Raffles showed him the pods, which he had immediately commenced propagating. 'When these sprout, and we are sure of what we have, you and I will take it to Calcutta to show Lord Hastings, and from there despatch it to London. It is quite the most remarkable thing I have ever seen.'

Teng bowed. 'It shall be done. But Stamford, you have found nowhere for us to remove ourselves to?'

'Remove ourselves to,' Raffles echoed. 'God, I wish I knew. We have seen nowhere that could possibly suggest itself as an improvement on Bencoolen. I suspect I am doomed to become more famous as a naturalist than an empire-builder, whatever the Prince's opinions.'

Yet, in the dry season, the colony was recovering, with the houses rebuilt, the school now operating under a master, the crops again being reaped, and his new son a healthy and vigorous lad. Only the row of graves in the cemetery, so many of them less than a year old, the knowledge that before long there would be another monsoon to contend with, and an overall deadening feeling that the colony had no future, and could never have a future, cast a gloom over their lives.

Yet they expected no immediate crisis and were prepared to do no more than welcome the Calcutta sloop which arrived about a month before the monsoon was due – and put ashore Edward Blaine, who was bristling with anger and outrage. 'Where is she?' he bellowed at Clive, who was waiting with the Governor to greet the sloop captain on the dock. 'I have come for her, by God, and this time you will go to gaol for abduction.'

'What the devil are you speaking about?' Raffles demanded.

'I seek my wife,' Blaine shouted. 'Oh, I know all about you, *Sir* Thomas Raffles, always ready to protect your friend. Well, it will not do. Wife-stealing will not stand up in a court of law.'

'Wife-stealing?' Clive shouted. 'You are mad.'

'Are you trying to tell me that Elizabeth is not here?'

'Of course she is not here,' Raffles told him. 'And you are behaving in a most unseemly manner. For God's sake control yourself and tell us what the matter is.'

'But if she is not here . . .' Blaine's shoulders suddenly bowed, as if he had been kicked in the stomach. 'If she is not here . . .' He looked from face to face, his expression sheer mental agony.

'You mean she is not in Penang?' Clive asked, aghast.

Blaine's head shook to and fro. 'She disappeared four weeks ago.'

CHAPTER FIFTEEN

The Hero

'And you thought she had come here?' Raffles asked, when they had taken Blaine to Government House and given him a glass of arrack to calm him down. 'Why?'

'Well . . .' He looked at Clive.

'Did she know that Clive had been widowed?'

'I did not know that myself. But . . .'

'Then I hardly think she would have attempted to throw herself on his mercy. Why did she leave Penang?'

Blaine stared at him.

'I see,' Raffles remarked. 'Domestic difficulties, eh? Well, has it not occurred to you that if she has fled your roof, it has almost certainly been with the idea of returning to her parents in England?'

'She did not go to England,' Blaine declared. 'I happen to know that. She boarded, clandestinely, a Malay prahu out of Kedah, and sought a passage down the strait. She stole money from my purse to do that. Where else can she have gone, save here?'

'Down the strait? In a Malay prahu?' Raffles was incredulous. 'A European woman, by herself?'

He looked at Clive, who looked at Teng Lee, instinctively.

Teng bowed. His face was the picture of misery. 'I believe she has returned to Singapura.'

'Singapura?' Raffles echoed. 'You mean the pirate isle? But, in the name of God, why?'

374

'How do you know that, you Chinese devil?' Blaine demanded.

Teng bowed, and repeated his conversation with Elizabeth in the cemetery two years before.

'Good God,' Blaine said when he was finished.

'Did you ill-treat her?' Clive asked quietly.

'Why, I . . .' Blaine looked from face to face. 'I maintained my prerogative as her husband.'

'You are a filthy swine,' Clive told him, still speaking quietly. 'And if you wish to regard that as a challenge, it is meant to be. We will break no laws. There is the mainland just across the water, where there is no jurisdiction.'

'Gentlemen,' Raffles said. 'I think your quarrel should wait until we have done something about Mrs Blaine. Are you seriously telling us, Teng, that she voluntarily returned to Perak Shah, because she was happy there, and because her son was there?'

'I am telling you what she told me she wished to do,' Teng agreed.

Raffles looked at Blaine. 'Did you know of this?'

'That she had had a bastard? Of course I did. But . . .' It was his turn to look from face to face, uncertain who knew what.

Teng sighed. 'I was sworn to secrecy,' he said. 'But I think I must break my oath. The child is Hammond's.'

Raffles looked at Clive.

'Mine?' Clive was clearly too amazed to have known.

'At least,' Teng said carefully, 'Mrs Blaine was always of that opinion. It is fair-haired and blue-eyed; Perak Shah still felt that it was his, but then, he did not know—if you will permit me, Clive—that you and Mrs Blaine had had a liaison on board the ship from England.'

'My God!' Clive said. 'And she never told me? *You* never told me?'

'That is what she wished,' Teng said, more carefully yet.

'My God,' Clive said again.

'You, sir, are an adulterous scoundrel,' Blaine declared. 'Why, sir –'

'Are you, or are you not, interested in regaining your wife, sir?' Raffles demanded.

'Why, your excellency . . . why, of course I am.'

'Over my dead body,' Clive growled.

'Clive,' Raffles admonished. 'Your personal differences will have to wait. We know there is a white woman who in despair' – he glanced at Blaine – 'has chosen to return to the clutches of a vicious pirate. We know too that there is in all probability a white boy also in captivity on Singapura, even if he is not aware of it. I would be damned for ever more if I did not determine to do something about that.'

He made them sit round a table, with Runsley and Evan Morton, to discuss the situation. 'You had better inform us exactly what is involved,' he told Teng.

'A direct assault would be very dangerous,' Teng said. 'And very difficult. The island is surrounded by reefs –'

'Through which you have sailed on many an occasion,' Clive interrupted.

Teng bowed his head. 'But my junk is not a warship.'

'You could con a warship through the channels.'

Teng glanced at Raffles, who stroked his chin; he knew that to risk one of his majesty's ships, supposing he could obtain one for such a purpose, and then perhaps to lose her, would mean the end of his career. 'Let us suppose we get through the reefs,' he said. 'What then?'

'The reefs would be the most dangerous part of the operation,' Teng told him. 'And as there are always look-outs, Perak Shah would know you were coming, long before you arrived. But once through the reefs, the ship would proceed up the river, which is easy of navigation, and then into the harbour.'

'How big is this harbour?'

'Oh, it is very big. It is one of the finest natural harbours I have ever seen.'

'But presumably very shallow?'

'No, no,' Teng said. 'There is amply deep water, with good holding ground. I have ridden out the fiercest of storms there without any mishap whatsoever.'

Raffles had stopped stroking his chin. Instead he was frowning.

'But it would be a mistake to assume that because you have got your ship into the harbour,' Teng went on, 'your task would then be easy. You would lie virtually in the centre of the Five Villages, surrounded by several thousand warriors.'

'Several *thousand*? On a tiny island?'

'Singapura is not that tiny,' Teng replied. 'And it is very fertile. It supports a considerable population. Oh, they are poor, but they are good fighting men, and they worship Perak Shah.'

'It really is nothing like Bencoolen, Stam,' Clive put in. 'There are mangrove swamps by the shore, of course, but inland the land is excellent, and somewhat higher, and thus easily drained. There is a considerable range of hills in the centre.'

'By God,' Raffles said. 'By God! Are you saying there is no malaria?'

Clive looked at Teng.

'There is some, of course,' Teng said. 'Malaria is everywhere. But no more severe than in Batavia.'

'And are there ever earthquakes?'

'Not that I have ever heard.'

'My God,' Raffles said again. He got up from the table and went to the window, and gazed out at his little community. After a few minutes he faced them; his face was glowing. 'I do believe, gentlemen, that the pearl we have been seeking has been lying at our feet for all of these years, and we have not noticed it.'

377

They stared at him. Clive was the first to understand what he meant. 'Singapura?'

Raffles held up his hand and ticked off his fingers. 'One, it is situated at the very bottom of the Strait of Malacca, where in fact the Java Sea and the South China Sea virtually meet – there can be no more strategic position in the whole of the East; two, it has a superb natural harbour; three, it has a relatively healthy climate; four, it is fertile enough to support a large population; and five, it does not belong to the Dutch.'

'It belongs to the Sultan of Johore,' Captain Runsley reminded him.

'Who has never, to my knowledge, made any use of it.'

'It belongs to Perak Shah,' Teng Lee said quietly.

Raffles glanced at him, then came back and sat down. 'By virtue of occupation. Two can play at that game. And if we can obtain legal title. By God!' He smashed his right fist into his palm. 'It can be done. I know it. It is forming in my mind. It may take a little time . . .'

'And Elizabeth?' Clive asked.

'My wife?' Blaine put in.

'The moment it was discovered that there was a British force attempting to invade his island,' Teng said, 'Perak Shah would cut her throat.'

'Despite being, as she claimed to you, so fond of her that he made her his favourite concubine?'

'He is a man given to sudden bursts of temper,' Teng said.

'It is certainly a risk we cannot take,' Clive agreed.

Raffles looked around their faces again. 'It will need careful planning,' he told them. 'And time. I must first of all go to Calcutta and talk with Hastings, and secure us the use of a frigate. And then, with his blessing, approach the Sultan of Johore and offer to buy the island . . .'

'Time?' Clive shouted. 'You are speaking of months. While Elizabeth . . .'

'Perhaps it will take a couple of months,' Raffles

agreed. 'But this is a time for looking facts in the face, Clive, however unpleasant they may be to you. Elizabeth returned to Singapura of her own free will. If Perak Shah was no longer interested in her, then he would have had her executed immediately. Am I not right?' He looked at Teng, who bowed. 'Therefore she is either already dead, or she is perfectly safe – because if she is still alive, that will indicate Perak Shah is indeed still fond of her and has taken her back into his harem.' Once more he looked at Teng for confirmation.

Teng bowed again.

The girl was very young; only sixteen years of age, Amina had said. Why, Elizabeth thought, that is half my age.

The girl was also terrified, and shivered, for all the proud expression on the face of her mother, who was standing beside her. 'She will please Perak Shah,' the woman said anxiously. 'He has looked on her already, and was pleased. She will please him more.'

'We shall see,' Amina said. 'Leave her.'

The mother hesitated, as if she suspected that these two senior wives might be about to sacrifice the girl to their own lust, or their own jealousy. Then she bowed, and shuffled through the door of the harem.

The other girls had crowded round the novitiate, much as they had done about her, Elizabeth recalled, all but ten years before. But this poor creature had less to offer them, for her colouring was as dark as theirs, and her breasts were as small. Only the sense that she was afraid attracted them.

'Take off your sarong,' Amina commanded.

The girl shivered again, then released the sarong and allowed it to fall to the floor.

'Now raise your arms,' Amina said, and began the inspection, in which Elizabeth shared. Elizabeth Blaine, she thought, taking part in the minutest examination of a young girl, like some madam recruiting a prostitute.

Well, perhaps that was indeed what she had become, although they were prostituted to but one man. And besides, she had done so many strange things these last few months – last few years, even – that to examine an innocent for blemishes might be considered almost commonplace.

How long ago seemed the memory of herself, shivering in fear, before the angry outrage of Edward Blaine. She had failed herself, there. The pride, almost arrogance, with which she had returned from Singapura to Penang did not last. She knew it was necessary to her survival, but just as no man can walk around for ever with his chest expanded to its maximum in order to impress his fellows, so she could not sustain so unnatural a state. And it did not seem so necessary, as she slowly grew to acceptance by the community and, she thought, by her husband, until that fateful day – six years ago now.

From that moment she entered hell. And at that moment she realized that the arrogance, even the pride, was all gone. Had he assaulted her like that on the evening of her return, she would have killed him, as she had threatened to do. And she doubted anyone would have held her so very guilty – they had hardly expected her to be sane. But after three years it was a different matter. Her spirit had weakened, and if her guilt was still remembered, her suffering had been forgotten. She possessed no defence. In the absence of Flora Raffles, she did not even possess a friend in the whole colony.

Thus she took refuge in dreams. Dreams first of all that Raffles, or someone else, would find it necessary to conquer Singapura, and that her son might thus be returned to her. Dreams that Clive might one day come for her, and if, after his marriage to Amalia, there had seemed no likelihood of that, dreams that Blaine might die . . . terrible dreams that she might kill him, even if she knew she was not the stuff of which murderesses are made.

Those dreams all faded into improbability with the passage of time, and thus were replaced by a single dream, based on the memory of the only period of her life when she had even approached happiness. That dream gradually turned into a plan. How it was to be implemented she had no idea. Singapura might be only four hundred miles away from Penang, but it could have been on the moon for all the contact between the two places. And in between was nothing but hostility. And then, quite without warning, she saw the *Dragon's Wake* riding at anchor in the harbour. She did not believe her eyes; it seemed too much like her dream come true.

But it was not her dream come true. When she screwed up her courage to a sufficient pitch actually to approach Teng Lee — reminding herself that he was a friend of both Raffles and Clive, and that he was, even more important, a man who made things happen, and that he had rescued her once before and would surely do so again — he refused her. It was as if she had been kicked in the stomach, she recalled, the most deadening feeling of despair she had ever known. And yet, the dream, having nearly become reality, then turned into a plan. She *would* escape Penang, with or without the assistance of Teng Lee or anyone else. It was a matter of watching, waiting, listening, observing, and then, when the moment came, acting without hesitation.

What the Malay captain thought of it she did not know. She did not know how much he believed anything of what she told him. He chose to believe her, both because of the stolen money with which she paid him, and because her story was well known. As was Perak Shah. And if she claimed the famous pirate chieftain had summoned her back to his side and would faithfully reward anyone who carried her there, then he was willing to see if it were possible to make a profit. The knowledge that she was the woman of Perak Shah protected her

381

more securely than a company of soldiers. And he did make a profit; she saw to that.

The dream at last came true. Perak Shah looked at her in consternation, and then he smiled, and then he roared with laughter. He knew that she had never been delivered to Rama, that indeed the whole thing had been a deception, and had assumed that Teng Lee wanted her for herself. Well, she did not disabuse him of that idea; she owed Teng nothing. Perak Shah's anger against his old friend was terrible to behold. But his delight at having her back was equally a pleasure to behold. She might never have been away, because she had not aged physically, that he could notice, save to grow more voluptuous. On the night she returned, he made her feel a whole woman again for the first time since she had left him.

Then came the reunion with Amina and the other girls, and the meeting with Ali. He was nine years old, and already living with the young men of the village, which was a disappointment. But as the son of the sultan he had more freedom than most, and he was allowed time to spend with his mother. At first he had no idea who she was, and yet he was able to recognize the yellow hair and the blue eyes which he had inherited as his own. Besides, Amina had often told him of his mother. Elizabeth supposed that to hold him again in her arms was the happiest moment of her life.

The months that followed were happy. She found it difficult to believe that she had actually done it, and succeeded, and half expected to see a frigate appear off the Dragon's Teeth and utter threats. But that was absurd; they had not sent a frigate nine years ago. And now she had turned her back on that life, for ever. That too she sometimes found it difficult to believe. Had she ever really worn buttoned boots and thick stockings, blood-restricting garters and corsets, clammy chemises and petticoats and skirts and blouses, piled her hair on top of her head and poured tea, or drunk it, with her little finger held aloft, while endless inanities flowed round her head? Were there actually people who did these things, day in and day out, for all of their lives, and never understood the freedom of going barefoot, of bathing beneath the sun or swimming naked, of wearing but a single garment and enjoying the sensation of total physical freedom, total physical health? Then the world was gone mad, and she the only sane person in it.

Amina, who was her friend, was as happy as Perak Shah to have her back. Now she smiled at her and said, 'I think she will do. I will prepare her for shaving. Will you tell Perak Shah?'

Elizabeth nodded, put on her yashmak and left the harem for the front verandah, where the chieftain was as usual talking with his sons, many of whom were now grown up – Bodaw Shan was twenty-seven, and very much his father's second in command, even if the two men differed on almost every point of view – airing his plans, although she supposed he knew that those plans would never now come to fruition. She knelt before him, and he placed his hand on her head. 'My sweet Lizbeth,' he said. 'What of her?'

'She appears to be healthy and unblemished, Perak Shah,' Elizabeth said, and listened to shouts.

Perak Shah heard them too, and frowned as he stood up. He was now in his fifties, but revealed no trace of ageing in his powerful muscles or his movements. 'What is it they say?'

'That a ship comes, Perak Shah' Bodaw Shan said. 'A Chinese junk. It is the ship of Teng Lee.'

'Teng Lee,' Perak Shah growled. 'Teng Lee,' he shouted, and glanced at Elizabeth. 'He has come seeking you.'

She was holding her breath. Teng Lee had told her that he could never return here for fear of being executed. Therefore, what reason could he have for risking his neck but to seek her? Although it must have been a pretty strong incentive, offered presumably by Blaine, to have brought him.

'You will not make me go with him?' she asked in a low voice.

'No chance of that,' Perak Shah said, and gave another shout of laughter. 'He is going to stay here with you. Oh, yes. Ring the gong,' he bellowed.

One of his sons hurried off to carry out his father's bidding, and the notes of the gong reverberated through the trees, bringing men hurrying from every direction. 'Arm yourselves,' Perak Shah shouted. 'Prepare the prahus for sea, but remain by your docks until the gong is struck again. We do not wish to frighten this Chinese scoundrel away.'

All was scurry and bustle, while Elizabeth, temporarily forgotten, withdrew into the doorway of the palace, where she was shaded from the street, and stared at the river, her heart pounding. However much she resented his refusal to help her, she did not really wish to see Teng Lee executed. But there seemed nothing she could now do about it, for the junk was in sight, slowly sailing up the river. She had no glass, and therefore could only tell that there were men on her poop deck, and yet . . . once again she caught her breath. Because surely two of the men were European.

The junk dropped its anchor, the sails came down, and the boat was swung out and lowered. The Five Villages now gave a deceptive appearance of calm, even indifference to the arrival, so much so that Elizabeth felt they should be suspicious – certainly Teng, who had been here often before. In place of the excited crowd he was accustomed to, there were only half a dozen people lounging on the docks, and instead of Perak Shah himself waiting at the landing to greet his visitor, there was only Bodaw Shan, standing alone, a tall, straight, very handsome young man. He was the next ruler of these people,

384

and knew it; Amina was very proud of him. Yet he was also a good friend and elder brother to Ali, which made Elizabeth proud of him too.

The boat pulled into the dock, and three men came ashore. Teng Lee was first, dressed in his finest green silk, bowing to Bodaw Shan as he gained the land. Next there was a tall man in a black suit with a white stock . . . Elizabeth felt a choking sensation as she recognized Clive Hammond. Oh, my God, she thought. Then her heart seemed to explode as she watched the equally tall, but thinner man in the red jacket over grey uniform trousers who had followed Clive ashore. 'Oh, my God,' she whispered. 'Oh, my God!' She shrank back further into the shadows.

The men came across the street to the palace, and Perak Shah rose from his stool. 'How do the minds of men become fuddled,' he remarked loudly. 'Are you demented, Teng Lee, you son of a treacherous Chinese whore, that you dare to enter into my presence? And who are these? Am I not sworn to kill all white men who fall into my hands?'

Clearly he did not recognize in the handsome, bronzed and remarkably tough-looking man at Teng's shoulder as the white-faced youth who had attempted to defy him ten years before.

Teng Lee bowed. 'I come neither in enmity nor in friendship, Perak Shah, nor do I come as a supplicant. I come as an emissary from your master, the Sultan of Johore.'

Perak Shah frowned. 'The Sultan?'

'It is true, Father,' Bodaw Shan told him. 'Teng Lee has letters from the Sultan.'

Elizabeth gazed at Clive. How handsome he looked, and how capable. How formidable! He could not see her, of course, but his eyes were darting left and right. He was seeking . . . she clutched her throat as she saw him half turn his head as a group of small boys gathered on the

385

street to watch the men talk. He knows, she thought. He knows, and has come for his son. Therefore the talk of the Sultan of Johore is all a bluff. But with Edward Blaine?

To commit suicide?

'Letters?' Perak Shah bellowed. 'What have I to do with letters?' He pointed at Teng Lee. 'You have come for the woman you stole from me. By Allah, but you are a bold wretch. Yet I will make you suffer for your effrontery. And your treachery. Hit the gong,' he shouted.

One of his sons had remained by the instrument, and now the stroke went crashing through the trees again. Instantly the whole of the Five Villages came to life. Armed Malays totally surrounded the palace, while a dozen prahus put out from their various landings, crammed with more armed men, to cut off the *Dragon's Wake* from the exit to the sea.

Blaine muttered something to Clive, and dropped his hand to where the hilt of his sword should have been – but like Clive and Teng Lee he was unarmed.

Teng refused to reveal any fear and continued to gaze at Perak Shah. 'It would be sensible for you to hear what the Sultan, your master, has to say,' he suggested.

Perak Shah snorted. 'It will not save your miserable skin, Chinese dog.'

Teng Lee bowed. 'You harm me at your peril, Perak Shah. I, and my companions, come here as ambassadors, protected by the laws of international usage. His highness the Sultan commands me to inform Perak Shah, so called Sultan of Singapura, that his highness, in his wisdom, has sold this island to the men of the country known as Great Britain, and that in accordance with this treaty, the men from Great Britain' – Teng paused to bow to Clive and Blaine – 'are forthwith to take possession of the said island of Singapura.'

'What?' Perak Shah bellowed. 'What are you saying?'

Teng looked at Bodaw Shan.

386

'It would be best for us to hear the rest of what the Sultan has to say, Father,' Bodaw Shan said. 'In it there is considerable hope.'

'Hope?' Perak Shah shouted. 'Am I a woman, or a beggar, that I must descend to hope?'

'It is the Sultan's command that you submit to the British rule,' Teng said. 'And in this regard, it is the British intention, should you not resist them, to deal with you fairly, and leave you in possession of your wealth and your palace, and all your goods, insofar,' he added hastily, 'as these can be reconciled with British law and custom.'

Fortunately Perak Shah had no experience of political double-talk, but he still looked ready to explode.

'It is a fair offer, Father,' Bodaw Shan said. 'We cannot fight against the British. You have heard the tales reported of their strength, you remember the fleet of great ships we saw sailing past our shores seven years ago.'

'Bah,' Perak Shah said. 'They will never find their way through the Dragon's Teeth. Besides, it is merely a trick to rob me of Lizbeth.'

'You are besotted, Perak Shah,' Teng said severely. 'Do you really suppose that great affairs of state can be concerned with the fate of a woman?'

'Ha ha,' Perak Shah bawled, stamping his foot. 'You have betrayed me too often, Teng Lee. Do you know that I sent ambassadors to Rama asking him to confirm the alliance you promised me? Do you know what he did? He bastinadoed two of them to death, and the third until he had no skin left on his back, then sent him back to me with the message that he sought no alliances with dogs or pirates. Me, Perak Shah! And now you have come here again with your childish attempts to deceive me? And brought these two Englishmen with you? Well, you are going to die. All of you. Seize them,' he snapped.

His guards had been slowly edging closer during the conversation, and now they grasped the three men by the arms.

'Strip them that they may be shamed,' Perak Shah commanded. 'And then confine them in the smallest cell we have. Let them consume each other with their fear and their heat and their thirst until tomorrow. Then we shall have sport. Then we shall watch the crocodile feast.'

'You would be making a terrible mistake,' Teng pointed out. 'If we are harmed, the British will raze your villages to the ground and hang you from the highest tree on the island.'

'I beg you to listen to the Sultan's command, Father,' Bodaw Shan said earnestly. 'Teng Lee is right. To oppose the British would end in the destruction of us all.'

'Bah,' Perak Shah declared. 'I fear no man. Least of all those white faces. And you are a white-livered coward yourself. Call yourself a son of mine? Beware lest I feed you to the crocodile as well, and call upon some other of my children to support their father. Take them away,' he said. 'Make them sweat and beg for water. Make them suffer and tremble for tomorrow.'

None of the three prisoners made any effort to resist as they were stripped of their clothing and had their hands tied behind their backs, to the accompaniment of jeers and kicks and punches from the Malays; they knew resistance would be useless.

Elizabeth could hardly breathe. The unthinkable had happened. Clive and Blaine had come together to rescue her, and Ali, and were now to suffer a horrible death, because their bluff had not worked. And she would have to watch them die . . . unless she could somehow save them. She knew that Perak Shah would never yield to her, while if he ever discovered that one of the men was her husband and the other her lover, what he would do to them *before* giving them to the crocodile did not bear contemplating.

To attempt to rescue them would probably cost her own life, with little prospect of success. But yet, she knew, it had to be done. If these men had come to destroy her

388

idyll, they had come because one at least loved her, in a way that Perak Shah could never envisage.

Suddenly she realized how there might be a way, as she watched Perak Shah stamping away behind his prisoners, and Bodaw Shan gazing after his father, his face twisted with anger and doubt.

'I feel I may have missed some of that,' Edward Blaine remarked, as the three men stood shoulder to shoulder in the tiny hut; there was no room to sit down. 'I am afraid I have never learned to speak Malay.'

'It is simply that Raffles' plan did not work,' Teng Lee said. 'I never supposed it would.'

'Yes, I sort of gathered that.' It was impossible to doubt the man's courage, or even to dislike him, Clive thought, when he was facing death in the most nonchalant of manners. 'But there is no need to be quite so gloomy. Raffles has promised to force the entrance tomorrow morning should we not signal him that Perak Shah had agreed to surrender.'

'I do not see how that will help us,' Teng pointed out. 'It will take at least one hour for the frigate to travel from the Dragon's Teeth to the Five Villages. That is ample time for Perak Shah to deal with us, and kill Mrs Blaine too, before anyone can help us. We have failed utterly, both in convincing him that he has no choice other than to deal with us, and in providing a diversion. Except' — he gave a grim smile — 'in so far as the Malays will be diverted by our deaths.'

'You are a pessimistic old devil,' Clive told him.

Teng bowed, as far as he was able. Naked, he seemed curiously larger than he had ever appeared when wearing his green silk. And far stronger than he had ever appeared, too; then Clive remembered the ease with which he had been thrown, not very far from here, when Teng Lee had chosen to exert his strength.

'How exactly are we to be killed?' Blaine asked.

389

'Perak Shah means to feed us to his pet crocodile,' Clive explained.

'It will not be so simple as that,' Teng said. 'I have seen him make an example of his enemies, those who have grievously offended him. First we will be castrated before the assembled populace. He will hope that we will beg for mercy, and in any event, it will be the most humiliating thing that can happen to us. Then, bleeding and destroyed as we are, we will be suspended from planks extended from the dock, with our feet dangling in the water, until the crocodile pulls us down — he lives under that dock. Again, the whole community will watch, and cheer, and jeer. It will provide them with a great morning's sport. It is best to hope that one is the first picked by the crocodile.'

'Hm,' Blaine said again. 'I must say, I find it difficult to remain optimistic with that hanging over my head.'

'You will be hanging over the crocodile's head,' Clive pointed out.

'I say, old man, do you suppose it is something we should joke about? Shouldn't we be praying, or something?'

'There isn't room to kneel,' Clive told him, 'and if we don't joke about it, we will go mad.'

'Hm,' Blaine commented. 'Yes, I suppose you're right. I say, Hammond, I would like to offer you an apology. It seems rather pointless to carry personal differences to the grave.' He forced a smile. 'I should have said, to the crocodile.'

Clive hesitated, looked at Teng Lee, who looked back at him, then shrugged. 'Apology accepted, and mine offered in return, Major.'

He stared out of the single barred window of the cell, where the two guards waited. Seeing him gazing at them, they began holding their water gourds high in the air and pouring the contents over their heads and faces, laughing as they did so. Well, he thought, he was certainly thirsty.

But that seemed irrelevant. They had all known, and accepted, the danger of the mission. It had been a very slim chance that Perak Shah might have learned some sense as he grew older; but there had been no one to teach him any. Yet it had been the only way in which they could get into the Five Villages. Now they were here, and it was up to others. Up to Elizabeth, surely. He refused to give up hope. Elizabeth must have learned by now that they were on the island, and prisoners. All depended on whether she had managed to identify them.

But even if she had, she had apparently returned here of her own free will, to Perak Shah. Why should she risk her life to help them now? And how could she, a mere woman?

How he longed for the sound of Raffles' guns. But even that could not help them if they could not escape from this cell.

It grew dark, but ever hotter. Now they were too thirsty to speak, and with their hands bound behind them they had no protection against the insects which filled the cell. They were so exhausted they could hardly stand; they leaned against each other in mutual misery, waiting for the dawn and the horrors which would attend the dawn . . . then heard a sound from outside. It was a moonless night, but even so Clive could suddenly make out that the guards were no longer sitting there, although he thought he could see the feet of one of them.

The others had heard the sound too, and stirred, to watch the door of the cell swing outwards. 'By God,' Blaine whispered.

Bodaw Shan stood there, and behind him a tall woman with a shawl round her head and shoulders.

'You must leave here,' Elizabeth said in English. 'Go into the forest and try to get across the strait to Johore. It is very narrow. If you have indeed come from the Sultan, then you will be safe there.'

Bodaw Shan had cut their hands free, and she held out sarongs for them to wear.

Clive worked his fingers to restore his circulation. 'You will come with us.'

'I have done all I can. I will not leave my son again.'

'We have come for you, and my son,' Clive said.

She looked at Blaine.

'Yes, indeed.'

'I have done all I can,' she said. 'I am not coming away with you. And you cannot reach your son. He sleeps with the young men, in a communal hut. If you entered there, you would be recaptured.'

'You don't seem to understand,' Clive said, switching to Malay so that Bodaw Shan would understand what was being said. 'There is a British frigate going to force its way in here at dawn. Teng Lee was telling the truth when he said the island had been sold to Great Britain.'

'My father will never surrender,' Bodaw Shan said. 'He will fight until the Five Villages are utterly destroyed. He must be replaced. With your help, white men, I can do this.'

'You mean, depose him and take his place?' Clive asked.

'I mean, kill him,' Bodaw Shan said.

Elizabeth caught her breath. 'No,' she said. 'You cannot. He . . .' She bit her lip.

'He will never accept deposition, Lizbeth,' Bodaw Shan said. 'And as long as he lives, the people will rally to him.'

Clive listened to a cock crow. Dawn was not all that far away; the frigate would be hove to off the reef, as yet unsighted by the Malays as she would have approached the island in the darkness, piloted by Li Yuan. 'There is a way we can preserve Perak Shah's life,' he said. 'Indeed, it will be necessary. Does anyone know that your son is also mine?' he asked Elizabeth.

'No. But . . .'

392

'Then his life is certainly in no danger unless the frigate has to open fire. Have you weapons for us, Bodaw Shan?'

'Only the kris.'

'That's what I was hoping you'd say. And you understand that if we do not succeed, we will be executed? We cannot surrender.'

Bodaw Shan nodded. 'I believe my father means to execute me anyway, one day, because I oppose him in so many things.'

'So let's go. Ever handled one of these things, Major?' he asked in English.

'I'm afraid not.'

'Well, you grasp it as you would a pistol, and thrust with it rather than cutting. How many guards are there in the palace itself?'

'Only four,' Elizabeth said. 'Two on the verandah, and two in the inner corridor behind which Perak Shah sleeps. Tonight he will be sleeping more heavily than usual, because he has taken a new girl to his bed for the first time. But you promise he will not be killed.'

Clive peered at her in the darkness. 'Not if it is humanly avoidable. Are you with us?'

She hesitated. 'I have no choice, now.'

The cock crowed again, and there was a distinct lightening of the darkness.

They ran through the still sleeping village, into the palace yard, shaded by the trees which cast a deeper darkness. Then they rushed the steps. The first guard saw them and shouted, raising his wooden spear. Bodaw Shan led them up the steps. 'What, would you oppose Bodaw Shan?' he demanded. The man checked his thrust, and Bodaw Shan stepped up to him and drove his kris into his stomach. There was a dreadful gurgling sound, and the man collapsed on the floor. Clive had already stepped past him and despatched the second guard as the man, who had been sleeping, reached his feet.

They burst through the doorway into the reception

chamber and looked at the inner corridor. The two guards saw them coming. One presented his spear, the other turned and ran. 'Stop him,' Clive shouted, side-stepping the man with the spear and killing him with another single thrust of the deadly weapon he had learned to use so well. Bodaw Shan leapt over him and ran behind the other guard, who was shrieking his terror to the world. The palace began to stir.

'Where is he?' Clive snapped.

Elizabeth pointed; she was panting with fear and excitement, and with uncertainty, too: she had not envisaged anything like this.

Clive broke down the door with a single charge of his shoulder, heard a high-pitched scream from the girl who was sprawled across the divan, and realized that Perak Shah was already on his feet and had armed himself with an enormous sabre. Now he advanced towards the three men, the sword raised. 'Treachery,' he bawled. 'Treachery, by Allah! Guards, to me.'

Clive darted at him, and he swung the sabre. Clive evaded the blow, getting inside it. He could easily have killed the pirate then, but he did want him alive. He dropped the kris and drove his fist into Perak Shah's belly. Perak Shah gasped, and Clive hit him again, clasping both hands together to crash them against his face and send him tumbling to the floor. Instantly, Clive leapt behind him, twisting his arms behind his back.

From the mosque there came the clang of the gong; the guard who escaped had fled there.

Blaine and Teng Lee were now helping Clive to drag Perak Shah to his feet and secure his arms. Perak Shah glared at them, then looked past them at Elizabeth standing in the doorway. 'By Allah,' he growled. 'Treachery. And from you, Lizbeth! By Allah, I shall not feed you to the crocodile. You I will impale upon a sharp stake, I will —'

'Shut up,' Clive told him. 'Do you not remember me,

Perak Shah? Once before you had me in your power, and let me go. That was a mistake. I am Lizbeth's lover, and I am the father of her son.'

'You? You? It cannot be . . .'

'There are people gathering outside,' Teng said; he had been looking out of the window. 'They have heard the gong and are wondering why Perak Shah does not appear.'

'Well, he's going to,' Clive said, picking up his kris. 'Where's Bodaw Shan?'

'I am here.' Bodaw Shan had returned. 'That man escaped me.'

'We gathered that.' Clive looked past him at the woman who had left the harem to stand next to Elizabeth; she was a Malay, he could tell, even though she was wearing the yashmak.

'My mother,' Bodaw Shan explained.

'You too, Amina?' Perak Shah asked. 'I am surrounded by treachery.'

'You would destroy our people, Perak Shah,' Amina said. 'And my son. You have ruled the Five Villages too long.'

'You will die,' Perak Shah said. 'You will —'

'Take him outside,' Clive said. 'Listen to me well, Perak Shah; if you try to escape, or do not say exactly what I tell you to, I am going to slit your belly open.'

Perak Shah glared at him, but this time made no reply. They forced him out of the door and along the corridor, stumbling over the dead bodies, and out on to the verandah. It was quite light now, and a large crowd had gathered. Bodaw Shan stepped forward to wave his arms at them, to attract their attention and bring silence. 'Listen to me,' he shouted. 'This island, Singapura, has been sold to the men of Britain. There is a British warship on its way here now, to take possession.' He paused to let that sink in, watching the Malays mutter at each other. 'These people are very powerful,' Bodaw Shan continued. 'They cannot be overcome. But they will deal fairly with us if we surrender to them. It is my father's wish that you do not fight them, but accept them as friends when they arrive.' He turned to Perak Shah. 'Say it, Father.'

Perak Shah snorted, and Clive pinked him with the kris. 'Say it,' he growled.

'It is my wish,' Perak Shah said.

'Louder.'

'It is my wish,' Perak Shah bellowed.

'Look,' Teng said.

Men were running down the path from the entrance to the harbour, waving their arms. 'A ship,' they shouted. 'A great ship, with guns, is entering the Dragon's Teeth.'

'That is the British coming,' Bodaw Shan shouted. 'Lay down your weapons and prepare to receive these men as your new masters.'

The Malays, men and women now, shuffled their feet and gazed at the water, and then one pointed, because, in the distance, but towering above the trees, could be seen the masthead of a ship.

'Hallelujah!' Clive said.

In that minute he relaxed. Perak Shah gave an enormous heave, threw off the arms holding him and leapt down the steps. 'Cut me free,' he bellowed. 'Cut me free.'

Clive bounded after him, but checked as several Malays turned to face him, weapons thrust foward. One was slitting the cord binding Perak Shah's wrists. 'Give me your weapon,' Perak Shah shouted, seizing the kris and turning back towards Clive. 'You, at least,' he snarled, and leapt forward, feet up, confident in his mastery of a weapon sure to be unknown to a white man.

Clive easily side-stepped the charge, swung to one side and thrust. Perak Shah saw the blow coming and brought down his own kris. The two blades met and screeched against each other, and the men in turn thumped their bodies together. The Malays stared in bewilderment.

396

They had been given no fresh instructions, knew nothing of what their Sultan had in mind. But presumably they also did not doubt the outcome of the fight.

Only Perak Shah knew that, for Clive's left hand, fingers closing like a vice, had seized his wrist, and he could not free himself; the two kris remained pressed against each other, haft to haft, the points only inches from their respective bellies. Perak Shah exerted all his strength to thrust Clive back, and found he could not. His eyes rolled and he panted, trying to get his leg round Clive's to throw him, and failing. Looking past Clive, he saw the masts steadily becoming clearer as the frigate came up the river.

'Allah curse you, white man,' Perak Shah gasped, and leapt backwards, dropping the kris as he did so. He hesitated for a moment, then ran on to the dock and stood there, waving his fist at the approaching frigate. The ship promptly fired her bow chaser. It was intended as a warning, and was aimed to send the ball plunging into the water some thirty feet from the dock, but there was an enormous splash and water flooded over Perak Shah, causing him to lose his balance. He staggered for a moment on the edge of the dock, and then overbalanced and fell into the water.

He went under, then surfaced, waving his arms. 'Help me,' he bellowed.

The Malays hurried forward, but checked on the water's edge. The long black shape of the crocodile, awakened by the shot, was between them and their chieftain.

While the marine band played the national anthem, Sir Thomas Stamford Raffles himself hoisted the Union Jack on the hastily erected flagpole outside Perak Shah's palace. The Malays stared at him in amazement. Never had they seen such pomp and power, the red-jacketed marines, the blue-jacketed sailors, the gold braid of the

397

officers, the immense power of the guns which remained trained on the village . . . their lives had been turned upside down in a few minutes.

Raffles stepped back and saluted the flag. Then he turned to Clive. 'I can hardly believe this day has come,' he said. 'I feel quite euphoric. Now I would have you meet John Farquhar, who is to be my deputy, and the Resident here.'

'I have heard a great deal about you, Mr Hammond,' Farquhar said.

Clive shook hands. He could not prevent himself from feeling disappointed; indeed, he felt as if he had been slapped in the face. 'Allow me to present Bodaw Shan, son and heir of the late Sultan. He is pro-British and is willing to cooperate with us in every way.'

'But that is splendid,' Raffles said. 'We must have a conference right away.'

'Then I will leave you to it,' Clive said, and walked away from them.

'Clive!' Raffles hurried behind him. 'I know how you feel, and I am sorry, believe me. I would have had it otherwise. But you know what the civil service is. You do not even belong to it, much less have any experience or training in it. They simply would not accept my recommendation.' He rested his hand on Clive's shoulder. 'You will never lack for employment, I promise you.'

'As your secretary,' Clive said bitterly.

'Well . . . until something better comes along. And you have regained your son, have you not?'

'Yes,' Clive said, and gazed at Elizabeth, standing by herself, the boy Ali next to her waiting . . . for what, he wondered? He had had the time to do no more than look at the boy.

'Well, obviously there will have to be some discussions about that as well,' Raffles said. 'Blaine . . .'

The major came towards them. 'I think Hammond knows the situation as well as I, your excellency,' he said.

'My wife is not, and has never been, in love with me. But she has proved herself a woman of great courage and resource, and perhaps she deserves better than she has endured. I will start divorce proceedings, if that is what Hammond wishes.'

'Should it not be what Elizabeth wishes?' Clive asked.

'Of course. However, I was taking that as read.' He hesitated, then held out his hand. 'I am pleased that we dared together, and won.'

Clive glanced at Raffles, and then shook hands. 'As am I, Major.'

'Well,' Raffles said. 'I must get down to work with Bodaw Shan. I am sure you have things to do, Clive.' He too looked meaningfully at Elizabeth.

Blaine went with him, and Clive was left alone, still gazing at her. Teng stood beside him. 'I feel that I have uncovered one of the mysteries of the universe,' he said. 'To how many men can it be given to arrive at a true meaning of yin-yang or wu-wei?'

'And you feel that you have arrived at that?' Clive asked.

'Certainly. It was fifteen years ago that I first stood on this very spot, and looked around me, and said to myself, this is where I shall make my home. Since then I fought and struggled to make that dream come true, and finally felt that I had to abandon it, so I sought other dreams. And now I am here, and Singapura will be my home, and my family will grow in comfort and security. So all the years of struggle were to no avail. What Fate decrees, so it will be.'

'Not exactly a Western point of view,' Clive said.

'Perhaps not.' Teng smiled. 'I still think that Fate requires a jolt from time to time. As in your case. You are disappointed in not being made Raffles' deputy, after having acted the role for so long.'

'Would not you be?'

'Indeed. But as he said, if you are not a mandarin, have

399

not been brought up to think with their minds and speak with their tongue, they will never trust you, never employ you, save where they can find no other. Why do you not break with them?'

'And starve?'

'And join me. We have a commercial empire to build, Clive. I see Singapura being the entrepôt of the East. I know my countrymen will flock to set up their godowns here, once they know they will be safe from pirates. I will make you a rich man, Clive. And you too now have a family to care for.'

'Do I?' Clive asked. 'She returned to Perak Shah.'

'She returned to her son, and because Perak Shah was preferable to Blaine. But she revealed her true self last night. I do not suggest the way will be easy, because you have both suffered too much in too different ways. But was any worthwhile goal ever achieved by the easy way? Go to her, Clive. She is waiting.'

Clive walked across the road to Elizabeth. She watched him coming towards her, her face expressionless.

'Blaine has agreed to divorce you,' he said.

Now colour flared into her cheeks. 'I am glad of that, Mr Hammond.'

'I . . .' He didn't know what to say. 'My wife has died,' he said. 'She was killed in an earthquake.'

'Oh, Mr Hammond,' she said. 'I am so terribly sorry.'

'Yes,' he said. 'She was a very fine woman, of whom I was very fond. But I do not think I ever loved her as I loved you. You do not have to go back to Penang, or anywhere,' he went on in a rush. 'I am going to remain here in Singapura, working with Teng.' He paused, and she continued to stare at him; but now there were tears in her eyes.

'I . . I have two other children,' he said. 'Waiting in Bencoolen. A boy and a girl.'

'I look forward to meeting them, Mr Hammond,' she said.

The founding of Singapore was the crowning achievement of Stamford Raffles' life, and as he had prophesied, within a very short space of time it became the greatest port in South-East Asia, from which British ships carried their trade to every corner of the Pacific and Indian oceans.

He personally was more gratified when the flower he and Clive had found in Sumatra was named after him *Rafflesia arnoldi*, although he discovered another rare plant in Singapore itself, which was to be called *Nepenthes rafflesiana*.

But for all his visible successes, he remained bedevilled by misfortune. To his continuing difference with the East India Company was added personal tragedy; four of the five children born to Sophia Raffles died in infancy. And his own life was soon to end. The headaches which had plagued him for so long grew worse, and on 5 July 1826, aged only forty-five, he died of a brain tumour.

His name will live forever.